EAST CLIFTON AVENUE

A FAMILY TRILOGY *Book One*

SICILY TO AMERICA | ORIGINI – ORIGINS

SECOND EDITION

Frank Plateroti, EdD

ISBN: 979-8-9887964-4-2
Library of Congress Control Number: 2024901732
Published by Plateroti Communications
Lincoln Park, NJ 07035

Dedication

To all the generations of people whose love and courage gave them the fortitude to leave their homeland and family and settle in a new land so their children would have the opportunities of creating a fulfilling and happy life for themselves and their family.

Most of all, to those family members who selflessly take care of their loved ones, making the hard, sometimes heartbreaking decisions, no matter how difficult the sacrifices.

"Praise goes to the families who can love and stay together."

Author Notes

My name is Frank Plateroti and I am not only the author but what you would also call the narrator of the story you are about to "experience." It is a story that recalls the life of two people who left their homeland for America, and then lived, loved, and died on East Clifton Avenue.

More years ago, than I care to remember, I was having lunch with my friend and famous actress, Helen Hayes, *The First Lady of the American Theater*. As we were reminiscing about her long theatrical and movie career, I was astounded at her memory of dates, places, and performances. She could even recite lines from what most people consider her most famous play about Queen Victoria, *Victoria Regina*, in which she performed on stage decades earlier. When I told her how impressed I was at her memory she leaned over and said to me, "My dear Frank, I may not be able to tell you what I had for dinner last night. Maybe I can't even tell you where I was a couple of days ago, but something happens when we get old. The past suddenly comes back to life and it is both a blessing and a curse. If you care to remember, write it all down before it's forgotten and gone forever."

I never forgot those words, "Write it all down before it's gone forever." Now that I am at *that* age, I can attest to the fact that the past *does* come back to comfort and haunt us.

The past that I am about to share is the early chapters of my life growing up with my mother's family, which had a great impact on my life. It includes my grandmother's life stories, the "whispered" family conversations, and the events I was part of and witnessed. Without documenting part of my family history, it would one day all vanish as it has for millions of other families. I believe family heritage is very important and I want to share these stories with my children by not only passing them on but also bringing these characters back to life, which was at times painful but at the same time joyous. A priceless memory I want to pass on is the unconditional love that both my mother's and father's family had for their children and grandchildren.

To tell the story of East Clifton Avenue, I needed to create a *non-fictional* and *fictional* framework and then interspersed the true events, which took place in Sicily, New York, and Clifton, New Jersey. Many of the characters are real, while some are fictitious, which helps connect the true stories. Otherwise, these stories would just be stand-alone, disjointed fragments without appreciating the full personalities of the characters involved. I am guiding you through the story of East Clifton Avenue through the *fictitious* Buonoforte family with me as the grandson, Dean Fonte, the narrator. Although some of the characters may be similar to actual real-life people, in no way is my intention to besmirch or villainize anyone. These are my memories and perceptions of events and the people involved.

Interwoven are life lessons that can be learned by not only the good things but the not-so-good things that, perhaps if one is keen-sighted, can be avoided. There are many underlying questions I wondered about growing up and observing life around me. For example, what do we have to offer future generations? Why do bad family behaviors repeat themselves? How do we not make the same mistakes past generations have made in the name of "blood"?

At one time, countries were bound by bloodlines, with the idea that a mixing of blood through children would result in peace and prosperity. But as time went on, those bloodlines were broken and chaos ensued. The same is true with family blood relations that are broken down and may result in much chaos and pain. True family bonds are cultivated with loving relationships and not just a biological connection.

I hope you enjoy them.

Frank Plateroti, EdD

Main Characters

The Buonoforte Family

Enzo Buonoforte The main protagonist in the story and the Buonoforte patriarch and unelected "Mayor" of East Clifton Avenue. He is warm, affectionate, and clever. Devoted family man. When provoked, he can have a temper.

Anna Buonoforte Enzo's wife and the family matriarch. She can be aloof but is affectionate and caring. She is the mother of eight children and godmother to Anna Avero.

Maria Buonoforte Lerino First daughter of Enzo and Anna. She can be cold and unaffectionate.

Antonino Lerino Maria Buonoforte's husband. A hard worker and more affectionate than his wife.

Giusepina Buonoforte Litto Second daughter of Enzo and Anna. She is warm and affectionate, the exact opposite of Maria.

Pietro Buonoforte First son of Enzo and Anna. Just like Giusepina, he is warm and affectionate. A family favorite, especially to his sister Chiara. He is in an arranged marriage. His untimely death at thirty-five leaves his wife with three young children that the Buonofortes help take care of, especially Chiara. His death shakes the family to its core and changes the family dynamic.

Francesco Buonoforte The second son of Enzo and Anna. He is serious and aloof and is sometimes mistaken for a Hollywood actor. A favorite of Dean's.

Rita Buonoforte Petteri The third daughter of Enzo and Anna. She became responsible for the younger children, especially Chiara. She is somewhat overweight, self-centered, and secretly resentful of Chiara, but can be warm and affectionate.

Dante Petteri Husband of Rita. Originally from Northern Italy. A very good cook. He is handsome and "continental." Likes to try to "live large."

Giacomo "Jack" Buonoforte The third son of Enzo and Anna. He is handsome and charming with an athletic build. Arrogant and narcissistic. He is Chiara's nemesis.

Margo Buonoforte Wife of Jack Buonoforte. She is glamorous and cunning. Disappointed in the direction her life has gone and is bitter. Can be warm to those whom she chooses. She likes to imbibe.

Chiara Buonoforte-Fonte The fourth daughter of Enzo and Anna. She is slim, stunning, and the most attractive of the Buonoforte daughters. Like her father, she is clever and loves unconditionally, especially her three sons and her husband. She is very social and devoted to her Buonoforte family. Mother of three boys, with Dean Fonte being the oldest. She is also "high-strung" due to the death of her brother Pietro, with whom she was very close.

Joseph Fonte Husband of Chiara. Warm, caring, and very handsome, with jet-black hair and deep blue eyes. Like his wife, he loves unconditionally, especially his three sons. He is devoted to his wife. When provoked, he has a temper.

Dean Fonte Chiara's son and narrator of the story. He witnessed the many events of the Buonofortes and knows the family's stories and secrets, mostly from the stories told to him while taking care of his grandmother. Very much like his mother and grandfather.

Donatello "Donny" Buonoforte The youngest child of Enzo and Anna. He has a place in everyone's heart. Very close to his parents.

Giuseppe Buonoforte Enzo's father. A widower who was forced to marry Julia, Enzo's stepmother. He is aloof and disappointed with his life and with the death of his first wife, Giulietta, Enzo's mother.

Julia Scarpa Buonoforte Enzo's stepmother—the proverbial evil stepmother who abuses Enzo and was made a widow from her first husband by a Mafia vendetta.

Rosalia Scarpa Julia's daughter and Enzo's stepsister. Opposite to her mother, she is warm and loves Enzo.

Francesca Scarpa Julia's second daughter and Enzo's stepsister. Like her sister Rosalia, she is warm and loves Enzo.

The Buonoforte Friends and Acquaintances

Tomasso Fassino aka "Old man Fassino" The Fassionos and the Buonofortes are close family friends since the Buonofortes moved on East Clifton Avenue.

Rabbi Merlino Enzo's teacher and mentor. A warm and affectionate man of God. A father figure.

Aunt Josephine Enzo's aunt on his mother's side. She is warm, affectionate, and considers Enzo her son after Enzo's mother dies. She leaves Enzo a small inheritance.

Antonino Scarpa Warm and caring. Uncle of Rosalia and Francesca who takes the two girls to live with him and his business partner Victor Roselli in Agrigento, Sicily.

Victor Rosselli A big, brawny man with a big heart to match. Antonino's business partner. Antonino found him in a street outside a bar where he was beaten and robbed. Antonino saved his life.

Angelina Maria Cesare A stunning, retired famous opera singer and restaurant owner who becomes Don Carlo's lover and mother of their daughter, Lucia.

Beatrice Ceasare Sister of Angelina and wife of Carlo Masseria after the passing of Angelina Maria Cesare

Carlo Masseria Also known as Don Carlo; runs a numbers racket because of his uncanny ability to calculate numbers and betting odds. He has a photographic memory. Lover of Angelina Cesare. With the changing times, Carlo invests in legitimate businesses and becomes a multi-millionaire.

Bruno Sessino Close friend of Carlo Masseria and Enzo Buonoforte.

Howard Johnson Also a close friend of Enzo Buonoforte and Carlo Masseria. A "colored man" who overcame bigoted obstacles, with the help of Carlo Masseria and Enzo.

Anna Avero Head of the Paramus nursing home with a secret that will dramatically affect all those around her, including the Buonofortes.

Stefano San Giorgio Birthfather of Anna Avero. Father of Anna's half-brothers, Morris and Luca, and half-sister, Loretta.

Chapter 1
"Am I Dying?"

Enzo Buonoforte walked out of his house and stopped to look up and down East Clifton Avenue like he had done a million times before. At one time he knew all the families in every house. There were many times when he would walk home from his grocery store at the end of East Clifton Avenue on Lexington, which should only take about ten or fifteen minutes, but would end up taking almost an hour by the time he arrived home. He would talk to so many people who stopped him on his way home, asking about what new cheeses, olive oils, or meats were coming into the store, or they just wanted to talk and gossip. When he did come home early or on time, his wife Anna would ask if something was wrong.

"Che male? Is something wrong? Are you ill?"

She knew there was no problem. She would tease him and he would laugh and pinch her cheek, scrunch his lips, and say, "Ti amo! I love you!" She would brush his hand away when he would try to pinch her on her bottom and they would play a little "cat and mouse" game. Over the years when Enzo came home early from work, Anna knew why. That little game they played led to the conception of many of their children.

Today, on this late January day, the snow is blowing off the trees and the telephone wires, and Enzo stands and asks himself, as he has so many times lately, *where did the time go?* He looks at his hands and wonders, *how did my hands get so old?* He takes his walking cane from his right hand and holds it in his left. With his right hand, he rubs his knee, which has become ridden with arthritis. He looks around and even though it is late January he sees that some of the houses haven't removed their Christmas lights and wreaths on the doors, but the fresh snow on the wreaths gives them a renewed freshness.

Again, Enzo looks down at the end of East Clifton Avenue, toward Lexington, where his grocery store once stood, and reminisces about his favorite holiday, Christmas, when he and his son Pietro sold Christmas trees and wreaths outside the store. He was proud thinking that no matter how challenging and difficult the times may have been, he made sure his family would have wonderful Christmas memories. He remembers how, together with Pietro, they would go down to the nearby Paterson Market after Thanksgiving and fill up their pick-up truck with Christmas trees and wreaths. They never made a lot of money, if any, selling them but they just loved the sight of them in front of their store. Pietro hung a long string of Christmas lights over them and he would get a large empty metal container and start a fire to stay warm as the people came by to haggle over the price of the trees and the wreaths, and end up in the store to shop and talk to Enzo. Enzo's daughters Anna, Maria, and Giuseppina would bring a hot dinner for Enzo and Pietro who would still be working late. They would serve passersby hot coffee, hot chocolate, biscotti, and even grappa, a strong liqueur made from the seeds, stalks, and stems leftover from the wine-making process.

On Christmas Eve, Enzo would close the store and he and Pietro would bring the trees that didn't sell down to the Sicilian Mussomeli Society in neighboring Passaic and give them away free in a lottery to families who couldn't afford to buy them. Enzo would always save one tree for his own family. Sometimes the tree he brought home was so sparse that Pietro would have to cut off branches from another tree to fill in their Christmas tree with wire or string.

Christmas Eve meant sitting around the potbelly stove eating oranges and roasted chestnuts. Enzo and Anna would sip hot expresso or taste homemade wine given to them by one of the neighbors or store customers. Even though at that time there wasn't much money to spend on toys, during the year Enzo would find toys that were being thrown away and he would fix them and give them to the younger children to open

Christmas morning. It didn't matter if it was a truck or a doll, it was a toy, and that was the best that Enzo and Anna could do. As the other children were born, Anna, being practical, would crochet slippers and scarves for herself, Enzo, and the children. Homemade Christmas decorations would be put on a sparse tree with small candles. A bucket of water was next to the tree not only for watering but in case the tree caught on fire from the candles. When they finished decorating the tree and lit the candles, they all sat around and talked about how beautiful it was. Enzo would lead the singing of Italian Christmas hymns.

Over the years, more Christmas traditions were formed. Enzo would still close the store for Christmas Eve until the day after Christmas Day and still his friend "old man Fassino" would say he was "pazzo," crazy, because he could do a lot of business on Christmas Eve. Enzo didn't care. This was a family time. Besides, he reminded all his customers starting before Thanksgiving that they had to get their orders in and pick them up the day before Christmas Eve, and most of them did.

Early in the afternoon on Christmas Eve, neighbors would call on Enzo and Anna and bring homemade bottles of wine and grappa, and every kind of cookies, cakes, pastries, and candies they either home-made or were sent from relatives in Italy. During past holidays, Enzo and Pietro would give the very needy neighbors groceries and other things the neighbors couldn't afford. As time went on, when these families' situations improved, they wanted to show their appreciation, so they would drop off cookies or cakes, handmade hankies, and other handmade gifts to show their gratitude. Enzo and Anna were reluctant to take anything but they realized that accepting a gift from these families gave the family the opportunity not only to express their gratitude but also helped them maintain their family pride and dignity. Sometimes there was so much food and so many gifts that Enzo would bring them to the church to distribute. He made donations to the local synagogue, in honor of his friend and tutor in Mussomeli, Rabbi Merlino, who had written a letter of introduction for Enzo to the local rabbi.

Enzo was extremely loyal throughout his life. Sometimes people would stop him and thank him for something he did years ago that he didn't remember. He just did what he thought was right and never forgot his hard times growing up. He wanted to thank God for leading him to where he was now. He was never a churchgoer, but instead, he lived his religion.

In the early Christmas Eve evening, neighbors who visited would all have a toast with grappa or wine and start singing traditional Italian Christmas songs. Then they would go to their homes for Christmas Eve dinner. Everyone would have variations of the same foods; keeping with the church rule of not eating meat on Christmas Eve. Instead, there was eggplant, antipasto with cheeses and pickled vegetables, spaghetti con sarde, sardines finished with fried breadcrumbs, baccala, a salted cod fish dried and then soaked for three days then baked with potatoes, black olives, onions, and fresh tomatoes. Everyone would stay awake and attend midnight mass at Sacred Heart Church. After Church, at the Buonoforte home, Anna would fry sausage and peppers for sandwiches, because meat could be eaten after midnight. All the other food that was put away before church would be brought out again. After everyone ate, the excited children would be off to bed and the desserts and coffee, and anisette, grappa, and other liqueurs, would be served.

On Christmas morning, Anna would be the first to wake and go downstairs to the kitchen to prepare breakfast before the children would wake. Despite her efforts, the anxious children would be up to see what was in their stockings and under the tree. Nothing was opened until Enzo was awake. The anxious children would try to wake Enzo, who would make believe he was sleeping. Then Anna would yell up the stairs for Enzo to get up and he would laugh and the children would pull his hands until he got up. They would help him put on his robe and slippers and come downstairs. By this time Anna had made coffee and put a turkey in the oven, if they were lucky enough to have a turkey or even a chicken.

When Anna and Enzo first moved to Clifton Avenue, Enzo peddled fruit, vegetables, eggs, and whatever else he could sell out of a horse-drawn carriage. Early on Christmas Eve, before anyone would wake up, he would go around town and see which butcher had an abundance of turkeys or chickens and then barter for eggs and vegetables from his peddler's cart. Enzo was a skilled barterer because almost always they had a small turkey or chicken and it would be served with all the trimmings for Christmas dinner. This didn't go unnoticed. When the children got older, they remembered their father made sure there was always plenty of food on the table and Anna made sure nothing went to waste. When Anna cut the bread, she made sure she gathered the breadcrumbs to feed their chickens. There was even a superstition that it was bad luck to spill olive oil since it was so expensive. As with the other thousands of immigrants, hard times were never forgotten, and the good times were never taken for granted.

A tradition everyone looked forward to was, a week before Christmas Day, Anna's sisters who lived in Buffalo would send homemade fig cookies and aprons or embroidered hankies. Anna would send back different cookies and knitted slippers. It was always exciting because it was almost the only time that packages were delivered to the house. It was just another reason to look forward to Christmas. Years later, it would be a tradition that Enzo's youngest daughter Chiara would continue after she got married. Her aunt Maria from Buffalo, who was also her godmother, would send a new apron and fig cookies individually wrapped in waxed paper. This went on for years until her aunt passed away.

As more children were born into the family, the gifts would be "store bought" and would be practical gifts, like socks, underwear, slippers, and shoes. There were even refurbished "hand-me-down" clothes. But Anna would make sure the younger children always got some new outfits. There would also be little trinkets that, although some would consider cheap, were cherished. The stockings that were hung near the potbelly stove were still filled with fruits and nuts, but now also candy.

When the older children still lived at home and started to go to work, they bought gifts for the younger children. As their siblings got married and left the house and had children of their own, the gifts became scarcer. Over the years though, the one thing that was always in abundance, especially on holidays, was food. Enzo still remembers so many times when as a child he went to bed hungry because his stepmother would feed her daughters first and there would be only scraps left for him. His stepsisters would even sneak food to him until they got caught and punished. Enzo swore that when he had children they would eat before him and they would never go to bed hungry. Even now on Friday nights, when some of their children would come over, he makes them eat first and walks around the table to make sure they are enjoying everything and then he sits down to eat his dinner, which for him because of his ulcer is warm milk and broken up bread.

As Enzo unlocks his car the memories keep racing through his mind, which causes some excitement; both happy and sad. As he takes the brush from under the driver's seat, he notices that it didn't hurt when he bent down. He's had trouble with his knees for years, ever since he fell off a grocery truck when he was younger, and then the arthritis started as he got older and he had to walk with a cane. He swore to this day that he was pushed off the produce truck, but he could not prove it. He always remembered the incident and who he thought pushed him. Many years later, he heard that the person he believed pushed him off the truck was killed because of some bootlegging vendetta. It didn't really make Enzo happy and he knew the man had a wife and children. He sent Pietro with a basket of food for the family and he wanted it to be anonymous. He hated overt gratitude. That is who Enzo is.

As he begins to brush off his car, Enzo turns to see if Anna is still at the front door of the house. She always watches Enzo as he drives away. As she admires the snow and watches Enzo, she suddenly remembers that she has the chicken cacciatore on the stove and runs back to the kitchen. Enzo turns around to wave to her but she is gone. He turns back to the car and begins to brush off the snow. As he lifts the brush, he feels a sudden pain that travels down his arm and he drops the brush. The pain travels to his chest and he feels weak. Then, as if in slow motion, he tries to grasp onto the car, but his hand slips from the wet snow and he falls to his knees. He tries to call out but can't. He slowly falls to his side. His face lands in the small pile of snow he has just brushed from the windshield of his car and he tries to blow it away. There is a profound silence and his only thought is, *am I dying?*

He doesn't know why he thinks this. It just seemed instinctive. It is the same feeling one gets when they are tired and begins to fall asleep. Even though Enzo tries to fight it, he knows that inevitably he will surrender. As falling asleep is a natural feeling, so is surrendering to death, and he begins to realize what is happening. He is no longer in pain from the arthritis that racked his joints for years. His knees, which were always stiff and sore, feel non-existent. He has no sense of the cold, no sense of his body, and no sense of time. It is as if time doesn't exist. *Am I dying?* again, he thinks. But he still sees his driveway and the house to the right of his house. He smells the aroma of lemon blossoms in the air and feels elated. It is as if he can remember everything that has happened in his life. All his memories clash and then stop. He remembers a discussion he had a few weeks ago at the Mussomeli Society with some of his friends about dying. They always joked about their final move to their "tiny apartment" in Calvary Cemetery.

The snow starts falling again on East Clifton Avenue as Enzo lay in the snow. He realizes his prayer is at last being answered, and he is not afraid. As he got older, he prayed that he wanted to be the one to die first. He couldn't bear to live without his Anna. He has a sense of what is to come, and how the experience is almost exactly how he envisioned it would be. He realizes that his life is passing in front of him as both an observer and participant. And yet, he doesn't know why. *Is it to resolve things? Is this the purgatory the church talks about? Am I going to be punished for things I did wrong? Will I feel the pain that I caused others, even if I didn't mean to?*

All these thoughts race through his mind at once. Then all he can remember is the last few seconds of seeing Anna at the front door as if in slow motion. He isn't afraid. He is trying to keep his eyes open. He thinks he sees his dead son Pietro and he gives out a small gasp. Pietro seems to be slowly walking from the driveway of his house toward him. Pietro's hands are reaching out to Enzo and he has a large smile and even begins to laugh. Enzo doesn't understand what he is seeing. Next to Pietro, Enzo thinks he sees his father and he is startled. But then there is a soft, white glow, and behind his father, he sees someone who must be his mother. He was so young when she died and he has only seen a blurry picture of her. When he sees her, his eyes water and he tries to call out to her, "Momma, Momma, Momma..." and he realizes his words are slurring. He can see the translucent shadows of other people behind Pietro who are also moving toward him. There are some he thinks he recognizes and remembers, but hasn't seen in years. Enzo tries desperately to concentrate. As they come closer, he feels more euphoric, with feelings that he never felt before. He wants to be totally enveloped in the feelings and run to them but he can't. The glow coming from them seems to be getting stronger. *Is this a dream? Am I just dying in my dream?*

He hears someone calling his name, and the visions of his son and the others disappear and he knows it isn't a dream. He is angry and becomes lucid and thoughts race again through his mind. *Who is calling my name? Was that real? Why did they leave me? Who caused them to disappear?* He gets angry.

He looks past the driveway and tries to focus and then he sees his close friend Howard Johnson. At that instant, Enzo is struck with the remembrance of when he first met Howard and why he felt so close to him. His mind is racing and time seems to stand still. Visions of times and places and people go through his head. Enzo hears Howard's voice again, and Enzo seems to be at the place where they first met. He can smell food cooking and there is talking and laughter. He looks around and he is in a restaurant kitchen. *Oh, dear God! Angelina Restaurante!* Tears begin to roll down his cheek. *What is happening? Anna?* He hears Howard, but he can only hear him.

"Enzo, Enzo! My God, what happened?"

Howard, seeing Enzo lying on the ground, drops his shopping bags, runs, and calls to him again. "Enzo, Enzo, my God, Enzo!" By this time Enzo is semi-conscious and he tries to speak to Howard. Howard picks up Enzo, cradles him in his arms, and carries him to the back door of the house screaming for Anna. Anna, seeing Howard from the kitchen window running to the back door as she is putting something into the refrigerator, is wondering what is going on. She hears Howard screaming her name and realizes something is very wrong. She runs to the back door and sees Howard holding Enzo, who is trying to speak.

"Anna, he must have collapsed as he was cleaning off the car. I'll bring him upstairs and you stay with him and I will call the police. He will be all right."

Howard knows he isn't going to be all right. Enzo is dying and he doesn't know why he even said that. Howard runs up the stairs and places Enzo on the bed with Anna following. Anna takes Enzo and places his head on her lap. Howard can hear Anna calling Enzo and speaking in Italian as he races down the stairs to call the police.

At first, Anna cannot fully realize what is happening. She remembers years ago when Enzo fell taking produce off a truck at the Paterson Market. Both knees were bloody and Enzo couldn't walk right since. Then arthritis developed and he had to walk with a cane. Anna thinks again this may be just something he will recover from. But Anna begins to understand what is happening.

Saliva is oozing out of Enzo's mouth and Anna cleans it with a hankie she keeps in her sleeve. She begins to cry and shouts for Howard and help. She tries to get herself together and again wipes Enzo's mouth. For a few seconds, Enzo looks at her and a tear runs down his cheek. It seems everything is happening in slow motion. Enzo tries to speak but his mouth is contorted due to the stroke that is taking effect. He tries to lift himself and points across the room in the direction of a Crucifix that is under a glass dome on a shelf outside their bedroom. He tries to say something, but he can't form the words. He keeps trying to point to the Cross and say something. Then he slowly lets his hand down. He is trying to raise his head and look past Anna, trying to talk to someone over her shoulder, and for a few seconds, it looks like he is smiling. Anna turns to look, but no one is there. Anna is confused. Again, he is trying to smile and say something. At first, Anna thinks Howard has come back from calling the police, but when she looks over her shoulder there is no one there. Enzo tries again to raise himself.

"Che Enzo? What?" she asks him through her tears. She thinks she hears him trying to say a name but his mouth won't form the words. After a few seconds, he stops trying and just looks at Anna. His body is limp. Anna knows he is gone. She takes his head into her lap, crying, rocking, and calling his name. His eyes are still open looking at her.

After Howard calls the police, he runs across the street and gets his wife. As they run back to the house and up the stairs, they can hear the sirens of the approaching police and the ambulance. Howard and his wife rush into the room and are about to tell Anna the police and the ambulance are on their way, but they both stop in their tracks. They see Anna holding Enzo and rocking back and forth. Enzo's right arm has dropped to his side. Howard gently places his arm on Anna's lap and steps back to his wife. They realize that Enzo is gone. They just stand there watching. Tears roll down Howard's face, and his wife buries her face in Howard's chest and cries hysterically. They hear the sirens getting closer and then the sirens stop. The back door opens and a policeman holding an oxygen tank rushes up the stairs and sees what is going on. He knows it is too late. The policeman realizes who the two people are.

"Christ, these are Jack's Buonoforte's parents."

Jack works for the city of Clifton and a couple of times he brought his father around to show Enzo where he worked and introduced him to some of the people in city hall. This policeman is one of the people who Jack had introduced to his father a few times.

The ambulance workers rush in with a stretcher. They can also see that Enzo is gone. The policeman gently talks to Anna and tries to get her to let go of Enzo. It takes Howard's wife to get Anna to let go of him. The ambulance workers slowly place Enzo on the stretcher, but his arm drops to the side. Anna quickly jumps up, kisses his hand, and embraces his arm. Finally, Anna moves away to let the ambulance workers take Enzo. Howard and his wife sit on the bed and embrace Anna. They watch Enzo leave his home for the last time.

Howard and his wife walk Anna down the stairs into the living room and place her in Enzo's chair. At first, Anna is a little reluctant to sit there, but she realizes it no longer matters. Howard's wife takes one of the dining chairs, sits next to Anna, and holds her hands. She is trying to stay calm for Anna's sake, but tears are welling up in her eyes. Anna is shaking her head and calling Enzo and speaking in Italian with such heartache and passion. Although Howard's wife cannot understand what she is saying, she knows what Anna must mean and what she is feeling at this moment. When Anna calms down, she calls for Howard.

"Please call Don Carlo and then Chiara, she will call my other children. The numbers are in the book next to the phone."

At first, Howard thinks it is a strange request, to call Don Carlo first. But to Sicilians, respect is very important. When he tries to call Don Carlo, no one answers the phone so he calls Anna's daughter Chiara and will try to call Don Carlo later in the afternoon. He calls Chiara but she isn't home. He speaks to her son Dean and then her husband Joseph and tells him what has happened.

Chapter 2
Everyone knew this would not be a typical Sunday visit to the Buonoforte home.

Chiara is the first of the Buonoforte children to arrive at the house after hearing the news of her father's death. Chiara had gone with neighbors to bring their neighbor's son to Fort Dix in New Jersey to serve in the military. When she arrived back home Joseph told her that her father had died. Joseph had prepared himself because he anticipated her reaction. She was hysterical and blamed herself because her father wanted to come to visit that morning but she said she was busy. Joseph tried fruitlessly to reason and calm her down to no avail.

"What difference would it have made if he was coming here? He was going to go to Donatello's house instead. The same thing would have happened."

Chiara was inconsolable. For Dean and the two other Fonte children, the death of their grandfather seemed unreal because this was the first time they experienced anyone dying. They stayed in their rooms because they couldn't stand to see their mother so upset and it was also not real to them yet and didn't know how to react.

There was one other time that Chiara lost herself in her emotions, and that was when her brother Pietro died. She suffered from what her doctor called a "nervous breakdown." It took almost a year for her to fully recover, and she had to be given vitamin B shots to keep up her strength due to her serious weight loss. Anna had her older daughter Rita, who was married at the time and close to Chiara, cook for Chiara and make her eat because she was losing too much weight.

Since then, Chiara learned to keep her emotions in check to survive. Although sometimes she would slip into a melancholy mood remembering when she rushed to the hospital and saw her brother being brought into the operating room to repair a bleeding ulcer, which also developed into pneumonia. Pietro was conscious and held Chiara's hand as she was sobbing uncontrollably. Pietro told her that he would be alright and not to worry. As the nurses tried to push her aside, she screamed for him to *promise* her that he would be all right.

"Chiara...Io promeso. I promise...."

As they rolled him away, he kept promising her, and she could see him nodding his head and waving his hand. Anna, Enzo, and Pietro's wife Nina and their oldest daughter were in the hospital waiting room anxiously waiting to find out about Pietro's condition. Minutes turned into hours and finally, the doctor appeared and they could all instantly tell that things did not go well.

Nina began to sob. Chiara, who was sitting next to Anna held her arm around Anna's shoulder but then stood up and went over to Enzo as if she knew what the doctor was going to say and she wanted to be near her father who was also standing.

"I am truly sorry. He lost too much blood and with the pneumonia, he was just too weak. He came to us too late."

Chiara collapsed into hysteria holding her father. The doctor tried to take Enzo aside but Chiara was holding onto Enzo so the doctor further explained what had happened.

"Mr. Buonoforte, your son's lungs were very damaged because of his heavy smoking. He even had a hard time breathing when I saw him last year when he had similar symptoms with his ulcer. I desperately tried to have him stop smoking and take better care of himself. I am truly sorry."

The doctor knew it wasn't his fault, but he also felt the guilt that doctors feel when they lose a patient.

Anna was screaming, as was Nina and her daughter. Chiara went over to them and embraced them both. Enzo went over to Anna who was sobbing uncontrollably. A couple of nurses came in and seeing what was going on began to tear up and tried to comfort the family. Finally, Enzo calmed them down and was pulled to the side by one of the nurses who discussed what was needed to have the body removed and suggested a sedative for anyone who needed one. Enzo said they would be alright and the nurses left. Anna calmed down with just tears rolling down her cheeks as she rocked a sobbing Chiara.

Even though the loss was devastating, Anna was strong. Part was her nature, and part was a familiarity with this type of loss she experienced in Sicily. Many families lost children either to disease or to vendettas. You had to be strong to survive in Sicily. You also had to keep silent and trust very few. She knew this, and that is why many trusted her with their problems. They knew that Anna would never discuss anything that was told in confidence. Most times she would not even tell Enzo. It did annoy some people that Anna never discussed any of her own family matters. Sometimes it gave the impression of Anna being "aloof." When some friends asked her what was going on in her family, she would just make small talk. She was used to keeping silent about her family, which was how she was the most comfortable.

As time went by, Pietro's death was never forgotten but also never discussed. The one time that Anna does show visible sadness is on March first, the anniversary of Pietro's death. Of course, the loss of a child is unthinkable. This loss was even worse. She never told anyone, not even Enzo, that aside from Chiara and Donatello, Pietro was her favorite. He was much like her own bother Pietro, who her son Pietro was named after. Anna was as close to her brother as Chiara was to Pietro.

Pietro would do anything for his family, but especially for his little sister, Chiara. One summer when Chiara was five, he took her to the park, where there was "Chico" the junk man. They both stopped to talk to him. It was a very hot day and the horse was very anxious. A small piece of metal fell by the wheel of the cart. Chiara bent down to pick it up and suddenly the horse bolted and the back wheel ran over Chiara's index finger. As she screamed, blood began gushing out of her finger.

Without hesitation, Pietro took off his T-shirt, wrapped up her little finger, picked her up, and ran all the way to Dr. Conserva's office on Randolph Avenue, a ten-minute walk. Although it was difficult, he never stopped to take a breather. As he was running with her, he kept promising that she would be all right.

As she was sobbing, she said, "You promise, you promise?"

Pietro kept repeating, "I promise, Chiara. I promise."

That would be their special bond. Anytime Chiara would start to misbehave and Pietro would scold her, she would promise to be better. Anytime Pietro said he would take her somewhere or get her something special, she would always make him promise. Neither one ever broke a promise except once. Pietro couldn't keep his promise that he would be alright the last time Chiara saw him.

When Chiara calmed down after hearing of her father's death, it was decided that Joseph would bring Chiara to her parent's house first, to shield their sons from the anticipated emotional hysteria, and then when things calmed down, Joseph would go back home to pick up Dean and his two younger brothers.

After Joseph drops off Chiara, he goes back home and waits to hear from Chiara. After a couple of hours, he talks to Chiara on the phone and it is then he takes their three sons and drives to the East Clifton Avenue house. In the car, Joseph tries to explain their grandfather's death, especially to the two younger children who aren't sure what is going on. Then he turns his explanation to Dean, who is twelve and can fully grasp the situation.

"Dean, we all have to die. The hard thing is that the person who dies will go to heaven, but for us left behind, we will miss that person. That is the hardest part."

After Joseph's explanation, there is silence for the rest of the ride. When the four of them arrive, the three boys first hug their grandmother and offer their condolences, as instructed by their father. Joseph watches Dean who is stoic. *Just like his mother,* he thinks. Joseph watches Chiara and her mother and can see how they are both trying so hard to keep from showing their emotions. Then he looks at Dean again. The same stoic reaction as his mother and grandmother.

As neighbors cautiously trudge their way along East Clifton Avenue and up the driveway to the back door of the house, Howard is trying to hurriedly shovel a path through the snow on the long driveway to the back door. It is hard to see who is walking in the pathway of the driveway because the wind is blowing the snow off the roofs into everyone's faces, so everyone who passes Howard just nods with a solemn hello and receives a quiet nod in return. Everyone sadly knows this will not be a typical Sunday visit to the Buonoforte home. This is a different kind of social call and it won't be pleasant. These Sunday visitors come to pay their respects to the Buonoforte family for the loss of their patriarch, father, and husband, Enzo Buonoforte.

Before entering the house, everyone does their best to wipe off their feet and shake the snow off their coats and hats. Whoever is nearest the screen door holds it for the next person. The mood is solemn and there is very little small talk.

Entering the house from the back door, there is a staircase to the upstairs living area and bedrooms. These stairs are not used in the winter because there isn't any heat in the stairwell. Another staircase was built inside the basement dining room for better access to the upstairs rooms during the cold weather. As you enter from the back door you turn left to three steps that go down to the French door that leads to the downstairs dining and kitchen areas. Any tall visitor has to bend down a bit due to the low header of the doorway. On the wooden header is nailed a horseshoe that has a thermometer in the middle, and next to it is the emergency switch for the oil burner that heats the house. As each visitor goes down the steps, they awkwardly balance themselves as they open the glass French door to enter the room. This results in people waiting in line to come into the house to the annoyance of some due to the cold air coming into the room.

When finally entering the dining room, there is a low hum of people talking and a waft of cigarette smoke mixed with the aroma of different foods being brought onto the dining table. There are people everywhere. Some of the Buonoforte grandchildren are sitting on the steps that lead to the upstairs, and women with aprons are taking the trays from the newly arrived visitors. At the same time, Chiara, and her sisters Maria and Rita bring napkins, plates, and flatware for people to help themselves.

It seems that everyone arriving proceeds the same way as the person before. Maria is collecting coats from the new arrivals and with the help of some of the grandchildren, they take the coats and put them on the upstairs living-room couch. Then as each visitor goes to pay their respects, they hold Anna Buonoforte's hand and in a low voice express the usual condolences and disbelief. Then still teary-eyed, they whisper a humble explanation of the food they brought as a small expression of their grief. As with other cultures, food is an important part of the Italian culture and a serious expression of pride for each family. Many prepared foods may be the same, but the preparations are different. Some families have not spoken for years due to arguments regarding how each family thinks their way is the best way to make tomato sauce, or as some refer to it, "gravy," or that their mother's meatballs are the best, and on and on it goes. As each person finishes their condolences, they take a sly inventory of what is on the dining table and make a quick comparison to the plates or trays they themselves have brought. As their eyes quickly leave the table, they greet others as they try to slowly make their way around the room to the overcrowded kitchen. Some even whisper comments to each other about the food, which in many cases is not complimentary.

With everyone in the crowded dining room, Anna still expects Enzo to walk out of the kitchen bringing her a cup of expresso. She looks toward the entry door to see if he is coming in from shopping talking a mile a minute about this or that. As each person bends down to talk to Anna, she is reminded that her Enzo is gone. She realizes she will slowly forget the sound of his voice, his smell, and the way he would smile and gently kiss her forehead. The person in the coffin will not be the man she fell in love with over fifty years ago. That person is gone, and she will wait until the time comes for her to join him. For now, she just wants everyone to leave. She does not need all that is going on to be reminded that he is gone. She does not need people to cry over her. She has had enough. Then she hears a voice that she welcomes.

"Zia, can I get you something to eat? Maybe a nice espresso?" Sofia leans close to Anna so she can softly speak to her. Anna looks at Sofia and smiles.

"Zia, my heart goes to you." Sofia leans in and gives Anna a welcomed hug and Anna makes a comment unusual to Anna's nature.

"Sofia, look at those cows. What do you think they are talking about? Did they come to see me, or gossip about everyone and what everyone brought? I never liked many of them but they are the wives of Enzo's friends. Such fakers, and I had to be a faker too. Not anymore. Now I don't have to see many of them anymore. Grazie Dio."

Sofia looks justifiably surprised at Anna's comment. Then Anna looks at Sofia who is looking around the room and whispers, "They're not here. They were here before but they left to go to the funeral home to find out about the arrangements. They will be back. I did not want them to go without me, but I will take care of that."

Sofia knows exactly whom Anna is talking about. She is looking for Anna's son Jack. It was before the war that Sofia introduced Margo to Jack as her boyfriend. Sofia took Margo to watch Jack play basketball at the Clifton PAL Center. Sofia had a strong infatuation with Jack and Margo knew it. When Jack went into the army, Sofia and Jack wrote to each other at least every week, even when he was overseas. But then Jack's letters stopped coming and Sofia just thought it was because of the war and the difficulty delivering mail back to the United States and the censors, or maybe worse. It was not unusual at that time. But that wasn't the real reason. What Sofia didn't know was that Margo was also writing to Jack when he was overseas.

When Jack returned from the war, there was a vague excuse to Sofia that letters couldn't easily be sent back to the States. Regardless of the explanation, he was different towards Sofia. She didn't know if it was because of the war or if it was just part of his nature. Jack's emotions were always erratic. When things were going his way, he could be charming, but he had a dark side and when he was angry, he could be cruel. Even though he would be quick to apologize, she didn't want to put up with that type of behavior in a relationship.

One example that made her really think about his dark, selfish nature was when he came back from the war and asked to borrow his sister Chiara's car. Chiara, who was working at Botany Village Mills then, had to take a bus to work, which was not only expensive but a big inconvenience. Time after time Chiara would try to explain to Jack that she needed the car and he had enough money to buy his own car. One day she met him as he was getting out of the car and told him she wanted to use it. As he got out of the car, he was yelling that *he* needed the car. Chiara had had enough at that point and told him to take the bus like she had all these months. He got so mad that he didn't see her hand on the car frame of the car and he slammed the car door on her hand and split the nail on her index finger so hard that blood was gushing all over the car. It was the same finger that she had hurt when the junk man's horse ran over it when she was a child. He took his handkerchief, wrapped her hand, and drove her to Dr. Conserva's, where they waited an hour to have it taken care of. Then he drove her back home and he again took her car. In many ways, he was more of a spoiled boy than a man. Because of his good looks, he got away with a lot and he knew it. The only problem was that Sofia loved the "bad boy."

Even though Margo knew that Sofia was in love with Jack, it didn't matter because Margo was used to getting what she wanted, and she wanted Jack. She wanted Jack even more because Sofia was in love with him. When Jack came back from the war, Margo knew exactly how to charm Jack and play to his boyish ego. She used every device to hook him, and he became hooked. At the time they met, Margo was trying to become a model. She did get some jobs posing in the Meyer Brothers store in nearby Paterson. She also modeled clothes in some other stores in Passaic when they would get the new season's fashions. Jack was impressed by Margo's modeling but as she got older, it was becoming harder for her to get jobs because she didn't have a soft look like the designers and stores wanted in their models. Also, due to her fondness for vodka, she was putting on weight. To get more modeling opportunities she had to commute to New York City where all the big stores and famous designers were and where there were more modeling opportunities, but the competition was tough. She was also getting into a routine that was making her look older and tired because she liked to stay out late and party, go to dance halls, and drink her vodka cocktails. She saw Jack as a way to stop working and stay at home, and for a time her drinking stopped and Jack and Margo decided to get engaged.

Of course, when Sofia found out what was going on with Margo and Jack, Margo and Sofia stopped talking for obvious reasons, but the engagement did not stop Sofia from having feelings for Jack. Margo chose Chiara to be her maid of honor, but it would turn out to be a rocky friendship.

Anna tells Sofia that she isn't hungry or thirsty, but asks Sofia to help her up so she can go upstairs to the bathroom and perhaps lie down for a while. Sofia slowly helps Anna from her chair. Anna's arthritis in her knees makes it very difficult for her to stand after sitting for long periods of time. Anna is on the one hand grateful for the help, but at the same time, she is resentful that she needs it. The years have been hard for Anna. Giving birth to eight children and hard work has taken its toll. Like most women of her social and economic way of life, she worked right up to the moment of giving birth. There were no hospital stays. All the children were born in the house with the help of a midwife. After only a day or two of giving birth, Anna was cooking, cleaning, and doing whatever it took to keep the family going without any complaints. It didn't matter to her how hard she had to work, she loved her husband and her children. This is what Sicilian women do. It's all about family.

When Anna first came to America, she weighed only one hundred and ten pounds and was five feet two inches tall. Now, at the age of almost eighty, she is forty to fifty pounds heavier and she has shrunk two inches. Most days she wears heavy black shoes with a small heel. Her ankles have grown heavy and are covered with support hose, which are pulled up her leg and attached with gray elastic garters that hold the stockings just below her knees. She wears loose-fitting housedresses that are buttoned halfway in the front with a small lace collar around her neck. Over her housedress, she wears a neatly pressed apron that ties in the back. There are two pockets on the front of the apron. One pocket holds a small handkerchief and the other pocket contains hard candies from Italy that are filled with different fruit jellies given to anyone who deserves a little treat. Her hands are pudgy extensions of her arms, which when outstretched, seem to have small hams hanging from them. When she hugs or embraces you with her large arms, the love radiates from her body and everything is right with the world.

Her hair had lost its color years ago, and is now snow white, and is covered with a thin netting to keep it neatly in place. Her face is round and her skin is clear and smooth with almost no wrinkles. From her elongated earlobes hang small, round gold earrings that were a surprise anniversary present from Enzo, too long ago for her to remember when. Her nose is somewhat bulbous and has a small mole at the right side where the nose connects to her face. She loves to laugh but tries not to show the few top teeth that she has left in her mouth, which she covers with her hand. Even though she has bottom dentures, they are very uncomfortable and Enzo cuts her food into small pieces and she tries to make the vegetables softer when she cooks them. Her eyes are dark and small and twinkle when she smiles. When she sees you, she looks right inside you, and you feel at peace with this seemingly quiet, unassuming little woman. People just gravitate to her, and the few times that she is sitting and relaxing, it is always with her husband and usually with two or three grandchildren at her feet.

Sofia helps guide Anna to the stairs. There are so many people standing around in such a small area that it would be very easy for anyone to fall. As Anna slowly climbs the stairs, Chiara, who is carrying a small platter of food, calls out to her.

Sofia explains that Anna is going upstairs to rest awhile. As Anna makes it to the top of the stairs, the people who are standing or sitting in the upstairs living room suddenly stop talking and some of them go over to greet her. Her son Donatello, also known as Donny, moves quickly to help his mother, who gives a small smile. Anna reaches up to Donatello's head and pulls it slightly down to give him a kiss. He walks her to her bedroom and asks Anna if she wants help to her bed, but she shakes her head. Sofia greets Donatello and says she will help Anna to her bed.

Donatello leaves and Sofia helps Anna sit on the bed so she can take off Anna's shoes. With Sofia's help, Anna lies down in bed and Sofia covers her with a blanket that is at the foot of the bed. When Sofia leaves the room and closes the door, Anna turns and strokes the pillow and imagines it is still warm from Enzo's head. She positions herself sideways on the bed facing the windows, so that no one will hear her and she softly cries bitterly into her husband's pillow. At this moment she wants to be with him more than she ever did all the years they were married. At this moment, she will gladly join him in death.

"Momma, Momma," Chiara whispers as she cracks open the bedroom door to check on her mother. Donatello walks behind Chiara and puts his hand gently on her shoulder and tries to see if Anna is sleeping.

He whispers in Chiara's ear, "I think she is either sleeping or she doesn't want to be bothered."

Chiara slowly closes the door. The moment she closes it, music from the clock radio on a bureau in the living area turns on and the music is loud. A couple of people jump up and fumble to turn the music off and just pull the plug.

"Who was playing with the clock radio?" Rita snaps. "Chiara, was your son Dean playing with the clock radio?"

"Shhhhh!" Chiara snaps louder. "Right away you blame my son. Did you see him up here?" She waves her hand in disgust and goes to check on her mother again, but her mother hasn't moved.

Rita doesn't respond and sits next to her husband who is annoyed at her and whispers to her to shut up. She doesn't respond. Chiara knows that it was probably her son Dean who was playing with the radio earlier, but she won't give Rita the satisfaction.

About an hour later Chiara and the others in the living room hear the door to the bathroom off the master bedroom close. Realizing that Anna is awake, everyone speaks a little softer. Sofia comes back upstairs.

"Chiara. Your brother Jack is on the phone."

Chiara, hearing Jack's name, grimaces as she starts walking downstairs after Sofia. Chiara takes the extension phone in the dining room.

"Yeah, Jack. Yeah. Tuesday and Wednesday and then the funeral on Thursday. No. I don't know if anyone is coming from Buffalo. If they come, they come. I can't worry about it now. Don't worry about the money, Jack. Don't worry, Momma has it. You won't have to give anything. I'm gonna warn you though, Momma didn't like that you and Margo went to the funeral home without her. Don't worry, she will tell you why. OK...Yeah...What? Why did you buy Papa a suit at Robert Hall? We have the suit he wore at their anniversary party they got at Moe and Arnie's."

Chiara, who is getting agitated, rolls her eyes at Sofia who covers her mouth to muffle her laugh.

"Good, take it back to Robert Hall and get your money back or you keep the suit." She looks at Sofia and hangs up the phone. "Christ."

"Chiara, I think more people have come in, and they are asking for your mother."

"OK, I'll help my mother get downstairs. Thanks."

Rita and Chiara help Anna back downstairs and get her situated in Enzo's chair. People who have just come in surround Anna. Chiara and Rita go up to the master bedroom to fix the bed and look for a sweater for Anna. Rita can see through the frosty front bedroom windows that Jack and Margo are arriving back from the funeral home.

"Chiara." Rita motions to Chiara to come look out the window. "Look at what Jack is doing. I think he is trying to give Howard money for shoveling the snow."

Chiara moves close to Rita and wipes some of the condensation from the window to get a better view.

"Oh my God! How insulting! He always treats Howard like a servant just because he's colored. What an asshole!"

Chiara shakes her head as she is talking and can see Margo trying to pull Jack away.

"Look at Margo with that fur-collared coat. Where does she think she is going, to a ball? Maybe she realizes he is making an ass of himself or is she trying to save him money?" Rita answers her own question. "Margo must realize he is making an ass of himself because whatever else you can say about her, she's not cheap. She's too used to paying for people to like her."

Chiara rubs her hands together, trying to dry them from wiping the condensation from the window, and then turns to Rita as she walks toward the dresser.

"Remember what happened at Momma and Papa's 50th anniversary and the coats?"

Rita rolls her eyes and says, "Oh my God! Was Papa mad! I will never forget that. What an ass Jack was."

Chiara grimaces and asks Rita, "What really happened again? I was with Momma."

Rita shakes her head. "My God. Don't you remember? Jack and Margo come in, and they see Howard, and they give him their coats to hang up. Then they give Margo's mother and brother their coats to Howard. Someone must have said something to Papa, because he came storming over, pushed Jack back in the corner, and the next thing I know Papa took everyone's coat from Howard who was trying to hang them up, and made Jack hang them up himself. Then after the party, Jack got everyone their coats when they left."

"I never knew what Papa said to Jack because I was afraid to ask. I did later ask Momma, but she just told me my brother has a lot to learn, and that was it."

Rita, again anxious to tell the story, looks at Chiara with some delight because she thinks for a change, she knows something Chiara doesn't know.

"I did find out from old man Fassino that Papa took over the coats that Howard was holding and screamed at him in Italian, 'Hang up the damn coats yourself, Jack and get that woman you married to help you,' but Jack hung them up himself."

Chiara, hearing this, just shakes her head. "I never knew that. No wonder Jack had such an attitude that day. I thought he was fighting with his wife because she was drinking so much."

Rita continues, "Jack was also probably always mad because his wife *was* drinking too much."

Chiara wants to end the conversation and opens the middle drawer of the dresser.

"I'll bring the dark button gray sweater for Momma."

Chiara walks over to Rita who is again looking out the window to see if anyone else is arriving. She sees one of the neighbors from Lexington Avenue carrying trays of food.

"What are we going to do with all this food? I guess all the food is what everyone was making for their lunch or dinner today. The families probably brought what they had prepared for the day."

"Oh look, Rita!" Chiara points down the street to a tall man walking toward the house. "Isn't that...."

"Yeah," Rita interrupts, "it's Vinny Petruzzi. You know, 'two- timin' Vinny.'"

Chiara laughs. "Yeah. I know who he is."

Rita gives Chiara a sneer. Rita never likes it when Chiara corrects her or calls her on something she says that is either a lie or not right. Rita is ten years older than Chiara and even though they have a close relationship, there is sporadic sibling rivalry. Rita constantly tells Chiara that being older earns her a certain respect that Chiara doesn't show. But Chiara waves her hand and shakes her head to dismiss Rita, which frustrates Rita even more.

"If you're so smart, Chiara, who gave him that nickname, 'Two-timin' Vinny'?"

With some delight, Chiara answers, "Papa did. You don't think I knew that! He gave him the nickname because Vinny answers everything he's asked with the same damn question first. Papa would ask him, 'Hey Vinny, how you doin?' Vinny would answer 'How I'm doin? I'm doing good.' Then Papa would ask him, 'Vinny, where are you working now?' Then he would say, 'Where am I working now? Oh. I'm still working at the mill.' And again, 'What kind of work are you doing at the mill?' Then Vinny's response would be, 'What kind of work am I doing at the mill?' and the whole conversation would continue like that until whoever was talking to him would just smile and walk away. It drove Papa nuts. Even though, Vinnie's a good skate."

Chiara looks out the window again and points, "Look, Rita." Chiara wipes the condensation from the window again with her hand.

"Vinny is talking to Howard. Poor Howard! Vinny will be there forever!" A moment after that comment Howard shakes Vinny's hand and continues to shovel the walk. "Good for you, Howard!" Chiara is impressed with the way Howard gracefully finished the conversation.

"Oh God. Does this mean the whole Petruzzi family is coming? Oh, God."

Vinny Petruzzi is the oldest child of the Petruzzi family. He has three younger sisters. Vinny's mother, Mary Petruzzi, had been friends with Anna since Mary was a frequent customer at Enzo and Anna's grocery store. Mary would always come into the store with a sigh and a complaint because one of her children was always sick. Enzo would listen with frustration and make comments to Anna when Mary left.

"Are those kids really always that sick? What is wrong with those kids? There must be something wrong with that family. It isn't normal that they are always sick. And what about Lucinda? What is wrong with her?"

Anna would listen and just shrug. Anna knew the real reason the Petruzzi kids were always sick, but she was sworn to secrecy and the secret was so sacred Anna didn't even want to tell Enzo. Enzo was usually very sympathetic, especially when children were involved, but he didn't like the Petruzzi girls, except for Lucinda. Lucinda walked with a limp and was small for her age but she was a very quiet and affectionate child. When Enzo sometimes saw Mary alone with Lucinda, he would have a smile on his face and always play little games with Lucinda and give her a little treat before she left the store. As far as the other Petruzzi girls went, he thought they were self-centered and were always gossiping about someone. If they came in with their mother or father, he would always comment to Anna after they left.

"Those girls never have anything nice to say about anyone or anything. There is something wrong with them girls."

Enzo was right. There is a problem with the Petruzzi children. It was a very closely guarded secret that would explain much of their behavior. Anna may be the only one who knew the truth but never told a soul. The secret finally did come out after the first Petruzzi daughter was married. It didn't cause as much embarrassment as Mary and her husband thought because most people had already guessed the Petruzzi secret. But there would be more problems related to it. It seemed that Mary Petruzzi had a hereditary disease that comes when ancestors marry their blood relatives, which was the custom years ago, especially with European royalty.

Chiara was at the window and again called over Rita. "There's the Violas."

Loretta and Paolo are walking up the drive with their son Charlie, who is about in his mid-thirties.

"Is Charlie with them?"

"Yeah. Poor Charlie."

Some single men were considered "confirmed bachelors." They lived at home with their parents long after their siblings got married and had kids. Many ended up taking care of their parents until their parents died. Meanwhile, they would be at odds with their parents who would ask them to find a nice girl and get married. There came a point as the parents got older that the parents realized they needed their son so they stopped telling him to find a nice girl because they needed his help or they understood why their son would never find a nice girl, because he already found a "nice guy." A movie that came out in the 1950s starring Ernest Borgnine called *Marty* told a similar story but Marty's story was a little different. In *Marty,* he wanted to find a woman but thought he felt he was too ugly. His mother, with her sister's help, began to realize maybe it would be better if Marty just didn't get married and took care of her. In reality, not all men wanted to, or could, get married so they lived a double life and took care of their parents.

It is getting dark and people are still coming in to pay their respects as others leave. Some of the women are taking the trays of food and desserts from the newly arriving visitors. Anna, who is still in Enzo's chair, is getting more anxious wishing that people would leave.

As a new crowd enters the kitchen, people leave to make room for them. The fresh arrivals are overtaken by the strong smell of expresso and cigarette smoke and the horrid smell of the men smoking little black

Italian cigars. As the new visitors come into the kitchen, they see all the open white cartons of pastries with names like Sorrento's, Paterson's, or Diana's Bakery, which had been filled with pastries and cakes. They look around to see where the pastries and cakes have been placed on the dining room table.

Even as people sit around and try to console Anna, a thousand thoughts run through her head as if it is on fire. The first thing that comes to her mind is that she is not going to let anyone sell her house and she sure as hell isn't going to live with any of her children. Although she loves all her children, there are some she doesn't like that much, or maybe it's just things about some of her children that she doesn't like. Enzo was more outwardly critical of them than Anna. Anna felt more responsible for their behavior. She knew that some of the characteristics of her children were inherited from her side of the family. She never discussed it with Enzo because in a way she was ashamed. That all doesn't matter anymore. She is now alone. She looks at all the people talking and all the people eating. Some are even laughing and carrying on until Chiara or Maria whispers something to them and they look over at Anna and whisper apologies.

It doesn't matter to Anna. She is in deep thought, trying to remember how she knows some of these people and when they moved to East Clifton Avenue. It was a lifetime ago. What would she do differently, she wonders, if she had the chance to go back to the time when they visited Enzo's step-sister Francesca and her husband Arnoldo? They were already living on East Clifton Avenue and a certain situation gave Anna and Enzo an opportunity for them to live in the neighborhood in a small house a few blocks down the street. How different would life be if they didn't live on East Clifton Avenue? Would they have been better off? That doesn't much matter now. It is the only life she knows. For over fifty years, their life and their house on East Clifton Avenue was their home, and now Anna hopes it will stay that way until she dies, even though the neighborhood has gone through some major changes. As Enzo always told her, the only thing that does not change, is change itself. She now understands fully what he meant. She looks around the room and she can see how even their house has changed. They live in a different world than when they first moved onto East Clifton Avenue. Back then there was more hope, optimism, and an exciting future...like for millions of others, a future unknown.

Chapter 3
East Clifton Avenue
For some, it became their street of dreams, for others, their nightmares.

It was many years ago in the early part of the 1900's that the second-floor master bedroom of the Buonoforte home, like some of the other homes on East Clifton Avenue, was originally the family living room. It had a front stairway that led onto an open porch that offered a broad view of East Clifton Avenue, with Lexington Avenue to the west and Randolph to the east, and it was the home's front door. On both sides of East Clifton Avenue, there were rows of different-sized houses built in different designs. Architectural integrity gave way to the need for additional living space. As with many of the houses in the neighborhood, the needed "renovations" were built for "function and not form" to accommodate a growing family. Rooms were built onto houses where rooms should never have been built. Where once large ceiling-to-floor windows let in warm summer breezes through a Florida-style sunroom, it later became a small additional bedroom for an unexpected newly born son or daughter. An oddly placed outside door led into small partitioned rooms that were hastily created to make an apartment for a widowed mother or father whose married son or daughter now lived in the main part of the house. Eventually, when grown children left their parent's house or were killed in one of the world wars, some of these rooms were turned back into sunrooms and porches; but instead of rebuilding them according to their original design, the exteriors were covered with the asbestos or aluminum siding to minimize cost and maintenance.

Now, on winter days generations later, the view from the large Buonoforte master bedroom is somewhat obstructed due to the condensation from the single-paned windows. In spite of this, one can still see smoke billowing against the gray winter sky out of the chimneys of the houses that make up the small neighborhood of East Clifton Avenue. Just as the houses are different architecturally, the perception on the outside is different from the reality of the families who live in each of the houses. Like the many neighborhoods in Clifton and the surrounding towns, it's about the families who created a "home." These homes were created by the sweat of hundreds of immigrants who traveled from Europe at the beginning of the twentieth century. They entered the United States at Ellis Island and moved into neighborhoods like East Clifton Avenue: For some, it became their "street of dreams," for others, their nightmares.

America had two things that the immigrants didn't have where they came from: hope and opportunity. With hard work, those who came here would be able to take advantage of all the opportunities that America offered to create a better life for themselves and the generations to come. As with other neighborhoods all over the country, many of the people who lived on East Clifton Avenue were able to achieve their goals and dreams by starting businesses from their garages, if they were so lucky to have a garage, selling fruits and vegetables from horse-drawn carts, or taking in wash, or whatever else could supplement the household income to survive. Hundreds of Clifton residents were employed at factories that sprang up like the Botany Village Mill on the other side of Clifton that produced textiles. Many hard-working immigrants worked in the factories in the surrounding towns such as Paterson or Passaic. Many parents, not wanting their children to have the same hard life as themselves, would stress the importance of education. The next generation became doctors, lawyers, and engineers, as well as achieving success in other professional fields.

There was the determination to work hard and sacrifice to achieve the "American Dream" of owning a home and becoming part of this great country. But the American Dream was hard to hang onto, and for some, hard work wasn't enough. This was also a time early in the century when there was no unemployment insurance or Social Security. Families had to make it on their own or they didn't eat. Many starved. It was made even more difficult because immigrants, as well as those already established in the country, had to endure bigotry and prejudice. Some immigrants were able to endure and rise above the bigotry, and others went back to their countries of origin and endured the "we told you so" from the families who remained there.

Many of the children of immigrant parents also fought and died in the wars that came and went, which further ingrained the families into the fabric of the country.

With the influx of immigrants, East Clifton Avenue became a blend of cultures. People from Italy, Germany, Poland, Hungary, and other countries throughout Europe and the world tried hard to hold onto and share their ethnic heritage, while at the same time acclimating to their new country. Many residents formed social and cultural clubs so they would be able to continue to enjoy and maintain their ethnic culture and pass it on to their children. But at the same time, they embraced the American culture and formed new traditions that were a blend of the new and the old.

There were traditions established by many Italian families on East Clifton Avenue, which took place each Sunday before and after going to church. Early in the morning, husbands would dress in their best Sunday suits and leave their homes to buy newspapers and groceries and gossip in lines while waiting for the fresh bread to come out of the hot bakery ovens. Everything would have to be fresh, including the gossip they shared as they waited. It had been pointed out on more than one occasion by the wives of the neighborhood that the men gossiped more than the women because the women were too busy keeping house and attending to the many children.

While the men shopped, the women were already preparing things for the afternoon and light evening meals. Some were making fresh raviolis or pasta that they dried on their beds when they ran out of room in the kitchen. They attended to the "sauce" or "gravy," depending on how each family refers to their tomato concoction. While mothers scream in Italian and "broken English" to their children to get ready for church, they also run around the kitchen toasting bread or heating leftover pizza for a fast breakfast to give to their children. After a couple of hours, the husbands return with the Italian Sunday paper, "Il Progresso." As they yell for their wives, they head for the kitchen carrying the bags of cold cuts, fresh bread, and groceries for the Sunday night meal, give the bags into the hands of their anxious wives, and ask for an expresso, "Per favore, prende il caffe subito!" Then they hang up their heavy wool coats smelling of cigarette or cigar smoke

After a quick trip to the bathroom to relieve themselves of all the espresso or coffee they already drank, they share all the gossip they heard while shopping to distract their wives as they break off the end of the freshly baked crusty Italian bread they just bought and dip it into the hot tomato sauce simmering on the sparkling white stove. Their wives scream and push them away from the pot while asking what took them so long, and the husbands continue to blabber about this and that. The wives don't even fully hear or care about what is being said unless it is about someone who is sick or has, God forbid, died. Perhaps it's some "juicy" new neighborhood scandal.

After fully interrogating the husbands, the wives shut the gas burner under the sauce, cover the steaming pot, throw off their aprons onto chairs, and leave the kitchen to help get the kids ready for Mass, while the husbands sit and read the paper, perhaps chewing on what is left of their Toscano cigars, or the like, they had smoked earlier. After all, the husbands know that getting the children ready and taking care of the household chores is the wife's job.

It is a well-orchestrated cacophony of confusion, which can take years of practice and a symphony of yelling. But not everyone can handle so many things at once. People still talk about Mrs. Nudio, who was in such a panic to get her family ready for church that she forgot to put her skirt on and left the house wearing just her slip. It was fortunate that it was winter and her heavy coat covered most of it, but it made for some teasing and laughs over cold cuts and homemade wine that Sunday evening sharing the story with her relatives.

Regardless of ethnicity, East Clifton Avenue families at first cling tightly together because that is all they have. For a time, blood ties and "la famiglia" is the most important aspect of their lives. But unfortunately, as families' fortunes changed, whether for the better or worse, the priority of the family would change as well, and a perfect example of that is the Buonoforte family.

Chapter 4

Praise goes to the families **who** can love and stay together.

When many families moved into their small houses, like those on East Clifton Avenue, there wasn't electricity, plumbing, or a bathroom inside the house. For the Italian families a place to "relieve themselves" was the typical "outhouse or back house" in the backyard, which was referred to in broken English as the "backous." Years later when family fortunes changed for the better, an inside bathroom was installed but was still referred to as the "backous" even though it was now in the house. Also, eventually, to make more living space as families grew, the basement was extended to include a bigger dining and living room area, with converted bedrooms on the second floor and perhaps even another bathroom.

This is what happened over the years for the Buonoforte family as their family grew. The original two-story, two-bedroom home with no indoor bathroom and a small basement kitchen, became a four-bedroom home with an upstairs living room, a large basement combined living and dining room, a large eat-in kitchen, a small bathroom, and a storage area. Every available space was occupied.

For Anna and Enzo, it was a joyous time, which, for Anna now thinking back, seemed like yesterday that their children were running in and out of the house, laughing and playing. They would wait for their father to come home from his grocery store, or on weekends they would help him skin the rabbits or pheasants Enzo shot hunting. Their dog Skipper would run all over the house excited after being in the woods and bringing back to his master the dead rabbits or pheasants. But that was years ago when the family grew. Like other families they all got married and moved out, leaving the parent, or parents, alone.

The Buonofortes have eight children: Four daughters and four sons. The first daughter is Maria. The second is Giuseppina. Pietro is the first son. The second son is Francesco. Rita is the third daughter. Giacomo "Jack" is the third son. Chiara is the fourth daughter, and Donatello "Donny" is the fourth son and youngest child. Each of the eight Buonoforte children is somewhat different and each has a distinct personality.

Maria, being the first child, received much attention and love. Perhaps that was why Enzo believed that as she grew older, she became very selfish and self-centered; even sometimes cold and unaffectionate. Although she most resembled Anna in appearance, that is where the similarity ended. Enzo even commented that she was so unlike himself and Anna that he wondered how she could even be their daughter. Although Maria gave the impression of being cold and self-centered, at times she could be affectionate. Anna often wondered if she was afraid of showing her emotions because she was afraid of being hurt. But her selfishness only made Enzo angry.

The second daughter, Giuseppina, is warm, affectionate, and loves to laugh. As she got older, she resembled the actress Sylvia Sydney, whom Giuseppina also loves, and she loved the comparison. At that time, movies had such an impact on society and were such an integral part of everyone's lives that people often referred to others as looking like this actor or that actress. If you wanted to describe a person, someone would ask, what movie star do they look like? For example, many people thought that when Francesco got older, he looked like the actor Don Ameche.

As Francesco is aloof, Pietro is warm and affectionate. He is close to both his parents, but he has a special place in Anna's heart, which can be seen when he is around her. Francesco is serious and aloof; very similar to Anna's personality, but he can also be affectionate at times.

Rita is more of a middle child and became responsible for the younger children, which she sometimes resented. She can be fun-loving, but can also be cold and selfish. Growing up she and Chiara were close.

Giacomo "Jack" grew to become a handsome and charming man with an athletic build. He may be emotional but he has a dark side that is not attractive and he can be abusive, which is accentuated by his icy stare. Because of his good looks, he is used to getting what he wants and he has a temper when he doesn't get his way. In reality, he is a coward, a bully, and braggadocious, and tries to hide it by being charming. Many times, he is just his worst enemy. He does, in his way, love his parents. To many, he is just an enigma.

Like her father, Chiara is clever and very social. She is also both emotional and affectionate, especially with her other siblings and parents. She is loyal to her family to a fault. Sometimes when questioned about her siblings' negative behavior she comments, "What do you want me to do, it's my sister." or "It's my brother." Chiara is the most attractive of the daughters and is selfless and warm-hearted, which she sometimes tries to hide. She doesn't like confrontation and does whatever she can to want everyone to get along, which can cause problems because issues are not resolved. Although Chiara can give the impression of being very strong, she is also insecure.

She witnessed the effect the Great Depression had on her family, but particularly with other families. At the time of the Depression, Enzo was in the grocery business and there was always food on the table, but Chiara, although young, could see how other families would almost starve. She would help Enzo deliver food to others in the neighborhood. She saw peoples' embarrassment at having to take what they thought of as "charity," and they would hug Chiara to show their gratitude, and many times the women would cry. The men, who otherwise were strong and proud, would bend their heads in shame, even if it wasn't their fault that their family fell on hard times. Enzo tried to do what he could by using his Mussomeli Club contacts to get friends' jobs. It was a life lesson that taught Chiara not to be financially frivolous, and to be compassionate and empathetic.

Donatello "Donny" is the baby of the family and has a place in everyone's heart. Donny and Chiara are the most similar in personalities. They are both emotional and affectionate and they have a close relationship. Because Donny is the last child, sometimes Anna would depend on the older children to take care of him. The one time that he evaded everyone's eyesight almost cost him his life. When he was about eight years old, he was sitting on the curb in front of his house and he was crying because he had a stomach ache and was afraid to tell his mother because sometimes he ate too much or things that he was not supposed to. However, on this day Rita's husband Dante pulled up to the curb, saw Donny crying, and asked what was wrong. Dante could see immediately that it wasn't a stomach ache because Donny was grabbing his right side, and Dante guessed he was having an appendicitis attack. He rushed him to St. Mary's Hospital in neighboring Passaic, where Donny immediately had an appendectomy performed, which saved his life. From then on, Donny was not out of anyone's eyesight. Both Enzo and Anna were forever in their gratitude for Dante saving Donny's life, and sometimes that created resentment with the other in-laws because of their obvious and continued gratitude.

As with other families, the dynamics of the Buonoforte family would change when the sons and daughters married and left the house. When Chiara and Donny were born, Maria and Giuseppina were married and moved out and Pietro would soon follow. As more of the children left the Buonoforte house, Anna and Enzo's world became smaller.

Many believe it is important to hold onto the past for mere survival and purpose. Maintaining routines creates a sense of security and many families try to keep their traditions alive after their children begin to have their own families and their own traditions. For Enzo and Anna Buonoforte, it was no different. But instead of continuing the tradition of the family coming on Sunday afternoons or evenings, which eventually became school nights when the grandchildren got older, some of the families would visit on Friday nights. They came to eat and afterward played the usual poker game and argued over the pennies they lost. That is how it was in the Buonoforte household every Friday night. But not all the Buonoforte children would show up. Sometimes their spouses would stay at home; sometimes they would come with the grandchildren and sometimes not.

Enzo discussed many times with his family and friends that when families first come to America they stay together because it is a matter of survival. Then when different members of the families become successful, jealousy and resentment soon develop. There would be arguments over little things and small incidents. A small inheritance would tear families apart for years until no one remembered what the argument was about. Reunions would take place at funeral homes when it was too late because the problems go deeper and over time the affection dwindles.

Enzo would die for his children, and fight tigers for Anna. Their marriage was different than many of the marriages of their friends and relatives. Marriages in their time were often arranged or were marriages of convenience that began before they arrived in America. The idea of *love* was, to a certain extent, a luxury that many couldn't afford. This was especially true in the small village of Mussomeli, where Enzo and Anna grew up in Sicily. Of course, they would have their bickering and teasing, but in the over fifty years they were married they never had a serious fight. Most of their squabbles were over issues regarding the children but were eventually resolved with a kiss. Any arguments about their children were kept to a minimum. When they thought that no one was looking, they'd glance into each other's eyes, which speaks volumes of their love. They had gone through many serious challenges, but instead of falling apart, they grew stronger. A deeply religious family, they clutched onto their faith without question. They both believed it was their faith that always got them through whatever challenges or hardships they were facing, and there were many. They did their best to instill their love of God in their children.

After the Buonoforte children were married and started families of their own, most of them made their parents their first priority. But this would change depending on the daughter, son, and respective spouse.

Maria married Antonino, who emigrated from Foggia, Italy. They met when Maria worked in Botany Village Mills cooking in the cafeteria.

At the time, Antonino worked in the boiler room. Although he was clever and knowledgeable, sometimes he couldn't read English and he needed help reading the boiler room schematics. They became close, and soon after Antonino grew tired of fixing and maintaining boiler rooms. Antonino loved to cook, so he bought a small cart and would make fresh food, like pepper and sausage sandwiches or a fresh huge bowl of pasta, and sell it to the people who worked at the mill. Soon there was enough business for both Maria and Antonino and Maria was able to quit the mill. They not only cooked lunch for the mill workers but for other businesses in the area.

After they were married, they sold the cart and opened a small restaurant near the mill, which became very successful. They had four children, and for the good and the bad of it, they raised them in the restaurant due to the constant attention running a restaurant needed seven days a week. They bought a big house in an "upscale" Clifton neighborhood and were very successful, considering the times. However, there was the cost of the lost "time" they could spend with the children due to working long hours in the restaurant. It was resented when the children got older. Antonino was from the "old school" of a hard work ethic, especially coming from a part of Italy where things were very bad for the poor, who never had an opportunity to come out of poverty unless they left Italy. Even with his harsh childhood in Italy, Antonino is affectionate and warm, as Maria is sometimes cold and distant. An odd combination, but not unusual.

Giuseppina is the second daughter to get married. She married a man not from Clifton but from Englewood, a few towns east of Clifton. She met Nino through a cousin. Nino is a tall, charming man who loves to drink and loves to go to the horse races. Being of the same fun-loving and warm temperament, there was an instant attraction and they married quickly. They had four children, and as anyone can tell, they are a close and loving family.

Pietro was the first son to get married. He married the daughter of a friend of Enzo's, whom Enzo met at the Mussomeli Society. It wasn't exactly love at first sight; it was more of an arranged marriage and they had three children. Pietro always stayed close to his family, especially Anna, whom he would visit every day on the way home from work. His untimely death changed the family dynamic drastically but the family kept together, with the other Buonoforte children helping to take care of Pietro's family after his death.

Francesco was the second son to get married. He was the first one to marry a non-Italian. Elisabeta's family was from Central Europe. She is slender and very attractive. As Francesco wanted to study to be a doctor, Elisabeta wanted to study to be a ballerina when she was younger. Her parents didn't support her ambitions and Francesco did not have the finances to support his ambition. Francesco and Elisabeta both would grow to resent their lost ambitions. Sometimes it would come up in an argument. They had one son named Lukas. As Francesco is aloof, Lukas is warm and fun-loving like his mother, sometimes locking horns with his father. Because of Elizabeta's worrying, which Lukas likes to ignore, Francesco has to enforce the close supervision that Elisabeta wants over Lukas. They live in a large two-bedroom apartment with Elisabeta's father, who takes great pride in Lukas. Unfortunately, Francesco likes to gamble.

The fourth daughter to get married was Rita. She met Dante at an Italian-American dance in Passaic. Rita was fascinated with Dante, who is very handsome and very "continental," always dressing as if he was living on the Italian Riviera. He emigrated from Northern Italy after his parents died. Rita married Dante secretly by the Justice of the Peace after just three months of their meeting. They have two daughters, and despite Dante's wanting to live large, they live in a small two-bedroom apartment over a butcher shop, which Rita quietly resents.

Jack was the third son to get married. Jack married Marta, or "Margo" as she prefers to be called. He met her through Sofia, a girl he was already dating. Margo is the second non-Italian whose family was from Central Europe like Elisabeta. At the time, Margo was exciting and wanted to be an actress and tried to model, but was not thin or tall enough. This excited Jack, who could show off with Margo's friends whom she met trying to be a model. Margo is somewhat like Jack. She has a mercurial personality. The one thing they don't agree on is Margo's drinking, which Jack has no choice but to put up with. Margo gave up her modeling ambitions right before she found out she was pregnant with what would turn out to be a son. Later in life, they had a second son. They live in Clifton in a two-bedroom house, which Margo hopes they can one day sell and move to a more fashionable part of Clifton, which to her frustration, would never happen on Jack's municipal salary.

Chiara was the third daughter to get married. She met Joseph Fonte through Joseph's cousin, Benny. However, Joseph was reluctant to meet Chiara because she was Benny's girlfriend's aunt, who unknowingly was around the same age as Benny's girlfriend. The first time they went out, Joseph was shocked at Chiara's unassuming beauty, her raven black hair, delicate hands, and warm personality. Chiara was also taken aback by Joseph's good looks, with his dark black hair, deep blue eyes, and quick wit. When Joseph told Chiara his full name, Joseph Francis Fonte, she almost laughed. Chiara thought it more of an aristocratic name, rather than southern Calabrian Italian. There was also something in his manner that seemed sophisticated, and in fact, she would later find out that on his mother's side, there was aristocratic blood. She thought it strange with Joseph requesting that he never be referred to as "Joe," because he felt that Joe was often used for "good time Joe," which to Joseph meant some-one simple and dumb. Chiara respected his request. What she called him didn't matter once she looked into his deep blue eyes.

Joseph lived a few towns away from Clifton and he would have to take a bus to see her so they would write letters back and forth. At first, it seemed Joseph was more taken with Chiara than Chiara was taken with him. Probably because she was seeing someone else at the time. But eventually, they fell equally in love. They have three sons and live in a town outside of Clifton that Enzo objected to. He wanted Chiara to live in Clifton. But Chiara is too much like her father, and she wants to make her own way with Joseph. After they got married, they lived with Anna and Enzo for a few months until their two-bedroom house was built. Anna is particularly taken with Joseph for his good looks and warm per-sonality. He became close to Anna. Joseph's family is very different than

Chiara's family. Joseph's Calabrese, Italian background is more "aristocratic," whereas the Buonofortes are more of a "peasant stock." However, he is in some ways more comfortable with Anna and Enzo, than the Fonte's more "rigid family."

Donny was the last child to get married and married another non-Italian named Dorothy. They have five children. To many, it seemed Dorothy was always pregnant, which was kind of a family joke. They too live outside of Clifton, but by this time Enzo didn't object. Especially because it is Donny. Chiara will never forget Donny's near-death episode either, and because of their similarity in nature, they are very close as "big sister" and "little brother."

With the change in the family dynamics when the Buonoforte children married, Enzo did not put up with any family bickering. He didn't take sides and would bully anyone arguing into making up and moving on. Sometimes all it took was a look. He told his children hundreds of times not to take each other for granted and to be true to "la famiglia," the family.

"That is the one bad thing about America," Enzo would sadly say. "Families just fall apart and eventually they 'eat each other.'"

As the Buonoforte children grew up, Enzo could see the difference in the lack of affection with some. He could split his children into two groups, seeing half as emotional and affectionate and the other half as emotional with little affection, even selfishness. Because of a lack of affection in some of his children, Enzo feared that his own family would fall apart when he and Anna were gone. But it wasn't only the lack of affection that made families drift apart; times were changing. As those who approach old age or are already elderly try to hang onto the past, sadly they realize the only thing constant is change. Values and priorities change, with some changes happening in the blink of an eye, which is bitter and very hard to take, like the loss of a child or a loved one.

Many realized that the world could not be limited to East Clifton Avenue. Some were reluctant to change, but they had no choice. Families were forced to make hard decisions, especially about elderly parents. Some parents were cared for, while others were all but abandoned. Some situations were driven by economics, and some of the saddest and most heartbreaking situations were driven by a lack of love and motivated by envy, jealousy, resentment, and grudges.

But there should be no shock or surprise. Sadly, Enzo admitted this was the way it was, the way it is, and the way it will always be. He said praise goes to the families who can love and stay together and not let the dark side of human nature destroy relationships. Praise goes to those who can rise above selfishness and hate, leaving a legacy of putting family above oneself for the sake of the family. Enzo was always concerned if his family would have an endearing and loving legacy when he was gone. If he died first would his children care for Anna? Would the Buonoforte children stay close? Ezno and Anna had their doubts, which they discussed many times with their close friend, Don Carlo Masseria. Perhaps it was also because of Enzo's sad childhood memories in Mussomeli that created such pessimism about his family's future. He would rarely discuss his early childhood and when he did, he would refer to it and Mussomelli with some bitterness. It wasn't the town of Mussomeli, it was the experiences with his early childhood and family. Ironically, one of his life's biggest regrets was that he and Anna never went back.

Chapter 5
Mussomeli, Sicily, Provincia di Caltanissetta

Mussomeli is located in the heart of Sicily, within the province of Caltanissetta, and was founded in the second half of the 14th century by Manfredi III di Chiaromonte. The name Mussomeli derives from the Arab term Manzil, which means "dwelling, farmhouse," and from Mel, which means "good." The village has a Medieval plan characterized by narrow streets and a beautiful ancient church with a stunning view. The weather is somewhat rigid and dry in winter, and warm and windy in the summer.

Enzo Buonoforte was born in Mussomeli, Sicily in 1885. At thirteen years old he worked at the farmer's market for Marco Giocare, selling fruit and vegetables at his large stand near the front of the market. This is a prime location because this is where most people first enter. Some of the villagers knew Marco and his pleasant personality and easy smile. He was also well known because of the quality and value of what he sold, which earned him customer loyalty and respect among the residents of Mussomeli. Within the two years Enzo has worked at the market sweeping the floors, stocking the fruit and vegetable stands, and doing whatever Marco asked him to do, Marco taught Enzo the best way to recognize quality fruits and vegetables and how to bargain to get the best deals from the farmers and the vendors. Enzo was an ambitious and quick learner. Customers were delighted with his quick wit, charm, and clever bargaining.

Enzo stopped attending school after his father Giuseppe married his stepmother, Julia. She wanted Enzo to make money for the household, in spite of the fact that Enzo's father worked on a ranch and made a good living. Also, Julia wanted him out of the house and Enzo's father, who wasn't home much of the time, didn't object despite Enzo's pleas to go to school. Giuseppe worked long hours transporting horses to different parts of the Sicilian Island and the Italian mainland.

After a year or two of living with his new wife, Giuseppe and Julia's marriage started to deteriorate and he would rather work than spend time at home with his wife. He soon realized he had made a mistake. Giuseppe was lonely after his first wife died, shortly after giving birth to Enzo, who he resented. Giuseppe needed someone to take care of the house and Enzo. His late wife's sister Josephine had no children and helped take care of Enzo and the house, but she didn't get along with Giuseppe. She thought he was not a good father.

Giuseppe was introduced to Julia by the Catholic church pastor, Father Gulio. Julia was a widow with two young daughters. Father Gulio told Giuseppe that Julia's two young daughters could be siblings to Enzo, and Julia could also take care of the house and young Enzo. Giuseppe thought it was a way to finally get rid of Josephine and Julia was so attractive. He knew little of Julia except that she was not Sicilian and was from Naples. This was all anyone really knew about her because she never talked about her past or her late husband. The only thing anyone knew was the rumor that her husband was killed because of some vendetta, which wasn't unusual in Sicily.

Giuseppe quickly found out he had married a dominating woman with a furious temper. Many of the women in the town needed to be strong to survive after being made widows as the result of being married to a weak man, killed by the local Mafia, or in many cases dying from a disease such as influenza. Good doctors were not plentiful and the few that were good were expensive. Most families relied on wet nurses, well-intentioned relatives, or homemade remedies. Sometimes the treatment was worse than the disease and the person died anyway. Blood-letting was a popular way of treating a disease until they realized that it caused people's deaths rather than saving them. Aside from disease and illness, many of the women who were once young, beautiful, and innocent girls grew to hate the men for the misery they brought to their lives, and Julia was such a woman. The difference was that a true Sicilian woman, in spite of her difficult life, took care of her husband, made many of the family decisions, loved her children, and would not only kill anyone who hurt them but sacrifice her own life to protect them.

In Sicily, like in many other countries, marriages were arranged. Some people got along and some didn't. Many men made the best of things, and some had a "goomah," a mistress. Many wives knew this and didn't care or looked at it as a blessing, not to have to deal with their fat husbands jumping on top of them when they went to bed. But then there was the exception when a man would see a woman and have "un colpo di fulmine"—the thunderbolt.

Giuseppe was one such man who experienced love at first sight and "un colpo di fulmine" for Enzo's mother Giulietta, who was a gentle, soft-spoken, beautiful woman and came from a respectable family. Many men wanted to court her, but it was Giuseppe who won her over with his good looks, sense of humor, and quick wit, which Enzo inherited. She had not yet learned the bitter lessons of a wife's Sicilian life.

Giuseppe knew Giulietta from childhood, but it was not until after she moved to Rome with her parents and then back to Mussomeli as a grown woman that they fell in love. Giulietta's father objected to the marriage because at the time Giuseppe wasn't settled in a career and just worked on horse farms as a stablehand. But fate would step in. A year after their return from Rome, suddenly Giulietta's father died from a heart attack. After a proper mourning period, Giulietta's mother didn't object to the marriage because they needed someone to help take care of them. Although Giulietta had an older sister, Josephine, they needed a man in "a man's world" to help and protect them. Giuseppe knew how hard life could be in Sicily, so he planned to immigrate with his new wife and in-laws to America as soon as he could save enough money. Plans changed when Josephine got married and didn't want to leave Sicily. Giulietta didn't want to leave her sister, so leaving Sicily would not come to be.

There were only a few years of happiness for Giuseppe and Giulietta. After a year of their marriage, Giulietta's mother died. Two years later Giulietta herself died, only a short time after giving birth to Enzo. After Giulietta died, Giuseppe grew bitter. He cursed God every day and when Enzo got older, he wouldn't allow Enzo to attend church or receive the sacraments, except for baptism, which Enzo received due to the insistence of Giulietta before her death.

It was years later that Father Gulio introduced Julia to Giuseppe and encouraged Giuseppe to marry her. Giuseppe welcomed Julia and her two children, Rosalia and Francesca, into his home. Although his feelings for Julia were not even close to his love for Giulietta, for a short time he felt content. Julia's restless spirit began to weigh on her and she became a bitter and angry woman as time passed. For Giuseppe, marrying Julia was God's way of punishing him for cursing God after Giulietta died and Giuseppe became bitter. To Giuseppe, it was as if the hand of God had worked through Father Gulio to punish Giuseppe. Although nothing was said to Father Gulio, Giuseppe had total disdain for him after his marriage to Julia and he would avoid him at all costs. That meant he would not attend church and would not allow Enzo to attend church either.

After a time, Giuseppe accepted God's punishment but would try to stay away from Julia and the house as much as possible. And in turn, he would also stay away from Enzo. When he did come home, many times it was after drinking too much wine. As long as he came home with his salary, Julia didn't care much but at the same time she would bitterly ridicule him in front of her daughters and Enzo, saying Giuseppe was just a "stupid horse jockey." At first, Enzo would try to protect his father, but after seeing how his father would take the abuse, Enzo lost respect for his father. When there was an argument between his father and stepmother, Enzo would just leave the house or go to his room.

Julia grew a little more bitter every day. She felt that she was married to a man who couldn't compare to her dead husband, and after a time Giuseppe and Julia would barely speak to each other. Another reason Julia stopped badgering Giuseppe was that Julia would also drink, but, unlike Giuseppe, she would drink secretly and not only wine but also grappa a hard liquor made from grape seeds and stems. She bought it from a man who made it in his home and she would sneak it into the house. She paid the man extra not to gossip about her drinking with the money that Enzo earned at the market. When Giuseppe would come home from the horse farms, she would be too drunk or too tired to argue. She just wanted the money he would come home with, and she would hide it in the basement in a gray metal box she kept behind a stone in the basement wall. She thought she was the only one who knew its location, but Enzo quietly followed Julia one day and saw where she hid it. To Julia, the money meant her eventual escape.

Although Enzo had pleaded with his father to be allowed to go to school, Enzo's stepmother insisted he go to work, and Enzo's father would not argue with her. It was finally a rabbi whom Enzo had met one day at the farmer's market, Rabbi Merlino, who offered to teach Enzo how to read and write. The rabbi had noticed that Enzo had a hard time reading the list of fruits and vegetables the rabbi had given him. At first, the rabbi thought it was a problem with Enzo's eyesight. The rabbi took Enzo on the side and asked him why he was having a hard time reading the list. Enzo was embarrassed at first. The rabbi had such kindness in his eyes that before Enzo knew it, he was explaining that his mother had died, and when his father remarried, his stepmother insisted that he go to work to help support the family. The rabbi said if he really wanted to learn to read and write, Enzo could come to him after he got out of work and he would tutor him. Enzo was reluctant at first because he was afraid of what his stepmother would do if she found out. After thinking about it for a while, he suddenly no longer cared about the possible consequences and he began going to the synagogue two or three times a week for about an hour after work to be tutored.

Enzo didn't know if the rabbi expected to be paid, and when he asked the rabbi, the rabbi smiled and said that he was just doing it so that Enzo would be able to read his shopping list, and they both laughed. Enzo was grateful and always brought something to the rabbi like oranges or lemons or whatever the market owner could spare. Marco had known

Enzo's mother Giulietta, and missed seeing her kind face, and he would let Enzo leave work a little early because he knew of Enzo's arrangement with the rabbi and he was touched by the rabbi's kind gesture. Marco also knew being taught was a secret and he would cover for Enzo if Enzo's stepmother or stepsisters came looking for him. Marco would say that he sent Enzo on an errand.

After a few weeks, Enzo was making wonderful progress and the rabbi was proud of his student. But then a problem arose. Enzo's stepmother needed some last-minute groceries and sent her older daughter Rosalia to the market where Enzo worked. When she came home, she told her mother Enzo was not there. Marco was delivering fruit and one of the workers said Enzo was at the synagogue. When Rosalia asked if he was making a delivery and when he would be back, the worker, not knowing of the secret arrangement, said proudly that Enzo was being taught to be a scholar and he started to laugh. Rosalia thought her mother would be proud of Enzo for wanting to better himself, but instead, Julia became furious and was determined to put a stop to it.

"How dare he take the time to be tutored when he could be working more hours at the market or helping around the house?" she screamed at Rosalia.

That it was Rabbi Merlino, and her past experience with him, made the situation that much worse in Julia's eyes. Seeing Julia's rage, Rosalia immediately regretted telling her mother. She never thought her mother would react so badly. *What have I done?* she thought, and tears streamed down her cheeks. Both Rosalia and her sister Francesca had grown to love Enzo for his kindness and loving nature toward them and they didn't understand why their mother was so mean to Enzo.

Later that evening, when Enzo came home, he noticed that his two stepsisters were at the top of the stairs as if they were waiting for something to happen and tried to warn him. It was so dark at the top of the stairs he couldn't make out what they were doing and thought they were just playing with him. But then when they whispered "pericoloso," danger, he guessed at that moment that his stepmother must have found out what he had been doing all these past weeks. This was his fear every time he came home after his lessons.

As he walked past the staircase toward the kitchen, he looked down at the Crucifix under a glass dome that was on the hall table and stopped for a few seconds. He looked at the figure of Christ hanging on the cross and he made the Sign of the Cross. He thought about the rumor regarding where the Crucifix came from and how his father received it. Giuseppe kept telling Julia to put it in their bedroom, but she ignored him. Enzo also knew how much his stepmother valued it and wouldn't let anyone touch it.

Before he walked into the kitchen, he made the Sign of the Cross again and suddenly realized he wasn't afraid of any consequences his step-mother would try to lay on him. *Strange.* He thought about the times she chased him with a wooden spoon under the kitchen table and behind the furniture. *Suddenly I have the strength to face the witch and I am not afraid.* So many times, he tried to avoid her wrath but not this time. He slowly walked toward the dimly lit kitchen and stopped at the doorway for a moment. He saw Julia sitting at the end of the dining table almost completely in the dark with a large wooden spoon in her hand. A soft light from the moonlight coming from the window above the sink was shining on the spoon. Enzo could see the shadow of his stepmother and thought it was as if the devil himself was lurking in the darkness ready to pounce. Enzo wasn't afraid, because he knew at that exact moment, that he had the strength to face her and was prepared for whatever would happen. He looked again at the Crucifix, turned back and for some moments there was silence. Enzo could hear his heartbeat pounding in his ears. Then his stepmother slowly rose from her chair, picked up the wooden spoon, and took a couple of steps toward him.

In a deep low voice made gravely by the grappa she had been drink-ing, she said, "Where have you been?" She lightly hit the large wooden spoon against the side of her leg.

He stood there, face to face, for a few moments with neither of them speaking. Julia was confused. She thought Enzo would cower and confess. Even though she was closer to him, Enzo could not quite see her. The moonlight from the window created a glaring behind her, which made

Enzo squint. When his eyes adjusted after a moment, he remembered how attractive she was when she was younger and that was what must have attracted his father to her. She could also be very charming and little girl-like when she wanted to be, like when she was with Father Giulio or trying to bargain for some trinkets from the local jewelers. However, this would not be one of those moments. This was the first time when Julia was angry that Enzo was able to look directly at her and make eye contact. Enzo could see that it took her aback for just a few seconds. He now had a gown-up authoritative stance that Julia had never seen before.

"I am not going to lie. Rabbi Merlino has been teaching me. He is teaching me to read and do arithmetic. If I know how to read and add and subtract, I can make more money and...."

Enzo stopped speaking as she took a step toward him. He foolishly thought if he could make more money, she would be appeased and leave him alone and maybe even encourage him. But he could see that she was either too drunk to understand and make sense of what he was saying, or so blinded with rage that she didn't care. She moved a little closer but Enzo stood his ground. Again, she was a little surprised that he didn't back away or look down as he usually did when she confronted him.

"Why have you lied to me?" She began hitting the side of her leg faster.

"I haven't lied. I...."

Before he could finish, she interrupted and her voice got louder.

"You lied when you came into this house and you made me think you were working, but instead you were with that dirty Jew."

As she finished, she could see he was getting angry. She saw him clench his fists at his side. She had never seen this side of Enzo before and she was a little confused about how to continue. She became concerned and said to herself, *what did that dirty Jew tell him?* she wondered. *Did he tell him of my history with the rabbi? Did he tell Enzo?* Enzo had a well-controlled temper and now it was Enzo's turn to speak loudly and with defiance. He took a step towards her.

"Don't you call him a dirty Jew. He's better than the priests who wouldn't help me after you made me quit school and work. I knew it was *you* who didn't want Father Gulio to teach me. It was *you* who made them stop teaching me, telling them that it was useless and I was just a stupid boy who wouldn't make his way!"

He couldn't believe he was talking to his stepmother in this manner. Then he continued as his anger increased.

"How can you call him a dirty Jew when you are so proud of that Crucifix under the glass dome you always brag about? Why? Because it is made up of gold? Who do you think is hanging on the cross? Don't you know that Christ was a *Jew!*"

Hearing that, she hit him with the spoon so hard across the face that she almost lost her balance. The spoon cracked his lip, and blood began to drip down his chin. Enzo surrendered to his temper he had been controlling, a temper he had controlled so many times over the years when he had to take all the abuse from his stepmother. He wiped his lip with the back of his hand and saw the blood. She smiled at him and waited for a reaction with the hope that he would just cower down and run out of the room as he had done so many times before. But this time was different. This time his eyes were ablaze with such anger she had never seen before. Then he looked straight at her.

"Who do you think you are, you stupid, ugly bitch?"

She was in shock, but instead of backing down, she attempted to hit him again. He took her hand with the spoon and he squeezed it as hard as he could until she dropped the spoon. At the same time, she tried to hit him with her other hand and he grabbed that too and twisted her arm. She began to curse him and tried to break free from his grip, but he squeezed even harder and she slowly stooped down and began to spit at him. He pushed her on the floor and stood over her. She tried to not let him see her in pain.

"This is where you belong. On the ground like a common animal with no feelings. A devil! A snake!"

She was afraid to get up for what he would do.

"Get out of this house! Go live with the dirty Jew! Go live with your fat aunt!"

And with that, she spit at him like a snake spits when it's angry. She stayed on the floor not out of pain but out of fear that he would hit her if she attempted to get up.

Enzo was in awful pain and his mouth and cheek instantly swelled. He was shaking from the whole experience. For a few seconds, he stood over his stepmother and considered kicking her. Instead, he looked around to see if he could find something to wipe his mouth. He looked down and grabbed her apron, which lifted her and ripped it from her waist so hard that she hit the ground and screamed. As she started to get up, he knocked her into a chair. He wiped his mouth with the apron and then threw it at her face.

She flinched as the apron hit her and yelled, "Get out, you bastard! Get out!"

He turned around to leave the kitchen and heard his stepsisters crying as they were coming down the stairs, but their tears weren't for their mother. They were afraid for Enzo and of the tirade from their mother after Enzo left. Enzo was always there to protect them, even taking the blame for them. He wouldn't be there for them this time. Not now anyway. They both hugged Enzo and begged him not to leave. Julia looked at the two girls. Couldn't they see that *she* was hurt? Their mother's hurt turned into anger and she screamed at them.

"Both of you go upstairs, or I'll do to both of you what I did to him."

They could see the blood dripping down his face and they hugged Enzo harder. Again, Julia was hurt, but that didn't stop her from getting out of the chair Enzo had pushed her into. He gently loosened the girl's grip. And walked toward Julia, who stopped in her tracks.

"Touch them. Go ahead. Try it and I will call on Don Antonelli to take care of you! He hasn't forgotten what happened to his dogs. I will tell him it was *you* who poisoned his dogs for coming around."

Julia quickly retorted in fear. "You liar! It was not me! It was not me!"

Enzo could see she was scared. "What does it matter? He *will* believe *me*. Even if he doesn't, how will you know? Are you going to ask him? I don't think so. You will live in fear always wondering if or when he will strike. You will have to sleep with one eye open if you will be able to sleep at all. Go ahead, hurt them. Just even look at them in the wrong way."

Julia knew she was defeated, but she would not let him have that satisfaction and yelled to the girls to go up to their room, showing Enzo some small defiance. With Enzo's encouragement, the girls ran up the stairs. Enzo walked from the house with tears running down his face from the pain. He felt a couple of his teeth were loose and bleeding. He went to the only person he knew would offer him any comfort, his mother's sister, Aunt Josephine.

Josephine was Enzo's mother's older sister. She was a widow and childless. Unlike Enzo's mother, who was petite and soft-spoken, Josephine was a big woman with a booming voice. She always wore an apron over her dress and kept her graying hair in a hair net, which made her look older than she was. Although she had a tough exterior, she had a heart of gold and loved her nephew Enzo. She didn't have to work because she was left with a small fortune from her late husband and lived well below her means. If someone wanted to keep their fortune in Mussomeli, it was a necessity not to be showy or brag.

After Enzo's mother died, Josephine wanted Enzo to live with her, but his father would not hear of it. Enzo's father's marriage to Julia had caused such a fight that Josephine and Giuseppe hadn't talked in years. Although Enzo was forbidden to visit his aunt, he tried to visit her as much as he could but hadn't seen her in a couple of weeks since his stepmother found out Enzo was visiting his aunt and forbade him to go there again. This is what always would happen, and he would just come back to see his aunt after a couple of weeks. Julia kept tabs on Enzo through the nosey neighbors, so Enzo had to be very sneaky. Now Enzo wasn't afraid for himself, but that his stepmother would find some way to punish his stepsisters because she knew that was the way to get to Enzo. His aunt would help him.

When Enzo entered his aunt's house, she saw the condition of his face and she frantically asked him what had happened. She took her right hand and bit her finger to show how in "simpatico" she was and wanted to show Enzo she shared his pain. As he told her what happened, Josephine soaked a towel and gently wiped Enzo's mouth until the bleeding stopped.

"I first curse your father for marrying such a woman."

Enzo didn't feel sorry for his father. One reason was that Giuseppe always blamed Enzo for his wife's death.

"My father always blamed me for my mother dying."

Josephine became enraged.

"NO! That's a lie. Your mother got ill. That had nothing to do with you. It happens to a woman sometimes, but it has nothing to do with you. Your father is a liar and a coward and didn't disserve my sister. You were the only good thing coming from that marriage."

After Enzo's mother gave birth to him, she immediately developed diabetes and the doctor said it was because of the pregnancy. Josephine and her husband helped take care of Enzo until Giuseppe got married again when Enzo was eight years old. It was a short time after Giuseppe married Julia that she began to abuse Enzo. Although Enzo told his father of the abuse, he brushed it off, siding with his wife's stories and lies about Enzo's disrespect and need for discipline. She even offered up her daughters as witnesses to his bad behavior by threatening to beat them if they didn't lie for her. Enzo's father was too proud to admit he had made a mistake and would rather sacrifice his own son's welfare for his Sicilian pride and scorn from Father Gulio. After a fight with Josephine about the way Julia treated Enzo, Giuseppe forbid Josephine and her late husband to come to the house or even see Enzo. But that didn't stop Josephine, who would sneak to see him, making him swear never to tell his stepmother.

Josephine gave Enzo supper and told him to get a good night's sleep. The next day Enzo woke up early and his aunt made him breakfast. His aunt told Enzo to finish his breakfast and wait for her in the house and she went to her bedroom. When she returned, Enzo could see that she had gotten a large hairbrush with a thick handle and put it in the pocket of her apron. Again, she told Enzo to finish his breakfast and that she would be right back. Enzo hurried to finish eating. Even though his aunt didn't tell him what she was going to do, he had a feeling it would be some type of retribution against his stepmother. He didn't want her to do that and left to stop his aunt. By the time Enzo got to his house, Josephine had already arrived and he could hear his aunt yelling loudly at Julia.

"How dare you hurt my nephew, you devil! There is only one way to treat someone like you and I am going to show you how."

Enzo opened the front door and saw his stepmother sitting in the kitchen drinking an espresso at the same spot Enzo had seen her the night before, but now it was day and the sunlight was streaming from the window onto the table where Julia was sitting. Josephine was a big woman and she had some weight behind her and was a formidable figure, yelling at Julia from the doorway. At first, Enzo could only see a shadow because of the bright light in the kitchen from the open back door. When Josephine had first arrived and came into the house, Julia was visibly startled, she wasn't expecting this and realized she had taken things too far. Enzo took a step inside and watched from the hall as Josephine walked over to Enzo's stepmother, who then stood up and tried to ignore Josephine and walked to the sink to wash the espresso cup and other dishes. Julia was at the sink with her back turned to Josephine, ignoring her in silence for a few seconds. Then Julia broke the silence without turning around.

"What do you want? Are you looking for that good-for-nothing "bastardo" nephew of yours?"

Julia knew Enzo probably ran to have Josephine console him and it was Julia's way of putting salt in the wound. She knew Josephine would only threaten her as Josephine had done in the past. But this time it was different. She had physically hurt Enzo. Josephine was a true Sicilian woman, something that Julia never understood. This time there would be consequences. Josephine stood there silent for a couple of seconds. Julia still had her back to Josephine.

"Well, what is it, old woman?" Julia said.

Josephine didn't say a word as she walked over to Julia, who was still washing some dishes, and suddenly grabbed Julia by her hair. Julia fell backward, tossing the dishes she was washing to crash against the wall across the room.

"This is what I want, you bitch!"

Without another word, Josephine dragged Julia by her hair on the ground. Julia crawled hopelessly, struggling to get up, cursing and screaming, and holding onto Josephine's hands to lessen the pain from her hair being pulled. Josephine dragged her out the front door past an astonished Enzo and into the middle of the street. Josephine turned Julia face down and straddled her with her back to Julia's head. By this time a crowd had gathered. Enzo at first was going to try to stop his aunt but she gave him a look and he backed off. Then Josephine pulled up Julia's dress and tore her undergarments to reveal her bare buttocks and began to beat them with the back of the hairbrush, leaving large, red welts. Some neighbors were now screaming while others were shocked to see what was going on and they began to laugh.

One of the neighbors who hated Julia began to scream, "Beat that bitch! Beat her good!" with a couple of other neighbors yelling similar things.

A man passing in a horse cart jumped down and stopped Josephine, who stood up panting, trying to break away from the man's grip.

"If you ever touch my nephew again," Josephine said panting, "if you ever hurt him in any way, I will pay the Mafiosi to cut off your hands so you can't hurt anyone again! Filglia di puttana!"

Josephine then spit at Julia and kicked dirt in her face. Some people cheered as Julia was crying and cursing, trying to hide her face in fear and shame as Josephine cursed her. Enzo stood in the doorway and could not believe what he had seen. This would be a story that Enzo would tell his children and their children would tell their children for generations. The retribution of how his Aunt Josephine changed his life and how important children are to Sicilians. Enzo, who had a soft heart, began to feel sorry for his stepmother. But that wouldn't last long. Enzo's aunt, still breathless, told Enzo to get his clothes and belongings and that he was going to live with her from now on, and she didn't care what his father said. She also said that if his stepsisters, who were crying and clinging onto Enzo, wanted to come too they could. Enzo knew that his stepmother would never let her daughters go with him and his aunt. It wasn't out of love. The two daughters did all the work in the house, and Enzo's stepmother would never let them move.

Enzo ran up the stairs with the two girls to gather his things.

"Don't worry. I won't let her hurt you. I will come for you."

Enzo told them as he made his way to his little room, which was just a little bigger than a coat closet. He began to tear up, thinking the two girls would now become the brunt of their mother's anger and wondering what he could really do. Then he remembered after the girls' father died, their father's brother Antonino would sometimes come to see them because he was the godfather of the oldest girl, Rosalia. But that quickly stopped because Enzo's stepmother didn't want the girl's uncle to influence the girls and find out how they were really treated.

After Enzo gathered his meager belongings, he pulled aside the oldest girl, Rosalia.

"When was the last time you heard from your Uncle Antonino?"

As Rosalia wiped her nose with her sleeve, she thought for a second. "Last Easter. He sent us a card and candy, but my mother took the candy away, saying the candy was no good for us but I know she ate it herself because I saw her."

Again, he whispered.

"Get every letter or card he ever sent you. Quick!"

Rosalia didn't know why Enzo wanted her uncle's cards and letters, but she knew that he would help them and maybe this was something he needed. She knew where their mother hid the letters and took them from the back of her mother's closet. Rosalia came back and handed him a stack of cards and letters wrapped in some string. He hoped there would be an envelope or card with their uncle's address. He stuffed them in his bag, kissed them both, and started going down the stairs. He stopped for a second. He saw the man who pulled his aunt off his stepmother helping his stepmother into the house. Enzo swallowed hard and slowly continued down the stairs.

When Julia saw Enzo, she yelled, "Good! Get the hell out! You good for nothing! I hope you join your mother soon...IN HELL!"

With rage in his eyes hearing what she said, he walked up to her, and for a moment he looked as though he was going to knock her to the ground. His stepmother flinched back. Looking straight into her eyes, he said, "You go straight to hell, you whore of the devil! Like my aunt said, 'figlia di puttana!'" Enzo took his left arm and put his hand to the middle of his right arm bent it a little and whispered so the girls wouldn't hear, "Vaffanculo puttana!"

Julia could see the girls crouched at the top of the stairs clutching each other and crying. She yelled to them, "Stop that crying or I'll give you something to cry about!"

With that, the two girls ran to their room and hid.

"If you hurt the girls, I will finish the job my aunt began, puttana!"

He stared at her for a second and she spit in his face. Once again, he held his temper, grabbed the bottom of her dress, and wiped his face. He pushed her and the man aside and left.

When Enzo got back to his aunt's house, she was sitting at the table all out of breath. When they made eye contact, they both laughed. Then he showed her the stack of letters and cards and said that he was going to have the rabbi write the uncle and have him come for the girls.

"Bravo, Enzo, Bravo. You have your mother's heart." A tear ran down Josephine's face, which she quickly wiped with her apron. They both looked at the letters and found the uncle's name and address in a fishing village near Agrigento. Even though Enzo would be happy to get his stepsisters away from their mother, he was sad that children have to be taken from their mother for their own good. For a second, he remembered the time he first met his stepmother, Julia. How beautiful and kind she seemed. Why did things have to come to this? Perhaps if he knew more about her things could have been different, but now it no longer mattered. She no longer mattered.

Chapter 6

Inside the box were two hands, with a gold wedding ring on one of the fingers.

Enzo brought the cards and letters to his aunt's house and after looking through, them, they found an address for Uncle Antonino near Agrigento, in the southeast of Sicily, not too far away from Mussomeli. They wasted no time in contacting him. Also, to their surprise when Josephine read through the letters, they found that Rabbi Merlino was mentioned in one of the letters. Why was he involved and why Taormina?

Enzo and Josephine ran to Rabbi Merlino and he told the rabbi what had happened. After seeing Enzo's face, the rabbi was shocked and tried to hide a smile when Enzo got to the part of his stepmother's beating. They showed him the letters with the uncle's address, and the letters with the address of a house in Taormina addressed to Enrico Glaudino. They wondered if this was the last name of Julia's late husband. They felt the letters might reveal some of Julia's background and history. But at this point that didn't matter, they wanted to contact the girl's uncle.

Enzo asked the rabbi to write a letter explaining what happened and to ask the uncle to come get the girls because he feared for their safety. The rabbi put together a letter explaining the situation and pleaded with Antonino to come and get his nieces because their mother would make life a living hell now that Enzo was gone. The rabbi took the letter and said he would get it to the girl's uncle somehow. Then Josephine and

Enzo showed him the letters mentioning his name and the rabbi felt he had no choice but to explain what had happened and why Julia and her daughters moved to Mussomeli.

Rabbi Merlino told them that Julia was originally from Naples where her father was the head of a rich and important family jewelry business. Julia's mother was from an aristocratic family in Milan, where the family now lived. When Julia came back to Mussomeli from Taormina after her husband died, she confessed everything to Rabbi Merlino about what had happened. Rabbi Merlino would tell Enzo and his aunt and be relieved to unburden the truth to two people he could trust...but he would not tell them quite everything.

He explained that Julia met her first husband, Enrico, when Enrico and his father, who was also in the jewelry business, were in Naples on business. Enrico was a tall, handsome man with dark black hair and deep blue eyes, unlike his bother Antonino who was a stocky, short man who lived outside of Agrigento at the address they had. When Julia met Enrico, she was only eighteen years old and he was about ten years older with a sketchy past, but she didn't care. To Julia, his age meant he was exciting and he could show her the world. She met Enrico while shopping for a gift in one of the jewelry stores where Enrico and his father conducted business. There was an instant attraction and they began seeing each other secretly when Enrico and his father made business trips to Naples. It wasn't too long before they wanted to marry. But neither set of parents would hear of it.

Enrico's family was Jewish and his parents forbid him from marrying a gentile. Julia's parents were against her marrying a Jew. They refused to be separated, so they made plans to leave Italy and move to Sicily, where Enrico's father had a brother-in-law in Mussomeli, Rabbi Merlino. Julia had met him a few times when he came to visit and because of her beauty and charm, Rabbi Merlino doted on her.

As soon as they could, Julia and Enrico snuck off to Mussomeli. When they arrived, they explained their situation to Rabbi Merlino who listened empathically but would not help them because Julia and Enrico were disobeying their parents and showed no respect for their parents and their parent's wishes, even though he disagreed with their parents. With nowhere to stay and little money, they would have to go back to Milan in disgrace where Enrico's parents had moved. After some pleading and outright begging, Rabbi Merlino agreed to let Julia stay if Enrico went back to Milan to reason with their parents. But Enrico had no intention of reasoning with his parents because he knew they would not be reasonable and they even threatened to disown and disinherit him if he married a gentile. Enrico knew it was not an idle threat. He knew they needed money so Enrico planned to rob one of his father's rich clients in Naples, which would give him and Julia enough money to either stay in Sicily or move to another country. He kept this plan to himself because if anything went wrong, he didn't want Julia involved. Also, she might try to talk him out of it, and he saw no other way.

When he got to the Italian mainland, he stayed in a little town called Pozzuoli, which was far enough outside of Naples so as not to be noticed by anyone. In the dead of night, he snuck into Naples and broke into the shop of Signor Scarpa. Enrico knew from visiting him with his father that Signor Scarpa kept a big inventory of jewels and gold and didn't bother to put everything in the safe when the store was closed at night as many of the other shops do. What Enrico didn't know was that the reason Signor Scarpa didn't secure his jewelry and gold was that no one would dare rob him because of his connection to the Neapolitan Mafia. To those who were close to him, Signor Scarpa was addressed as Don Scarpa and was a man of honor who demanded respect and knew how to administer retribution. This was something Enrico failed to have any knowledge of. The fact the Mafia even existed was denied by any of its members because they swore "Omerta." It is secrecy to the death. Omerta possibly descended from a form of resistance against the Spanish kings who ruled over Southern Italy for over two centuries. For that reason, only rumors abounded and no one would take a chance on crossing someone they even thought was connected to the "nonexistent" Mafia.

When people needed what they considered "justice," they would secretly go to someone like Don Scarpa for an "accommodation." He would quietly offer them a glass of grappa or anisette, listen to their request with little comment, and perhaps later the accommodation would be made. This would leave the one making the request in debt, with no limit, but Don Scarpa was fair and because of that he was a popular man but still feared. To a man like Don Scarpa, and others in similar positions, showing a lack of respect alone could be fatal. Enrico foolishly had no idea of what he was getting himself involved in.

When Enrico broke into the shop, his eyes lit up and he quickly took as much as he could fit into the leather satchel that he brought with him. He left the shop with his pockets, as well as the satchel, filled with diamond rings, gold bracelets, necklaces, and anything else that he could get his hands on. He was proud of himself and lacked any guilt because he was doing it for love. But without Enrico's realization, he left behind something that would tie him directly to the robbery. When he was filling his satchel, a letter he had begun writing to Julia fell unnoticed onto the floor. In the letter, he explained that he would not be coming back to Sicily and he would write her where they should meet. Other than that, there was no way of tracking the person writing the letter or who was writing it, but Don Scarpa had his sources.

When Enrico got back to where he was staying in Pozzuoli, he forgot about the letter, thinking he had already mailed it. He left the next day at dawn before the jewelry store opened and headed to Taormina on the northeast coast of Sicily where he rented a house. He sent a letter to Julia, who had been waiting for weeks to hear from him, instructing her where to meet him and only to tell Rabbi Merlino that both sets of parents finally relented and to thank the rabbi for his generosity. He also wrote that Julia should tell Rabbi Merlino that she was meeting him in Naples, but of course, she was meeting him in Taormina, a few hours away.

Enrico had already given Julia money for the journey. When Julia finally arrived at the house in Taormina, she was over the moon with excitement. After they made love, she got dressed and they sat on the balcony and she asked him what really happened and how he got the money. At first, he wasn't going to tell her. But after some insistence, Enrico explained exactly what he did and the situation they were in. He was afraid she would be outraged or afraid, but she was neither; just the opposite. She said she didn't care and was even excited about the robbery. To Julia, it would be paradise because they had enough money to live on for years and years. Julia also had news. She told Enrico she was pregnant. Enrico was excited about the pregnancy, and, as quickly as they could, they were married in a little church in the Taormina under different names: Mr. Vincenzo Leone and Mrs. Anna Mae Leone.

After a few years, they had two children: Rosalia and Francesca, but the life that Julia was leading with Enrico after a time was not enough. Enrico didn't work because they lived off the stolen goods, and they started to get on each other's nerves. Many afternoons Enrico would come home after playing cards, or just drunk. This led to arguments. She also missed the busy and exciting life in Naples and Milan. She missed the lifestyle and she missed her friends. She missed living in a large home where the cook prepared dinner and the maids did the cleaning. Julia now felt trapped and she was not fond of motherhood. She was also not fond of living an unexciting life, but she still loved Enrico and she put up with it. She had no choice. Enrico was a fugitive, and she would suffer with him if anyone found out and if he was arrested, or worse.

Then fate had an unwanted twist for Enrico and Julia. One Good Friday, Julia, Enrico, and their two daughters were in the center of town where Julia liked to drink expresso at the cafés and watch all the people who came into town to celebrate Good Friday and Easter. Although Enrico was always uncomfortable, he did it to please his wife. Every year that passed only increased the guilt and fear of the theft. It was eating away at him more and more. He wondered if it was the guilt or the fear of being eventually caught and realized that was the reason he was drinking more and more. He kept swearing to Julia he would stop drinking, but he needed to dull his guilt and fear. They even talked about leaving Sicily, but they were afraid. Their names were a lie and they didn't have the proper paperwork to leave. They thought somehow they would be caught.

There in the café, as they were having expresso, they spotted Rabbi Merlino walking toward them. They turned away to avoid him, but he had already seen them and walked over to their table. They tried to act surprised and greeted Rabbi Merlino warmly, introducing their two daughters. The rabbi said he was so surprised to see them and assumed that everything was settled with their family but he didn't ask them any questions. Rabbi Merlino introduced them to his companion, Father Leonardo whose family lives in Taormina. Rabbi Merlino had been coming to visit Father Leonardo and his family every Good Friday and Easter since they were young and serving mass in the local church for Good Friday and Easter at The Cathedral of Taormina - The Fortress Duomo. Enrico and Julia looked surprised and Rabbi Merlino could see their surprise in their greeting. After all, a rabbi being friends with a priest, especially on Good Friday? Didn't the Jews kill Christ? Rabbi Merlino was used to the puzzlement, but instead of ignoring it, he began to explain.

"I know. A rabbi celebrating Good Friday and Easter?"

But what the rabbi didn't know was that it wasn't the fact of a rabbi and a priest being together on Good Friday. Rabbi Merlino brought the robbery fresh to Enrico's mind, and with it the fear of being caught. Now someone knows that he and Julia are in Taormina. They would have to move. They couldn't take a chance. He knew something like this would happen. *God was working through this rabbi,* Enrico thought. Stealing is against one of the Ten Commandments. Enrico would have to hide his fear and focus on the rabbi's explanation. He could not look guilty or afraid. Julia reached down and squeezed Enrico's hand. She could sense his fear.

The rabbi explained he had been a friend of Father Leonardo's family since they were young. Rabbi Merlino's father owned one of the big hotels in Taormina. One Easter, years ago, Father Leonardo's family had come to the hotel to have Easter dinner. At the time, Father Leonardo was called Lenny, and Rabbi Merlino was called Franco. After dinner, the family sat on the hotel patio. Lenny went down to the pier to try to feed the small fish and he suddenly fell in the water. He was screaming because he couldn't swim. Without a thought Franco, who had seen him fall in, jumped into the water and saved his life. From then on Father Leonardo's family insisted that Rabbi Merlino celebrate Easter with them because they said that Christ sent Rabbi Merlino to save their son.

Rabbi Merlino could see that Enrico was not interested in his story, so after some cordial goodbyes, Rabbi Merlino and Father Leonardo walked toward the square. Rabbi Merlino had been so busy talking about himself that he forgot to ask if both Enrico and Julia were in contact with their parents. Also, in the excitement, he forgot that Enrico and Julia's parents wrote to him a few years ago and wanted to know if he knew where they were. The letter stated that their parents missed them and were heartbroken and they didn't care if they were to marry as long as they came home. Rabbi Merlino had written back stating they were not with him and assumed they had gone back to Naples or Milan. He never received another letter and assumed everything was worked out.

Rabbi Merlino regretted not asking Julia and Enrico about their parents, but with Father Leonardo present he didn't want to embarrass them in case they were estranged from their parents. When Rabbi Merlino turned to go back and talk to them again, they were already gone. The rabbi was a little suspicious, but just shrugged his shoulders. He took Father Leonardo's arm and they walked on.

When the rabbi returned to Mussomeli, he looked for the letter that was sent to him from Enrico and Julia's parents to find their parents' addresses. He then wrote to their parents that he was overjoyed to run into them in Taormina and they were safe and doing well. Rabbi Merlino, although with good intentions, didn't realize the wheels he had just set in motion. Actually, the letters Enrico and Julia's parents wrote to the Rabbi had been cajoled by Don Scarpa whose sources led him to Enrico as the thief, since his parents were asking everyone if they had seen their son. Don Scarpa had told Enrico's parents he knew through his sources that Enrico stole the jewelry and showed them the unfinished letter to Julia that was carelessly dropped on the floor of the jewelry store. Enrico's parents recognized Enrico's handwriting. Don Scarpa swore that no harm would come to Enrico. He just wanted his jewelry back. The parents, in fear, said they would pay the value of what was stolen as long as the children were not harmed. Don Scarpa agreed to their generous offer, but he had his pride. If anyone knew of the agreement, he would look weak, and someone in his position could not afford to look weak. No.

He wanted both the money first and justice second.

A few weeks from the time that Enrico and Julia met Rabbi Merlino and Father Leonardo on Good Friday, Julia went shopping with Rosalia and Francesca in the market. Later that day, when she returned to the house, she saw a box in the middle of the table wrapped in a red ribbon. She moved toward the box. She saw that the planter near the window had moved. It was the place that Enrico used to hide money and the remainder of the jewelry he stole. She smiled and figured he had bought her a gift. After all, they had been arguing more than usual. She looked outside to see if Enrico was hiding and was going to surprise her. She looked back to the table where the box was and yelled at Rosalia, who was starting to pull the ribbon. Julia pulled the ribbon the rest of the way and opened the box. It was filled with a beautiful red silk handkerchief. She put the top of the box down and then slowly she moved the silk handkerchief to see what was in the box.

The first layer of silk revealed an envelope. She opened the card and as she read, she gasped and dropped it. As their neighbor Signor Capusso was walking past Enrico and Julia's house, he heard a scream, unlike any scream he had heard before. He ran into the house and saw Julia and the two girls screaming and hanging onto their mother as they looked at the box. Signor Capusso slowly walked to the box, moved the silk handkerchief, and suddenly moved back and made the Sign of the Cross as he looked at Julia and her daughters. Inside the box were two hands with a gold wedding ring on one of the fingers. They were clearly Enrico's hands.

Julia, hysterical, pointed to the card on the table. Signor Capusso picked up the business card slowly. It read simply Scarpa Jewelry with the address of the store in Naples and the word, "Giustizia," justice, written in what looked like blood on the back of the card. Not knowing that it was Rabbi Merlino who had unwittingly tipped off Don Scarpa, Julia quickly left Taormina and took the children to the only person and place where she felt they would be safe, Rabbi Merlino. When Julia confessed everything to Rabbi Merlino and told him what had happened, he didn't tell her about the letter he had sent to her parents but he was grief-stricken. *Was it because of the letters he sent?* Rabbi Merlino shuddered to think, but he knew Mafia justice and he would not say anything to anyone, especially Julia. After all, what good would it do to even tell Josephine and Enzo? It was something he would keep to himself and had to live with and always wonder about.

Enrico and Julia's parents went to try to find Enrico and Julia, but there was silence in Taormina. They finally sent a letter in care of Rabbi Merlino to Julia and in the letter, they stated because of the disgrace of the robbery and with things changing for their parents' families in Italy, both Julia and Enrico's parents fled to America. Also, because of the pain that they had caused both families they never wanted any contact with their children again. When Julia read the letter, she tore it up with almost no emotion.

Rabbi Merlino set them up in a small apartment next to the synagogue and told Julia not to use her last name even though he knew now that justice was done according to Don Scarpa, and he would not come after Enrico's family. After a time, Julia's fear subsided, and because of that her contentment wouldn't last. She was looking for a more exciting and different life, but she wouldn't find it in a small town like Mussomeli; quite the opposite. To further protect her and her daughters, she felt she was forced to marry Giuseppe Buonoforte.

Chapter 7
If you don't sign the paper, the two girls will be orphans.

Rabbi Merlino kept his promise and had the letter brought to the girl's uncle by one of his congregation who knew the area of Agrigento. Within a week of receiving the letter the girls' uncle arrived at Rabbi Merlino's with a huge man at his side he introduced as Victor. They met with Enzo at his aunt Josephine's house. Enzo told them again what had happened and the conditions the girls were living in. Antonino said that he would go with Enzo and Victor to collect his nieces and he had the legal paperwork to be their custodian. Then he told Rabbi Merlino he should not be involved. The rabbi cautioned Antonino.

"Don't do anything bad or unlawful for the girls' sake."

"No, Rabbi. I am not a foolish man. We are prepared with the proper legal papers."

He gave the rabbi a small sack of gold coins, which the rabbi accepted and said he would share with his small congregation. They all thanked and hugged the rabbi, especially Enzo, who was too choked up with emotion to speak but just nodded to Rabbi Merlino, who nodded back.

With Rabbi Merlino returning home, Enzo, Antonino, and Victor went to meet with Enzo's stepmother. When they arrived, the uncle knocked at the door but didn't wait for a response. He opened the door and all three quietly walked in. Enzo's stepmother was in the kitchen leaning over Francesca, who was crying because she was being yelled at. When Enzo's stepmother saw the uncle, she was taken aback. She gained her composure and told Francesca to go to her room. When Francesca saw the two men and Enzo, she gave Enzo a little smile and he motioned for her to do what her mother had told her. Then Julia stepped forward.

"What do you want?" She looked at Enzo. "Didn't I tell you not to come into this house again?"

"This is my father's, it's my house, too."

Julia ignored his response and was more composed. She'd had time to realize she'd made a mistake and now she knew things were going to get worse. The girl's uncle ignored what she said, walked up to her, took a leather bag that he was carrying, and placed it on the table. Enzo and Victor stood behind Antonino. Julia stood by the table but didn't sit. Antonino looked directly at her and gently instructed her. "Julia, sit." She stared at him for a second, pulled the chair from the table, and sat down. She then wanted to take control from him.

"Alright. I am sitting. What do you want?"

Antonino sat down, reached into his leather bag, and removed some papers. He quietly explained why he was there, but all the stepmother did was give Enzo a deadly stare., Enzo stared right back. Staring at Enzo, she regretted what had happened, not out of remorse, but because she didn't think things would get to this point. After Antonino explained that he was going to take the girls, she hesitated for a second, looked at Antonino, jutted her head back, and just laughed.

"Who do you think you are, coming into my house and telling me you're taking my daughters? Get the hell out of my house."

"My father's house," Enzo quickly responded. Again, Julia ignored him.

She began to stand, but Victor walked forward and pushed her back down in her chair, which startled her. She was now duly intimidated.

Antonino leaned toward her and talked to her just above a whisper.

"I am not some stupid fisherman like you always called me. I am smart enough to have a good business and to have the money to take care of my two nieces."

He pointed to the clean white papers that had a name and address at the top. She could tell it was an official paper and from a solicitor. Antonino stood up straight and further explained.

"These are legal papers that give me custody of my nieces. You are a drunk and an abusive parent. We know the man who supplies you with liquor who will be a witness to the amount of grappa you buy."

She just pushed the papers away and didn't look at him. Again, Antonino gently pushed the papers in front of her. This time she pushed them aside and spit at the papers. Antonino took a step back. He looked over and nodded to Victor who was standing behind him. When Antonino nodded to him, Victor moved next to Julia, pulled her hair, and she grabbed the table so as not to fall. Antonino stood up straight and shook his head.

"I wanted to do this nicely."

Antonino grabbed her hand that was grasping the table, took a big fishing knife from his leather pouch, and slammed it into the table right next to her forearm.

"I wanted to do this nicely, but now puttana, if you don't sign the paper, your two girls will be orphans and then I am going to take them anyway and small parts of you will be scattered to feed the animals."

Again, Julia spat at the papers. "Fungol!"

Then Victor pulled a knife from inside his waist and jammed it into the table on the other side of her forearm. She was now physically shaken and tried to hide her fear. She cursed both Victor and Antonino and tried to free her hair from his grip. Victor pulled back her hair again. She knew she was defeated. She told him she would be happy to be rid of the girls. Antonino nodded to Victor again and Victor allowed her to pull away from his grip.

Julia signed the paper, after which Victor and Antonino signed and witnessed Julia's signature and Julia cursed them and told them to get out. Enzo left the kitchen and ran upstairs where the girls were listening and told them he would help them pack their things and they would leave with him and their uncle. Enzo hurriedly threw their belongings in pillowcases and anything of theirs he could find. He wanted to get out of there just in case his father showed up. When Enzo and the girls came downstairs with their things packed, the girls looked at their mother, perhaps for the last time. Their mother was holding back tears and told them to go, get out of her sight. Rosalia slowly approached her mother to embrace her, and then quickly stepped back.

"Get out! Go! You're both my ruination. Get out!"

At that moment, Julia, in her own strange way, realized she loved them and would miss them, but it was too late. She would never let them know how she felt and it made her even angrier.

"Get out of my sight, you little brats! I'm better off without you!"

With that, everyone left but Rosalia was the only one to look back. She could see her mother was on her knees crying. Enzo hearing Julia cry, thought to himself that maybe she did love them. For a second, he felt sorry for her, looking so pitiful kneeling on the floor. When Julia realized they were both staring at her, Julia took off one of her shoes and threw it at them, hitting Enzo in the leg. He picked up the shoe intending to throw it back. Rosalia put her hand on the shoe to stop him, and looking up at Enzo, she shook her head.

"No. Please. Enough." Enzo knew she was right and dropped the shoe.

Julia wiped her face with her apron, got off the floor, walked over, and slammed the front door. Without a word, Rosalia and Enzo both turned and left. Antonino and Victor were waiting ahead with Francesca who was crying because the whole incident was so frightening.

That was the last time any of them would see Julia. They would all stay at Josephine's for a few days until they could make arrangements to travel back to Agrigento.

After the beating incident, Enzo rarely saw his father because his stepmother blamed Enzo for the beating and the embarrassment to his family. Enzo's father had no choice but to side with his wife because otherwise, she would make his life a living hell.

As fate would have it, almost a year to the day of Julia's beating by Enzo's aunt, it was raining and Julia slipped while crossing the street in front of her house and was killed by a horse and cart that was coming around the corner. Ironically, the cart driver was the same man who stopped Josephine from hitting Enzo's stepmother with the hairbrush. It was determined by the local officials to be an accident and no charges were brought against him. It was whispered that the man was not punished because Enzo's stepmother was so disliked by everyone in the town that it must have been God's way of punishing her.

At Julia's funeral, only Enzo's father and Rabbi Merlino attended. Father Gulio said the mass and presided over the funeral. Enzo's father never attempted to contact his stepdaughters. After all, their mother never attempted to contact them, so why stir up emotions? But it was after Julia died that Enzo's father found a large stack of letters that were sealed and addressed to the girls but were never mailed. He never opened them and just threw them away with all his dead wife's belongings. He realized later, that it was a mistake and regretted throwing away the letters. Maybe he should have mailed them. Then again, he thought maybe it was for the best. What value would there be to have the girls know their mother died? Let them live happily in ignorance.

After the girls left Mussomeli, Enzo had been living with his aunt Josephine who was thrilled to have him since she was a childless widow and lived alone. Unfortunately, after a couple of years, she died, but before she died, she gave Rabbi Merlino a small inheritance to hold for Enzo. She left a note telling him how much she loved him, hoping that one day Enzo could leave Sicily. The aunt's landlord told Enzo he could stay there as long as he wished because his aunt helped to take care of the landlord's sick son before he died. Now Enzo really felt alone.

Enzo remembered the gray box with money that Julia had hidden in the basement. One night he went to sneak into the house to take the box, but he saw his father in the kitchen at the table. For a moment he wanted to talk to his father, but then changed his mind, remembering all the pain his father had caused him, so he waited until the next day. He went back in the morning and watched for his father to leave for work, and after a few minutes, he snuck into the basement and found the box hidden in the wall behind one of the stones in the foundation where he had seen

Julia hide it. He took the box and placed it on an old fruit crate. He was shaking as he contemplated opening it, but it was locked. He looked for something to break the lock and found the head of a hammer with the handle broken off. He hit the lock once and the lock broke. He waited a few seconds to open it. He was shocked by what he found. There was a stack of money, some gold jewelry, and something on the bottom of the box wrapped in a red silk cloth. Enzo stuffed the money in one pocket and the jewelry in the other.

As he looked at the red silk cloth, he thought it must be something really valuable considering it was wrapped in such a beautiful fabric. Then he remembered what Rabbi Merlino had told him about in Taormina. He slowly opened the cloth, and when he saw what it was, he stopped himself from screaming and the box dropped to the floor. After a few seconds, he pushed back the cloth with his foot and made the sign of the cross. He bent down slightly to make sure it was real. Something gold caught his eye. It was a gold ring on a withered human hand. It was Julia's husband's hand. He couldn't believe what he was seeing and didn't know what to do next. He looked around, even though he didn't know why. Perhaps it was because maybe somebody saw him enter the house and was watching him. He took the red silk cloth and placed it over the hand, held his breath, and picked it up. The light weight of the hand surprised him. He placed the hand in the box and then slowly carried the box over to the hole and put it as deep inside as he could. For a second it came into his mind to take the ring. But it would be almost sacrilegious in a strange way, and he wanted no part of it. There are many superstitions in Sicily, like spells and giving the "evil eye." Enzo was thinking that this was so strange there must be something evil about it.

After he put the gray box in the hole and replaced the stone, he took some dirt from the floor and tried to fill in the cracks around the stone. *No one should ever know what is in there.* He backed away from the stone and snuck out of the house without anyone seeing him and rushed back home. When he returned home, he hid the money and jewelry under a loose floorboard in his bedroom and covered it with a small rug. He intended to save as much as he could so he could leave Sicily for a new life in America. Enzo lived in his late aunt's apartment, worked at the market, and saved as much as he could for the next few years until he met someone who would change his life forever: Anna Maria Arnone.

Chapter 8

Anna and Enzo have a passion for each other that is deep-seated in Sicilian heritage.

Gino and Beatrice Arnone had six children and lived in a nice section of Mussomeli. Anna was the oldest child and her father's favorite. She was a thin, beautiful woman with black raven hair and almond-shaped eyes. There were four younger sisters, Sarah, Maria, Giovanna, and Daniela, and the youngest, her brother Pietro, who was Anna's favorite sibling. He was a tall and handsome man with a body that was more like a Greek athlete than the average Sicilian farmer or ranch hand. Years later sometimes Anna would see Pietro in her own son Jack's looks, but that is where the resemblance ended. Pietro was a talented singer and loved music. He would play guitar and sing Sicilian folk songs he learned from farm workers and musicians who would come to the village during fiesta. Many people were in awe of his talents and tried to encourage him to take his ambitions further. He really had no desire and was happy working in the fields and training his father's horses.

Gino didn't show affection to his children as much as his wife Beatrice did. Gino loved his children with a passion, well known to Sicilian parents, but at the same time, Gino did not know how to show affection. He was emotional, but not affectionate, unlike Beatrice who was both emotional and affectionate. As Anna got older, she began to see her father as a distant and cold man who was only interested in what he thought would make his family happy: money and power.

But Gino was a contradiction. At times he seemed to be distant and cold but in reality, he loved every one of his children and would suffer great guilt when he would scold or punish them. Only Beatrice knew of his demons. There were times he would have bouts of depression and in a state of ignorance he blamed God for all his troubles and would smite Him. Gino only attended mass to put up a front to appear as a strong family man. As he got older and more powerful in the community, he didn't see the necessity for appearances, but he continued to attend Mass. Perhaps it was because he began to take an inventory of his life. Or perhaps it was because he asked God to forgive him for the way he treated his children when they left for America.

Enzo first met the Arnone family when he worked in the market in Mussomeli. He was particularly interested in the older sister Anna, but it was Anna's younger sister, Sarah who was interested in Enzo. When Anna, Sara, and their mother Beatrice shopped at the market, Enzo would ignore Sarah, in spite of her asking useless questions about the fruits or vegetables, and he would intentionally cut peaches or oranges for Anna to taste. Sarah would then ignore Enzo and talk to some of the other boys working at the market thinking it would get Enzo's attention, but he didn't care and, in fact, he was relieved. Sara thought if she could get her father to intervene, then maybe she would have a chance with Enzo. She told her father that Enzo was making rude advances to Anna and he should talk to him to have him stop. When Gino did go to see Enzo, Marco intervened and said it was a lie and Enzo was always a gentleman. Gino didn't care because he didn't want his daughters involved with a "fruit and vegetable seller" and warned Enzo off. That only excited Enzo more and made Anna even more appealing, which resulted in Anna and Enzo being forced to meet on the sly.

The Arnone family was well known in Mussomeli because not only did Gino Arnone have a profitable farm and horse-trading business, but he also worked for the government as a local administrator. This made it hard for Anna and Enzo to meet, but with the help of a sympathetic mother who chaperoned the meetings, they met at a friend of Beatrice's who kept the meetings respectful and secret.

Anna and Enzo had a passion for each other that was emotionally deeply seated in their Sicilian heritage. It was a love that grew rapidly. It was a passion that was part of their heritage and had been passed on as part of the heredity of their ancestors, which later would be passed on to future generations. It was not a passion that could be cooled or be extinguished by any interference. After a couple of years, it was obvious that they wanted to marry and Anna would defy her father who was against the marriage because of Enzo's lowly position. With the help of Anna's mother, the father finally agreed to the marriage only if Anna and Enzo stayed in Sicily, which they agreed to do. They were married and, for a time, planned to live where Enzo was living till they could save enough to buy their own home. However, fate would have another plan for the couple. Enzo had heard from a friend who worked with him at the market that his father had died and that there was an inheritance involved, but that Enzo would not be alive to receive it. Enzo didn't know if it was true or just to scare him off. Whether true or not he kept the information from Anna.

When Enzo told Anna's father, he was able to find out that what Enzo had heard was true and he was now in danger. As hard as it was for Anna's father to admit it, Anna and Enzo would have to leave Sicily and go to America, but for both Anna and Enzo to leave at once was also too dangerous. Without telling her why, it was decided that Anna would have to leave first, and then a few months later Enzo would sneak off and meet with Anna. It was not unusual for a wife to do what she was told to do without any reason from her husband, so Anna accepted her father's and Enzo's plan.

Enzo would have to live in Anna's father's house under his protection, but his protection would only last for a short time. When she would eventually arrive in America, Anna made her father promise to write to her and tell her exactly why Enzo was in danger. She also made her father promise to keep her sister Sarah away from Enzo. Anna still remembered the times in the market when Sarah tried to sabotage her and Enzo's relationship. Anna's father promised he would keep Sarah away from

Enzo and write to Anna telling her what really was going on.

When Gino realized he would be losing his favorite daughter, it was one of the first times he showed some real paternal emotions. Gino knew the situation was serious and he knew he would probably never see Anna again. Beatrice was heartbroken when all but one of her children left Sicily, even though she wanted them to have a better life. She learned to live with a broken heart. Many parents lived with the same heartache when their children left Sicily. Many of the women began to wear black, even though their loss wasn't due to a death.

When Enzo confided to Rabbi Merlino what was happening, he told Enzo he had a cousin in New York who would gladly help settle Anna into an apartment while she waited for Enzo to arrive a few months later. There was even a part-time job for her at the docks in lower Manhattan at the new Fulton Fish Market where his cousin had a booth and was always looking for people to work. The appropriate letters of introduction were given to Anna. It was getting too dangerous for Enzo to stay at his in-law's home so Enzo hid out in a little room in the rabbi's home until he could get safe passage to America.

When it was time for Anna to leave for America, Anna said goodbye to her mother who stayed home and couldn't handle coming to the train station to say goodbye. Anna spent as much time as she could with Enzo. It was decided Enzo would not see her off. When the time came to leave, Enzo almost didn't let her go. He grabbed her and whispered in her ear because if he faced her, he would burst into tears.

"My life is nothing without you. I know that we will be together because I have faith. Nothing ever will keep us apart. This is God's way of testing our love and after this, we will never be apart, even when we die, we will again be together in heaven."

Anna was crying so hard she could only shake her head. When her father saw them from the doorway he was taken aback. He could see how much they loved each other and what a crime it would have been to keep them apart. He wiped tears from his eyes.

"Grazie Dio."

Gino felt a door open on his emotions. As he took her bags and was waiting for her, he was still shaken that two people could love each other so deeply and so hard. He would have to show his wife the same love, and it was sad to him that he waited this long to show his feelings.

Anna left with her father for the Mussomeli train station to board a train to Palermo. From Palermo Anna would get on a boat to Naples where she would board a ship for the Atlantic voyage to New York City. This was not a journey to look forward to and it wasn't a journey for the weak. Depending on the weather, it would be an arduous three-month journey to get to New York City, and many didn't survive.

When Anna and her father arrived at the small station to catch the train to Palermo, her father took an envelope with money from his pocket, put it in her large purse, and hugged her as he had never hugged anyone in his life before.

"I don't know if we'll ever see each other again but I promised your mother that we will try to come see you someday. I know I haven't been the best father but I know I love you so much because my heart is breaking."

Anna fell into her father's arms, crying. She could only try to say I love you through her tears.

"You promised to write to me. Don't forget."

Her father nodded.

A second later the train whistle blew, announcing the train was getting ready to leave. With tears running down Gino's face, he helped Anna onto the train.

"Don't talk to strangers and hold on to your belongings. Do you have your papers and the address of Rabbi Merlino's cousins?"

She took it from her purse to show him. At that second, Gino wanted to pull her from the train to make her stay, because he was so nervous about letting her go alone. But a couple of acquaintances of Anna's were also going on the same train and Gino felt a little better. Anna quickly found a seat, opened the train window, leaned out, and grabbed Gino's hand as the train was leaving. For a few seconds, Gino ran along the train holding Anna's hand until he finally had to let go as the train sped away.

"I love you. God keep you safe and...."

Gino had to let go of Anna's hand and couldn't speak because he was crying so hard. The train whistle was like a death knell in his ears. *Will we ever see each other?* Gino asked himself as he saw the train getting smaller in the distance. He took his hankie from his back pocket and wiped his eyes. Then someone behind him, who had observed them, put his hand on Gino's shoulder.

"You will see her again. God will see to that."

Gino didn't know the stranger who was walking away from him, but for a moment he was comforted with the thought that he would see her again somehow.

Hmmm, it may not be in this life on earth, but I will see her again as God is my witness.

Chapter 9
"I was born Giancarlo Antonio Francesco Buonoforte in Palermo, Sicily."

After Enzo dies, Howard thinks it is a strange request that Anna asks him to call Don Carlo before he calls their daughter Chiara.

A great deal is not known about Don Carlo's background. To everyone he knows he gives his full name as Giancarlo Antonio Francesco Masseria and says he thinks he was born in Palermo, Sicily. Enzo and Don Carlo share the same birthday, October 15th but it is not known the exact year. Enzo was born in 1885 and Don Carlo's birth year is believed to be between 1883 and 1888. Don Carlo met Enzo when Enzo and Anna were living in a cold-water flat on Mulberry Street in Little Italy. Some thought that they could be brothers because their appearance was so similar. They both were about the same height and physique, with wavy dark brown hair. The biggest difference was that Don Carlo had deep blue eyes, and when he looked at you, you knew he meant business. They had similar values and morals, especially when it came to a wife and family. Many men had a wife and kept a mistress. Neither man criticized that behavior, but they also didn't condone or believe in it. "If you can't be with one woman forever then you should never get married," they would sometimes remark when they heard of some friend or neighbor getting kicked out of his home because the wife found out they were cheating on them. There is also the desire for *Love*. Both men believed in "unconditional love," which was unusual for a time when arranged marriages rather than love were considered the norm.

When the phone rings, Don Carlo walks into the living room and sees his daughter Lucia answering. Lucia doesn't recognize Howard's voice at first.

"Yes. Yes, hello Howard, how are you? He's here. Let me get him. What?"

There is a hesitation and then Lucia's whole demeanor changes.

"Dear God...Oh no...Yes...Yes, he's here. Just a few seconds...Yes, I understand."

Don Carlo can see that it must be something serious by the hectic tone in Lucia's voice. He walks over and without a sound, Lucia hands him the phone. She stands right next to him, anticipating he will need help sitting. Tears are welling up in her eyes as she helps her father to a chair. Their eyes don't meet. Don Carlo takes the phone almost reluctantly, knowing it is bad news.

"Hello. Oh hello, Howard."

There is silence for a few seconds. He turns away from Lucia and holds the phone in his hands because he has a premonition of what he is going to hear.

"Oh...Thank you, Howard. Yes. We will be there. Yes, please call back about the arrangements. Thank you for letting us know."

Don Carlo slowly hangs up the phone and avoids making eye contact with the fear of becoming too emotional. He didn't ask how Enzo died. It didn't matter. He was gone. Lucia holds onto his arm and helps him into his study. She knows he will want to be left alone with the bad news of Enzo's death.

For a few moments, there is an awkward silence.

"We have to go to Clifton. Enzo died."

"Yes, Howard told me."

"We'll go to the house tomorrow morning. We won't wait for Howard's call. Tomorrow, call the Buonofortes in the morning and tell them we would like to come by and ask if there is anything we can do."

Don Carlo's daughter can see he is physically shaken.

"For a time, Enzo and I had a falling out. I can't even remember what it was about but it was my fault. He is, was, the closest thing I had to a brother. It was strange that he was an only child. For that time in Sicily, I think it was, his mother died shortly after he was born. Then his father married again and it wasn't a good thing for Enzo. He never really talked about it, but one day I stopped over to taste some homemade wine he had received from a neighbor. Enzo had given the neighbor the grapes that were growing on his fence in his garden and his neighbor gave Enzo a couple bottles of wine that were made from the grapes. We sat in his yard and drank both bottles and Anna brought out some pepper and egg sandwiches and fruit."

Don Carlo smiles and laughs for a few minutes thinking about eating the sandwiches that tasted so much better than a steak or any other fancy meal.

"I still can remember the smell of his garden and the basilico, the basil. The smell was so strong, you could almost taste it in the air. You should have seen his garden. He would graft fruit trees with different varieties of the same fruit, like the pear tree he did for me in our garden. Three different pears on one tree. Amazing. Genius. For some reason, maybe it was about the garden or the fruit, or the wine, he talked about the oranges and lemons in Sicily. He brought up some things about when he was young and his mood suddenly changed. He talked about his mean stepmother. As I said, his mother died shortly after he was born and he was an only child. He missed not having a mother and carried a small photo that was blurry and torn that he kept in his wallet. The only remembrance of his mother."

"You are so different from one another. How did you first meet and become friends?"

"Are we so different from one another? Hmmm."

Don Carlo just shrugs. So many times, his daughter asks about things in her father's past but he always puts her off saying, "The past should stay in the past." Lucia knows little of her father's background and youth but now with Enzo's death he becomes melancholy and he feels it is a good time to discuss his background before he too passes away. It didn't matter much now what his daughter thinks of him, she felt his love and devotion over the years and it will overshadow any judgments she would have. Besides, he knows that there are rumors and it would be better to tell Lucia the truth now and squash the rumors.

"I want you to know everything that is the nearest to the truth of my youth. When I was little, my mother made me keep a diary and for a good part of my life, I wrote in entries over the years. Who knows, when I'm gone, you can sell it to Hollywood and they can make a movie.

"Oh, Papa!"

"Go in my bedroom. Behind my closet is a large gray box with a few black books. Take the one that has my name engraved on the bottom and bring it here."

Lucia is both shocked and delighted that at last, she will get to know who her father really is. She runs and returns with the book, sits next to her father, and hands him the book. He runs his fingers over his engraved name and hands it back to his daughter.

"Here, you read it before I change my mind."

She slowly opens the book and it creaks like leather-bound books do when they haven't been opened in a long time. There is a slight smell of mildew. She looks at the writing. It is in an almost perfect cursive script. She gently runs her hand across the first line and then begins to read.

<u>August, 1940</u>

"I was born Giancarlo Antonio Francesco Buonoforte in Palermo, Sicily on October 15th I believe in 1885."

Lucia shocked, stops reading.

"What?! What is this?"

Don Carlo laughs. "Just read."

"At that time birth years were not really kept..."

"Papa, that is not what I mean."

"Keep reading. I know. Meeting Enzo was not an accident. The truth will reveal itself."

"Alight. My God."

She continues to read.

"When I came to America with my mother and young sister Stefania from Sicily, the only relatives we had in America were my mother's cousin Anita and her son Bruno. Anita's husband was killed in Sicily due to some vendetta and they were forced to come to America because it was feared her son Bruno might be killed as well. There were towns in Sicily that hardly had any men left due to vendettas and warring families.

My father's name was Giancarlo Francesco Buonoforte. He had a vendetta set against him from one of the up-and-coming Dons in Palermo, Sicily. The last we heard, he is part of a tough group of men that protect each other against other groups in Sicily and he is either still in hiding somewhere in the mountains of Sicily or he is dead.

Everyone thinks that all Mafia are bad and Sicily is a bad place but what about America and the gangsters? They are not all Italian. They are not Mafia. They are not honorable. Some men are bad and others have to protect people from the bad ones in any way they can from the greed and power hungry. This is how it has been since time began. This is how it will always be.

To many people in Sicily, as years went on, my father had become somewhat of a folk hero. He fought against many of the groups who took advantage of the lawlessness within the outlying farm areas. These are the huge landowners who ruthlessly consolidated power by intimidating farmers and peasants for money and land. They are also crooked government people. What is the difference? There were many victims of the warring group's ruthlessness. One began to threaten my father, who was widely respected for counsel and protection. It was not always this way. It was, one lucky stroke of luck at first that fate played a role in our lives that changed everything and then later fate reared its ugly head and changed our lives forever.

Don Carlo took the diary from Lucia and thumbed through the pages. He handed the book back to here. "This entry told to me by my mother, later explained a great deal."

<u>August 1889</u>

During the first week in August, my parents would take us for a week's holiday at a small pensione near the east coast of Sicily in the resort town of Taormina. One of my mother's cousins, Ernesto, worked as the head chef in a luxury resort on a cliff above the beach right in Taormina. Ernesto was very good friends with the hotel's assistant manager. When the manager would take a couple of days off and the assistant manager was in charge, he would let us use the facilities. The hotel had a large pool and access to the beach with cabanas, lounge chairs, and umbrellas. On one of these days, while we were on the beach, we heard a woman screaming. She was violently waving her arms and running into the water. Suddenly people began to gather and my mother told my father to go over and see what was happening. As my father ran to where the screaming was coming from, he could see a couple of people were trying to go into the water, but because the sea was rough and they were wearing heavy swimwear, they kept getting knocked down by the waves. My father looked in the direction of the commotion and he could see a man and a small boy trying to keep their heads above the water and swim unsuccessfully toward shore. My father took off his shirt and shoes, grabbed a swimming tube from a man who was just watching the events unfold, ran into the water, threw the tube ahead of him, and dove under the oncoming waves. He grabbed the tube and swam as fast as he could toward the man and young boy, and when he reached them, they tried to climb onto him in a panic. My father gave the swimming tube to the man and he was able to swim on his own. Then my father took the exhausted boy's arms around his neck and pushed him over his back. The boy grabbed his neck so hard he was choking my father, who had to free up the boy's arms so he could breathe while my father was trying to swim to shore. Halfway to shore, a couple of other men swam toward them to help. One man helped with the little boy and another guided the man in the tube, who was exhausted and was no longer able to swim and collapsed on the beach. When they reached shore, a man ran into the water, scooped up the boy, and ran to the others who were anxiously waiting. My father was exhausted and laid on the beach to catch his breath. The man's wife was hugging the man and the little boy on the shore. When my father finally was able to get out of the water and stand, the woman and man went over and hugged and smothered my father with kisses. They began to walk back to their lounge chairs when an older man walked up to him, and with tears in his eyes, threw his arms around my father and thanked him again and again for saving his son-in-law's and his grandson's lives. My father tried to wave him off, saying that it was nothing, but the man would not hear of it. The man, whose name he found out was Alberto Giammanco, implored him to come over to his family because they would like to thank him for what he had done. As I remember and I was told, my father was a proud and humble man and did not accept praise and appreciation very easily, but promised to come over when he had rested a while.

While sitting in the lounge chair a waiter brought over soft drinks and a bottle of champagne. My mother told the waiter that they hadn't ordered anything. As the waiter was opening the champagne, he said Don Giammanco ordered it and would also like to have you and your family be his guests for dinner that evening. When my father and mother looked over to where the Giammancos were sitting, an old man, presumably Don Giammanco, raised his cane and nodded in recognition. Giancarlo and his wife then felt obligated to personally thank the old man. As they walked toward the Giammanco family, the boy's mother and father ran up to him, again hugging and thanking him repeatedly. Then Don Giammanco and his wife came over and the man offered his hand, and he said for the rest of the afternoon he would be thinking of ways to repay my father for saving his son-in-law and grandson. My father was genuinely embarrassed and said that was not necessary. Don Giammanco asked my family to please join them for dinner. My father and mother looked at each other, smiled, and said that they would be delighted.

As they gathered their belongings, a waiter and the assistant manager came over to my parents as they returned to their lounge chairs. The assistant manager said that Don Giammanco had inquired about who my father was and where he was staying. When the assistant manager explained the situation to Don Giammanco, hearing that they were not guests of the hotel, Don Giammanco then asked the assistant manager to meet him in the hotel lobby. When they met again, we later found out that Don Giammanco directed the assistant manager to arrange for Giancarlo and his wife and family to stay for the rest of August in the hotel with all expenses paid. He also asked the assistant manager to arrange to have the finest clothing stores in Taormina, and in Palermo, if necessary, to bring everything in their inventory so an elaborate wardrobe can be put together for my father, my mother, my sister, and me. Characteristically of Don Giammanco, he saw to every detail and requested the appropriate luggage be bought to transport the clothes back to their home when it was time to leave. Don Giammanco also made private carriages available at the hotel for any sightseeing the family may desire and then, finally, to bring them home. He also gave the family unlimited credit for anything they would like to buy in the hotel, and if it wasn't available in the hotel, the assistant manager was instructed to carry out any of their wishes.

When my parents were informed of this, they were dumbfounded. "Who was this man?" they asked the assistant manager. The assistant manager told them that Don Giammanco and his family have been coming to the hotel since it was built, and if his information was correct the Don put up much of the money when the original hotel had burned down ten years earlier. The assistant manager suspects that Don Giammanco is the real owner of the hotel but he doesn't want anyone to know, which is a typical Sicilian strategy of someone powerful keeping a low profile from both his friends and his enemies with the philosophy, "Always keep them guessing." He said that Don Giammanco is the head of the most powerful 'family' in Palermo.

The assistant manager told my father it is believed that Don Giammanco is very powerful and operates through other families, because he does not want any attention brought on him and his family, and lately there had been a problem with the other families who feel as if they are a protective shield, which is exactly what they had become. The other families feel that they take all the risks and Don Giammanco reaps the rewards. This information sent a chill down my father's spine. He knew firsthand how things are done by lesser powerful men, and a word from

Don Giammanco could be a matter of life or death with no questions asked. The assistant manager, still seeing the look of concern on my father's face with what he was told, took my father aside and told him that saving Don Giammanco's son-in-law's and grandson's lives was more important to this man than his own life, and he is not going to have his generosity refused. It is a matter of personal honor and it would be the same as refusing to make an accommodation to Don Giammanco, who doesn't ever hear the word "no." My father said he would accept Don Giammanco's generous offer. He thought he would simply be finished with it when he returned home. The assistant manager winked at him again and then led him to his office. When they arrived at the office, the sign on the door read "manager." My father looked at the assistant manager and he laughed and said that his fate was tied to my father and he was made manager when Don Giammanco realized the assistant manager was responsible for allowing Giancarlo and his family to use the hotel's facilities. My father asked what would happen to the manager.

"He will be offered another position at another hotel. An offer he can't refuse." The manager then winked at Giancarlo and thanked him.

The next few weeks were like living in another world. Not only was every luxury laid at our family's feet, but my father began to grow a genuine affection for the old man who took my father under his wing and was going to play the role of my father's benefactor. Could everything he heard about Don Giammanco be really true? Could this loving family man have his enemies disappear? My father was being indoctrinated into a whole different world and he put all those questions about Don Giammanco out of his head.

Late in the afternoons, when the wives and children would take their daily nap, my father and Don Giammanco would sit on the beach and smoke cigars. Don Giammanco was never blindly generous nor would he offer his services without knowing the person's background that could possibly be disguised as an enemy or a friend of an enemy. The Don had my father thoroughly investigated during the time they stayed at the hotel, which was another reason that we were kept at the hotel. When Don Giammanco was convinced that my father was not connected to any of *his enemies and was an honorable man, he gave himself over to my father and treated him like a son. More like a son than his own son, who didn't have the intelligence or the stomach for the business that Don Giammanco was involved in. His son would turn out to be a covertly jealous adversary of my father. Don Giammanco's hopes rested with his grandson, but his grandson was young and Don Giammanco was an old man. He worried about who would counsel the grandson after he died. Who would inherit the business? He believed that fate had given him the answer in my father; and, to a certain degree, he was right.*

Again, Don Carlo took the diary and had Lucia read only the next two entries. That is all he wanted her to read for now. "This explains my father's fate and why we had to leave Sicily and start a life in America with a new name."

<u>September, 1921</u>
Our family's life would be completely different from this point on. Don Giammanco made my father his assistant, his "consigliere," but he would have to be careful because there were many people who would be jealous of this upstart who had been in fate's favor. As my father began to gain power, it didn't sit well with many of the powerful groups that were benefiting from bullying the locals. Nobody wanted a war and the other families realized they would wait until the old man died and they could then take advantage of the situation and take control. But now the situation has changed. There was someone young, my father, who was under Don Giammanco's wing and who would easily be able to step into his shoes. Both men were naïve to think that power would easily pass from Don Giammanco to my father. Plans were already being made to be put into action after Don Giammanco's death, which of course would directly affect my father and our family.

<u>January, 1924</u>
It took about three years and finally, Don Giammanco died from a battle of influenza and what would turn out to be the remnants of the

Spanish flu. It didn't take long before the plans that were to be put into place after Don Giammanco's death were now set into motion, but it would not be. Still grateful for saving the life of his son, Don Giammanco's son-in-law came to our home and told my father what would happen to him a couple weeks after his father-in-law's funeral at a meeting of the families to discuss new business. It would look like an assassination by one of the rival families, but in fact, it would be Don Giammanco's own son who wanted the assassination of my father to be carried out by one of the rival families for an exchange of some power. Don Giammanco's son-in-law gave my father money and made arrangements to send us to America, but my father had to hide in the hills because there was no way to get out of Sicily by any commercial routes not seen. The next morning my father made the arrangements telling the Giammancos that we were taking a vacation but my father was staying behind. Then arrangements were made for my mother, sister, and myself to go through Messina and then make our way to America, but not under the Buonoforte, name but under the name, Masseria. A name given to them by Don Giammanco's son-in-law along with all the travel papers changed to that name, just in case there were plans to kidnap my family if they could not find my father.

Before Lucia can read the next section with the title, *Enzo Buonoforte*, Don Carlo takes the book from Lucia and closes it. As Lucia gives her father back the book, a small flyer drops to the floor. When she picks it up her father takes it from her hand and for a few seconds stares at the writing at the top, Grand Opening *Angelina Restaurante*.

"Papa, what is that?"

"Hmmm...a big part of my life that I try to forget since the time I designed it."

He takes the flyer, folds it, and gently places it back in the book.

"That's enough for now. Some of the things that happened are still upsetting."

"I understand, but when did you change your name to Don Carlo, I know why it was changed to Masseria."

"There was this Chicago gangster named, Joe 'the boss' Masseria.

My cousin Bruno stopped working with me and wanted to make more money so there was an opportunity to work for Joe Masseria. After a time, he told Joe about me and said that I had a great memory, could calculate odds in my head, and didn't have to write anything down. Joe Masseria said I must be some cousin and he wanted to meet me and have me work for him. That was the last thing I wanted to do. Bruno really built me up because he wanted to stay on the good side of Masseria. Also, that is the first time the name Don Carlo was used when he said that I was a don in Sicily and I have a lot of connections. When Bruno called me and told me this, I could've killed him. I tried to avoid coming to Chicago as long as I could but Joe Masseria was getting impatient, and as Bruno told me, you 'don't say no to Joe.' So, I left the country and went to Italy, which is another story, and then I heard he was killed in April of 1931. When I heard that, I came back to America and I kept the Don Carlo name because the rumors about who I was, or was supposed to be, gave me some power.

"When did you meet my mother?"

"Many years ago, when she had the restaurant that was named after her, Angelina Restaurante. She was probably the most beautiful and stubborn woman I have ever met."

"Oh...That was the flyer."

Don Carlo gently takes his daughter's hand.

"You have all her beauty and heart, and you can be stubborn when you want to be."

"Tell me more about her."

Don Carlo looks away and his mind goes back in time.

"I will. This is enough memories for one day. Look outside. I hope we don't have problems traveling to Clifton.

The weather fluctuates from cold to unseasonably warm and then to cold again. The snow on Long Island has melted, but with the cold weather returning, the melting snow turns to ice.

Very early the next day as Don Carlo is getting dressed to visit the Buonofortes, he can see how the water in the birdbath in the backyard has frozen and it makes him shiver. Suddenly he is tired and has to sit down. When he finally finishes getting dressed, he asks his daughter to make him a cup of expresso and bring it to his study in an hour. He gets to his study and sits in his chair facing the window with a view of the gardens. He looks around his beautiful study and thinks of how in an instant everything can be gone. He sits back with his eyes closed letting his mind think back to the times in his life he has tried to shut out of his mind. *How did I get here?*

After Carlo bought the estate, he had the entire house renovated and decorated. No cost was spared. Don Carlo and his daughter ended up being the only ones living in the house, however, his daughter was in boarding school much of the year and would just come home for holidays. Summers were for vacations and traveling. The rest of the year Don Carlo only used the kitchen and the master bedroom on the first floor most of the time. It didn't matter that Carlo was the only one living in the house, the servants came and cleaned the house every week. Even rooms that no one ever went into.

On the grounds of the estate, the vast gardens were redesigned by famous landscape architects that Don Carlo had brought over from Italy. These were the landscape designers who restored the gardens of the Villa D' Este hotel on Lake Como, the Boboli Gardens in Florence, and the Vatican Gardens in Rome. Again, no cost was spared. The gardens are where Don Carlo escapes to enjoy his solitude.

He instructed that the gardens and the house never be considered complete. Over the years, he installed huge fountains. Flowers and plants were constantly changed according to the season. In the fall and winter months, vegetables and flowers were grown in greenhouses to supply the house, the staff, and the neighborhood with fresh produce and fruit nearly all year long. He wandered the gardens and would have lunch brought to a small summerhouse that contained a living room with a fireplace, a study, and a bathroom. Connected to the summerhouse was a gazebo that overlooked Long Island Sound, where he took his daily naps on a large lounge chair.

On the other side of the property was the heated pool, which Don Carlo had rarely used but must be kept crystal clean and constantly at 85 degrees. One of the servants once asked why he keeps the pool heated. He answered that he may one day want to go in and he wants to make sure it is warm. He would sit and stare at the fountains around the pool for hours. Even when he broke his hip a few years ago and couldn't get around as easily, he made sure everything was maintained according to his detailed plans. He would supervise everything from a salon on the first floor of the house which was also his office. It has an expansive view of almost all the gardens. In the main master bedroom on the second floor of the house, there was an even more expansive view of the gardens right to the docks on the Long Island Sound. Someone gave him a copy of Fitzgerald's *The Great Gatsby* and told him there was a familiarity between him and the mysterious Gatsby, especially living on Long Island Sound like Gatsby. At first, Carlo was excited, until he read the book and didn't like the comparison and made sure the person who gave him the book knew of his displeasure and they had a long and sometimes heated discussion. When it came to persuasion, Don Carlo learned to be very articulate with his English.

"In spite of what you have heard, or what you think you know of me, unlike Gatsby I have made all my money through honest American investments and not in mysterious ways like Gatsby."

He of course conveniently left out his gambling business with his cousin, but overall, it was true. He lived modestly and invested heavily in real estate during the Depression when people were desperate for money. He also made sound investments in businesses that were always profitable. This is a murky area, because Don Carlo always made sure he got paid first, and the few times a business wasn't profitable he took over the business and either had someone run it or sold off all the assets. However, he always made sure the family of the business owner didn't suffer and had the owner work off the debt. A few of his gardeners are examples of business owners who went bankrupt, who now worked for Don Carlo, and were happy to work for him.

Before Don Carlo bought the house he would go back and forth to Italy and told his sister that he had businesses he was selling in Italy, but that was all he said. He felt that his business was his business and he would tell her the full story when he felt it was the right time. The last time he returned to the United States he did not return alone. He came back with a four-year-old girl he said was his daughter Lucia. He then told his sister about Angelina and his daughter, which she had already guessed knowing the circumstances. He said that Angelina wasn't able to travel because she was taking care of her elderly mother and father who were afraid to take a long ocean voyage. Eventually, Angelina's father died of a stroke. The plan was that they would all leave Naples, but Angelina was waiting for her paperwork to leave Italy. Angelina insisted that Don Carlo and Lucia go ahead and he would buy a house and get it ready for her arrival. Those were the only details he told his sister but it wasn't the whole story and it wasn't the whole truth. It wasn't Angelina he was talking about. It was Angelina's sister Beatrice, Don Carlo's wife.

What Don Carlo didn't tell his sister was that Angelina and he were not married when she gave birth to their daughter. They told Angelina's parents and everyone else that they were married in America. Giving birth out of wedlock is a huge scandal in the church and society. It is even worse for a celebrity like Angelina.

When Lucia was about three-years-old, Angelina was getting sick. At first, she hid it from Don Carlo, telling him to go to America with Lucia and that she, Beatrice, and their mother would follow when they had the proper papers. Don Carlo found out Angelina had been seeing a doctor. It had become obvious because of her symptoms that she had lung cancer. She refused treatment because she would have to travel and at this point, she was too ill.

She made Don Carlo promise to marry her sister Beatrice so that Lucia would have a proper and legitimate mother. A couple months after Angelina died, Don Carlo was secretly married to Beatrice by a priest who was a close family friend. Although heartbroken, Don Carlo found comfort in Beatrice, who was as beautiful as Angelina but had a quieter nature.

Don Carlo began to make plans to return to America with his new wife, Lucia, and Beatrice's mother. He was able to get the proper papers for Lucia, but there was a problem with getting them for Beatrice and her mother. They insisted that Don Carlo and Lucia leave because they were afraid Don Carlo might run into a problem leaving if they waited. It was in Lucia's best interest that they go. Beatrice assured him that because of their celebrity status and their connections, they wouldn't have a problem. Everyone agreed that Don Carlo and Lucia would sail home and when Beatrice and her mother got the proper papers, he would arrange for them to sail to America. That was not to be.

After Don Carlo bought the house on Long Island, he immediately began renovations and repairs so the house would be ready. However, during this time things in Europe began to change. Hitler came to power in Germany and Mussolini came into power in Italy, and the fascists were taking control of all the towns. It became harder to communicate outside of Italy. Both Don Carlo and his wife wrote letters back and forth, but the international mail was erratic. Don Carlo thought of contacting his connections in Sicily, but that didn't go anywhere. He was afraid to travel to Italy because he feared that he wouldn't be able to get out and might be recruited into the Italian army. Things became even more concerning when Mussolini created an alliance with Hitler. Europe was on the brink of war.

Months went by, and then the Nazis came into Italy. They took anything they wanted and killed or sent anyone who opposed them to concentration camps. Both Don Carlo and his wife sent letters, but they were never received. World War II broke out. There was no way his wife could travel to America. Communication was cut off. Don Carlo was beside himself with worry and could not do anything about it. It was too late, and Don Carlo blamed himself for the situation. He should have gone there and brought them to America. He could have paid a doctor and nurse to come back with them. He blamed himself but still tried to make contact. All communication stopped, and he presumed the worst.

After the war, Don Carlo tried to find out what happened to his wife and her mother and he even traveled to Naples. Of the few who still lived in his wife's neighborhood, no one knew what happened. Many were either killed or sent to Germany to die in concentration camps. Then in 1956, Carlo received a letter from the Italian government sent through the U.S. State Department questioning if the woman in the enclosed picture, who claimed to be his wife was actually his wife. Carlo instantly recognized her and had his lawyer wire the Italian government stating that the woman, Beatrice was, in fact, Don Carlo's wife. The letter further explained that she and her mother had been sent to a concentration camp where the woman's mother quickly died. Don Carlo's wife was sent back to Naples, Italy with some neighbors who had also been in the concentration camp. The woman was suffering from "dissociative amnesia" that had been caused by traumatic events she had experienced during the war.

The letter further went on to say that in early 1956, one of the older nurses who began working at the Naples clinic recognized Carlo's wife from an old Italian magazine. She had seen the story of the family of a famous opera singer. Together with the doctors who were treating her, she was shown the pictures from the magazine and they were able to slowly bring back her memory. Finally, getting a letter from Don Carlo's lawyer with pictures of her and Don Carlo and background information, made all the pieces fit together.

When Don Carlo realized she was alive, he was overwhelmed with joy and planned to travel to Naples to bring her back to the United States, but his passport had expired and he would have to wait possibly weeks to get a new one due to a backlog of everyone applying for passports and traveling to Europe. He also needed a passport for Lucia. He wouldn't go without her. He didn't want to wait, so he contacted the clinic and said he would pay for a nurse to accompany his wife, and for the nurse's return back to Italy. He wanted the same nurse who helped his wife recover her memory, so he could do something to reward her for what she had done.

Arrangements were made to have them sail on July 17th on a ship that was labeled the "floating art gallery"–the *Andrea Doria*. But the reunion was ill-fated. A few days into the voyage on July 22nd, the Swedish passenger liner the *Stockholm* struck the *Andrea Doria* and fifty-three passengers died. Don Carlo's wife and the nurse were among the dead.

Don Carlo was inconsolable and blamed himself for not waiting for Beatrice's passport. Nothing and no one could console him. He said he only wanted to live because of his daughter, but even Lucia could not break through his depression at times. He became a recluse in his own home, living a sometimes eccentric existence. Rooms that were never occupied or rarely used he insisted should always be cleaned. Even lights were turned on at night in different rooms on different nights because he didn't want to feel the house was empty. The wine cellar had its own sommelier, who monitored the hundreds of bottles of wine to ensure they were properly stored at the right temperature and that the bottles were turned to address sediment, even though Don Carlo didn't often drink wine or liquor.

Don Carlo's yacht, *La Diva Davina,* was still brought out of dry dock and moored at his dock at the edge of his property, with a three-man crew who ensured it was always ready to sail. No one could remember the last time it was taken out to cruise. Years have gone by, and now Lucia is married with a daughter and a son, and they moved into the guesthouse. They use the yacht on weekends. Don Carlo sometimes joined them and wondered why he never used it before Lucia and her family. He loves to be with his two grandchildren, who are the only ones who can pierce his wall of invulnerability. With them, he isn't afraid of showing an affectionate side. Although Lucia regrets that he wasn't the same with her as with her children, she forgives him because she understands him. In many ways, she is like him.

It was not only his yacht that Don Carlo made sure was ready at a moment's notice. He had his cars maintained, even though they were rarely used. Expensive cars like two Italian Bugattis, a large chauffeur-driven Mercedes Benz, a Rolls-Royce, and a red Ferrari. He never did anything for show. He appreciates quality and craftsmanship and if he owns it, he wants it taken care of or he will get rid of it; and he rarely gets rid of anything. He enjoys what he has and says it is because of all the sentimental feelings associated with what he owns. Many antiques and family heirlooms in his home were chosen by him and Lucia's mother when they were in Italy and shipped to his warehouse in the United States. He is a contradiction of emotions. On the one hand, he doesn't like to discuss the past, which may bring on certain feelings; yet he keeps inanimate objects, like his antiques, to remind him of past times and still has a sharp memory of where and when every item was purchased. Then again, sometimes he feels his memory is a curse because with a good memory comes pleasure but also heartache of what has been lost: another contradiction of emotions.

When he can't sleep because of the past he wanders from room to room. It's as if he is looking for someone or something. And even though he knows he will never find what he is looking for, he still wanders the halls of his huge mansion.

Things changed when his architect son-in-law Andrew's uncle died and left him a house in Newport, Rhode Island. It was among the Gilded Age mansions on Bellevue Avenue and was named "Le Bord de L'eau," because it was on the water. The huge iron gates were rusted shut and the grounds were in dire need of maintenance. Although the electrical service and plumbing had been updated, it had been done in a "mish-mosh" by unskilled workers. With ten bedrooms, ten bathrooms, a huge dining room for eighteen, parlors, a billiard room, a ballroom, and outdoor spaces, it would take a team of skilled artisans and other skilled and specialty craftsmen to repair plaster moldings and ceiling paintings.

Andrew seemed overwhelmed, but Don Carlo was as excited as a child on Christmas morning, running from room to room, making notes, in awe of the artwork and the skill of Italian artists and craftsmen. Lucia and her husband could see that this was what Don Carlo needed to get him out of his depression: it was a Godsend. Don Carlo would leave his mark on this house that would be there long after his death.

As they walked around the neighborhood, they saw empty lots where some mansions had already been torn down or were turned into offices or schools. Andrew, having an appreciation for old homes and their history, had a hard time deciding to sell the house, rather than renovate it. Don Carlo, who was enamored with the house and all of Newport, told his son-in-law that he would back the expense of renovating the house for him and Lucia and their children. He would spare no expense. Since the house was on the water, they would renovate the dock and boat house first. Immediately after the docks were repaired, they took the yacht and sailed it to Newport to supervise the renovations. At the same time, Don

Carlo and his son-in-law got involved in trying to establish some sort of preservation society to stop having the other historical homes torn down.

Although it would take time to find the artists and craftsmen and skilled electricians, plumbers, and other workmen, it didn't matter. It gave Don Carlo a new sense of purpose, even though it was just a house.

As the renovations began, like in Long Island, many of the surrounding neighbors asked other neighbors and town shopkeepers about Don Carlo. Who was he, where did he come from, and how did he amass such a fortune to live in one of the biggest estates in Newport right next to the Vanderbilt mansion? Some of the workers on the estate who were also asked said they honestly didn't know or even care. Even if they did know or suspect, they had all grown fond of Don Carlo, who wasn't afraid to roll up his sleeves and get his hands dirty. Their fondness only grew and they wouldn't betray him. Also, Don Carlo paid them very well and they didn't want to lose their job. There was also another reason: Fear.

The workers heard a story from one of the garden workers whom Don Carlo had brought over from Long Island. The worker told them about an incident that happened a couple of years ago. There was food missing from the kitchen and when the chef asked the sou chef Fabrizio about the missing food, he told the chef that he saw the dishwasher, Alexandro, stealing food and was sure he was selling it. When the chef asked Don Carlo what to do, Don Carlo told him to say and do nothing and he would look into it. Don Carlo had learned years ago that anyone can lose their temper and jump to conclusions. He never tried to show any emotion, especially anger, which he felt showed weakness. He saw men in powerful positions lose respect because they were foolish enough to react emotionally instead of getting the facts. Then, when they found out the truth and knew they had reacted wrongly, they looked foolish. If they reacted with a fatal act, the problem was even worse, which could result in retaliation and retribution.

Don Carlo was smart enough to ask questions first, get the best proof possible, and then act accordingly. He had his suspicions about the accuser, Fabrizio, and asked his secretary Rosemary to try and get some information about who was the real thief. Don Carlo had paid for Rosemary's son's operation that saved her son's life and she swore complete loyalty to Don Carlo so he knew he could trust her. In a couple of days, Rosemary got the information from a few of the kitchen staff who were loyal to her. As Don Carlo suspected, it was Fabrizio, the accuser who was the thief.

A week went by and Don Carlo asked Fabrizio to take a ride with him into Little Italy in lower Manhattan to shop so that Fabrizio could carry the large quantity of imported cheeses, olive oil, and other food stuffs that Don Carlo personally liked to pick out. This was not an odd request because other kitchen help had been asked before and they knew that Don Carlo loved to shop in Little Italy and visit the stores and shopkeepers he got to know, many of whom he had helped over the years. However, this time instead of driving directly to Little Italy, the driver took them to the Meadowlands in Secaucus, New Jersey, and drove them to one of the garbage businesses Don Carlo owned. Again, it wasn't so unusual for him to occasionally pay a visit and make the cash collection himself, look over the trucks, and talk to the workers.

Fabrizio began getting nervous as Don Carlo got out of the car. Don Carlo put his arm around Fabrizio and walked him over toward the huge piles of garbage.

"How many acres do you think this garbage is on?

By this time, Fabrizio was really nervous because he had never seen Don Carlo get that familiar with anyone.

"Don Carlo, I don't really know."

Don Carlo took his arm off Fabrizio's shoulder and laughed. "Neither do I!"

Fabrizio laughed nervously and then Don Carlo looked him in the eye and asked him another question.

"How many bodies do you think are dumped here every year?"

Fabrizio was almost in tears and just shook his head. Don Carlo put his arm around Fabrizio's shoulder again, this time walking toward one of the trucks dumping the garbage.

"Now, you tell me. Do you still think that Alexandro is the one stealing from me?"

Don Carlo squeezed the accuser's shoulder as two men approached. Fabrizio was shaking and would now tell Don Carlo the truth.

"No, Don Carlo. It was me. It was me. Please, I am sorry." Then the man broke down in tears.

"Ahh. A thief, a liar, and a coward. Why did you steal? And don't lie. Please tell me you wanted to feed your starving family, or you needed the money to buy medicine for a sick family member."

Don Carlo took his hand off the accuser's shoulder and raised Fabrizio's head because Fabrizio was afraid to make eye contact with Don Carlo.

"To pay off gambling debts or I would be killed."

This was something that Don Carlo was familiar with and felt guilty about. Yes, in the old days, he had provided gambling, but it was up to the man gambling to make sure he didn't get in too deep and not be able to pay. Regardless, he knew of too many men who let themselves and their families come to ruin because of gambling. So, he did have a certain amount of empathy, especially since Fabrizio had been a good worker for many years, but he couldn't get away with stealing and most of all accusing an innocent person. Don Carlo knew what to do to not lose respect and his honor.

Don Carlo got close to Fabrizio, looked over his shoulder, and quietly asked him close to his ear, "How much do you owe?"

"Twenty-five hundred."

"Hmmm, you're a big loser."

"Don Carlo, I am sorry. Please, Don Carlo, I have a family.

"You should have thought of that before gambling over your head and worse, accusing someone else of stealing. What should I do with you?"

At this point, Fabrizio was shaking so hard that he began to wet himself.

Don Carlo motioned to one of the men, who came over to Don Carlo. Don Carlo whispered something to the man and the man walked over to the office. Fabrizio was so sure he was going to end up in the garbage dump, he quietly began praying. Don Carlo stood waiting for the man to return with an envelope that he gave to Don Carlo.

"In this envelope is three thousand dollars. You pay off your debt and keep the rest. If I ever see you again, here is where you will end up for eternity."

Don Carlo handed the envelope to Fabrizio whose hand was shaking so much that Don Carlo had to put the envelope in the man's hand and squeeze his fingers around it. Then Don Carlo walked to the limousine with Fabrizio following him. Don Carlo stopped and turned. Fabrizio stopped in his tracks.

"Thank you, Don Carlo. Thank you." Then Fabrizio tried to kiss Don Carlo's hand, but Don Carlo pulled it away. Fabrizio kept following Don Carlo to the car. Don Carlo stopped and turned to Fabrizio.

"Where do you think you're going? You're not coming with me to stink up my car with piss in your pants. Even if you didn't piss yourself, what makes you think I want to even look at you. Get out of my sight. You walk to wherever you want to go."

Then Don Carlo got into the car and it drove away, leaving Fabrizio standing there shivering from wetting his pants with the men around the garbage trucks laughing at him.

This was one of the stories that would get around, with everyone who heard it wondering the same things. How close was the accuser to ending up in the dump and was Don Carlo responsible for anyone rotting in the garbage? Some heard the story and admired Don Carlo's generosity. But anyone who heard the story also feared Don Carlo, who doesn't mind being feared because he hates to be patronized. He learned something a long time ago in Sicily; keep your friends close and your enemies closer. Since you can't tell who your real friends are, consider everyone your enemy until they earn your trust. With that philosophy, Don Carlo had developed a keen sense for the people he would rather stay away from.

For example, at Christmas, Don Carlo would have bottles of wine and flowers from his greenhouses brought to neighbors. Or he would make a rare visit, which he did around the holidays. Because of the mystique that was a part of "who Don Carlo was," it was both an asset and a liability. No one knows how the "Don" became part of Carlo's name. It doesn't matter. Some people are fascinated with how this handsome and kind-mannered man could be the subject of such rumors. Also, how could this man have had men killed? There was also the confusion of the Masseria name, which was what Don Carlo wanted; the confusion of Chicago's Joe "the boss" Masseria, even though he was killed years ago. Nevertheless, they respected him. Others looked down on him because he was a "nouveau riche" foreigner. Others stayed away because they just feared him or were resentful. Regardless, everyone wants to know who is the real Don Carlo. There were the rumors and the reality. But whether it was out of fear or fascination, most welcomed him and were charmed when they met him, either by fascination or fear.

No matter if it was in Newport or Long Island, he was aware of the questions and rumors. Now, especially at his age, he doesn't care. His life is his life. He makes no apologies. He takes responsibility for what he has done in the past, for the things that he did to survive, the same things thousands of others who wanted to survive had done. But now, years later, looking back at his life, he does have one big regret and the catastrophic decision that he made because of his stubbornness. Aside from his late wife, Beatrice, is the only other woman he has ever loved and considered his "soul mate." A woman who to this day still haunts him; Angelina.

Chapter 10

La Divina was fascinated by Don Carlo, but she would not fall in love with him; she would not allow it.

Angelina Maria Cesare, or *La Divina,* as she was better known, was a very famous opera singer who stopped performing when her manager, who was also her husband, was killed in a car accident. A short while after his death, she stopped performing and took some of her money and invested in a small trattoria-style restaurant on Mulberry Street, close to Canal Street, with her cousin, Fabrizio, and her parents, who were in the restaurant business in Naples, Italy. For a time, it was a good way to keep her parents busy helping to run the restaurant. When Angelina and her family lived in Naples, they owned a restaurant, but her parents sold it to concentrate on Angelina's singing career. With her cousin Fabrizio and her parents, they set up the restaurant and put the menu together from old family recipes. With Angelina's connections in the music world, the business instantly took off.

After a few years, Fabrizio decided to retire and go back to Italy and Angelina bought out his share. The restaurant outgrew its original location and Angelina's parents wanted to retire and went back to Naples soon after Fabrizio left. Now Angelina was on her own but she was determined to make the new restaurant successful. With the staff of the original restaurant, Angelina moved down the street, occupying three buildings that

Angelina was smart enough to buy, rather than rent, on Mulberry Street, closer to the newly established Columbus Park. When the tenants left, she completely gutted the three buildings to build one huge dining space with a mezzanine and grand staircase that resembled the foyer of the Naples Opera House. No detail was ignored, including a new menu, which included some French dishes.

At first, the restaurant was frequented by the usual, "uptown crowd." However, the business didn't take off as fast as she thought it would, and she became concerned because she had spent much more than she intended on the renovations. Also, she lost the rental income from the apartments in her old building so she was dipping into her savings, and her accounts were getting depleted fast.

Years earlier, Don Carlo, having a passion for Italian Opera had his friend Luca, a booking agent who knew Angelina, arrange for Don Carlo to meet her after her performance in *La Boheme*, at the Metropolitan Opera House. They had an instant attraction to one another, but because of their conflicting schedules, nothing went any further until years later when she stopped performing.

Don Carlo had heard about her new restaurant opening downtown in Little Italy. Don Carlo and Luca went to the restaurant a few months after it opened and sat at the bar waiting to once again, meet Angelina. When she was told they were at the bar she rushed to see them and was happy to see both Don Carlo and Luca, but especially Don Carlo. She invited Don Carlo and Luca to her private upstairs salon for some drinks. Angelina was surprised at how knowledgeable Don Carlo was about opera and opera history and argued if Enrico Caruso or Feodor Chaliapin was the better tenor. They talked until dawn, with Luca snoring on Angelina's living room divan.

Angelina was taken with Don Carlo. She had had a brief affair with a man about a year ago, but their interests clashed and she ended the relationship. There was another reason for her interest in Don Carlo other than their mutual interest in opera. There weren't many men who could stand up to her and remain charming. She knew that she could love this man. Angelina was a few years older than Don Carlo and she wondered if that would be a problem if she had a relationship with him. The age difference didn't really matter to Don Carlo. Although he loved strong and independent women, he would never want to have a relationship with one. He knew his own personality was too strong. Also, in some ways, he was too "old school" when it came to a woman's place.

Don Carlo had his "lady friends" and was content to leave it that way. Don Carlo knew with an independent personality like Angelina's, the relationship would be too much work and the passion would burn out. This wasn't just theory. He learned this hard lesson from past experiences. He was too fond of Angelina to risk it. She, however, began to have feelings for him that she would block out. She could sense that he wasn't fond of her in the same way that she was fond of him. She never let him know how deeply she really felt. She liked him too much to make him feel uncomfortable, and she valued their friendship and did not want to do anything to put it at risk. Don Carlo was one of the few people she knew who was honest and didn't expect anything from her except friendship. She also knew that his personality was as strong as hers, and this would cause the relationship to burn brightly and then burn out, like a candle lit at both ends.

A few weeks after the new restaurant opened, Don Carlo came by again, this time for dinner with some friends. He was surprised to see that the restaurant was so empty. What was worse was that it was a Saturday night, which should be the busiest night of the week. The mezzanine was even closed. He could see with the reduced staff that Angelina was really concerned about the drop in business. To add to her troubles, both her parents had gotten sick in Italy and the money she was sending for their medical bills was costing a small fortune.

Don Carlo looked around the restaurant. He had once been to the old restaurant hoping to see Angelina, but she was not there that night. The new restaurant was so very different than the old one. The old restaurant had more of a country or Tuscan feel. It had warmth. It had charm. The new restaurant was fancier to cater to the uptown customers, but it was cold and seemed unwelcoming. Even the new menu was too sophisticated. It now included some French dishes that he felt didn't have a place on the menu and were just thrown in to be fashionable. The "uptowners" came to Angelina's to get away from this type of sophisticated environment. They wanted a place to relax, have great food and talk, without feeling like they were being watched. The new restaurant had no real "cuore," heart. They left and Don Carlo planned to come back the next Saturday.

Once again, Don Carlo came with some friends and after dinner, Don Carlo asked his friends to go home without him because he wanted to talk to Angelina. After the last customers left, Angelina came over to Don Carlo's table. As she sat down, she took out a fan from her dress pocket, opened it, and fanned herself, and without making eye contact, she remarked how hot the weather in June was in the city. She knew what Don Carlo was thinking, and she was too embarrassed to refer to the empty restaurant. He leaned over and looked directly at her.

"Angelina, what is going on here? I had heard the restaurant wasn't doing big business, but 9:30 on a Saturday night and the place is empty—what's wrong?"

Angelina was looking at the floor and twisting her foot in and out of her shoe from nervousness. She slowly started to speak, looking down, and then looked up and shrugged her shoulders. She had tears in her eyes, which instantly went to Don Carlo's heart. Then she looked at him and began to explain.

"I don't know. I tried changing the menu so many times I began to lose track of what was changed. I know the service is good because I'm here day and night. I don't know, but if things don't change, I am using all my savings and I am going to have to cut my losses and a lot of people are going to be put out of work."

As she finished speaking, she bit her lip and a tear rolled down her cheek. Don Carlo took his finger and gently wiped the tear from her face and she again looked at the floor. He saw how vulnerable she could be and it touched his heart. He lifted her chin and tried to make eye contact.

"Listen. I have some ideas. First, completely shut down for at least three weeks, maybe four. It's the end of June and it's hot. It's a perfect time. Maybe it's another reason why people don't want to be in the city.

Now they go to Long Island or Newport for the summer."

She wiped her eyes with the lace handkerchief she had stuffed into her sleeve. Don Carlo could see from the damp and limp handkerchief that this wasn't the first time tonight she had been crying. Angelina composed herself, sighed, and looked at the beautiful painting on the ceiling. Don Carlo kept talking.

"Go back to the original old menu. Don't put as many things on the menu, and take the French shit off it!"

She gave a small laugh, looked at him, and listened seriously. She knew he was right, and she was anxious to hear more.

"Write the menu in Italian with English underneath each dish. Offer specials. Things that are available in the market that you can make a lot of and offer as the specialty of the day. Another thing, advertise that your menu will be seasonal because you want to offer the freshest of ingredients that are available to your customers."

He made a grand gesture by waving his arm.

"If you want this type of décor, make it over the top. Something people will talk about. The type of restaurant that a grand opera diva would design. Not this French style, mixed with Italian Baroque. Make it classy, and sophisticated. Get in an architect, a designer."

These were good suggestions. He was passionate. La Divina was fascinated by Don Carlo, but she would not fall in love with him…she would not allow it.

"And instead of calling it *Angelina's Restaurant*, rename it *Angelina Restaurante*. It has more of a European feel. Also, let your customers come to see YOU and not the restaurant. The food will be a bonus. The customers will be your guests, and that should be the reason people will come to eat and drink here again and again. *And* make the bar much bigger for the late crowd. Make the grand foyer on the side entrance smaller and set up small areas for people to sit in privacy."

Then Carlo rose from his chair and moved to a place by the far wall and almost started yelling.

"Most of all, get a piano and entertain the customers a couple of times during the evening. And YOU should be the person doing the entertaining!"

He stopped and thought Angelina would blow up and get upset, but her response was not what Don Carlo expected. She looked at him and just laughed.

"Me, sing! Forget it. I want the customers to come in, not to leave!"

Before she could make another objection, he slowly walked over to her and shot back, "You can still sing. You quit in your prime. I've heard you in the kitchen when you think no one is around to listen. You still love it. It's in your blood and your soul. You don't have to sing arias that go on and on. Improvise. Sing whatever you like. Give the people a reason to come all the way downtown. No one has heard you in years. You have a great sense of humor. Joke with the customers. People would love it! You used to sing to standing-room-only audiences. Take down the latticework in the front, install the old opera posters, and light them up. Think about it. You don't have to sing all night. Go and get that voice coach at the Metropolitan you used to always brag about to get you in shape. Hire opera students as waiters. Let them sing at the tables. Think about how wonderful it would be!"

As Don Carlo was talking, he could see that he was convincing Angelina. In reality, she had stopped listening and just stared at him. She agreed to everything he suggested as long as she could hire Don Carlo to oversee the renovations. He agreed to help on a short-term basis, and he would only take a small percentage of the profits after expenses. She agreed half-heartedly. She wanted him around for a long time. If it worked, great. If not, he would also be taking the risk. He insisted a contract should be drawn up. Business was business. She agreed and they shook hands.

"There is something else that's gonna make a big draw. I have the contacts. You're gonna have to serve liquor. I don't mean that bootleg crap. I'm talking about good rum from Cuba. Champagne from France, good wines from Italy, and gin and vodka wherever I get it. I don't mean going into the bootleg business. We're not going to sell liquor and I'm not going to use your place to sell liquor from. I don't want to get involved in that. I know the people to buy it from and I have the protection from the police so there won't be a raid. You also have big-shot politicians and they are going to want a place downtown out of the spotlight to have dinner and drinks to show off with their showgirls. Serve it in glasses, coffee cups, or whatever you need to do. You, the food, and the drinks will make this place. On second thought, forget the bar on the main level. We'll build a bar on the mezzanine with a backway up and a hidden exit to your apartment and out the street level, just in case.

Don Carlo put on his hat and left reluctantly. He would not let her in. No. He couldn't bear the pain he knew would be inevitable. He didn't want to marry for love. If he ever married, he would marry for convenience. His convenience.

As it was planned, the restaurant closed for August, and, if needed it would be closed at the beginning of September. Instead of a designer, the décor changed with the help of a friend from the scenic department at the Metropolitan. Angelina had made a lot of friends because when she was *La Divina,* she was unlike the other opera singers. She was "one of them." She was part of "the crew," all the people behind the scenes who made the opera possible. She never forgot where she came from. Her parents taught her to be true to herself and that her gift was from God, and he could take it away if she didn't treat others the right way.

The set designer brought over two huge crystal chandeliers and had the Metropolitan electrician install them. Mirrors on the back and side walls were installed to make the restaurant seem even bigger. Large portraits of Angelina in costume from the different operas she performed were taken out of storage and hung from the ceiling, centered over the mirrors, which gave the restaurant more interest and warmth. A baby grand piano was also on loan from the Metropolitan. But the Metropolitan had a catch. Sure, they would give her anything she needed, but she had to perform at least four times during the year for fundraisers. She agreed.

Angelina had one of the music students play during the renovations, and it made all the work and preparations seem like a festival with people singing and sometimes dancing. It was a magical time. Angelina and Don Carlo served food and drinks to thank everyone who was doing the work, some without wanting to be paid, just to be near Angelina. A famous conductor came to help because when he was starting at the Metropolitan, his mother was ill and Angelina paid for a nurse to sit with her so the conductor was able to work.

The menu was changed with daily tastings. Nothing was put on the menu without Angelina and Don Carlo getting everyone's feedback, and then Angelina and Don Carlo would give the final approval. While this was going on, Angelina was studying almost every afternoon with Signor Rossetti, her old voice coach. He was amazed at how good she still sounded. Although she had to sing in a lower register, her voice was richer than ever.

The plan was to open the restaurant on the second Thursday in September. Many of the invited guests had second homes and Don Carlo felt no one could use the excuse about having to leave their country homes to come to the city. The hours of the restaurant would also be changed. They would open for lunch, so new dishes could be tested. Then they would close at three, open again at five, and then close without a definite time for anyone who wanted to come downtown after a show. A lighter, late-night menu after eleven was made available at the bar. Two late-night chefs were being trained the entire time the restaurant was closed to accommodate late-hour customers. Just because it was a late-night menu didn't mean the food wouldn't have the same care and quality as during the dinner hour in the dining room.

Gold-trimmed invitations were sent out and some people who didn't receive them contacted Angelina. She thought it was either a good sign, or it would be a boycott retribution for not being invited. Transportation was made available for customers to hire taxis if they didn't have a ride home. Don Carlo and Angelina tried to think of everything. Now if it would just all work.

The night before the opening, workers were putting last-minute touches on the décor and placing the tables as close together as they could, while still leaving room for the waiters to serve. Angelina decided to have her piano player come in for a last rehearsal so she could get a feel for the room; where to stand, how to walk around the tables, and basically how to entertain a room that hopefully would be packed with customers. It was thought that the best time to sing was while most people were having their appetizer or their dessert since all service would stop during Angelina's brief performance.

The rehearsal went better than expected, but it was hard to move around, so Angelina decided to do some songs from the front and others in different places in the restaurant. An elaborate theatrical dimming system was also installed by the electricians. As a signal that a performance was about to take place, the lights on the sconces would be lowered to one level and the chandeliers would be raised to another level, which added to the drama. Liquor, wine, and champagne were brought into the restaurant in the middle of the night by four men with shotguns and Don Carlo supervising. Everything was brought into a specially designed basement and an inventory was taken of everything that went in and came out.

When the doors were locked, two German Shepherds were locked between the inner doors and outer doors each night with enough food and water. It would take a blast to get in so Don Carlo was confident that no one would try to get into the "booze vault," as it came to be known. Bartenders were also rotated and their backgrounds were investigated. Don Carlo kept a close watch of the inventory.

On the night of the opening, Angelina decided to wear one of her costumes from her favorite opera, *La Traviata*. She wore the ball gown from the first act. It would be a challenge to wear such a heavy dress, but at the last minute Don Carlo suggested she take off one of the petticoats, which made the dress lighter and it didn't flow out as much, making it easier to get around the tables.

For the opening, with Don Carlo's suggestion, Angelina hired a few violinists to greet the guests as they arrived. As finishing touches were made it was finally seven o'clock and the guests began to slowly arrive, happily surprised to be greeted by the violinists. Angelina could see this was another brilliant suggestion of Don Carlo. By 7:30 the room was full. Everyone, plus others who weren't invited, came to the opening and had to wait at the new formal bar area where high cocktail tables and secluded bar seating areas were installed. If someone was doubtful about attending when they received the invitation, others reminded them of the many things that Angelina did for so many people when she was *La Divina* and they would humbly agree to attend.

Having the restaurant full caused an embarrassing problem. Now that every table was occupied, and the lounge, which was formerly the bar room was also full Angelina came up with her own brilliant idea. She went outside to personally apologize to the guests and told them they would be escorted to wait in her suite of rooms above the restaurant. Unknowingly, she had begun a tradition that lasted until she sold the restaurant. The guests were amazed that she would personally apologize and offer them a place to wait. As she greeted and apologized to each guest, a waiter would get the names and number of guests in the party. She then instructed the waiters to take two of the violinists and lead her guests to her rooms. She could hear the whispering and she knew that the quests were impressed and excited about the experience.

"Imagine," one guest remarked. "We're going to wait and be entertained in 'the diva's' rooms. How exciting!"

When they entered from two large wooden double doors at the side of the restaurant, each guest gasped to see a grand staircase that was a duplicate of the staircase in the restaurant with a large chandelier that was dimly lit. The foyer was magnificent. What the guests didn't know was that all the furnishings and artwork were borrowed from the Metropolitan Opera House. Eventually, as the restaurant flourished, each piece of furniture and artwork was either purchased from the Metropolitan or replaced with something as beautiful that was taken out of storage that was once in Angelina's Long Island home that she sold after her husband's death.

As Angelina personally welcomed each guest, she was confident that this would be a good night and realized it was all because of Don Carlo. She was both happy about it and threatened by it. She shook off the feeling because it was going to be a wonderful night.

Angelina and the staff tried to prepare for any unanticipated problems that always arise when opening a new restaurant. Oddly enough, almost everything went as planned. The only problem was with Angelina's dress, which kept getting caught on the bottom of the chairs, so she couldn't move as much as she liked. It got some laughs the couple of times it happened, but it was endearing. She decided to sing in the middle of the grand staircase so the people in the mezzanine could also see her. She was radiant. They loved her. She was *La Prima Donna Diva* once more. *Thanks to Don Carlo*, she thought to herself.

Don Carlo had brought his mother and sister to the opening. Angelina spotted them right away and was concerned about who they were. She would never question anything about his personal life but she was obviously jealous. Don Carlo could see she had a standoff attitude when she came near their table and he surmised she was jealous and wanted to have some fun. He stood up and took her hand.

"Angelina. Let me introduce you to the two most important women in my life."

At first, she was embarrassed and reluctant to come to the table. When she realized it was Don Carlo's sister rather than another woman, she was elated. She laughed as she shook their hands. His sister and mother were at first a little taken back at the laughter. When Angelina left, Don Carlo explained, and they too got a laugh out of it.

Right before the dessert course, Angelina made an announcement wishing to thank Don Carlo for his help in making *her opening night* such a success. Angelina had an ego and she wasn't about to let all the credit go to Don Carlo, even though most of the suggestions were his. Although Don Carlo didn't care that she referred to the evening as "*her* opening night," he realized two things: first, if there were to be a relationship there would be a battle of egos and second, perhaps the battle of egos made her extremely attractive to him and he was having deep feelings for her. At the same time, he knew the relationship would be a disaster and he would shake off those feelings.

It took until four in the morning for the last guest to leave. It wasn't because of the dining or the drinking. The accolades and congratulations from the patrons and friends of Angelina were overwhelming. And the whole time Don Carlo was at her side. She looked at him from time to time and knew that she wanted him and damn anything else. When the last person left, Angelina asked Don Carlo to meet her after he made sure everything was locked up. When he arrived in her apartment it was dark and only lit with candles. A bottle of champagne and two glasses were set on the side table. Angelina came out of her bedroom wearing a sheer nightgown. Behind her Don Carlo could see that the silk bedding on her large bed was turned down. She walked over to the champagne and poured it into two glasses. She handed one glass to Don Carlo and took the other. She clinked the two glasses.

"Thank you. Thank you for everything."

They each took a sip. Don Carlo took Angelina's glass with his and put them on the table. He took her in his arms and kissed her as she caressed the back of his neck. Don Carlo was helpless for the first time in his life. Without another word, he looked into her eyes, scooped her in his arms, took her into the bedroom, and closed the doors. Their relationship was about to change forever.

In appreciation for everyone who had helped her with the opening, Angelina arranged an elaborate dinner party the following Sunday when the restaurant was closed. Angelina and a few of the celebrity guests entertained everyone for almost two hours. She even had the famous theatrical producer Florenz Ziegfeld send down a couple of his performers from his Follies to try out their new acts and entertain. At the end of the evening, Angelina gave out expensive gifts for everyone, which included the kitchen staff. For Don Carlo, she formally presented him in front of everyone with an engraved, custom-designed pocket watch that played the Waltz from *The Merry Widow*, one of Don Carlo's favorite pieces of music.

Opening night and the nights that followed, were a time Angelina would never forget and everyone would talk about for years. Don Carlo was happy it was over and was anxious to move on to other projects. He hadn't given up running numbers and was getting into more legitimate business of his own, as he planned for the future, his future, a future that included Angelina.

From opening night, the restaurant became a huge success and the place to go "downtown." Without Angelina knowing, Don Carlo paid off, or in some cases threatened, some society writers and newspapers to report on who was in town and who had dined at *Angelina Restaurante*. It had become the "chic place" to see and be seen. Lovers met there. Politicians dinned for hours, and every known celebrity had their picture taken with Angelina. The restaurant was so successful that within a short time, Angelina eventually replaced all the things she had borrowed from the Metropolitan, including the baby grand piano, which was replaced by a Steinway grand. She was able to recoup the money she lost when the restaurant went downhill. Instead of performing for the Metropolitan's fundraiser she just donated the money.

After a couple of years, the restaurant's clientele slowly changed. More local, as well as out-of-town people, would come for special occasions, and tourists who had read and heard about Angelina Restaurante would want to eat there and experience the beauty. She enclosed the mezzanine for her personal or important guests and the room was booked months in advance. She also entertained guests in her rooms if the night was particularly busy. As the business became steady, Angelina wouldn't be at the restaurant every night. She and Don Carlo would get away as much as they could. Also, instead of the gambling, Don Carlo began buying up real estate and businesses. When the restaurant business seemed to be slipping a bit, Angelina would be at the restaurant more and it would become a sort of cycle.

After the restaurant was firmly established, Don Carlo stopped by the restaurant less and less. Angelina tried everything to make him stay. She even offered him a percentage of the restaurant ownership if he stayed. When he refused a partnership without having to put any money up, she was really impressed. *He is his own man and can't be bought*, she thought to herself. *What a rarity this man is.* Eventually, he moved in with her but he kept his apartment on Beekman Place, which they also used. From the first time they met, Angelina had wanted him and she always got what she wanted. But could she keep him?

Chapter 11

Enzo couldn't believe his luck: he was working at the famous Angelina Restaurante.

When Don Carlo first met Enzo, Don Carlo had been involved with illegal gambling and running numbers for his cousin Bruno. It wasn't by chance Don Carlo met Enzo. He had heard the name from one of the men who gambled and thought because of the last name there may be a connection. When Don Carlo told his mother of the possible connection, she already knew of the Buonofortes from Mussomeli. She was told by her late husband that they were somehow related. Not having any relatives in America, that was good enough for Don Carlo. However, he would keep the information to himself. He didn't know what type of person Enzo was and Don Carlo didn't want to be taken advantage of. He had seen how sometimes blood relations could be poison and he was very cautious. He had had some bad experiences with his cousin Bruno, and he no longer had any business dealings with him. And because of that Bruno went back to Italy. After Bruno left, Don Carlo became involved in helping to run Angelina Restaurante. He also had been buying up legitimate businesses. One business he knew would be lucrative was the garbage business in Manhattan. He believed there would always be garbage and, as with his other business investments, he was right.

At the time when Enzo met Don Carlo, he never used the moniker, "Don Carlo." To Enzo, Carlo just seemed like he was just a nice guy who ran the numbers. After a time, Don Carlo took a real liking to Enzo, but Don Carlo kept to the Sicilian philosophy, "Trust no one until they earn it beyond any doubt, and even then, keep three eyes open."

At the time, Enzo was working in the kitchen at Lina's on Mulberry Street. Enzo met Don Carlo when he would come to the back of the restaurant at the kitchen entrance to collect bets. Don Carlo would wait until the owner left and the kitchen was being cleaned to pay the winners and collect from the losers. The owner of the restaurant didn't like his employees to gamble. It wasn't as much looking after their welfare, but that they would try to get an advance on their salaries to pay off their debts when they lost. The owner said he would never give anyone an advance because he claimed maybe they would never come back to work off their advance.

The owner of the restaurant was so cheap that he would make the cooks reuse food that the diners didn't finish and feed it to the help. The owner would always get comments on how attentive the waiters were while the patrons were eating their dinner and took the plates as soon as the waiters thought the customers were finished. What the waiters were really doing was watching who was eating what to see what the patrons would leave, because they knew they would get it and there was a competition for the leftover food no matter how disgusting the idea was of eating a stranger's leftovers. Times were tough, especially for immigrants.

Enzo knew about Don Carlo but Enzo would never make any bets. He saw how so many men lost and would then have to tell their wives or they would be working just to pay their betting losses. Enzo worked hard for his money and he was not going to waste it on a long shot. What Enzo didn't know was that Don Carlo wouldn't let him make any bets and did his best to show that the people betting hardly won, and many ruined themselves and their families. The difference between Don Carlo and the other numbers runners was that Don Carlo kept track of what the people were losing and cut them off or discouraged them from betting by reminding them of their wives and family obligations. When the employees complained that they lost, Carlo would remind them that a bet is a bet and they better pay up or suffer the consequences. The losers would say they weren't scared, but Don Carlo had a reputation and they didn't want to find out whether or not it was true, so they always paid up except for one time. Besides, the losers knew his cousin Bruno who did the dirty work. They also knew the name Masseria, and when the word got out, with the help of Don Carlo, for many that was enough.

This one night it was raining pretty hard and Enzo could see Don Carlo trying to keep dry by standing under the restaurant awning at the back door. Enzo let him in and told him to wait behind the walk-in refrigerator. Don Carlo had arrived before the restaurant closed because one of the dishwashers who owed Don Carlo money didn't wait around to pay him. The dishwasher would sneak out of the restaurant before Don Carlo got there. Don Carlo knew it set a bad example if someone kept getting away with not paying, so this time he confronted the dish-washer and the man did pay him, especially when Don Carlo moved the side of his suit jacket and the man saw a gun in a holster.

It was a harsh winter. One night it was snowing and the snow was mixed with rain. The wind was blowing hard and while Don Carlo was waiting at the back door of the restaurant, he was getting soaked. Enzo opened the back door and told Don Carlo to come in. He didn't have to hide because it was Tuesday night and the owner of the restaurant would meet with his mistress every Tuesday. They both made some small talk about the weather, where they were from, and about each other's families. This went on for a few weeks on every Tuesday night until Don Carlo confronted the same dishwasher because the guy kept putting him off and they got into an argument about having to pay him for losing some bets. The dishwasher accused Don Carlo of cheating him. Don Carlo calmly went over to the dishwasher, picked him up by his neck, and pushed him hard against the wall.

"Don't you ever accuse me of cheating. The only cheater here is you. You cheat your family by gambling too much. No one puts a gun to your head. I warned you about losing too much."

Don Carlo let him go and the man fell to the floor, stunned. The dishwasher took some bills out of his pocket and handed them to Don Carlo. Don Carlo threw down a twenty-dollar bill. "You still owe me.

Take care of your family. You know I'll be back."

Everyone just watched as Don Carlo walked toward the door to leave.

"You've got one week to pay the rest. Otherwise, I'll get the money from your wife. If she doesn't have it, I'll tell your boss. If he doesn't give it to me, I'll have your arms broken and then try to wash dishes."

Don Carlo brushed off his coat and slammed the door behind him as he left. The dishwasher made a gesture with his arm and yelled, "I'm not afraid of you!" But he was afraid. Everyone who knew Don Carlo was afraid of crossing him. There was only one time his cousin Bruno questioned the weekly numbers take. Bruno counted the money and made mention to Carlo.

"Carlo, I'm not questioning you. Hey, maybe somebody might have shorted you..."

Before he could finish Don Carlo walked up to him nose to nose, "No one will ever short me. Count it again."

That was the last time Bruno ever questioned Don Carlo. Bruno was afraid of Don Carlo because Don Carlo had already earned a reputation as an honest man; fair, but also tough as nails. He had a bad temper, which he was able to control most of the time. But when he was provoked, he blew up and was not afraid of a fight, no matter how big the other guy was. A big man from another part of Little Italy tried to scare off Don Carlo by physically threatening him. Don Carlo beat him so badly that the man ended up with a broken jaw, a broken nose, and two broken ribs. He also threatened to shoot the man. The word quickly got out

Many people who knew Don Carlo and had observed his behavior found him to be a man full of strong convictions and contradictions. As they got to know each other Enzo and Carlo realized they had many similarities to the point that it was uncanny. On the one hand, Don Carlo could be ruthless, but at the same time he would help countless people in a variety of ways, but do it anonymously. He could be generous, but if his generosity was taken for granted it could change relationships. He was loyal, but betray him once and he would completely end the relationship no matter who it was. Unlike most other Sicilians, Don Carlo constantly reminded himself that blood could be more of a liability than an asset. There were too many times that he had seen families quickly turn on each other in spite of their family "blood bonds." It's the petty jealousies and resentments within families that Don Carlo detests and wouldn't tolerate in his own family when the time came for his sister to marry. "You don't marry a man," he would always tell his sister. "Be careful. You marry his family!"

Don Carlo, like Enzo, had seen so many times when families come from Italy, they become close to relatives who have already settled in one neighborhood or another. After a time, the different families prosper and then jealousies and resentments build. Instead of supporting each other, they turn on each other. Don Carlo was weary of these situations and judged people by the history of their deeds. He would distrust someone first until they earned his trust, and he would never take the loyalty and trust of others for granted. Blood was never a reason to build relationships; if anything, families took advantage and could hurt each other more than anyone else outside the family.

The day after the incident with Don Carlo and the dishwasher, the restaurant owner heard about what happened from one of the cooks who was shaken up. The owner didn't want Don Carlo in the kitchen anymore and wanted to know who let him in. When he heard that it was Enzo who let him in, he fired Enzo on the spot. When Enzo asked for his salary, the restaurant owner refused, saying Enzo had to pay for upsetting everyone in the kitchen. Enzo would never beg. He took his apron off, threw it in the owner's face, and knocked over a whole crate of eggs, which splattered all over the floor.

"Keep the change, bastardo!"

The owner started yelling and walking toward Enzo. He was bigger than Enzo, but Enzo didn't care. Again, like Don Carlo, when provoked Enzo had a temper. He turned around, took in a deep breath to expand his chest, and raised his two fists. The owner instantly backed down.

Enzo opened the door, turned, and before he left, he shouted to the owner, "Your food is shit! That's why this place is never busy. Merda, merda, merda!"

Enzo slammed the door so hard that some dishes fell off the shelf and broke when they hit the floor.

Enzo and Anna sat in their little kitchen counting their money and trying to figure out how they were going to make ends meet until Enzo could get a new job. Jobs were not easy to find, especially for someone who didn't speak fluid English. Anna had left the Fulton Fish Market when she had baby Maria. To save on the rent, she had made a deal with the landlord and cleaned the apartment halls and stairs. She had waited on tables when waitresses didn't show up at the restaurant where Enzo no longer worked. It didn't matter because Anna hated the restaurant owner, who would steal tips off the table and lie about it, cursing the customers behind their backs and lying to the waiters that the customers didn't leave any tips. But all the waiters knew better and went after the tips before the owner got to them. For that, and other reasons, there was a lot of turn-over of wait staff. Ironically years later the owner of the restaurant would be found floating in the river for not paying his gambling debts. Many suspected Don Carlo, but Enzo knew better, although Don Carlo let everyone believe what they wanted.

As they were putting the money back in a shoe where they always hid it, there was a knock on the door. For an instant they thought someone was there to rob them, so they hid the shoe under the small couch in the living room and Anna quickly sat on the couch. Enzo asked who was at the door. It turned out to be Don Carlo. Enzo looked at Anna who shrugged her shoulders and Enzo opened the door. Don Carlo stood there with his hat in one hand and a bag of groceries in the other.

"I am sorry to disturb you and your wife. I found out from one of the waiters where you live."

Anna listening, stood, and told Carlo to please come in. She knew from Enzo's description who he was. Enzo also quickly asked Don Carlo in, and he introduced him to Anna, who asked Don Carlo to sit down. At first, Carlo refused and handed the groceries to a surprised but pleased Anna. Don Carlo seemed so different than when Enzo saw him at the restaurant. He now looked well-dressed, very serious, and humble, al-most like a priest who was coming to give a dying man his last rites. When

Enzo asked him again to sit, Carlo finally sat down. He said when he had heard that Enzo had lost his job, he felt very badly about it. Enzo said that he was sick of working for such a pig and was a little relieved that he wouldn't have to listen to the owner complain and yell at everyone.

"I also heard from one of the dishwashers that you told the owner that I am an honorable man and should be respected."

With some embarrassment, Enzo shook his head.

"I see how fairly you treat people. I don't agree with your business, but I have seen how others are, and you act with honor."

Don Carlo smiled and didn't respond, understanding exactly and agreeing with Enzo about his business. It was the way Don Carlo made a living for himself, his mother, and his sister and it was his business what he did; but he respected Enzo's honesty.

Suddenly, they heard a baby crying from the next room. Anna ran quickly and picked up the baby who stopped crying and brought her into the living room.

"This is our daughter Maria. I think she needs changing and feeding. Please excuse me."

"Signora Buonoforte, she gets her beauty from you."

Anna thanked Don Carlo and left the room so the men could talk. Enzo asked Carlo to have a seat at the dining table outside the small kitchen.

"Signor Carlo, would you like an expresso, or perhaps some grappa? A man down the street makes it in his basement. It really isn't that bad."

"Grazie, no thank you."

Don Carlo asked Enzo if he had another job. Enzo said that he was going to start looking in the morning.

"Enzo, I know someone at Angelina Restaurante on Mulberry Street and they are looking for help if you are interested."

Enzo said, of course, he would love to work there. He knew Angelina Restaurante was a very popular restaurant where people from "uptown" would come "downtown" to get a real authentic Italian meal. Some politicians and cheating husbands came with their girlfriends, away from the prying eyes of those who would report them to their wives—or worse, to the press—if they saw them in midtown. But aside from being away from the society of uptown, or the wonderful food, everyone also came to see the owner Angelina in person. A celebrity in her own right, she was someone that her fans would stand in line for hours to see at the Metropolitan Opera House just a few years ago, and Enzo was one of them.

Carlo arranged to meet Enzo in front of Angelina Restaurante the next day at noon. Anna came out with the baby and Don Carlo excused himself and said he had to leave for an appointment. As he left, he felt some envy of Enzo and his wife. *With what little they have, they seem so happy*, he said to himself. He wondered if he could have the same happiness with Angelina, but he was becoming doubtful. With the restaurant and his other businesses, how could they find the time?

Enzo arrived early and was dressed and ready to go right to work if need be. Instead of meeting outside the restaurant, Don Carlo had been inside talking to the chef about a new recipe he wanted him to try using ground basil, pasta con pesto.

When Don Carlo saw a nervous Enzo at the kitchen door, he opened the door and guided Enzo in to meet Angelina. Angelina insisted she know everyone who was working for her. She shook his hand and guided him around the kitchen. Although Enzo was in awe of meeting Angelina, he had never seen a kitchen like this one. It was huge, with so many stoves, pots and pans, and people everywhere. The aroma of the food made his mouth water and he tried not to smile. He wanted to seem serious, but he was already enjoying himself. Angelina introduced him to one of the two chefs, who reluctantly shook his hand when Angelina gave him her famous cold stare. Angelina knew that Enzo would work out because Don Carlo would not even think of hiring someone who wasn't good at their job.

Before Enzo could thank Angelina, she was gone. Enzo thanked Don Carlo, as Don Carlo introduced Enzo saying Enzo was his cousin and to take good care of him. Don Carlo then winked at Enzo, patted him on the back, and left. The chef handed Enzo an apron and showed him where the sink was, which was filled with dishes and pots from the night before. Enzo looked around and smiled. He would wash dishes and scrub floors. He didn't care. Enzo couldn't believe his luck: he was working at the famous Angelina Restaurante.

After a couple of months, from time to time, Anna was able to serve meals in the mezzanine. She had an elderly neighbor watch Maria in exchange for cleaning her apartment. Anna was the only female to serve the guests. She was beautiful and had a quiet charm. She was also a hard worker. For a while, Enzo was still washing dishes and cleaning the kitchen after the restaurant closed. They were both making more money than they ever imagined and it made saving for a house easier. Their luck would continue.

One day one of the assistant chefs seriously cut his hand right before the dinner crowd and had to be taken to the hospital by another assistant chef, which made them seriously short-handed. Enzo saw how dire the situation was and offered his services. At first, the main chef said it was out of the question, but Enzo knew the main chef was in trouble and Enzo insisted. The chef, realizing that Enzo was right, relented. Enzo knew what the opportunity could mean and he worked as hard as he could to anticipate the chef's every need. The whole kitchen staff was impressed. Enzo worked flawlessly assisting the chef and others, anticipating their needs. He also cleaned the dishes and the kitchen after the restaurant closed.

When the injured assistant came back to work two weeks later, Enzo realized he would be back washing dishes, but the main chef didn't want Enzo's efforts to go unrewarded. He talked to Angelina and they came up with a position that would not only help in the kitchen but would be a great opportunity for Enzo. It was very hard to get fresh vegetables and fish in the late morning. Most of the best produce, meat, and fish were bought in the early mornings, but it meant that the assistants had to do the shopping in the morning and then work until the late evening. The main chef saw how Enzo was able to pick out the best ingredients that were in the restaurant and make suggestions about what produce or fish would be the freshest. Many times, over the two weeks that the injured assistant was out of work, Enzo took it upon himself to go to the Fulton

Fish Market at five in the morning and bargain for the freshest fish. Because of his hard work and talents, Enzo was made the "buyer" for all the ingredients for the restaurant. This not only meant that he didn't have to wash dishes, but it gave him a respectable position that he loved and more money.

After six months, Enzo was well known all over Little Italy as the buyer for Angelina Restaurante. He was respected, demanding the best products at the best prices. After a time, he was offered "kickbacks." Not only didn't he accept any money or offer of products, he would not deal with anyone who made him an offer. He also reported it to the head chef. He never became friendly with any of the dealers he regularly bought from, even though they invited him and his wife over for dinner or drinks. The only time he accepted any gifts was around Christmas or Easter but he would bring them in the restaurant and share them with everyone.

There was only one incident that upset Enzo. A meat market owner was frustrated with Enzo for not buying any of his meat products. The owner kept trying to get Enzo to do business with him, but Enzo felt his meats were inferior for the restaurant and expensive as well. The meat market owner even sent his cousins to try to strong-arm him to buy his meats, but Enzo wanted no part of it. Then the meat market owner and his wife were having dinner at the Angelina Restaurante and ordered the veal piccata. When the dinner came, they tasted the veal and told the waiter to take it back because it was an inferior cut of veal. He asked to speak to the manager. Angelina was in Naples tending to her parents and sister, and Don Carlo was running the restaurant in her absence. Don Carlo walked over to the table. "How can I help you?" Carlo quietly asked. The meat market owner had planned exactly how he was going to approach the situation.

"Sir, this is an inferior piece of veal, and my wife and I are surprised that you would serve it."

Don Carlo looked at the veal and wasn't going to argue.

"Would you like to order something else?" The meat market owner then became indignant.

"I don't understand how a restaurant like this will serve such bad veal. I should know. I deal with meat. If your buyer wouldn't ask for money under the table, I could offer you better veal than this."

Don Carlo smiled at the man and excused himself. A few minutes later Don Carlo came out of the kitchen with Enzo and the chef.

"Sir," Don Carlo said loudly enough for everyone around the table to hear, "is this the man who won't take any kickbacks from you?"

The man and his wife were stunned. The man stuttered, "Uh, well, I...."

Don Carlo turned to Enzo and the chef. "Thanks, Enzo. You can go back to the kitchen."

Enzo was looking directly at the man, and then without saying a word he looked at Don Carlo, smiled, and walked back to the kitchen with the chef without saying a word. Don Carlo picked up the coat check that was on the table, again excused himself, and returned with the woman's wrap.

"Madam," Don Carlo said, "here is your wrap. Now both of you get up and leave quietly, or I will personally throw you out."

The wife started to get indignant as she stood up and tried to put on her wrap.

"Well, I never!"

"Oh Madam, I sure you have!"

Don Carlo even tried to help her. The meat market owner got up and was going to speak, but Don Carlo walked right up to him almost nose to nose, and interrupted him.

"Sir, say one damn word and I will drag you out of here by your ass! Then your hands will be broken so badly, you will never be able to even pick up a knife to cut your wonderful meat."

The people around the table who had been listening and watching the scene unfold began to laugh and applaud, and the couple left with Don Carlo closely behind them. As they were leaving, Carlo began to realize that he had now become a "bouncer." This wasn't what he intended when he agreed to help Angelina. He let his feelings get in the way of his good sense, but love has no logic he realized.

He shook his head as he walked back into the restaurant. Now he felt trapped in the restaurant. A feeling he did not like. *But how to get out? How to get out without hurting the relationship with Angelina?* He would just be reduced to a bouncer. Angelina's personality would not let him be in charge, and he would have to take a back seat, which is something that he wasn't used to and something he would never allow. He didn't allow it when he was younger, and he wouldn't allow it now. He learned from the past and would not make the same mistakes.

Growing up in Sicily, either you show strength or you don't survive. He hated when people who thought they were better or stronger took advantage of others. The next time he helped someone the circumstances would be much more dramatic. As fate would have it, the person he helped would be a young colored man, whose name would later be shared by a restaurant chain he had nothing to do with: Howard Johnson.

Chapter 12

"Angelina, we have it figured out. Howard says that he could do the chef's job."

Howard Johnson is a young colored man who left Georgia after his mother died when he was eighteen. His father was killed by some Ku Klux Klan members when they mistakenly thought his father attacked a white woman. Although the truth came out years later, some white people said it didn't matter and it was an honest mistake "cause them niggas all look alike." The despicable attitude angered other white people. and they formed a group to expel the Klan from their town. It didn't matter, though, because when the truth did come out many members of the Klan quit and denied being involved if they were asked. There were just a few ignorant people who still belonged to the Klan, but they were forced to leave town or face arrest, or even worse.

After the restaurant that bore Howard's name opened, some people teased him asking if he was named after the restaurant, Howard Johnson's. They asked if his mother worked there, or maybe he was born there when his mother worked as a waitress. A ridiculous and offensive question, since Howard was born in 1900 and the restaurant wasn't even around. Howard later found out that the Howard Johnson restaurant was established by a man named Howard Deering Johnson, who founded the restaurant in 1925 and then turned it into a franchise. Some people said Howard should change his name, but Howard said that was the name his mother gave him and that was the name he would stick with. He also thought it was a way to help determine if he had to be wary of someone. If they started making fun of his name, rather than just making an innocent inquiry, he knew to stay clear of that person. The person was a bigoted idiot.

Many people considered Howard stupid because of the color of his skin and because he was quiet; but, he was extremely smart. He always believed he inherited his faith in God from his mother and his intelligence from his father. He had dreams of becoming a doctor, but his chances were slim since he probably wouldn't get into medical school, let alone pay for it. Before his father Isaiah was killed, he worked for a lawyer, who tried to defend him, but his father was lynched before they could get to court. The lawyer was so disgusted he moved up North to defend poor colored people who were in trouble. That didn't last, because he couldn't make a living from it and he had a wife and kids to support. He eventually taught law at Columbia University in Manhattan and would also some-times take "pro bono" cases for colored people who were really in trouble and where there was a good chance justice would not be served. That also had to stop, because his life and the life of his family were threatened by someone opposed to him defending a "stupid nigga." When he passed away, there were lines of colored people at Riverside Church in Manhat-tan to pay their respects for a man whom they considered a champion for people of color who found it hard to find justice.

Don Carlo met Howard who was working in a small trattoria where Don Carlo would frequently eat; Tony's on the lower end of Mulberry and Canal Street. He didn't always have dinner at Angelina Restaurante. He would have an early dinner at Tony's when Angelina was rehearsing or resting then he would have a late dinner with Angelina. He liked Tony's because it had a limited menu and the food tasted familiar to Don Carlo because the chef was from the same region of Palermo, Sicily where Don Carlo was born. The pasta dishes were like something Don Carlo's mother made, especially the eggplant with pasta. The restaurant wasn't fancy, but it was clean and the service was quick. Don Carlo would come in with a newspaper, order his food, read the paper to avoid any chitchat with the owner, have his cup of expresso, a cannoli, his favorite Sicilian dessert, and then leave. Although the owner was friendly, Don Carlo didn't like the way he treated the help. Many times, there would be screaming in the kitchen and Don Carlo couldn't understand why the chef stayed working there until he found out the talented chef was Tony's brother-in-law.

Don Carlo first noticed Howard when Howard was a busboy at Tony's. Don Carlo saw how hard he worked and the terrible treatment Howard had to endure. Even so, Howard always had a smile on his face for Don Carlo, and Don Carlo was pleasant and respectful to Howard. Don Carlo couldn't imagine working under those conditions. Don Carlo had seen how some of the people in Sicily were treated by some of the landowners, and unless you were "connected" there was no opportunity to make a good living.

Not knowing if the tips were split among the waiters, Don Carlo always quietly handed Howard a dollar, which was a lot of money at the time. What Don Carlo didn't know was another waiter would sometimes see Howard accept the dollar and Howard would have to split it with the other waiters, or they would threaten to tell Tony. It was hard for a colored man to get a job, so there wasn't much Howard could do. But fate would quickly change Howard's situation due to the ignorance of one of the restaurant's patrons.

One night when Don Carlo was in the restaurant there was a small party in the opposite corner of the restaurant, and they were very loud. Don Carlo could hear from the loud conversations that one of the men was a cop uptown. The cop was loud and rude. At one point the cop's wife needed something and the cop yelled to Howard, "Hey boy, get over here." This wasn't the first time the cop was in the restaurant and treated Howard the way he did.

"Hey, boy. I'm calling you."

Howard walked over to the table. He didn't know what came over him but he looked directly at the cop.

"Howard, sir. My name is Howard Johnson."

Don Carlo, overhearing Howard, said under his breath "Uh oh."

"Howard Johnson!" The cop laughed and a couple of the people followed suit.

"Well, Howard, you're a real uppity nigger, aren't you."

The restaurant suddenly got very quiet. The cop's wife whispered to her husband, "Stop it. You're embarrassing us. Stop it." But the cop ignored his wife. He was too drunk.

"Listen, Howard Johnson, you be a good little nigger and get my wife another expresso."

Howard brought another expresso to the table and went about his business.

Later Howard was stooping down and putting some dishes in a cupboard outside the kitchen and the cop was coming from the bathroom. He saw Howard and intentionally bumped into him, which made Howard drop some of the dishes on the floor. Then he tried to make it look like it was Howard's fault.

"Why don't you look where you're going, you dumb nigger!"

It looked like the man was going to kick Howard, who said nothing and just tried to stay down and pick up the broken pieces. Suddenly Don Carlo jumped from his chair, threw his napkin on his plate, grabbed the cop by the back of his neck and the back of his pants, and dragged the startled cop to the front door. The man's wife started screaming as Don Carlo threw him out of the restaurant with the cop's wife following and yelling. The cop landed on the sidewalk and was about to try to get up, but stopped. Don Carlo looked down at him and slowly pulled open the left side of his jacket to reveal a shoulder holster with the butt of a gun sticking out. Seeing the gun, the man froze and told his crying wife who was squatting next to him to shut up.

"Hey buddy," the cop shouted up at Don Carlo, "do you know who I am? I can have you arrested and taken to jail!"

Don Carlo spit at the man's feet and put his hand on his gun in the holster.

"Do you know who I am? You won't make it to the telephone alive to make the call." Don Carlo turned to the man's wife, who was shaking.

"Lady, get your husband out of here before you become a widow."

Meanwhile, the rest of the cop's party hurried out of the restaurant past Don Carlo and helped pick up the cop, who was yelling while his friends were trying to shut him up. The cop got up and tried to fix his jacket and stand erect. He shook off his friends who were helping him and stumbled away with his wife, who was taking his arm to guide him.

One of the cop's friends whispered to the cop, "Do you know who that is? Don Carlo Masserria, Mafioso. Don't fuck with him. By the time he and his friends get done with you, parts of you will be scattered all over the East River."

The cop just started walking away. "Dumb fuckin wops."

The restaurant owner, hearing all the commotion, had come out of the kitchen and saw Howard picking up the dishes and immediately blamed him for the encounter. Without even asking him what happened, he told Howard to get out, he was fired. Don Carlo came back into the restaurant, and seeing how Howard was being treated, threw down some bills on the table and yelled to the owner.

"Hey, Tony. Not only was the veal tough, but you have some real asshole customers. It's too bad. I don't think you'll be in business too long when the word spreads. When I spread the word."

The owner just stood there in the restaurant with all the customers staring at him and Don Carlo. Before Tony could even try to make amends, Don Carlo grabbed his newspaper and walked out. When Howard came out of the restaurant, he saw Don Carlo and was embarrassed. Don Carlo handed Howard a card with the address of Angelina Restaurante on Mulberry Street and told him to go to the restaurant tomorrow at lunch and he would see to it that he got a job. Howard was shaking with fear. Without a word, Howard gave Don Carlo a nervous smile and nodded. Don Carlo took an interest in Howard because he remembered back in Sicily someone once helped him. This was a sort of payback.

Enzo started working at Angelina Restaurante around the same time that Howard was employed as a dishwasher. Although young, Howard was hard-working, quiet, and minded his own business. There were many times that Howard picked up any slack and helped Enzo finish up his work so Enzo could leave early to be with his wife. As time went on Howard felt comfortable enough to talk to Enzo and they developed a close working relationship and became close friends.

Then one day, Howard's fate changed dramatically. One of the assistants to the chef cut his finger badly and Howard offered to help. At first, the chef was reluctant but had no choice. No one else was around. Enzo was doing the buying and wasn't always around so the chef agreed. Howard worked hard and was a fast learner. The chef liked him because he was able to anticipate the chef's needs, which made the chef's life much easier.

After two years of working as a chef assistant, another opportunity changed Howard's life again. It was Christmas Eve and the restaurant was fully booked. There were many friends of Angelina's as well as the usual local celebrities. In the morning, the chef was sitting in the kitchen and said he wasn't feeling good. Enzo and Howard came over to the chef, who said he just needed a few minutes to rest and then suddenly collapsed on the floor. A doctor and the police were called, but it was too late. The chef died from what they were later told was a massive heart attack. Angelina was beside herself. The chef had been with her for years, even back when he was her personal chef when she and her husband lived on Beekman Place in Manhattan and she was performing at the Met.

An ambulance took the chef away and she told Enzo to go into the dining room and get Don Carlo, who was with some friends who dropped by early before going home. He didn't want anyone to know what had happened so he gave them some drinks and then escorted them out. When Don Carlo came into the kitchen, he was told Angelina was in the small office at the back of the kitchen. He found her behind the desk crying hysterically. Don Carlo went over to her, and when she saw him, she got up and threw her arms around him. He made her sit back down and tried to calm her. She was shaken and upset about the chef's death. Then it dawned on her and she looked at Don Carlo.

"My God. What should we do about tonight? I know we can't close."

Don Carlo gently picked up her head and quietly said, "Let's go in the kitchen and discuss what to do. First, dry your eyes and freshen up."

Don Carlo kissed her on her forehead. Don Carlo had no idea what they were going to do. A few minutes later, Angelina came into the kitchen and asked Enzo who took the chef away and if the chef's wife had been informed. He said that everything had been taken care of. Angelina said she wanted to speak to his wife because she was going to pay for the funeral.

"Tomorrow I will need someone to come with me to pay a visit to his wife. I want to bring some food and I just don't want to go alone."

Enzo instantly said that he and his wife would go with her. Then everyone was assembled in front of her and before she could speak, Don Carlo walked toward her.

"Angelina, we have it figured out. Howard says that he can do the chef's job. He has been assisting him for two years and knows all his recipes and knows exactly what needs to be done."

Angelina looked directly at Howard as Don Carlo smiled and patted Howard on the back. Angelina shrugged her shoulders and said, "Alright. Our fate is in your hands, Howard. Make us proud."

On the outside, Howard was his usual calm, unassuming self. On the inside, he was both excited and scared. He knew this was a chance he would never have again. At the same time, he was sad about how he had gotten the opportunity of a lifetime. He was upset that the chef had died and wanted to make the chef proud for the faith he had shown in him. A month before he died, the chef had been tasting some new wines that had come in and was in a good mood. He saw Howard getting some utensils ready before the chef was ready to start cooking. The chef put his hand on Howard's shoulder and whispered in his ear, "I have worked with many men who call themselves experts in the kitchen. They were never as good as you are. I am proud of you and I am sorry I have not told you sooner. I never want anyone but you to work with me for the rest of my life. Thank you."

It was the first time the chef saw Howard really smile and look at him straight in his face.

"Thank you for teaching me, Chef. I hope I can always work with you."

Howard thought about that day and whispered to himself, "Chef. Wherever you are, I want to make you proud. God, please give me strength."

Howard wrote out a list of things that he needed. Enzo saw him writing and went over to him.

"Howard, tell me what you need and I'll help you as much as I can. Both our asses are on the line." Howard then smiled and handed Enzo the list.

"Madonna Mia! You really can smile!"

Angelina didn't stay in the kitchen. She just prayed that everything would go without a hitch. When the people began to arrive, Angelina forgot about what had happened that afternoon and was as charming as possible, with the hope that even if the food wasn't good and the service was slow, maybe it would be overlooked if she could charm her guests. But as the trays of food started coming out of the kitchen, Angelina was surprised and then shocked. The food was being served hot and the service was quick. As Angelina moved from table to table, almost all the customers commented on how good the food was and how prompt the service was. Angelina decided to go into the kitchen where she was surprised to see this colored man who barely spoke a word before this, tasting the food, calmly shouting out commands, and in complete control. Angelina was delighted. She walked over to him and put out her hand to shake his. When he put out his hand, instead of shaking his hand, she gave him a warm embrace, and for a moment there was silence in the kitchen. She stepped back, took his two hands, and simply said, "Thank you."

She began to walk away but then stopped, turned around, and said to everyone, "I would like everyone to welcome our new chef, Howard Johnson!" With that, she began to clap her hands and was joined by everyone in the kitchen. Enzo, who was standing next to Howard, could see a tear roll down Howard's cheek.

When Angelina left the kitchen, things went right back to filling trays, the sound of dishes being washed, and Howard shouting waiters' names and giving instructions.

The night was a complete success and it was the beginning of a new chapter in everyone's life that Christmas Eve, especially for Howard Johnson.

For the next few years, Howard worked as the head chef and his cooking surpassed anything that was done before him. Howard never forgot how Enzo helped him and made sure they always worked and shopped together.

Things might have been going right in the kitchen but they were not going right with Angelina and Don Carlo. When the restaurant was doing good business, their relationship was thriving. But things started to change. There were rumors that Prohibition was going to end. A little man named La Guardia was an American attorney and politician who represented New York in the House of Representatives and wanted to be the 99th mayor of New York. La Guardia made one of his platform promises to stop bootlegging illegal liquor. Pictures in the New York Times cover page of La Guardia smashing beer barrels and breaking whiskey bottles were a pure indication of his promise. Because of that and more competition, it was harder for Don Carlo to get good liquor. He turned out to be right about making liquor a big part of the business because of the high overhead of the business, liquor kept the restaurant afloat. Also, with the gangster troubles in Chicago, the heat was turned up in New York and protection and payoffs were not only getting scarce, but more expensive. The politicians were getting very nervous, which more than trickled down to the police commissioner ad the police. Don Carlo now thought it was a good time to sell the business, especially if there was someone interested. He was going to meet with Angelina in the apartment after the restaurant closed and it would be a good opportunity to discuss their future plans.

When he went to the apartment, he looked around, and waiting for him was a chilled bottle of champagne with two glasses, a tray of freshly made sandwiches, a fire burning in the fireplace, soft music playing on the radio, and Angelina looking radiant. The first thing he did was take off his coat, throw it on the couch, turn off the radio, and turn on some lights. She looked at him, at first puzzled, and then she got angry.

"What is going on?"

He took her hand and sat with her on the couch next to him.

"I have some plans I want to talk to you about. There is a dim future for the restaurant. It's getting harder to get good booze. Customers, good customers are starting to complain and I mean the good customers who spend. It's no secret that the booze is keeping the restaurant going. The politics are changing. This guy La Guardia is dead set on going after bootleg liquor and he wants to become mayor. There are also rumors that Prohibition is going to be repealed very soon. Political winds are shifting big."

Angelina lit a cigarette and Don Carlo took it out of her mouth and put it out in an ashtray on the coffee table.

"I told you to stop smoking. What's wrong with you?"

Angelina got up from the couch and made a dramatic turn.

"Angelina, you're not on stage. Cigarettes are bad for your health, not to mention your voice. I know you've been sneaking it. I smell it in the office so don't lie."

Angelina ignored his comments.

"What's your big plans?" she asked.

"I want to sell the restaurant now that someone is interested before things go belly-up and move to Florida."

She became indignant.

"Sell the restaurant! Florida! Are you crazy?"

"Listen Angelina. I know people. I keep my ears open. I was right about changing the restaurant and I am right now. The big Florida boom in Palm Beach is over. The hurricanes destroyed a lot of properties, developers need money, and property is dirt cheap. When things calm down the rich who were coming from Newport, Boston, and New York are eventually going to go back. There are luxury hotels that are being repaired, like the Breakers and the Royal Poinciana that will still attract the wealthy. The Vanderbilts, and the Astors, all have homes or vacation there and they will continue to come in their private rail cars for the warm weather. The real estate and business opportunities are there and we are going to be part of it. I am telling you the time is now to..."

Angelina lit another cigarette, leaned against the table at the window, and shook her head.

"I hate the heat and I hate Florida. My husband's family had a house in Palm Beach and I hated it. Bugs and Heat. Bugs and Heat. I am not selling this restaurant. DO YOU HEAR ME! I am not selling this restaurant. NO!"

She took the cigarette and smashed it into the ashtray with sparks landing on Don Carlo's pants that he quickly brushed off. He stood up and took his coat that was right next to him.

"Well like hell I am staying here just to be a fucking bouncer! I have two train tickets. If you don't want to go, I'll go alone."

Angelina stomped her foot and threw a small figurine from the table she was leaning on.

"Then go! Get out! Now!"

Don Carlo left without saying a word. The next day he called the restaurant and her apartment and she would not talk to him. He took the train to Palm Beach. Angelina quickly regretted her tantrum realizing that Don Carlo was right about everything and he was only thinking of their future. The next day she called his apartment several times but there was no answer. She went to his mother's apartment and she said that he left for Florida and didn't say when he would return. Angelina left word with his mother that if he called, please have him call her.

A week went by without any word. Angelina called the man who wanted to buy the restaurant and they came to an agreement. She sold the restaurant for cash, which made the deal that much faster. She had hoped she would hear from Don Carlo so she could tell him she sold the restaurant and she would meet him anywhere. She would also tell him he was going to be a father. When another week went by and she hadn't heard from him, she bought a ticket on the Mauretania, which sailed in a few days to Europe. She would then find her way to Naples.

As it turned out, Howard and Lena, a waitress who became a good friend of Angelina's, were the only people she told of her plans. Everyone else was left in the dark to be introduced by Howard to the new owner, who fired Howard the next week and brought in his own people. As Don

Carlo predicted, the restaurant began to fail forcing the new owner to mortgage the property and shortly after that, the new owner went bankrupt. The only person who landed on his feet was Howard. Before she left, Angelina gave him a thousand dollars with the instructions that if Don Carlo called not to tell him where she was and to tell him to go to hell. Angelina was certain Howard wouldn't do what she asked. When Don Carlo did call before Howard left the restaurant for good, like Angelina figured and hoped, Howard told him she went to Naples. Immediately Don Carlo made plans to follow her. But what if Howard followed Angelina's instructions and didn't tell him? How things could have been so different just by a chance decision of a colored man whom Don Carlo helped. Loyalty and appreciation.

Chapter 13

Once again, Enzo's and Francesca's fate would be tied together, this time not in Mussomeli, but on East Clifton Avenue.

Beginning around the 1900s, East Clifton Avenue was a fast-developing neighborhood with large new homes being built at the top of East Clifton Avenue and Randolph. Enzo's stepsister Francesca and her husband Alfredo have been living in New Jersey for over a year. She met Alfredo Buonocosa when he came from Palermo to Agrigento to visit Alfredo's family's relatives. When their eyes met for the first time, as the Italians say, they were both hit by the "capo di fulmine"—the love thunderbolt. It was love at first sight, and for about a year Alfredo would frequently come down from Palermo to spend time with Francesca, of course properly supervised by Sister Marie Antello in and around the convent where Francesca was then living. When a formal engagement was to be announced, Sister Marie traveled with Francesca to Palermo to meet the rest of Alfredo's family and plan the wedding. After a few months, Francesca and Alfredo were married in Palermo, which was at first a disappointment because Francesca wanted to get married in Father Giovanni Brunelli's church in Agrigento. Alfredo knew that Francesca was disappointed, so he paid for travel and accommodations for both Father Giovanni and Sister Marie and made arrangements for Father Giovanni to marry Francesca and Alfredo in the Cathedral of Santa Maria Assunta, one of the oldest churches in Palermo. Alfredo paid for Rabbi Merlino to be there, which made Francesca very happy. Seeing a rabbi at the reception, some rude person asked what a rabbi was doing there. Rabbi Merlino overhearing what was said, took a small cross from his pocket that his friend Leonardo had given him, and showed it to the person.

"I am representing this guy."

They all nervously laughed.

Within a year, the couple moved from Palermo to Agrigento and finally to Clifton, New Jersey so Alfredo could take charge of his family's import business, which was out of Newark and Manhattan. Alfredo's father had relatives living in Clifton, so it made it an easy transition. Sending letters back and forth to Rabbi Merlino, Francesca was able to find out where Enzo and Anna were living and working in lower Manhattan, in "Little Italy" on Mulberry Street in a four-story walk-up. When Francesca and Alfredo were finally settled in their home on Clifton Avenue, they made a surprise visit to Enzo, Anna, and little Maria. As expected, it was an emotional visit, especially with little Maria. It was also somewhat awkward for Anna and Alfredo since Francesca didn't know Anna and Enzo didn't know Alfredo. They planned to get together one weekend at Francesca and Alfredo's home.

They picked a date about a month out so Enzo could take off work. Arranging a visit to New Jersey and Clifton at that time was considered quite a distance and complicated, especially with a small child. It was also difficult since Enzo and Anna didn't have a phone. Alfredo would make the travel arrangements and send the tickets with one of his workers to escort them onto the Hudson Ferry to the ferry station in Jersey City, where he would pick them up on the agreed-upon weekend.

Finally, after a few weeks, early on a Saturday morning, a young Sicilian, Silvio, met Enzo and Anna at their apartment. With their borrowed suitcases, Silvio took Enzo, Anna, and a small child by horse and cart to the ferry station. Enzo tried to tip Silvio but he refused and even though both Enzo and Anna insisted, Silvio said he was given strict instructions not to take any money.

"I don't go against what my boss, Signor Alfredo says. He pays me."

Enzo and Anna laughed but the boy was serious.

Once they arrived in Jersey City, ordinarily they would have to take a horse and carriage, but Francesca and her husband were fortunate enough to own a car so they picked them up. When they met at the station, Francesca and Enzo again hugged and it was an easier meeting than when they first met a month earlier. At that time, Enzo and Francesca cried almost uncontrollably. They cried not only because they were so happy to finally see each other, but because they hadn't seen each other since the death of Rosalia. For Enzo, it made her death more of a reality. Also, Francesca never had the opportunity to really thank Enzo for what he had done for them and the deep appreciation of how their life turned out in such a wonderful way, which would have never happened if they had lived with their mother.

Enzo and Anna had never been to New Jersey, so as they drove through the countryside they were fascinated by the land and the new houses that they saw being built along the way. Everything seemed so spread out until they approached East Clifton Avenue. The houses there were a little more packed together, like the small homes in Mussomeli, just newer and architecturally different.

Francesca and Alfredo, or "Fredo" as everyone referred to him except Francesca, owned a big house on a double lot on East Clifton Avenue near the juncture of Randolph closer to the Passaic River. The house had three bedrooms, electricity, indoor plumbing, and two bathrooms, which was not that common at the time. In the back of the house was a large vegetable garden painstakingly cared for by Alfredo and a gardener. Francesca tended to the flower gardens on the side and in front of the house, also aided by a gardener. Within the garden, there were beautiful fountains intentionally reminiscent of the villas in Sicily.

After they arrived at the house, Anna asked if there was a place to have Maria nap. Francesca already had a small crib set up in the den, next to the garden where they would be sitting. Francesca gave Enzo and Anna a brief tour of the living room, not wanting to impress them. Enzo was very complimentary and Anna was her usual reserved self, and both were duly impressed and wondered what Alfredo did for a living to own such a house. They didn't ask, but when Anna and Francesca were getting some wine and biscotti in the kitchen to bring into the garden, Francesca mentioned that Alfredo was in some type of importing business with his family.

"I don't ask Alfredo about his business, but I know where he goes and when he comes home. He is a good husband and I love him."

Without another word, Anna and Francesca brought the wine and biscotti to the back garden where Alfredo was proudly showing Enzo his garden. As they sat at a small table, Francesca poured some wine and handed it to Anna, who politely refused and went to check on Maria.

As Anna came back out to the garden and handed a glass to Alfredo, Francesca asked,

"Enzo, do you and Anna ever think you would go back to Sicily for a visit? Alfredo and I were talking about it."

Enzo just looked at her. It became clear that he didn't want to discuss it, at least not then. Anna broke the silence.

"Francesca, did you make these biscotti? They are so good."

Francesca was intentionally distracted. Enzo and Anna rarely talked about Sicily.

"Oh no. There is a new Italian store with a bakery on Lexington Avenue a few blocks away. We have some cheeses and meats I bought there to make sandwiches for later."

Again, there was an awkward silence, broken when Francesca stood and filled Enzo's glass with wine. Enzo then responded to Francesca's question.

"I don't think I will ever go back. At least not right away. Although I would like to see Rabbi Merlino and maybe some of my friends from the market where I worked and, of course, it is Anna's dream to see her mother and father again."

Silence.

Francesca spoke, the awkwardness again broken. "Oh my God, Enzo! Do you remember that big man and his little wife? How she would always holler at him in front of everybody in the market? He killed her."

Enzo gave out a shocked, "Madonna Mia!"

"Yes," Francesca continued. "Well, that is what everybody thought. They think he poisoned her, but they couldn't prove it, so nothing really happened. Anyway, everyone at the market didn't care, because she was such a penny-pincher and troublemaker. After she died, her husband found money hidden all over the house. He gave the house to his wife's sister, which may be why nothing ever came of an investigation. Anyway, he moved to Genoa where his brother lives."

Francesca stopped for a moment, shook her head, and then laughed.

"Rosalia would follow her through the market and just laugh watching the scenes she would make trying to bargain down everyone. Enzo. you were the only one who knew how to handle her."

Francesca saw that Enzo had begun to get teary-eyed when she mentioned Rosalia. She didn't think he even heard the story she was telling.

"Enzo, I know that Rosalia would want to thank you for saving us. It was very difficult for Rosalia because she was older and had more of a closeness with our mother. She did feel guilt that she left her, but we both knew we had to leave. If it weren't for you, we don't know what would have happened. She was drinking more and more and getting out of control with her anger."

Enzo interrupted before she could continue, "Francesca, you never really told me what happened with you after Rosalia, your uncle, and Victor died. What happened? Your letters and cards didn't go into too much more than about what you were doing in school, and your cards around the holidays were just about the holidays."

Francesca intentionally broke the train of the conversation and turned to Anna. "Anna, would you like something to drink? I made lemonade."

Anna smiled. "Yes, I would like that."

Before Anna even finished, Alfredo got up.

"I will go."

Francesca smiled at Alfredo and nodded. Then Francesca turned to Enzo and Anna.

"When Uncle Antonino died, Rosalia and I were his only living relatives that we knew of and he left us a sizeable amount of money as well as part of the business he had built up over the years. We eventually wanted the business to go to Victor, but he didn't want to accept it because he felt it wasn't his place to own it, but he had worked so hard for Uncle Antonino."

She could see the expression on Enzo's face, so before he could ask, "Who is Victor?" Francesca anticipated the question and she continued.

"Remember? Victor was the huge man who was with Uncle Antonino when they visited my mother to take us with them." Francesca was a little upset with the memory but continued.

"Victor's full name was Bacso. He was Hungarian. Remember that big head that didn't fit with his body? His hands were also huge and when people first met him, especially women, he could be a very frightening figure."

They all laughed because of the huge gestures Francesca made as she spoke, which lightened the mood.

"But as he was big, he was a gentle soul with a heart as big as the rest of him. Uncle Antonino had found him in the street outside a bar near the docks and he looked to be drunk. But Uncle Antonino realized that Victor was not drunk, but had been beaten and robbed. He took Victor back to his house and got Father Giovanni and Sister Marie to stay with Rosalia and me because he thought that Victor was going to die and he wanted him to have his last rites. But he didn't die. Uncle Antonino nursed him back to health and gave Victor a job and he continued to live in the shed behind Uncle Antonino's house. Father Giovanni and Sister Marie would come to visit us to see how Victor was getting along. I think they wanted to make sure that Victor was not a dangerous character, but it wasn't long before they realized what a good soul Victor was. Father Giovanni and Sister Marie were also hearing gossip about why two men were living together with two little girls. Father Giovanni quickly made it known to the gossip mongers that he and Sister Marie often visited their home, which was a wonderful place and the girls were living in a very healthy environment."

Alfredo was back with the lemonade and handed it to Anna. It was a good opportunity for Francesca to take a sip of wine. Then she continued.

"After a time, Uncle Antonino and Victor even took us to church, where the community could see for themselves how well we were being taken care of. We always had beautiful clothes and were well-behaved. Uncle Antonino and even Victor made many friends and they were very generous. Sister Marie became our tutor. Victor showed his gratitude toward Uncle by helping him build up his little fishing business, and, as it turned out, Victor had a great head for figures and a photographic memory, which helped him compare the prices the other fishermen were charging for their fish so Antonino could get a good price when they took the fish to the markets and the restaurants. Victor was also good at bargaining because people would be a little frightened of him, although he would always be generous with the people who he knew were struggling."

Francesca stood for a couple of moments to again fill Enzo and Alfredo's glasses with more wine.

"Both Victor and Uncle Antonino built a successful business and were generous, especially with the church, donating food and money for all the holidays. Victor would never accept money for his work because he really didn't need anything nor did he ever ask for anything. Uncle Antonio gave him anything he needed, like clothes, without Victor asking. He was generous with Victor, which only made Victor more loyal and the two men became committed to each other. Like two old married people. Il due Sposi Vecchia!"

They all laughed because they could picture little Antonino and huge Victor, as Francesca described them.

"Uncle Antonino spared no expense on the celebrations for the both of us with open invitations for our birthdays and communion and confirmation, which endeared the townspeople even more to all of us. When Uncle Antonino died, the whole town mourned. Shops closed and there were hundreds in the church and at the cemetery.

Enzo interrupted Francesca. "How did he die?"

"Victor got a very bad cold, which turned out to be pneumonia. Uncle was not as strong as Victor, and while taking care of Victor, Uncle too caught pneumonia and died. Victor was inconsolable. Especially since

Victor felt it was his fault. Then as things were so wonderful, things went so wrong. Victor became silent and didn't show any emotion. We never brought up Uncle Antonino. Sister Marie took care of us, but we did most everything on our own. We still lived with Victor, even though Sister Marie said we could live at the convent.

Francesca stopped for a moment, took the little hankie she kept in her sleeve, and wiped her eyes.

Enzo interrupted and asked when Rosalia died. Francesca looked down and Anna gave Enzo a dirty look and kicked him. Francesca looked at them, and because of Anna's gesture, she smiled.

"No, Anna. He should know."

Francesca was again serious.

"Rosalia began getting sick after Uncle Antonino died. We thought she was just depressed because she was always tired. She coughed a lot and she said she was fine. She refused to go to the doctor until I asked Father Giovanni to please try to talk to her. When he did come to the house to talk to her, he became startled because she looked so thin and pale and he immediately wrapped her in her blanket and took her to Dr. Molinari, who has a small clinic near the church. The doctor knew right away what was wrong, and insisted that she stay there in quarantine, and warned everyone not to say a word because he didn't want to start a panic in the town. The doctor didn't even tell me what was wrong but we knew people could catch what she had. Victor didn't care about the quarantine and stayed with her day and night. Father Giovanni came and gave her communion every day. She was there for a week, and it was so hard for her to breathe. The doctor kept giving her medicine but said her lungs were no longer working, and he gave her enough medicine to go peacefully to sleep. I guess it was a mercy killing, but you should have seen her trying to catch her breath."

Francesca again stopped to wipe her eyes. She placed the hankie in her sleeve and continued.

"Victor couldn't be consoled. He was holding Rosalia in his arms when she died. We were all there and it took Father Giovanni to finally convince him to let her go. When he did let go, Victor looked up to heaven, shook his fist, and screamed, 'Perche! Why?' He screamed so loud the priest saying mass in the church next to us stopped and blessed himself we were told. Then he ran out of the room and back to the house. Dr. Molianri said in all his years of treating patients he never saw anyone as devoted and broken as Victor. I can't imagine how Uncle Antonino would have been."

At this point, everyone was fighting back tears except for Enzo, who was openly weeping. Francesca just continued, hoping to distract everyone.

"I think everyone in town came to church for the funeral because there were crowds out to the street. Then everyone walked behind the carriage bringing the coffin to the cemetery. We tried to have food at the convent but there were just too many people. Some of the restaurants and coffee shops set up tables outside and gave food away. It was something that no one would ever see in that town again. We never realized how many people Rosalia knew and would talk to every day. I was so busy with school, which came easier to her so she had a lot of time. She would babysit and wouldn't take any money...the stories people told us after she died were unbelievable. It was like she inherited all the goodness from our mother who had none."

Enzo could see that Francesca was getting emotional and changed the subject.

"What happened to Victor?"

"Well, it wasn't too long after Rosalia died that poor Victor became lost. I had already met Alfredo, so I was with him a great deal of the time, but we always tried to include Victor but he didn't want to be with us. He said he was too busy or tired. I think he felt he was in the way. I also think that Victor was drinking but he would hide it. The fisherman that worked and took care of the business told us that Victor would just stay in the house and would visit the cemetery every day and lay flowers for both Uncle and Rosalia."

Enzo again interrupted and asked how Victor died.

"At the time I was living at the convent with Sister Marie, and we would go every day to take care of Victor and bring food. Victor said it would be better for me to be with the sisters and I didn't want to go, but he insisted. I think he was worried about gossip. I had gone to Palermo with Alfredo for the weekend and Sister Marie brought him food, but she also had gone to see her brother on that Friday for the weekend and Victor said he would be alright. On Sunday when one of the fishermen went to check on Victor, he found him dead in his bed. Everyone said he died of a broken heart because Uncle Antonino and then Rosalia had died. A note had been left with Father Giovanni. Victor couldn't really write well, so he had his friend Salvatore write his will. Victor's share of the money that Uncle Antonino left him that was in Father Giovanni's care was to be divided among the church and the five fishermen who worked in the business. Victor and Uncle Antonino's home and personal belongings were left to me. Father Giovanni is taking care of Uncle Antonino's house that I inherited, so I give the church half of the rent and he sends me the rest."

The mood had become very heavy. Francesca was about to change that. She picked up the almost empty wine carafe.

"Alfredo, take Enzo and show him that wine cellar you're so proud of and get some more wine. Take your time. Anna and I have to talk. And don't get Enzo drunk."

Enzo looked at Francesca and wondered what that was about.

Francesca gently grabbed Anna's hand in a gesture of affection.

"Va! Go! I want to have some girl talk with Anna. And take your time but don't get drunk!"

Alfredo took the pitcher from Anna and he motioned to Enzo, who was getting up from his chair. Both men were talking, gesturing, and laughing as they were walking to the back of the house to the entrance of the wine cellar. Francesca pulled her chair closer to Anna.

Then she smiled right at Anna as the two women made eye contact. "I think we are going to be good friends. I can feel it in my bones."

Both Francesca and Anna laughed. Anna felt the same way as well. Her comment was prophetic because little did either of them know that they would be good friends and more like sisters for the rest of their lives.

"I have a couple of things for Enzo that may bring some bad memories, but I must give them to him. I need to know what he told you about how his father died and what happened afterward."

Anna looked a little startled, wondering what it could be, but at the same time, she had a good feeling that she could trust her.

"Enzo told me about what happened after his mother died, and he told me why you and your sister had to leave. He told me bits and pieces after he had had a couple of glasses of wine. I never wanted to pressure him. He never said much about his father. I always thought it was because he was so mad at him. I know you and your sister were always in his thoughts, and when we went to church, he would always light a candle for you and your sister and even your mother."

Francesca looked shocked at Anna. "My mother! The way she treated him?"

Anna smiled. "That's Enzo."

Francesca looked down as if to say she should know better. She then shook her head in understanding. "Yes. That's Enzo."

After a couple of moments of silence, Francesca continued.

"I just have to warn you. There may be some things that Enzo does not want you to know or is embarrassed by, but he needs to face them now. He has never done anything bad but I think he has shame and he shouldn't. He had to practically raise himself and I look at you and know that he has done a good job, otherwise you would not be with him."

Anna smiled. The two men were returning laughing and gesturing, revealing that they had had more wine.

Francesca got up from her chair and took the wine carafe from Alfredo and gave him a dirty look. "Alfredo, help me make the sand-wiches."

Anna started to get up. "Francesca, let me help."

"No, let my old man here help me." And they all laughed.

When Alfredo and Francesca were in the kitchen, Francesca looked at Alfredo sternly and whispered, "What did you two talk about?" Before he could even answer, she continued. "Don't you offer him a job. I don't want him involved with what you do. Don't think I don't see the secret meetings behind closed doors and the whispers. You told me your business is your business and I accept that. I understand that, but I don't want Enzo involved. He is like a brother to me. He saved Rosalia and me, and I will never forget it. We can help him in other ways. What I am going to give him will help him a lot, so let it be."

Alfredo was a little taken aback because although Sicilian women are tough, they also know their place. He took her seriously. He knew better than to disobey her wishes. Francesca felt she made herself clear. The other thing about Sicilian women was don't cross them and especially don't hurt the ones they love.

She gestured to Alfredo. "Come. Take that tray outside and come back for the olives. I will bring out the napkins and the rest."

After they had their lunch, Anna and Francesca brought everything back to the kitchen. Alfredo brought in the wine carafe and put it in the sink. Anna went to check on Maria, who was still sleeping, and went back outside into the garden. Francesca asked Alfredo to get the box and the envelope that were in the living room and bring it outside.

Alfredo walked into the garden and placed a box on the table. Francesca walked over to Enzo and handed him a large brown envelope. He just looked at her, surprised, and before he could say anything she put her hand on his hand and the envelope.

"In the envelope, there is a note and another envelope with a couple of stacks of lire."

Enzo looked at Francesca, and again she anticipated his question, and before he could ask, she continued, "No. The money is not from me. Indirectly, it is from your father, or I guess your father's estate. There is a letter explaining everything, but I will tell you what happened."

Enzo was in shock. "I don't understand. Who wrote this and how did you get this?"

Francesca took Enzo's hand.

"Rabbi Merlino? My God. Of course. The money is from him?"

"No. I told you, it's from your father's estate. Your inheritance."

Enzo was in shock.

"I tried to get it and even sent Anna ahead of me to America, but I never got anywhere."

"I know. After we left with you, my mother had no one but your father to take her anger out on. Rabbi Merlino tried to help your father and my mother, but my mother would have none of that until your father finally tried to throw her out of the house. But she wouldn't go and when she was drunk, she tried to stab him when your father tried to throw her clothes out the window. Rabbi Merlino interceded with the authorities. But Rabbi Merlino said he would be responsible for your stepmother. One day she went out of the house. It had rained and she slipped and a horse cart killed her. That is all I know. What you and none of us knew is that your father had another house and a small horse farm outside of the city. That is why many times he would not come home."

"Yes, I knew that. My aunt told me. I went there but they scared me off. After a couple of times, I just gave up." Enzo avoided making eye contact with anyone and just shook his head.

Anna looked surprised but just looked at Enzo waiting for an explanation.

Enzo looked back at Anna.

"I never wanted to discuss going there because of what happened afterward. I didn't want you to be scared. That is why I wanted to leave Sicily after we got married. Aunt Josephine left me the money, so we were able to leave. I didn't think it was fair that my father's inheritance not go to his son. He put me through enough."

He could tell that Anna wanted more of an explanation but she didn't need an explanation because her father wrote to her as he promised before she left Sicily and told her everything. She felt guilty and didn't tell Enzo that she knew the truth, but she also felt it was better to leave the past behind them.

"I don't know how my father died. I was living in Aunt Josephine's house and a man came and told me that my father died. He first looked for me in the market and they told him where I lived. He said that there was going to be a funeral the next day and I should come to the cemetery. I asked him where my father was living, and he said that it was at his house, way outside of town. The man told me where it was, next to the big Malatesta horse farm. I went right away to see Rabbi Merlino and told him what happened and that I wanted to go see my father before he was buried."

Enzo took a sip of some wine. Anna could see he was starting to get a little upset. His hand was shaking as he sipped his wine.

"Rabbi Merlino and I went to the house, and there were two men with rifles standing on each side of a large wooden gate. One of the men came and asked us who we were and what we wanted. After we explained, he rode back to the house, and another man came out with a gun. He got off his horse and told us my father was in a coffin in the barn, and if I wanted, I could see him, but they were going to bring him to the cemetery in the afternoon and bury him. I was so nervous I was shaking. The man led us to the barn and there on the side was the coffin. The man opened it and my father lay there dressed as if he was sleeping. I almost fainted because I was so upset and scared. Rabbi Merlino had to hold me up. Rabbi Merlino asked what happened, and the man closed the coffin and said my father just died. We went outside, and the rabbi sat me down on a bench. He went to talk to the man who seemed to be in charge. I couldn't hear them talking, but I could see the rabbi gesturing to me, and the man nodding and not looking interested in what the rabbi was saying. Then the man just walked away."

Enzo took another sip of wine. There wasn't a sound, in anticipation of what was going to be said next.

"Rabbi Merlino motioned for me to leave with him, and after we were far from the house, he told me that the man he was talking to owned the farm, the horses, and everything with my father. Of course, the rabbi asked when I was going to get my father's share, and that is when the man walked away. The rabbi then told me, and I will never forget this—that I should leave Sicily. I looked at him and asked why. He told me that he got the feeling that my father was killed to get his share and I may be next."

Anna gave out a gasp. Enzo looked down and shook his head.

"Rabbi Merlino knew the man and his reputation. Anyone who got in his way would not be in his way for long. So, Anna and I got married and planned to leave as soon as we could. I thought about it and was more angry than scared, so I sent Anna ahead and said I had some business to take care of. I went back a couple of times, but they scared me away, so I gave up and left to meet Anna a few months later. I knew that she was being taken care of by the rabbi's relatives. My father-in-law heard that I was going to be 'taken care of,' which we knew what they meant. If they wanted to scare me off it worked."

Enzo looked at Anna and grabbed her hand.

"I couldn't take the chance that you would be hurt, so we decided that you leave and I follow. It was the hardest decision I and your family ever had to make. I saw how frightened your father was so I took him seriously, especially letting you go to America alone."

There were a few seconds of silence, and then Anna asked about the money.

Without saying a word, Enzo opened the envelope and took out two stacks of lire in large denominations and a letter. Enzo handed the money to Anna and quietly commented, "That is a lot of money."

Francesca smiled. "It may be enough to buy a nice little house down the street here. It just went up for sale and we know the owners."

Enzo and Anna looked at each other and smiled, and Enzo didn't take his eyes off Anna.

"That is good because Anna is pregnant again."

Francesca screamed with delight and went over and hugged Anna, and Alfredo shook hands with Enzo. Then Francesca hugged Enzo and the two women cried.

Francesca took her hankie from her sleeve and wiped her eyes. "What a wonderful day for us. A joyous day." Then Anna remembered to check on the baby.

"Speaking of babies, I have to check on Maria."

Anna returned with Maria who was just waking up and let Francesca rock her.

For a time, they made a fuss over Maria and they all talked and laughed. It felt for all of them that a weight was lifted from their shoulders. It was truly a joyous day.

After a time, Anna handed the unopened letter to Enzo, who took it and opened it.

"It's from Rabbi Merlino. He explains more."

Dearest Enzo and Anna,

I pray this letter and money get to you. I sent it through trusted friends, and that is why it took so long to get to you. I was afraid if I posted it to you, it would be stolen or lost.

After you left, Enzo, a man came looking for you. I was so afraid but relieved that you both had left Sicily. He asked if I could get something to you. He gave me the money that, if you are reading this, is hopefully in your possession. I asked him why he was giving it to you. All he would say is the man who owned the farm with your father sold the farm and here is the money that would have been your father's share. I asked him how your father died. He told me that your father fell off a horse and broke his neck. I asked him why we weren't told that. He said he thinks the man who owned the farm wanted you to be frightened because he was afraid you would come after him for your share, and he didn't want to do anything to hurt you, but he also at first intended to keep the farm to himself. He said that was the agreement that he made with your father. In case one owner died, the survivor owned the farm. He said the man was heartbroken when your father died because they were very good friends and they trusted each other. So, when he sold the farm, he wanted you to have some of what would have been your father's. However, I also understand that Anna's father had something to do with it. Because of Anna's father's influence, he met with the man and forced his hand. He told the man how angry he was that his daughter had to leave for America alone and if he did the right thing, there wouldn't be any problems. What problems... I don't know, but it doesn't matter. Just know that I believe this is in a way Anna's father's gift to both of you. Anna's father was able to sell your father's house and that is part of the money you hopefully are in possession of. Again, a gift from your father. It should give you some relief how things turned out and to know that your father was not killed and the man did the right thing, with Anna's father's help. I hope you will come to visit me one day now that things have turned out the way they

have. God Bless both of you. Shalom.
*   Rabbi Merlino*

Anna was holding the money and crying because it was going to change their lives. She was so happy about what her father did for them but said sadly she couldn't thank them in person.

Then Francesca handed the box to Enzo. "This is also for you."

Enzo was clearly emotional as he began to open it. The box was filled with crumpled Italian newspapers. He gently removed the papers and there was an object wrapped in what looked like a lace blouse. He slowly pulled the lace down and was amazed at what he saw. Francesca was smiling.

Enzo looked at Francesca with tears in his eyes. "How?"

Francesca's eyes also began to tear. "This is from Rosalia."

Anna leaned over and looked in the box. What she saw was a Crucifix within a glass dome. She looked at Enzo and then looked at Francesca.

"After we left your father's house and you went to stay at your Aunt Josephine's, Rosalia snuck out and went back to the house. She saw our mother in the kitchen sleeping at the table, probably passed out from drink. She wrapped the Crucifix in her blouse...and here it is."

Enzo stared at the cross in the glass and gently touched it. He took Rosalia's blouse and wept in it for what seemed like five minutes. He could still smell the lavender soap she used. Anna helped calm Enzo and he looked down at the Crucifix in the glass dome.

Francesca anticipated that Enzo was going to take it out of the box. She placed her hand over Enzo's, and said, "Leave it in the box. In a couple of weeks, Alfredo and I are driving to New York to see his cousins and we will bring it to you."

Enzo took his hand away, and Francesca closed the box and put it back on the table.

Francesca looked at Anna. "Anna, you must be tired. Would you like to lie down for a nap?"

"That would be a good idea. Give me Maria. She will lay with me."

"Alfredo, please show Anna to her and Enzo's room, and then go to the bakery and get some dessert for tonight."

Alfredo shook his head and smiled. Anna stood up and took the baby from Francesca. Alfredo guided Anna and the baby into the house. When they were out of sight, Enzo took Francesca's hand.

"You have grown up to be a strong Sicilian woman."

Enzo kissed her on her forehead. Although usually the men would appear to rule the house, in most Sicilian marriages it is the woman who has the strength and turns a man's head toward what the woman wants without the man even realizing it. Francesca took a brown envelope out of her pocket and handed it to Enzo. Before he could take it, she still held on to it. He could see it had a wax seal that he couldn't make out. Then she let him have it.

"Enzo, the Crucifix is 'molto pericoloso'...very dangerous."

Enzo looked intently at Francesca and before he could ask a question she continued.

"Father Brunelli is a friend and the pastor at Sacred Heart Church right here in Clifton. He couldn't be here today but he gave me an envelope to pass on to you. He is from Palermo and he is the one who married me and Alfredo, so we trust him. When I was still in Sicily, I told Father about the Crucifix and told him that I wanted to send it to you, but Father Brunelli said he was going to America to be a pastor at a church in New Jersey. He was the one who told us about Clifton and later gave us the information about this house. He said he would bring it with him and keep it for us until we got settled. We trusted Father Brunelli, so it seemed natural that he would help us. When we got to Clifton, we went to see Father Brunelli and he told us to open the box that was heavily packed. When we uncovered it and Father Brunelli saw the Crucifix, he first looked at it with curiosity and then his expression turned very serious, but he didn't say anything. It seemed he knew something about it or saw a picture of it. He studied art in Florence and Rome when he was younger, so we thought naturally he was familiar with such things. His family is very wealthy and wanted him to be a lawyer but instead, he studied art. He went to Assisi to study the frescoes of Giotto. Instead of returning to his art school, he followed a 'calling' and became a Franciscan Priest."

Enzo was listening intently. He was both excited and anxious. Francesca continued.

"He didn't tell us much, so we packed up the cross and took it home. A few months later he had gone to Rome for an Ecumenical meeting at the Vatican. When he returned, he had this sealed envelope with information about the Crucifix. He only told us that having the Crucifix is very dangerous and not to tell anyone we have it, and it should be you who sees what's in the envelope. He didn't want to keep it any longer. We didn't know what to think, and I told Alfredo it was none of our business and I hid the envelope."

Enzo and Francesca nervously looked at each other and laughed.

"It's like a mystery novel, I know. As you can see, of course, I didn't open the envelope. Don't read it now and don't even let Anna know you have it. I think Alfredo forgot about the whole thing. He is not really a church-goer, so he is not interested in Crucifixes and things like that. I think once you open and read what's in it, put it with your other important papers. Also, when you do have the Crucifix in your home, don't display it where anyone can see it. Maybe keep it in your bedroom. Father Brunelli at first wanted to keep it in the church but he was concerned about it being in his possession. He said since it was your father's, it must be God's intention that it go back to you. I really think he is scared to have it."

They both heard Alfredo walking back to them from the house. Enzo shoved the envelope into his jacket. In his mind, he could feel the envelope burning through his pocket. He would have to read it the first chance he got. Alfredo told Enzo that Anna and the baby were resting and asked Francesca if there was anything else she wanted him to get at the bakery. She said just come back, and they all laughed. When Alfredo left, Enzo took Francesca's hand. "Francesca, let's go to the wine cellar."

Francesca led Enzo to the wine cellar in the back of the house. When she opened the door, they could feel the damp, cool air as they entered. She switched on the light and closed the door. They sat at a small table among what looked like hundreds of bottles of wine stacked up on shelves. Francesca randomly grabbed a bottle, took two glasses, and handed the bottle with a corkscrew to Enzo.

"Here. Open this. In case Alfredo comes back it will seem like we're just having some wine. I need to know anyway what is in that envelope!" They both laughed.

"Hurry, give me the papers."

Enzo wasn't surprised that Francesca wanted to know what the Crucifix was all about. After all, she not only lived with it but it sounded like she took some risks. Enzo took the folded envelope out of his pocket and handed it to Francesca. She broke the seal and opened it. There were some pictures and other printed papers. Then she saw the note that explained what the Crucifix was.

"Enzo, the note is not in English. It looks like Latin. I can understand some words. You would really have to have someone you can trust to read it. We should bring it to Father Brunelli. He is the one who gave it to us, but he is not the one who wrote the note. I can't make out the signature."

Francesca tried to read the note and periodically stopped so she and Enzo could try to understand what she had read. When she stopped, they both silently looked at each other. She took out another piece of paper from the envelope, which was a black and white photograph.

"Enzo, look. This looks like it's a photo of the Crucifix in a painting, but the photo is only a small part of the painting. Enzo, maybe we should have left this is Sicily. Put these papers away and don't let anyone see this."

Enzo looked at Francesca and really didn't know what to say.

"How did your father get this?"

Enzo looked at the envelope and then Francesca. "I don't know, but it was always in the house. I don't know if it was my father's or my mother's. I really don't know. It was always there. I think it might have been there before your mother was there because it was in my father's bedroom and had a silk cloth on it or something. I snuck a look under the cloth a couple of times but I was afraid my father would catch me. I thought the cloth might have to do with my mother's death. Wanting to shut Christ out or something."

"Do you want me to keep it here until you get settled into a house or bring it to you like we talked about?

Enzo looked at Francesca and they both laughed. "I just think you want Anna and me to move here. This whole thing is made up!"

Enzo knew it wasn't something to laugh at. The note was real and the information was true.

"Please keep it here. Keep the papers with it." Then he thought for a moment. "I don't want you to take any risks. Maybe we should see if Father Brunelli would keep it in the church."

Francesca poured some of the dark red wine into the two glasses.

"I love Father Brunelli, but I don't think he would do it; he knows too much. Maybe I'm going to tell him you sent it back to Sicily, to another relative. Better it be kept a secret."

They both took a sip of wine and didn't say another word. A couple of beads of sweat fell from Enzo's temple almost into his wine glass. He took a hankie from his back pocket, wiped the sides of his face, and then took another sip of wine.

"Take your wine glass and the bottle. Let's forget about this for now."

Enzo put the envelope in his jacket but left the wine glass and bottle. He was getting a little drunk.

"Thank you, Francesca"

"I don't think you should be thanking me, Enzo."

They both nervously laughed as they walked out of the wine cellar toward the garden. Enzo turned to Francesca.

"Let's go see that house you're talking about. Maybe it's time to move. I need a place for the Crucifix. I still think the whole thing is just a way to get us to move closer to you."

Francesca smiled.

"I love you, Enzo." She placed her arm in Enzo's and kissed him on the cheek. "We have come a long way."

"We have. I love you too, Francesca."

Enzo kissed Francesca on her cheek and they walked toward the gardens to wait for Alfredo and for Anna and Maria to wake up. Once again, Enzo's and Francesca's fate would be tied together, this time not in Mussomeli, but on East Clifton Avenue.

Chapter 14

Everyone was careful not to say anything hateful to Enzo about the "colored neighbors."

Enzo had already left Angelina Restaurante before it was sold in 1933 during the midst of the Depression and the end of prohibition. Enzo and Anna had settled in their new home on East Clifton Avenue with Anna, baby Maria, and another baby on the way. The new owner of the restaurant said he didn't want a colored chef in an Italian restaurant, but then without a good chef, no one wanted to come downtown. Also, fewer people were going out to eat because of the depression, and now that Prohibition was over, without the bootleg liquor that was served in the restaurant, anyone could get a drink wherever they wanted. They weren't going to pay the high prices at Angelina Restaurante.

The high rollers had thrown themselves out of skyscraper windows so they weren't around anymore. Even in midtown the restaurants where almost all the "former wealthy millionaires" and celebrities would party into the night, had closed. They were replaced by Horn and Hardart automats, which were started in 1888 and were now everywhere. Where else could you get a cup of coffee for a nickel and a sandwich for a dime? Broadway was dead and the banks owned more theaters than the producers. Many of the producers, actors, and script and songwriters moved to Hollywood and became part of the booming movie industry.

The new owner of Angelina Restaurante finally lost the building as it went into receivership to the bank that held the mortgage. When the mortgage was sold to another bank, the building stood empty and it started to fall into disrepair. What was at one time an elegant and pristine structure designed after Villa Carlota on Lake Como, was now badly deteriorating. When the building was eventually sold to a local investor for pennies on the dollar, the beautifully sculpted architectural details that did not fall off were taken off, leaving an ugly cement building. The summer roof garden and fountains where Angelina would take her special guests on hot summer evenings, were all removed. The imported Italian statues that could not be taken off the roof easily, were smashed. The restaurant space was subdivided into shops and Angelina's luxurious suite of rooms above the restaurant was divided into small, cold, flat apartments. Although the neighbors complained about the destruction of a building icon, nothing was done.

When Enzo and Anna moved to New Jersey they tried to keep in touch with Howard. The last time they had heard from him he had written them that he was moving to Atlanta to work for his cousin who had a restaurant. It was a couple of years after the last letter that they received a Christmas card that was postmarked from New York. They figured that he moved back to Manhattan and was working somewhere at another restaurant but they didn't know where.

Finally, one Sunday Enzo and Anna took a trip to Little Italy and tried to find out if anyone knew where they could find Howard. One of the waiters at Angelo's restaurant on Mulberry Street said that the bakery around the corner, Tarantoli Bakery, may know where he is. Enzo knew where the bakery was because they used to deliver bread to Angelina Restaurante and he remembered the baker's son Jerry who made the deliveries. They went in and asked the woman at the desk for the owner's son.

"Hi, my name is Enzo Buonforte and this is my wife, Anna. Is Jerry around?

"Jerry is away at college, but his father is here. What is this about?"

"Jerry used to deliver bread to Angelina Restaurante and I am trying to find out where someone that I used to work with there, is working."

"Maybe I can help you. I'm Mrs. Tarantoli and Jerry is my son."

"Oh. How do you do? We're looking for a man named Howard Johnson."

"Oh, Howie, the colored chef at Angelina. He's a great guy. Before he was the chef, he used to come in here to pick up bread orders early in the morning. He didn't say much in the beginning, then he opened up. Great guy."

Anna was getting anxious.

"Do you know where we can find him?"

"Sure. He left La Cisterna Restaurant up the street when they went bankrupt. A lot of restaurants are closing, which is why we now have to go uptown to deliver bread. Anyway, he went to Atlanta to work but that didn't work out so he and his wife..."

Anna quickly interrupted.

"His wife? He got married?"

"Oh yeah, a pretty, little thing. She's a teacher."

"Anyway, he came back here and tried to find a job but no luck. We heard that a restaurant, well it's more like a bar that serves food in Hell's Kitchen, was looking for a chef so we told Howie about it. It's a clean place run by a husband and wife and they're very nice. He's too talented for that place, but people aren't going to high-class places like they used to so you have to take what you can get."

She took a piece of paper and wrote the address.

"Here's the address and here are the subway trains to get you there. Be careful. It's still early so you shouldn't have any trouble."

Enzo took the address and since she knew so much about the neighborhood, he asked what happened to Angelina and the restaurant.

"We loved that restaurant and we went there a couple of times for our anniversary. Actually, when Howard was the chef, that's how we knew how talented he was. Anyway, what the rumor was, was that she had a fight with her boyfriend who just left her. She sold the restaurant to a guy who owned a restaurant next to Café Ferraro's and kept pestering her about buying it. She finally sold it to him and left. He fired Howard and then just went bankrupt, like so many other restaurants. My cousin...."

Anna didn't want to hear about her cousin and interrupted her.

"Do you know where Angelina went?"

"The last we heard was that she went to Italy after the guy left her, being pregnant with no father after all, people talk."

Anna looked at Enzo who asked further.

"How did you know this?"

"My cousin that I was going to tell you about was a waitress at Angelina's and I guess a friend to Angelina and she knew what was going on."

Anna was annoyed.

Enzo was now anxious to find Howard and thanked Mrs. Tarantoli and they left for the subway. Both Anna and Enzo were shocked at the story and wondered first if it was true and second if the father was Don Carlo. They also wondered what the fight was about.

When they walked down Mulberry Street and passed what was once Angelina Restaurante on the way to the subway, Anna began to cry. It was now just an ugly cement building with yellow demolition signs on the once beautiful oval-topped double oak doors, with graffiti painted all over them. No one looked like they were living in the upstairs apartments and there weren't any stores occupying the retail space. How things had changed. Now it just looked like the building was being torn down by a developer.

But that wasn't all. The whole of Little Italy was no longer what it once was. People were trying to sell things on the street, drunks were sleeping in doorways, and the streets were full of trash. From the boarded-up stores and restaurants, instead of music and laughter from happy customers, there was an eerie silence. The open restaurants were struggling, doing whatever they could to try to lure customers inside, with barkers holding menus, almost begging people to come inside.

In a melancholy tone as he looked around trying to find the building they once lived in, and it too was boarded up, Enzo remarked, "Thank God we left. Thank God for Francesca. And I hate to say it, thank God for my father."

When Enzo and Anna got to Hell's Kitchen, they found the restaurant with the address the woman had given them, Bernie's Bar and Grill.

The woman was right, it wasn't even a restaurant but more like a bar where food was served. The place was clean and it was a nice atmosphere. When they asked the bartender for Howard, he asked if they were friends. Enzo explained who they were. Then the bartender went in the back to get Howard, who was surprised to see them.

"How did you find me? How...."

Anna interrupted him and they all hugged with tears in their eyes.

"We went to Little Italy and the woman in Tarantoli Bakery told us. She said you are married?"

"Yeah. The job, working for my cousin didn't work out. He was more interested in drinking than working so I left. But while I was there, I met one of the customers. A beautiful girl and we hit it off and after a while, we got married. She's smart, she's a teacher. We saved our money and after the school year we came up here and I got this job. The owners are real nice and sometimes I can make a fancy dish as a special but it's mostly burgers and fries and that kind of stuff.

Anna and Enzo could see that Howard had changed. For all he went through he was stronger and more outgoing. Then Anna asked about his wife.

"Where is your wife?"

"Oh, Della. She is a teacher in a Harlem school. She really likes it."

"Where do you live?"

"We live upstairs. The owner gives us a good rent and it's a nice place. I'll show you. Della's upstairs. The only thing is, well, she's pregnant and this isn't a place to raise a family."

Anna screamed with joy.

"Pregnant! How wonderful!"

Then Enzo broke in.

"We have some good news for you but let's sit down first because we have some questions."

They sat in a booth and Enzo was anxious to ask about Don Carlo and Angelina.

"We want to know if you have seen Don Carlo and know what happened."

"I had seen him and he did tell me what happened. I saw him when I was working at this restaurant, La Cisterna before it closed. He had heard that I was working there and he came in to see me with his daughter. He told me that he and Angelina had an affair. They were deeply in love but both stubborn. He wanted her to sell it to this guy who was anxious to buy it. Don Carlo could see what was happening with the depression, politics, and the end of Prohibition. Business was not what it used to be. They had a big fight. I think because she didn't want to sell. Then she went to Italy without telling him because he took off to Florida to set up a real estate business. Before she left for Italy, she agreed to sell the restaurant, and because there was nothing in writing with Don Carlo, that was it. He called after she left and I told him the restaurant was sold and she went to Naples. He followed her there and that was that. He came back four years later with a four-year-old daughter. He made a fortune in Florida buying properties for pennies on the dollar and holding on to them until the market changed. He even offered me a job but I live in the kitchen.

Anna interrupted. "What happened when he went to Naples?

"When he found out he was a father, he was really happy. They finally had the pressure of the restaurant off them and for a few years, they were happy. Angelina's father died and then she got sick. She got cancer and he took care of her. Her last wish was that Don Carlo marry her sister Beatrice and leave Italy with his daughter. Angelina did not want a stranger bringing up her daughter and Lucia loved Beatrice. They also thought that it was the only way they could get out of the country because Mussolini was in power and things were getting bad.

Angelina died and Don Carlo married Beatrice. He said he was truly in love with her, but he couldn't get her out of the country because she didn't have her papers and it would take weeks. Don Carlo got his daughter's papers and his wife convinced him to get out before he got recruited into the army or something happened to him. He reluctantly left and she said she would follow. The family still had some prestige because of Angelina so they were convinced Beatrice would quickly be able to get out. That is all I know because I just saw him that one time."

For a few moments, there was silence hearing the sad news. Enzo broke the silence.

"Well, it's good that you want to leave here because we have a plan for you. There is this moving company that is across the street from us and they agreed to rent you an apartment over one of the garages. We also got you a job at my daughter and son-in-law's restaurant."

Enzo told Howard to give two weeks' notice and gave Howard their phone number. Enzo asked if Howard could use the pay phone in the bar. Howard said it was ok and he was thrilled.

"How did you know you would find me."

Enzo laughed.

"We just knew. We are too connected not to be together."

"You both are a Godsend! Wait till we tell my wife. Come on upstairs."

When Anna and. Enzo returned to Clifton, he told his daughter and son-in-law that Howard had agreed to take the job. They really had no choice. Enzo's daughter Maria, and her husband Antonino, knew how angry Enzo could get when Enzo didn't get what he wanted, and they didn't argue with him. They knew it was Enzo who helped to get them started in the business.

Howard working for Enzo's daughter and son-in-law was a good fit. Howard was a hard worker, and Enzo's son-in-law Antonino showed his appreciation with a good salary. He truly liked Howard. There were times when a couple of customers made a comment about a colored cook and asked if he was clean. Both Maria and her husband told the customer to leave and never come back. Although embarrassed, Howard said nothing but showed his gratitude by working as hard as he could. He never wanted to take a vacation and would always be willing to work on the Christmas and Easter holidays. For years, Enzo tried to put a stop to having the restaurant open on holidays by making them feel guilty.

"Why aren't you home with your children?" he would say. And then when the children got older, he would scold them, "How could you make your children work on Christmas? What kind of parents are you? Working Christmas and Easter is a sin against God!"

Enzo shamed them so much that after a couple of years of hearing it, they finally agreed with him and closed the restaurant at least on Christmas and Easter. But the real reason was that the children refused to work on the holidays.

Over time, Howard had two children, saved enough money, and bought the entire garage. He turned it into a beautiful little home with gardens and beautiful flowers that Howard's wife took care of. No one in the neighborhood objected to a colored family living there, because Enzo made sure that Howard was treated like family. It would be a personal affront if anyone said anything either to Howard or Enzo in front of, or behind, their backs. Anyway, it wasn't hard to be nice to Howard and his family. They were soft-spoken and kind. After only a short time, they were one of the most liked families on the block. Everyone was careful not to say anything hateful to Enzo about the "colored neighbors." When one neighbor, George Mayer, said to Enzo that it was OK that a family of color family lived on East Clifton Avenue because the Johnsons "were clean and knew their place," Enzo stared at him and after a few seconds said that if George ever said that again, or if he even heard that George had said it, that George would find *his* place in Calvary Cemetery. After all, there were rumors about Enzo's "connections."

The years passed and everyone believed that things would continue as they had and the times would never change. But again, like Enzo used to say, "The only thing that doesn't change is change." Enzo's death is a testament to his wisdom.

Chapter 15
The rumors were true. It was the room where Enzo hid people from the police or worse.

The day after Enzo's death, his funeral arrangements are being discussed by the Buonoforte children, but not with Anna, which they are going to find out is a big mistake. They agree that the wake and funeral will be at Conte's Funeral Home, where Pietro was laid out years ago. The first viewing will be for three days: Tuesday, Wednesday, and Thursday. It is felt that three viewing days are needed for people who will be coming from Buffalo and other areas and will have the weekend to stay over on Saturday or Sunday. The burial will be on Friday at Calvary Cemetery, in nearby Paterson, where Enzo had bought a burial plot when Pietro died. Enzo bought a plot for himself, Anna, and Pietro's wife Mina.

The Monday after Enzo dies, Joseph takes off from work to get the boys to school so Chiara can stay with her mother. Chiara gets up early because she expects more people to come the day before the wake and she wants to get things ready. The reality of her father's passing has not become a reality for Chiara yet and the first thing she thinks about is the food. She knows Don Carlo and his family will be coming in the afternoon. There is no worry because there is plenty of food from the day before. Most of the leftover food was wrapped and had been stored in the garage. They put it in the back of the garage so it wouldn't freeze. Fortunately, it was a mild night.

Rita is dropped off by her husband before he goes to work. Chiara is already upstairs getting her mother's clothes out so she can change and have breakfast. When Rita comes into the house, she sees that no one is in the kitchen and dining room, so she goes upstairs where Chiara is helping Anna get up from bed. They didn't realize that Enzo was always there to help get Anna up from bed. They knew that Anna sometimes needed help getting up from her chair, and again Enzo was always there. But what to do without Enzo will be discussed another day. When Rita walks into the room, Chiara is helping her mother put on her shoes. Rita stands back and wonders how Anna will be able to stay alone in the house. Chiara has been aware of it for a long time. The phone rings and without saying anything Rita takes over helping her mother. Chiara goes downstairs to pick up the phone. It is her brother Jack calling from the funeral home.

"Hi. No. I don't know where the cemetery paperwork is. Alright...I'll look again. We also have to get the will. The lawyer might have a copy, but I want to see if it's here. It's gotta be in the house somewhere. OK. Bye."

As Chiara comes upstairs, she is trying to think what places her father would have kept his will and other important papers. She thinks her mother and even Rita may know.

"Chiara. Who was on the phone?"

"It was Jack at the funeral home. He wants to know where the paperwork is for the cemetery plot. I looked. I don't know. Ma, do you know where Papa kept the papers?"

Anna, who is now dressed and standing, just looks at Chiara. She can tell Anna is angry.

"Why is Jack at the funeral home again?" Anna asked. "Who told him to go there? I wanted to go there myself. Chiara, look in the bottom drawer of the dresser and see if the papers are there. We keep the bills and the bank books in the bottom drawer. I want to go to the funeral home now. Who told Jack to take over the arrangements?"

Chiara looks at Rita and neither one is going to argue with their mother.

"Ma, I already looked in all the drawers and I couldn't find anything."

Chiara is mad at herself for not asking her father where the papers were when he was alive. At the time she didn't want to face the fact that someday she may need them and she was in denial that her parents would die, even though it was common sense. She also didn't want to scare her father or make him nervous. But the truth is that she did anything to stay in denial, especially after her brother Pietro died.

Anna usually didn't show her anger. She left that up to Enzo, but this time is different. She is alone.

"Chiara, take your father's car and take me to the funeral home. I should be the one picking out the coffin and making the arrangements, not your brother."

Chiara doesn't argue with her mother. They all go down downstairs. Chiara is getting Anna's coat and they are preparing to leave when the phone rings. Chiara goes to pick up the phone.

"I hope it's not Jack again."

"Yes, hello. Thank you...I appreciate your concern...Yes, and I will tell my mother. Yes. 1:00 clock is fine and we have plenty of food, so please stay for lunch. I hope so. See you then. Good-bye."

As she hangs up the phone and before Rita can ask, she tells her and Anna who was on the phone.

"That was Don Carlo's daughter. They're coming here at 1:00. My God, I haven't seen him in years. What happened between him and Papa?"

"Yeah, Momma, what happened between Don Carlo and Papa?" Rita repeats.

There is silence for a moment. "Let's go." Anna isn't going to answer the question.

Chiara and Rita look at each other. They don't make any comments because they can see that Anna just wants to leave.

"I'll tell you in the car. Let's go. Andiamo."

Chiara helps Anna get into the back seat of the car and once they pull away, Anna begins to explain.

"I don't know everything but I could guess some of it. Your father wanted to keep me in the dark, but it was pretty obvious what was going on. I didn't ask questions, but I knew something. You know your father. They did talk. Don Carlo and your father talked on the phone, especially around the holidays. Sometimes they would talk for hours."

"Soooo, Momma, what happened?" Rita asks.

"After Pietro died, I think it was a couple of weeks, it was early in the morning; it must have been real early because it was still dark out and we were in bed. We heard a loud knock at the door. At first, we thought it was thunder because it was pouring rain. Then we realized that it was someone knocking. Your father got up and ran downstairs to answer the door. He thought he could get there before the knocking woke me up, but I was already awake. I heard some talking and I could tell it was Don Carlo. He was excited, which was unusual for Don Carlo because he was usually so quiet. Your father comes back upstairs, sees that I am sitting up in bed, tells me to go back to sleep, and closes the bedroom door. I hear footsteps and someone is coming in the living room and they're whispering, and then your father is getting either excited or mad—I couldn't tell. Then there is silence and I hear a lot of moving around. I tried to go back to sleep, but now I'm scared. Someone is going in and out of the house. I looked at the clock and it was almost four in the morning. I did fall back to sleep, and then your father came back into the bedroom and woke me up. He said it was Don Carlo and someone else. Later I found out it was Bruno Sessino and Don Carlo's father, Giancarlo. For years we all thought he was dead. He had been with a group of men in Sicily led by this man, Salvatore Giuliano."

Chiara interrupts, "Who is Salvatore Giuliano?"

"He was some kind of bandit hero to the people. Your father was interested when he heard that he was killed in 1950. Remember them talking about him with old man Fassino?"

"Yes. Now I remember. Something in an Italian paper that he brought over to show Papa. What does that have to do with Don Carlo's father?"

"I don't know. Something happened and Giancarlo left Sicily and went to Argentina or Tunisia. He got into Canada and then he snuck into the country here. He made contact with Don Carlo through some people in New York, but someone told the police that he was in the country. Don Carlo couldn't hide him at his house, but he needed time to get him to a safe place to live, so he brought him here and wanted your father to hide him until he could get him somewhere safe."

Both Rita and Chiara give out a gasp and look at each other.

"How did you find all of this out?" Chiara asks.

Anna ignores the question. "Your father hid him in the attic."

"Momma. What attic? There is no attic in the house," Rita says.

"That is what your father told me after we left that afternoon. Don Carlo paid for us to stay at Villa Roma in the Catskills, but your father was mad anyway."

"Yeah, I remember that. I thought it was a gift for your anniversary."

"When we came home, I guess he was gone. It was never discussed again."

"Then what happened?" Rita and Chiara ask almost at the same time.

"Your father was mad as hell because if Don Carlo's father got caught in our house, we would get in trouble. They are both stubborn and the relationship wasn't the same after that."

"Yeah, but what happened to Don Carlo's father?" Chiara asks.

"We really don't know. When we got back home, he was gone. I never saw him. On the dresser, there was an envelope with money but your father gave it back and told Don Carlo that he is a friend and doesn't need to be paid. But still, the relationship wasn't the same. We did see him a few times, like when his daughter had a christening for her baby and things like that, but it wasn't the same for your father. I also think your father was embarrassed by the way he acted, you know his temper, but he also didn't want Giancarlo to be hidden in the house. Your father never wanted to talk about it with me. And it wasn't the first time we had to hide someone. But that was a long time ago. One time we hid someone in the basement where we keep the meats and vegetables. Your father stayed in the house, and you remember the rest of us stayed with Maria and Antonino in their big house. Your father told them work had to be done on the boiler or something. They didn't believe him, but it didn't matter."

Before Anna can continue, they arrive at Conte's Funeral Home. Chiara parks the car and helps Anna out of the car. They see that Jack's car is in the parking lot and he is still there. As they walk into the funeral home, they can hear Jack, Margo, and the funeral director talking loudly and even laughing. Jack and Margo are shocked to see Anna. With Chiara and Rita at her side, Anna walks right up to Jack and ignores Margo.

"What is so funny? Are you having a party?"

Everyone can see she is angry. This is something they have rarely seen. It was usually Enzo getting mad at situations. Anna would listen and only say something if she disagreed with Enzo, but most times it was behind closed doors.

The funeral director, feeling the intensity of the situation, changes his attitude and offers Anna a chair in his office. Jack and Margo think they will follow, but Anna intercedes.

"You wait outside. Chiara and Rita, come in with me."

Jack doesn't like hearing that. "Momma, I already took care of everything and...."

Anna shoots back, "It's my husband. Chiara, help me."

Chiara and Rita don't say anything and walk in with their mother. They can hear Margo whispering something in Jack's ear, and Jack motions her away. Rita doesn't want to go into the office and sits outside and avoids making eye contact. The funeral director closes the office door. Margo and Jack walk down the hall to avoid talking to Rita.

After about twenty minutes, the door opens and they can hear Anna thanking the funeral director. Chiara walks out of the office with a folder and Rita gets up from her chair and helps Anna out of the office. Jack walks back up to the office and when he sees the folder and tries to take it from Chiara, she pushes his hand away.

"You ask your mother."

He backs off.

Jack goes right over to Anna.

"Ma, do you want me to look at...."

Anna looks at him. "No. We took care of everything. The funeral director is going to put the times in the newspaper. Now I want to go pick out your father's coffin."

Chiara can feel Jack's anger but she doesn't care. This is what her mother wants. Like Anna said, "It is my husband."

Anna doesn't wait for everyone to follow her and turns to Jack. "We are only going to have two days and then the funeral, not three days. Whoever can come, comes. The weather is bad anyway. Chiara is going to make the arrangements at Johnny's for the family and anyone who wants to come after the wake."

Jack interrupts, "Ma, what are you talking about? You know how much that..."

Anna cuts him off, "I'm paying for it."

Jack tries to interject again. He is getting angry. "Do you know how much...."

Anna cuts him off again. "You mind your business. This is what I want. This is what your father would want. You mind your business. Go home."

Then Margo chimes in, "Momma, Jack is only trying...."

Anna stops in her tracks.

"I don't care what Jack is trying to do. And don't you call me *Momma*! I am not your momma," Anna says in a mocking tone.

Chiara and Rita are surprised at the way their mother is talking to Margo. They've waited years for this. Who is this woman? Anna walks closer to Margo who backs away.

"How do you treat your mother? Do you treat *me* the way you treat your own mother? When was the last time we were at your house for even a cup of coffee? When did you ever come over on Christmas or other holidays? You come the day after. When do your kids ever come to see us? They are always at *your* mother's house. No. Everything is about *your* family. Enzo knew these things but he always said, 'keep the peace. keep the peace.' I don't care about the peace anymore, because you are not going to tell me what to do or sell my house. I can live alone.

I don't need you. If I need something, I can call someone. I can call Chiara or Rita or someone else. You are not going to sell my house."

Jack says, "Who said anything about selling your house?"

Anna moves close to his face. "Do you think I'm stupid or just off the boat? I know what you worry about. I don't need you to do anything for me."

"Ma, I'm just trying to help. I'm...."

"You only care when it does something for you or your wife. Did you ever take me to the doctor? When did you ever take me to the store? No! But you drive your wife's mother all over the place. When did you ever ask me if I needed anything, huh? We buy your kids' clothes. I never see the kids dressed in those clothes. We give your son some money for a car when he gets his license. Does he ever come to see us? Never! I will tell you now like I wanted to tell you for years but your father stopped me. Everything is for your wife's family. Don't tell me what to do. You have not earned that right."

"Ma, I don't know what got into you."

They continue to be guided by the undertaker to pick out a coffin.

Chiara also can't believe what Anna is saying, but in reality, it is and was the way things were and are, and she has to defend her mother. Before Jack can interrupt Anna, Chiara stops him.

"Jack, did you listen to her? Everything she says we see. And you know it, too. Papa should have kicked your ass years ago."

Anna has had enough. "OK. Basta. Enough. After I'm done here, I want to go to my house. Jack, you go to your own house. I had enough for today."

Anna picks out Enzo's coffin and they go back to the house without anyone saying a word in the car. When they drive up to the house, they see Maria and Antonino's car. Anna just shakes her head. "And now we have another opera. Chiara, I've had enough. I want to go to my bedroom when we get in the house."

As they walk into the house, the phone rings and Rita runs to answer it. Maria and her husband kiss Anna and want to help her to "Papa's chair," as they still refer to it. "I don't want to sit down here. I need to rest. I am going upstairs...by myself."

Anna doesn't want help climbing the stairs and goes to her bedroom. Chiara goes into the kitchen with Maria to get the coffee. When Rita hangs up the phone, Chiara yells out to ask who is on the phone.

"It was Don Carlo's daughter. Her father is not feeling well and they called the doctor."

Maria comes out of the kitchen holding an expresso coffee pot.

"How sick is he?"

"His daughter sounded a little upset. She said since he heard about Papa, he hasn't been feeling well. She said she would call back. They were waiting for the doctor."

In the afternoon, more people come to pay their respects. Chiara tells the visitors that they will convey their respects but her mother is resting. Around five o'clock the last visitor leaves, and then Joseph and their three sons come for dinner. Chiara asks the boys if they finished their homework and wants to know about what is going on in school. She also fills Joseph in on what happened during the day.

"Joseph, do you know where my father kept his papers by any chance?"

Before Joseph can answer, Dean speaks up.

"They're in the closet. I once saw Grandpa take a metal box into the closet one time when I was coming up the stairs. It looked like a little pirate's chest. He didn't see me. I went back downstairs before he came out because I thought he wouldn't want me to know."

Chiara shakes her head. "It's not in there now."

"Ma, when he was in there, I heard some rumbling noises. It was weird."

Chiara looks at Joseph, and he shrugs his shoulders.

"Maybe it's under the floor boards and that is what Dean heard."

Before Joseph can finish, Dean runs to go upstairs to look. Chiara and Joseph follow him. Dean takes the few shoes left on the closet floor and the coats that are hanging and puts them on the couch. Joseph gets a flashlight from the bedroom bureau. As Chiara shines the light on the floor, they can see that the floor is solid linoleum.

"There isn't any hidden opening. It's not under the floor."

Then Dean, who is looking from the doorway, notices something.

"Dad, there's a piece of towel under the wall in the back."

Joseph shines the light on what looks like the small corner of a towel. He pulls it and the corner of the back wall moves. He is able to get his hand behind the wall. When he pulls the bottom half of the wall below the shelf, the wall moves out completely. He pulls that part of the wall out of the closet. When he shines the light inside the closet, he can see a small room that goes alongside the area where Anna said at one time there was supposed to have been a large storage closet before there was a staircase. Joseph hands the flashlight to Dean, who goes into the small space. He can see there is a cot, a little table with an old flashlight, and on top of the cot is a medium-sized sealed cardboard box. The rumors were true. It was the room where Enzo hid people from the police or worse.

Dean shines the light underneath the cot and he sees a gray metal chest that looks like a pirate's treasure chest. Dean pulls out the cardboard box and then the metal chest.

"Great job, Dean. We probably would have never found these things."

They all look at the small metal chest, which Dean is trying to open.

"Maybe it's full of gold coins!"

"Dean, you have a great imagination as usual!" says Chiara.

"Well, Ma, you never know!"

Chiara opens the cardboard box and sees two large brown envelopes. On one envelope is the name "Fassino," and it is sealed with a lot of tape. On the other envelope, which doesn't have a name, the seal is ripped so someone had already read the contents. Chiara places the envelopes in the box without opening them. Silently, Joseph tries to open the metal box but it is locked.

"Chiara, is there a key in the box?"

Chiara looks and shakes her head.

"No. Nothing."

Then Dean asks, "Where are Grandpa's car keys?"

Chiara looks at Joseph. "Of course. That small, old-fashioned little key that was always on his key ring. He said he kept it for luck."

Dean runs down to the kitchen where the keys are hanging behind the door.

He runs up and gives them to Joseph, who finds the key that fits and unlocks the box. When he opens it, Dean yells, "Wow!"

He tries to grab what he sees but his father stops him. It is a gun.

Chiara looks shocked. "Why did my father have a gun?"

Then she remembers. It must have been when Don Carlo's father was hiding in there. Or maybe someone else. She tells Joseph the story that her mother had told her. Both Joseph and Dean are as shocked as Chiara had been.

"Dad. Is the gun loaded?"

Joseph picks up the gun and clicks open the bullet chamber. "No."

Joseph takes out some papers and envelopes and among them are old gas ration books and immigration papers. At the bottom of the box, they see about eight bullets. Chiara is more interested in the papers and takes them from Joseph.

"The cemetery deed must be with these."

Dean hands the chest to his mother. She takes out the stack of papers that were still in the chest underneath the bullets and hands them to Joseph to examine.

"OK. Here's your father's will...and here's the cemetery deed. Oh...here is a copy of your brother's Death Certificate."

Chiara wants to ignore that. "What else is in there?"

Joseph takes out a stack of papers wrapped in an old, crumbling envelope with an elastic band.

"Chiara. This has your name on it."

Chiara takes the stack of papers and removes the elastic band that crumbles in her hand. When she removes the decaying envelope, she sees there is a stack of United States Saving Bonds with her name on them. "Oh my God! Look at this! I forgot all about these." She counts them. There are eleven bonds with different denominations that add up to $1,050.

"Mom. Are these yours? Where did they come from?"

"Yes, these are mine. They're from grammar school. The school used to have us open savings bond accounts and we would put in money every week. My father used to give me the change from his pockets and I used to go around and look for soda bottles to redeem them for pennies. I can't believe it. I forgot about these. They matured to over a thousand dollars. I now remember I gave them to my father to hide them for me. Yeah. They are mine. Joseph, wrap them up with what's left of the envelope and I'll put them in my purse. I can't believe this. Dean go downstairs and don't say anything and just get my purse."

When he returns, Dean hands his mother her purse and she takes the savings bonds and stuffs them in the bottom. She then takes the envelope marked Fassino.

"I bet I know what's in here."

She takes the unmarked envelope and opens it. There are old, yellowed papers; two pages of a handwritten letter, some other papers, and a black and white picture of a crucifix under glass. She hands them to Joseph. As Joseph is reading the papers, Chiara takes the picture of the Crucifix and walks over to the Crucifix under glass on her mother's bureau. Joseph walks in with the papers and looks at Chiara.

"You have to read this. It's not in English and it has a lot of dates and a lot of people's names and places in Italian. We need to get someone to tell us what all this means. This paper looks like it is written in Latin or Greek."

Chiara shows the picture to Joseph.

"And look at this picture. There is something written on the back in Italian and a stamp but it is blurred. We should put them in a very safe place until we can figure out what to do. This seems like really serious stuff. In the meantime, let's pack up the crucifix and bring it home. We can't keep it here and we definitely can't tell anyone; especially my brother Jack. Who knows what he would do."

"I know what he would do."

Chiara rolls her eyes and puts the papers back in the envelope.

Chiara is still looking at the picture and the Crucifix on her mother's dresser.

"It's the same cross, but it looks like it's in a painting. The rest of the painting is cropped out. I wish it was in color."

Joseph takes the picture and compares it to the Crucifix on the bureau.

"My God almighty. It is the same. What the hell?"

They both look toward the living room and see that Maria and her husband have come up the stairs and are looking at the box.

"Chiara go in there. I'll hide the papers in your mother's bedroom. Don't say anything."

Chiara walks into the living room and tells Maria and her husband that they found the papers they were looking for.

"No money," she says half-kidding and half-serious, because knowing Maria that is all she wants to know.

"Just some old papers. It must be old bills and stuff like that. Here, take a look at Papa's will. He must have just left everything to Momma. We have to have a new one made up for Momma."

Maria scans the will and doesn't seem interested since it has nothing to do with her and puts it on the coffee table.

"Chiara, Antonino, and I are going to leave. I think everyone is going anyway. I'll call you tomorrow. I'm going to say goodbye to Momma and leave."

Chiara and Joseph are happy that everyone is leaving.

"OK. Call me tomorrow. Where's your husband?"

"He's getting Momma a sweater in case she's cold."

"Ok. Tell him we'll see him tomorrow."

As they left, Chiara went into the bedroom.

Joseph hid the papers underneath the mattress.

"Until we can get the papers out of here, your mother is going to sleep on them. When everyone leaves let's show the papers about the cross to your mother and see if she can translate them. Maybe she even knows a lot more about it than what's in the envelope."

"That's a good idea, but I don't want to do it until after the funeral. You should have been there today when she went after Jack and Margo. I don't know what got into her, but whatever it was I'm glad. I'm sick of always being the bad guy. My mother had enough drama for a while. You should have been there. Margo almost died. The expression on her face! I wish I had a camera!"

They hear Anna calling Chiara.

"Be right down, Ma."

When she goes downstairs, Dean is sitting next to Anna holding her hand.

"Dean said you found the papers. Is the deed for the house there?"

"I think so. There were some old mortgage papers and I thought I saw a deed with them."

"Get me the deed. I am holding on to it and don't tell anyone I have it. Then have them try to sell the house."

Chiara doesn't know what to say. She will do what her mother asks. She looks at Dean and knows he must have given her the idea. Clever boy.

"Ma, we also saw some papers about the Crucifix," Chiara says.

Anna looked at Chiara for a second. "You bring that Crucifix to the funeral home and put it next to your father."

Considering the papers she just read about the Crucifix, Chiara says, "Ma, I don't think that is a good idea."

Anna quickly cut her off. "I want it there."

Chiara knew it was not good to argue with her mother.

Chapter 16
Summer, 1964 - As Jack reviews the bankbook, his jaw drops.

On East Clifton Avenue people live in their homes until they die or move in with one of their children. After the Buonoforte children married and left the house, Anna and Enzo planned to live out the rest of their days in their Clifton Avenue home, not even considering ever having to leave, but for Anna, that would not be and time would change everything.

A few months after Enzo had passed away, it had become more and more difficult for Anna to live alone. Except for Chiara, none of Anna's other children could or were willing to offer to have Anna move in with them. It was Chiara, the seventh of Enzo's and Anna's eight children, and Chiara's husband Joseph and their children, whom Anna had been living with for almost three years. Anna stays in Dean's room, the oldest son, now fifteen years old, where there are two twin beds, a chair, and a small dresser. Dean keeps his clothes and belongings in the hall closet.

But now, because of Anna's failing health, there seems to be no choice but to provide Anna with full-time care. As a young girl in Sicily, Anna was a slim and petite beauty. She had dark, almost black hair, which was always piled on top of her head. She had a beautiful smile and skin like alabaster. After years of struggles, and having eight children, Anna is now heavyset, with almost no teeth and difficulties wearing bottom dentures, where she has no teeth. Her hair is still piled on her head but it's now completely white. She is close to eighty and her age and weight make it difficult for her to even get out of a chair without being helped. Once she gets up, her knees are in almost constant pain, and the hardening of her arteries, which affects her equilibrium and her ability to balance, makes walking very difficult. Also, Anna has had to make trips to the emergency room because of cuts on her head that needed stitches due to a fall when she lost her balance in the middle of the night while going to the bathroom. As Chiara's husband Joseph puts it, "The mind is willing, but the flesh is weak." The time is coming close when Anna will need constant attention, but that is not on the minds of the other Buonoforte children, especially Jack and Maria. Their concerns are elsewhere.

For it was Jack who, almost immediately after his father died, was not concerned about his mother but about whether the money was all being deposited in Anna's bank account. Even after being reassured by Chiara, Jack tried to find out the account balance and the account's activity by going directly to the bank, but the bank refused to give out that information. Jack even asked friends who worked at the bank to look into his mother's account, but the bank employees would not put their jobs on the line. Jack's failure resulted in an "unholy alliance" between Jack, Margo, and his sister Maria and her husband Antonino. Jack tried to recruit his other brothers and sisters, but they didn't want to be involved. Finally, with Margo pestering him, Jack was pushed to directly confront Chiara about Anna's bank account. He figured he would go in the afternoon when Chiara's husband Joseph was at work. Joseph has a temper and has little patience for the nonsense that Chiara's family is putting his wife through. Joseph has a history of problems with Jack, and it was only because of Chiara's pleading that Joseph didn't knock Jack "into the middle of next week," as Joseph put it. No, Jack didn't want to face Joseph.

One Thursday afternoon when Joseph was at work, Jack arrived at Chiara's house unexpectedly. When Chiara opens the door to let him in, they kiss and are cordial with one another. Chiara isn't surprised because she knows why he is there. *It was only a matter of time*, she thought. Jack goes into the living room where Anna is sitting, kisses her, and makes some small talk. The conversation is brief. Anna wonders why Jack is there, but she knows it isn't to see her. How unusual. It isn't strange when Chiara's youngest brother Donny drops in to see Anna and Chiara. But it is strange for Jack. He wants something, and Chiara knows exactly what it is. Chiara doesn't go into the living room with Jack and Anna but stays in the kitchen filling a teapot. Then after a few minutes, Jack walks into the kitchen. They make little eye contact. Jack sits down at the table and offers some small talk about how Joseph and the kids are, and Chiara reciprocates with the same about Margo and Jack's sons.

"Jack, do you want a cup of tea?"

Jack doesn't respond. Chiara gets two cups and saucers anyway and puts a teabag in each cup. There is a deadly silence. A few moments go by and Jack finally gets up the nerve to ask what he came for.

"I want to see Momma's bank book."

Chiara was right. This is what he came for. She doesn't look at him and calmly continues what she is doing, taking the hot tea kettle off the stove and pouring hot water into each cup. *Wow,* she thinks to herself, *right to the point. How nervous he must be.* She will just play along. Without saying a word, she puts the tea kettle back on the stove.

"Why are you so interested in Momma's bank book?"

Chiara knows exactly why he is interested and she wants to make it as uncomfortable as possible for him. Jack is speaking just above a whisper and Chiara is talking louder than normal. *Let Momma hear,* Chiara thinks, *I'm so sick of hiding everything and protecting her.* But at the same time, she can't stand to see her mother hurt. This time she doesn't care. She tries to fight the small resentment because of her mother, but sometimes it rears its ugly head. Now Chiara will be subjected to this questioning. Anna is also not the same woman who challenged Jack and Margo so openly after Enzo died. Even though it was only three years since Enzo's death, Anna has aged rapidly. Now she just ignores things that would have ordinarily bothered her. In some ways, she gave up and let Chiara bear the brunt of many things and Chiara knows it. She also knows she has no choice and that is the root of the resentment.

"Chiara, I only just want to see how much she has in it."

"Why? Do you want to make a contribution?" she asks mockingly.

Jack doesn't answer.

Chiara takes a small pitcher of milk out of the refrigerator, places it on the table, and then looks at him almost eye to eye and pushes him again.

"Why Jack? Why do you want to see Momma's bank book?"

"I am just curious. I want to make sure she has enough in there..."

"Jack, that's bull. Who are you kidding?"

She stands over him with her right hand on her hip. "I know why you want to know."

She leans over him. "Jack, the money is all there. You can't take my word for it?"

A moment of silence goes by and then the tone changes as she stands back up.

"Goddamn it! All you care about is the money! Or maybe it's your wife who cares. It is always about your wife and money, isn't it, Jack?"

She sees Jack is nervous and stirring the tea without looking at her. Then he looks up.

"Chiara, do you have to yell, for Christ's sake?"

Jack is more than startled. He has never seen this side of Chiara. *My God*, he thinks, *what can of worms did I just open?*

"What are you worried about? Huh? Your mother may hear? Why don't you ask your mother to see the bank book? It's hers. See what she says. You know Papa would knock you on your ass if he was alive. But then again, you wouldn't try to pull this crap with him."

"I just want to see how much is in there."

"No, you don't. You really only care if I'm using the money. Or your wife is worried about if I'm using the money. Who the hell are you kidding? And you know what? If I want to use the money, I can. It isn't fair that my husband has to work to help support us, AND my son has to share a room with Momma, *AND* I have to entertain everyone who comes to see her."

Jack's eyes widen because he thinks this is Chiara's way of rationalizing that she should use the money. His wife, Maria, and Antonino were right! He has caught her in the act, and he will insist he takes care of the account. Then Chiara turns the conversation around.

"What do you do to help? We all agreed that you and the five others would take turns taking Momma for one Sunday so we could take the kids out for the day. And what do you and your wife do when it's your turn? You pick her up late and bring her back early. That's a real big help."

Normally Chiara tries to avoid confrontation so everyone can just "get along," but now her nerves are rattled and she can no longer hold her tongue.

"I have to take care of this house, do the cooking and cleaning for my husband, my three kids, and now Momma—I don't mind doing it, but who the hell do you people think you are questioning me without doing a goddamn thing? My son is a teenager and Momma is sleeping in the same room, in HIS room, and he has to help her in the bathroom at night. Now Momma needs more and more attention. You come here and bring her some bullshit candy and everything is great. Maria and Antonino saw what happened a couple of weeks ago when they were here."

Jack doesn't look at her. "Yeah, I heard."

"Yeah, you heard."

Chiara doesn't care if he heard. She tells him what happened anyway. Chiara had asked Maria and Antonino if they could come early to sit with Anna and the kids while Joseph and she went to the doctor. Dean was sitting in the kitchen with Maria and Antonino serving them tea. Anna was sitting in the living room watching television. Suddenly they all heard a thump and a bang. Without asking for help, Anna got up and went to the bathroom. She lost her balance and fell into the bathtub. Maria, Antonino, and Dean ran to the bathroom. Dean and Antonino helped Anna get up. Maria was visibly shaken. Anna wasn't hurt this time. When Anna was settled into her chair, Maria scolded her.

"Momma. Ask for help. We'll help you."

Anna just waved her hand. Then for the first time, Anna spoke up.

"When will you help me? Later tonight? Early tomorrow morning?

When, Maria?

Maria didn't answer. She didn't know how to answer. Anna just looked away at the television. Without saying a word, Maria and Antonino returned to the kitchen. Dean, seeing how upset Maria was and how awkward the situation escorted Maria back to the kitchen.

"Aunt Maria, now you know what my mother goes through."

Neither Maria nor Antonino said a word. That comment set the stage for their realization that Anna needed constant care and it was impossible for Chiara and her family to provide it.

After Chiara tells Jack the story, she gets louder.

"Did Maria explain it to you like that? I can't relax without worrying if she is going to fall and get hurt. How can I be related to you? You and your sister Maria...what kind of family are you? How could you treat me, your sister, who is taking care of *our* mother with such selfishness, never mind your mother? How can you treat *our* mother, your father's wife who he loved and would want to be taken care of after he's gone, and you don't do a damn thing to help but worry about her bank book. Shame on you. Shame on all of you."

Jack doesn't want to acknowledge what Chiara is saying. "Would you quiet down, Momma is in the other room."

"She knows what's going on. You think she's stupid. She knows who gives a shit and who doesn't care."

Chiara is right. Anna knows exactly what is happening. Jack and Margo don't care about her. And what about Maria and Antonino living alone in their big house? But Anna suspects it is mostly Maria and not Antonino who is concerned about the money. Maria is lazy and Anna is an inconvenience. Anna knows that when it is Margo and Jack's Sunday to take her for the day, Margo will make Jack take her back sooner than agreed with the other brothers and sisters. Anna sees how Margo's mood changes in the early afternoon. She wants Anna home. Anna only goes to Jack and Margo's to give Chiara a break. Secretly, Anna disliked Margo from the first time Jack brought her home. Margo would fuss over Enzo, and sit on his lap and Anna resented it. Women just didn't do that kind of thing. She tolerated Margo to keep the peace. Even with her own children she tolerated a lot, but kept quiet to "keep the peace." Then there was the business of Margo stealing Jack away from Sofia. Sofia could have made a man out of him instead of the coward that he is now.

Jack shows no concern that his mother needs full-time care. Instead, he insists again, "I wanna see the bankbook."

Chiara looks at him for a few seconds and doesn't say a word. She goes into her bedroom, and when she comes out, she flings the bankbook in Jack's face, almost hitting his eye. She doesn't care. She is more hurt than angry.

"This is what we've come to. Here! Look for yourself. You can't take my word."

Jack gets the bankbook and thinks he has won. As Jack reviews the bankbook, his jaw drops. He is in shock. For the past three years, there have been only deposits. Jack and the others were sure Chiara was using the money. Jack sees there is not one withdrawal, just deposits on almost the same day of every month for both the rent and Anna's Social Security checks. Now he knows Chiara will pounce. And in a strange way, he knows he deserves what is coming.

"What do see, Jack?! Huh! Disappointed?! You and your wife and Maria and Antonino only give a damn about the money. What do you see? Only deposits! You only give a damn about the money. What do you do to help your mother other than worry if I'm using the money?

There is silence.

"Va! Go tell the others the money is safe, but don't be too sure. If you piss me off, I may just empty the account and there isn't a damn thing any of you can do about it, because I have *power of attorney.* Do you know what that is, Jack? I can take everything. I can sell the house, take the money, and there isn't a damn thing any of you can do. So, I suggest you don't piss me off, Jack, and tell the others the same." Chiara tries not to show that she is shaking, but it is hard.

Now Jack wonders if he should even tell the others about Chiara's threat. Maybe it was a mistake to even confront Chiara. No. He won't tell the others. They would ultimately blame him if she did take everything. After all, the money is still in the account. He feels Chiara won't touch the money. At least that is what he convinces himself. As he begins to leave, Chiara speaks again.

"And remember, it's your turn to take Momma this Sunday. Don't pick her up late and bring her back early like you usually do. We have plans. Don't think you're gonna call and say you're leaving to bring her back. We won't be home until dinner time. Just make your wife a couple more drinks."

Jack doesn't say a word. Chiara has the upper hand. He isn't used to Chiara talking to him this way, and he wants to avoid any arguments. He doesn't want his mother, who is sitting in the living room just a few feet away, to hear any arguing. He also doesn't want to piss off Chiara. No. He doesn't want to piss off Chiara. She is arguing from a position of strength.

Jack puts the bankbook on the table without saying a word or making eye contact. He knows Chiara is right. *Damn, Margo*, he thinks. Before Jack got married, Chiara and Jack were close. But as time went on, they grew apart, mostly because of his wife Margo, but also because Jack was somewhat different than some of his brothers and sisters. He had a darker side; a cold side, an unaffectionate side. That was one of the reasons their relationship grew further apart. Jack's attitude toward their parents and the family was different than hers. Now, after this confrontation, they probably would never get close again. Jack's wife had too much of a grip on him and she was tearing the family apart. People were also beginning to suspect her outbursts were being fueled by alcohol, so they stayed away.

Chiara looks straight at Jack as she picks up the bankbook, and then pokes him on the chest.

"Say goodbye to your mother before you leave. And, by the way, when was the last time you brought your sons over to see your mother? They are never there when you take Momma over to your house; they're always at your in-laws. Unless of course, it's a birthday, Christmas, or Easter. Then they make sure they see her for their card and money."

Jack doesn't say a word or look at Chiara. She puts his teacup in the sink, turns away from Jack, goes into the bedroom, and slams the door. Jack goes into the living room where his mother is watching TV, kisses her, and says goodbye.

"State bene," Anna says as Jack kisses her on the cheek without looking at him.

Anna has heard almost everything that was being said. She knows it was about her and her money. After Jack leaves, Anna is reminded that she loves all her children, but there are a couple who she just doesn't really like. She fights back her tears. She never likes to show her emotions. It is something she learned when she was a young girl living in Sicily. Showing one's emotions was considered a sign of weakness when no one could afford to look weak in order to survive.

Chapter 17

"Just sell the damn house."

After three years of living in the Fonte household, with Anna falling and incontinent, she needs constant attention. She can no longer handle basic personal hygiene chores, like bathing and going to the bathroom alone. There seems to be no other choice but to place Anna in a facility that can take care of her on a full-time basis. A nursing home seems the only choice. The decision is difficult but necessary.

Anna's care is taking a toll on Chiara's health. Her nerves are frayed worrying about her mother's wellbeing, as well as the growing tensions with some of her brothers, sisters, and in-laws. It is taking a toll on Chiara's family, too. It is Joseph who makes Chiara realize the situation with her mother is taking time away from him and their children, and that if anything happened to her mother, Chiara won't forgive herself. The decision has to be made, but for Chiara, it seems like she is abandoning her mother. There is no choice.

For some of Chiara's brothers and sisters, it is an emotional decision, but for others, it is first and foremost a financial concern. You can split them into two groups: those who are concerned for their mother and those who are concerned about the money. There is another aspect of the situation that it seems no one talks about except when Dean discusses it with his father.

"Dad, does anyone care how Grandma feels?"

In a way, Joseph is surprised at Dean's mature perception of the situation; sometimes around his brothers, he can be so immature.

"That's a good point. I think you're talking about her 'dignity.' The idea that all her life she was proud and strong and now she has to hide the embarrassment that her body is failing her."

"I heard Mom talking on the phone and saying that Grandma is failing. I kinda figured that is what she meant. I can't talk to Grandma about it. I can't."

"That is not your responsibility. Your mother and I are doing that. Remember something. It doesn't matter what everyone else does or doesn't do. That is something you have to learn. Don't concern yourself with that. There is no such thing in life as, 'what's fair and not fair.' It doesn't matter. There are reasons for things happening that we may not have the answers to. Do what is right and in your heart and learn from it. The Man upstairs sees. Also, no matter what happens during this whole thing, don't hate or ever use the word hate. You know I don't want any of you boys using that word. I hate that word!"

They both need a laugh. Joseph feels things are getting too serious. He doesn't want to go on because he sees that Dean is trying to make sense of everything, and like his mother, he hides his emotions. Joseph realizes that for Dean, his grandfather's death, was just the beginning of a lot of heartache that Dean will experience in the future. With Chiara being the seventh child and Joseph being the third child in his family, everyone is getting on in years. Joseph will try to prepare Dean for what is to come over the next few years, but because Dean hides his emotions, it may be hard for Joseph to see if he is getting through to him. For Joseph, as a parent, and for the first time seeing their child grow into an adult, knowing the hardships ahead they will face, is a sad experience.

After the decision is made that Anna needs twenty-four-hour care, a family meeting is held at Chiara and Joseph's house with Anna's sons and daughters and some of their respective spouses. A decision must be made on how to finance the nursing home. The cordiality of everyone arriving leads to an awkward silence with sudden bursts of small talk.

Joseph quiets everyone down and reminds them that since Anna moved in with them and the East Clifton Avenue house is rented, the money from the rent and Anna's Social Security will almost cover all the monthly nursing home fees. Another odd thing, but not surprising, is there is no mention of any gratitude for taking care of Anna for over three years, not to mention it was at Chiara and Joseph's expense as well.

The difference needed could be taken from Anna's small savings, and when the savings run out, they could all share the difference. While Joseph is talking, Dante and a couple of others begin to nod; but even before Joseph finishes talking, Jack stands up in his typical arrogant stance, completely disregarding what Joseph is saying, and begins in his usual obnoxious bravado, "Just sell the damn house."

Chiara looks over at Jack's wife Margo and knows what Margo is thinking. Margo will never want to help her mother-in-law, and at that moment Chiara wants to take a wooden spoon and smack Margo in the middle of her face because Margo has the phony smile she wears when she is with the Buonoforte family. Margo was eventually referred to by some as "faccia brutta," "ugly face" or "shark eyes," because of her dark, and black, dead eyes. When Margo is with Jack's family, she just sits on the sidelines with her phony grin and gossips with anyone willing to listen to her. Unless she is with her mother and brother, Margo is not happy. Because of Jack's usual bravado in front of everyone, it is a surprise that he is so weak and allows Margo to push him around. The only arguments Chiara and Joseph seem to have are over how Joseph feels some of Chiara's family take advantage of her. Whenever something needs to be done for her parents, it seems Chiara is the one to get the call. Most times Joseph doesn't mind because Chiara is so good to Joseph's mother and family, but sometimes there are limits with Chiara's family.

There was this one time when Chiara, Joseph, and their kids were visiting on the usual Friday night at the Clifton Avenue house. When Jack, Margo, and their two sons arrive, Jack comes in like he owns the place and starts to bark out orders. Margo walks in with a box of cookies as if it is gold. Most of the time she has either a scowl or that phony smile on her face. It becomes known to everyone that Margo only likes to be with her own family.

The last straw for Joseph and the Friday night visits was when on one

Friday, Jack walked in and told Chiara and Joseph's oldest son Dean to stand so Jack's older son Donald could sit. Joseph told Dean to stay seated and his stare at Jack had him backing off with Jack telling his son to go get a chair in the kitchen and bring it in. From then on, Joseph and Jack were just civil to each other and Joseph and Dean stopped coming on the usual Friday nights, but Chiara continued to come with one of her other sons. Joseph was one of the only people who could intimidate Jack, and Jack knew it.

The family meeting is taking way too much time, with way too much tension. A few moments after Jack says the house should be sold, tensions can be felt as everyone is now talking over each other trying to get their points across regarding how to pay for Anna's nursing home care. Antonino also suggests selling the house, but Chiara insists the house be rented because if they sell it, Anna may outlive the funds from the house, and then what would they do? There is silence.

Over Chiara's objections, the decision is made to sell the house. Social Security will pay for most of the cost of the nursing home and the rest will be paid with the money from the sale of the house. They also agree that a certain amount will be put aside for funeral costs, which doesn't matter because it is something Chiara has already taken care of.

Everyone can see that Chiara is fuming. No one except Joseph and Donny came to her side. It even took a brother-in-law, Dante, Rita's husband, to come to Chiara's side. It is no surprise because it was Dante's idea to increase the amount of money they gave to Anna and Enzo each month, to the subtle but vocal resentment of some. Out of the corner of her eye, Chiara sees that Margo is whispering something to Jack, and then Jack looks at Chiara. Chiara knows what Margo was whispering and Chiara is ready to say that the money will stay in her control. She gives Jack a cold stare and he doesn't say anything because Jack already knew the money wasn't being touched after he saw his mother's bank book. He never said anything because of Chiara's threat to use the money if anyone steps out of line. Margo looks at Jack, but he ignores her. Chiara is ready to tell everyone what happened that Thursday afternoon. The gloves are off.

There is silence until Chiara speaks up, looking at Jack and smiling. "Don't worry, Jack. Maybe Momma will die before the money runs out."

Maria and a couple of others gasp.

Chiara looks around. "Come on. I'm not stupid. Don't think I don't know that's what you're worried about."

Silence

Before the meeting ends, Chiara stands and says there is one thing more. She looks directly at Jack. "You decide who is going to do it, but one of you is going to tell Momma. We've done enough. By the way, I don't have the deed to the house. You're going to have to ask Momma for it."

But as it happens and no surprise, no one volunteers and time is running out. The next day, with the boys out of the house playing, Chiara and Joseph sit down with Anna and it is Joseph who explains the situation. Chiara doesn't say anything because she would just break down. Characteristically, Anna doesn't show any emotion and just accepts it without any questions. Joseph walks Anna to her room and helps her into her chair. Anna tells Joseph to go to the dresser and get the deed to her house. Too weak to fight, she gives up.

After Joseph leaves the room, Anna tries to muffle the sound of her gentle crying. "How did things come to this?" she quietly says to herself. She thinks of Enzo and the two of them in Sicily. Maybe they should have gone back there. She looks over at the top of the dresser and sees the heavy hairbrush with the tortoiseshell back and silver handle, and goes from crying to laughing. She laughs so hard she has to muffle the sound, thinking that her daughter and son-in-law will think she has gone crazy. She and Enzo had many laughs about the hairbrush. She feels a little better for the moment. But just for the moment.

Chapter 18
"God's waiting room."

Life was hard in the early part of the twentieth century, and people didn't live long enough or have the money to be put in a nursing home. For many the idea was just unheard of. When parents couldn't take care of themselves or when a parent outlived their spouse, they either lived alone or were forced to live with one of their children until the parent died. Unfortunately, some elderly parents were just abandoned by their children who moved away or didn't care, and it was left up to relatives or kind neighbors to help care for them. Worse case, the state had to step in.

As time went on, with the help of new medical discoveries, people were living longer and things began to change. Because of the increasing mortality rate of older people, children of elderly parents now had an alternative. Nursing homes were becoming more popular but were also becoming more crowded. And like other families with elderly parents, it wouldn't be easy to get Anna into a nursing home. There are long waiting lists, and unless you have more money than the next person, or you know someone who could put you at the top of the list, the wait could be months and even years.

The nursing home closest to Chiara and Joseph is the Paramus Nursing home, only about a fifteen-minute car ride. It has a good reputation, but like several other nursing homes, it is at capacity. Plans are being made for an addition with more rooms, but that will be a couple of years away. It is fortunate that Chiara's sister-in-law, Dorothy, her brother

Donny's wife, knows the head nurse at the Paramus nursing home and at least was able to get her an appointment with the woman in charge of the nursing home, Mrs. Avero. But it would not be as simple or easy as just knowing the head nurse to get Anna a room. It would almost take some luck or maybe a miracle.

Chiara pulls into the nursing home parking lot and sits in her car trying to collect her thoughts. Joseph was at work, and unless one of her brothers or sisters volunteered to come with her, she would rather go alone. She has her pride, and sometimes it is to her detriment. There were times when she should have said something but didn't. Even though there may have been honorable intent, something should have been said. This is one of those times. Chiara never thought about what would happen if either one of her parents died, and of course never thought of ending their days alone in a nursing home in Paramus, New Jersey. It is a town neither Anna nor Enzo ever traveled to or were familiar with...not as if that would make much of a difference. To Anna, it is the other side of the world and a world she doesn't want to live in. Clifton was her home for most of her life, not a world where people sit in a wheelchair watching the other nursing home residents "waiting" in their different stages of decay in a place some refer to as, "God's waiting room."

After sitting in her car for what seems like an eternity, Chiara grabs the door handle of the car and tries to think. *Isn't there a better solution than this?* She lets go of the car handle and thinks of the conversation in the kitchen with her son Dean when Chiara and her husband told him that his grandmother was going into a nursing home. Thinking about the reality of the situation upset her again because Dean was telling it how it really was going to be, which they tried to ignore and concentrate on what had to be done.

"You mean that Grandma is going into a home where she doesn't know anyone and she is going to stay there for the rest of her life?"

Joseph looked at his son and he saw the anger building up in him. Dean was much like his mother in that respect. Like his mother, he did not like to show his emotions, but Joseph saw in his face that his emotions were building. Joseph glanced at Chiara to pick up where he left off.

Joseph was resentful of Chiara's family for being put in this position; for Chiara being put in this position. Joseph could see that Chiara wasn't going to further explain. Joseph was going to have to and he chose to explain things sternly.

"Your grandmother cannot be left alone. She has hardening of the arteries, and it affects her equilibrium and she loses her balance. You see what happens when she falls. She doesn't listen to your mother when your mother is trying to work around the house, and she gets out of her chair and falls. Your mother is getting sick over this."

Dean ignored his father and looked directly at his mother, who was fighting back tears. Joseph could see that Dean was getting teary as well.

"Why can't we get help? When I get home from school, I sit with Grandma and do my homework. I comb her hair and wash her feet. I take her to the bathroom. It isn't hard. Why can't we get help from your family?"

Chiara knew why. Some of her brothers and sisters' families do not have the finances, or they have a large family and no room. Others who do have the room and the means just won't do anything. She is both ashamed and protective even with being put in the position of placing Anna in a nursing home and trying to explain it to her son. She ignored Dean's question. Joseph continued the conversation. Joseph was trying to check his anger, not because he was getting mad having to explain the situation, but the resentment that was building up against Chiara's family.

"Dean, your grandmother needs constant care. She is getting too old and her mind is also getting old where she can't think about things like she used to."

Dean ignored his father's explanation.

"Ma, your family should help. Talk to them. Don't they know she is going to be living like in a hospital? Don't they care?"

Chiara wanted to stop the conversation. Again, Joseph tried to explain.

"She's going into the nursing home because they can take care of her better there. It's too much here. There is no choice. We've tried. That's it."

Chiara couldn't look at Dean. She wasn't only upset at the situation but she was ashamed of her brothers and sisters. No. She felt the resentment probably more than Joseph.

Dean got up from his seat and pushed his chair hard into the table.

"This is bullshit. And your family is bullshit. All that some of them care about is money. I heard what went on in that meeting. I heard you talking to Dad. This is all bullshit."

Joseph spoke up.

"Hey! Watch your language in front of your mother."

Dean ignored him. "I am never talking to your family again. I would never do that to you and Daddy. Never! And I don't care what you told me. I HATE them!"

Joseph ignored his comment. Was he beginning to hate them?

"Dean, this is hard on your mother. How do think she feels? Your grandmother is failing. She is wetting herself more often. And she keeps falling. How would you feel…"

Dean loudly interrupted, "I take her to the bathroom all the time. Put some diapers on her. I don't know but…."

Chiara didn't want to hear anymore. It was difficult as it was and she wanted to end the conversation.

"Look. This is the best thing for her. I'm getting sick over this, and I am no good to anyone if I'm sick." She was starting to get more upset.

"Mom, I get it, but this is still bullshit."

He walked away.

"BULLSHIT!"

He walked into his room and slammed the door. He didn't want to see his mother cry. He also had to shield his emotions. Dean was glad that it was Sunday and his grandmother was not around to listen to the argument about the nursing home.

In the kitchen, Chiara turned to her husband. "He's right. This is bullshit." She stood up and went to their bedroom

"Yeah," Joseph whispered to himself. "This is bullshit." He stood there and tried to decide whether to leave Dean alone in his room or again try to explain the situation. Instead, he went to comfort Chiara because the decision to put her mother in a nursing home, even if for no one else, for Chiara would be heartbreaking.

It was planned that the situation would be discussed on a Sunday and Anna was picked up by her son Donny for the day, which was a delight for Anna. As Dean sat on his bed and looked at Anna's empty chair, he could hear his parents talking through his bedroom wall, which was up against his parent's room. He then leaned back and looked at the ceiling. "Bullshit." He already knew his mother made the appointment with the nursing home and there was nothing he could do about it.

He began to remember so many times he would make jokes before he and his grandmother went to sleep. One time when she just started falling asleep, the room was dark and he tickled her on her neck with a feather he had found outside that day. She kept brushing it away cursing in Italian, thinking it was a bug, until she realized it was Dean. They laughed so hard and loud, that Chiara had to come in and see what was going on. Anna was laughing so hard she couldn't explain what happened and Dean ran after his mother with the feather, with her running and screaming, "You're going to drive me crazy, stop!" Then Joseph came in and it started all over until Joseph put a stop to it.

"Go to sleep! Now stop."

Dean lay in his bed and remembered how his grandmother and he laughed themselves to sleep that night.

"She's not going to no nursing home. I'll figure a way to put a stop to it."

But he couldn't and he knew it.

Chapter 19

"Dean, you're right.
There has to be another way."

Chiara finally steps out of the car, stands there, and takes a couple of seconds to look at this big house that has been converted into a nursing home. She walks up to the steps and again whispers to herself.

"Dean, you're right. There has to be another way. But what?"

When she reaches the top of the stairs and opens the door, she sees a janitor mopping the floor. When she steps inside the foyer, she is instantly greeted with the smell of antiseptic cleaners and urine, which is strong enough to almost take Chiara's breath away. It is a smell that will stay with her for a long time. Her expression is of disgust, but she tries not to show it. As if walking in slow motion Chiara looks around for the reception desk. She hears the muffled sound of someone moaning from what must be one of the bedrooms toward the far end of the facility. An elderly patient in a wheelchair to her left is asking anyone who passes by if they know where her mother is. A couple of nurses are running from one room to what looks like a storeroom, taking out sheets and towels and running into one of what she thought must be bedrooms. Toward the back of the large reception area, she sees wheelchairs lined up in front of a television. Some residents look like they are watching while a couple of others are rocking back and forth and mumbling. One of the residents is crying to what looks like her daughter, who is trying to comfort her.

Near them on another couch, an old man is just staring into the distance while someone who might be his son is ignoring him and reading a newspaper. Everything seems to be whirling around Chiara, which increases her sense of sadness, anxiety, and hopelessness. What appears like the normal activities of a nursing home seem to Chiara like organized chaos and she is overwhelmed.

"How can I leave my mother here?" she says to herself. Suddenly, a passing nurse startles her. At first, Chiara doesn't know if it is a real nurse or a resident. The nurse has flaming red hair, bright red lipstick, rouged cheeks, and false eyelashes.

"Excuse me, honey. Can I help you?"

The nurse can tell Chiara isn't there to visit someone because she looks so disturbed and disoriented.

"Oh, oh, I am here to see the administrator..." Chiara looks at the paper she takes out of her pocket, "...a Mrs. Avero about my mother."

"Follow me, honey. The receptionist is over there to the left."

Chiara timidly nods, follows the nurse, and is introduced to Ms. Peterson, the receptionist.

The receptionist smiles at the nurse and thanks her, "Oh, by the way, Mrs. Peterson, Mrs. Mayer is asking if the doctor is going to come today to see her leg. It's still swollen."

"I will check it out and let her know. Thank you."

The receptionist, like everyone who first sees the nurse, is a little shocked.

"That is Mrs. Preston. She is a very good nurse."

"Oh. I am sure."

"Now how can I help *you?*"

Chiara gives her name and the receptionist looks at the day sheet where all the appointments are written and she sees Chiara's name and hands her a few papers.

"Mrs. Fonte, your appointment is for 1:00. Please fill out these papers at that table over there. When you're done, please bring them up and I will bring you in to see the nursing home administrator, Mrs. Avero, at 1:00."

Then suddenly an old woman comes up to the receptionist. "Lollipop, lollipop!"

Without even looking at the woman the receptionist hands the old woman a small lollipop. The old woman unwraps it and walks away with a big smile on her face. Again, Chiara is startled as she watches the woman walk away wondering if it is a wise thing to give the woman a lollipop. What if she choked? Then Chiara slightly leans over the counter. She wants to get out of there as soon as possible. *Why did she come alone?*

"Do you think there is a little chance for my mother?" Chiara quietly asked as she takes the papers and looks at the receptionist, waiting for an answer. She wants any sign of hope. The receptionist shuffles some papers to avoid eye contact, and answers in a very business-like tone. She is used to this question and after a while, she has little patience. After all, it isn't up to her.

"What I know is that there is a long waiting list, but you never know."

The receptionist looks up and sees the desperate look on Chiara's face. It is a look she is not unfamiliar with. But she pities Chiara, just like she pities many of the other people either trying to get their parents in the nursing home or leaving them there to live. But she continues in her business tone.

"Now please fill out the papers I handed you. Please fill out both sides and bring them back to me, and I will bring them to Mrs. Avero, the nursing home administrator at 1:00. Also, make sure you print your name and sign it at the bottom of the third page."

Silently Chiara shakes the receptionist's hand. She doesn't know why she just thinks it is the thing to do. She takes the papers to a small table by a large picture window, sits down, and begins to fill them out. She stops and stares at the papers, and again she realizes that this is how her mother would spend the last days of her life. Her desperate feelings begin to overwhelm her.

After all those years of struggle, sacrifice, and brief periods of happiness, this is how it ends? This is it? She doesn't make the statement in reflection but in anger.

Chiara leans back into the soft cushioned chair. She stares out the window and begins to remember the stories her father told her about growing up in Sicily and the struggle to come to America, eventually first settling in Little Italy in the lower part of Manhattan with thousands of other immigrants. Some of the only jobs available in Little Italy were working in the hot kitchens of restaurants, where Enzo and Anna were lucky to find work. Thinking of her father telling her the stories of those times puts a smile on Chiara's face, remembering how her father told her everything with so much emotion and passion. Suddenly she realizes the image of him and the sound of his voice are already growing fuzzy. She would have to keep the memories alive somehow or they would be eventually forgotten. Yes. She will think of his stories and remember as much as she can, especially of his struggles growing up in Sicily and their struggles as immigrants. There was no social assistance of any kind. Even if there were, she knew her father wouldn't have taken it. He was too proud. She is like him. Living through the depression herself, Chiara learned many lessons and never took anything or anyone for granted. She is independent: A survivor.

Chiara sees out the window some of the residents being brought to the garden in their wheelchairs. Six of them are being lined up in a row in front of a small fountain. A couple of the residents are talking to each other, and the remaining few are either rocking back and forth or falling asleep. An attendant tries to calm down a man who is waving his hands and yelling. The resident spits at the attendant. For a moment Chiara thinks the attendant is going to hit the man, but the attendant wipes his shirt and seems to tell the resident not to do that again. The resident drops his head down and the attendant walks to his side and hugs him. Seeing this, a couple of tears ran down Chiara's cheeks. *How could things come to this?* she thinks and shakes her head. She keeps thinking that with everything her parents did for their children, why can't her brothers and sisters help their mother now knowing this is their mother's fate? Even though the whole process of the nursing home was discussed with Chiara's brothers and sisters, no one else came besides Donny and his wife to see the facility and talk to Donny's wife's friend to get the appointment. Chiara knew that everyone else would suddenly be too busy, just not interested, or too afraid and guilty to visit the nursing home. No. Chiara must bear the burden, but she doesn't care. As she said to Joseph, "She's my mother. I don't care what everyone else does."

Joseph, thinking of his own mother, just nodded.

Chiara looks down at the papers. She sees them as a blur through her tear-filled eyes. A couple of tears fall on the papers and begin to smear the ink, and she wipes it, making the smeared words even worse. As she tries to wipe the tears from the paper, a woman walks up to the table with papers in her hand and startles Chiara. The woman asks if she can sit down. Chiara, momentarily embarrassed, wipes her cheeks, smiles, and gestures to the woman to sit down. The woman pulls out the chair and sits down. Then after a few moments, the woman breaks the silence.

"This is a horrible thing to have to do. I never thought in a million years I would be putting my mother in a home. She was so active. So alive."

It doesn't seem to matter whether or not Chiara is listening. The woman has to say what is on her mind probably even if no one was sitting there. Chiara nods and asks after a moment, "Are you placing your mother or your father?"

The woman seems annoyed that Chiara hasn't been listening. She shuffles through the papers and says again, "My mother."

Even though the woman is still talking, Chiara is too distracted to really listen, but the woman continues, "My mother is only going on a waiting list so I don't know if this is a waste of time. We just can't take care of her anymore. My father died two years ago and my mother has what the doctor calls 'dementia.' She is getting worse, and I am an only child. I have two children and they help, but it isn't enough. My mother gets up and wanders off looking for my father. Do you have any children?"

"Yes. I have three boys. My older son is..."

The woman starts to cry, interrupting Chiara, who doesn't know what to say to comfort her and just reaches out and holds the woman's hand; but the woman can't stop crying. Finally, the receptionist comes over with tissues, puts her hand on the woman's shoulder, and calms her down.

Mrs. Peterson sees the situation is uncomfortable.

"Mrs. Tanner, would you like to take those papers home and bring them back when you finish filling them out?"

The woman takes the tissues, dries her tears, and looks up at the receptionist, "No, I'll fill them out. At this point, it probably doesn't matter. No, I'm all right. I'll fill them out. Thank you."

The receptionist pats the woman's shoulder and looks over at Chiara, "Mrs. Fonte, are you alright?"

Chiara smiles and shakes her head. The situation upset Chiara. She has never seen anything like this before or even known that it existed. Everyone takes care of their own. No one goes into a nursing home. She takes some comfort in the fact that the woman is also upset, realizing she isn't alone. Others have to deal with the same situation and decisions. The receptionist smiles and goes back to her post. At this moment Chiara feels compelled to explain her own situation. She doesn't care if the woman listens or ignores her.

"My mother can't walk on her own. She keeps falling. It's her equilibrium, the doctor says. She loses her balance. My husband and son help but it is too much now. I think she is also getting senile."

The woman does listen to Chiara, and as she listens tears well up in her eyes because she feels she is in the same situation, and hearing it makes it even sadder. She looks out the window and sighs.

"All my life my parents, especially my mother, did everything for me. She anticipated everything I needed. I took it for granted and sometimes I wasn't nice. Now when I can do things for her, she sometimes doesn't even know who I am. And now I worry all the time like she used to worry about me. So now I not only have my two daughters to worry about, I have to worry about my mother and I feel guilty because I resent it."

She turns her head from the window, looks at Chiara, and again asks, "Do you have any children?"

"Yes, I have three boys. I worry all the time about my sons, and now I have my mother to worry about. I do resent it because..." Chiara looks down and doesn't want to admit her resentment. The woman can sense Chiara's sadness. Chiara continues, "I have brothers and sisters and they help but it's not enough. You would think the oldest would take charge, but that's not how it is. I'm the next to the youngest of seven children. I guess that doesn't matter because it is what it is and..."

The woman nods her head in agreement and interrupts Chiara. "We can only do what we can do. My aunt, my mother's sister, is going through the same thing as my mother. She has three children, but for her, the oldest is the one taking care of everything. The second son helps but the youngest hardly does anything. Everything is about his wife's family. I'm sure you know how that goes."

She sees Chiara's reaction and continues, "I do guess you know that 'whatever goes around,' by the sound of it. It doesn't matter older or younger. It's whatever's in your heart. You do what you feel you want to do, or what you have to do...Oh, well."

Seeing that the conversation is getting uncomfortable for Chiara, the woman stands up to leave.

"I think I am going to fill out these papers at home after all. Not that it matters." The woman reaches out her hand to Chiara. "I wish you luck."

Chiara shakes the woman's hand, "Yes. Good luck to both of us."

The woman pushes into her chair and leaves.

To distract herself from the woman leaving, Chiara turns her head to look outside. It is the beginning of spring and the trees are in bloom. She remembered her father's stories about the lemon and orange trees and the smell of the blossoms. She will never forget the stories her father told her over the years. They had a special relationship. "Chiara, sempre mia picolla bombina," he would often say to her. Then she looks down at the papers. *What a sad day,* she thinks. She fills in her father's name, Enzo Buonoforte, on the application and checks the box "deceased."

"Papa, this is probably one of the last times I will ever write your name." After Chiara wrote in her father's name, she saw the next question: home address.

Chapter 20

"Goddamn it! It's their mother too!"

Chiara has to finally stop thinking of her father and finish filling out the papers, home address: 105 East Clifton Avenue, Clifton, New Jersey. She stops for a minute. Maybe her son Dean was right. She thinks she should leave and try to find another solution. She will force her brothers and sisters to help. *Goddamn it! It's their mother too!* Then the receptionist comes over to her, and Chiara is forced back into reality.

"Excuse me, Mrs. Fonte. Mrs. Avero, the office administrator, will see you now."

"Oh, but I haven't fini...."

"That's alright. You can finish it later. Mrs. Avero has a late lunch meeting and she needs to leave in a few minutes."

A few minutes, Chiara thinks, *just enough time to tell me there's not enough room.*

The receptionist knows the lunch meeting isn't true. Mrs. Avero hates to tell people that there isn't any room for their loved ones and needs an excuse to end the meeting. Many times, there are tears and it is a very difficult situation. It is an easier way of getting people to leave, so she will always say she is going to a previously scheduled meeting. The only reason Chiara is being seen is because of the connection to her brother Donatello's wife, who knows the head nurse and who got Chiara an appointment.

The receptionist leads Chiara into the administrator's office, introduces her to Mrs. Avero, and leaves.

"Hello, Mrs. Fonte. Please have a seat."

Before Chiara sits down, she hands the administrator the papers.

"I'm sorry, but I didn't finish filling them all out." Chiara figures what does it matter anyway. There's no room for her mother.

"That's alright."

The administrator shuffles the couple of papers that Chiara handed her so she doesn't have to make immediate eye contact. This is the part of the job she hates. There are two types of people who want to place their parents in a nursing home: the ones who are heartbroken and realize they don't have a choice and it is for their parent's own good and the ones who just want to place them and rarely will ever come to visit, if at all. Both types upset her, for different reasons. She can tell that Chiara is the former and not the latter, and they are the most pitiful.

"Well, Mrs. Fonte, I am sorry that at this time we do not have any vacancies, or rather the couple of vacancies we have are already spoken for by people who have been waiting. However, I contacted a colleague of mine in Suffern, New York and there may be a possibility there. The home is older than this one but I understand they offer very good care."

When she hears this, Chiara is thinking about the idea of having to drive all the way to Suffern, New York. How could she see her mother every day? And for some of her brothers and sisters, it would be a good excuse not to visit, and again the burden would be on her and her husband.

"My husband and I were really hoping for my mother to stay here because it is so close to our home. And, also, for my sisters and brothers."

Mrs. Avero doesn't give her time to finish. "Yes, I understand. How far is Suffern from where you live?"

Chiara doesn't answer her, because she is becoming overwhelmed with the idea of Suffern.

Mrs. Avero looks down at the application to see where Chiara and her husband live. "You live in...."

"East Paterson," Chiara quickly states.

"Oh, I see. East Paterson." Then the administrator notices her mother's name. "Oh, your mother's name is Anna. That's my name, too."

The administrator smiles and tries to put some lightness into the conversation because she sees how upset Chiara is getting with the idea of having to deal with the distance of Suffern, New York. Then the administrator suddenly stops, looks at the paper again, and then looks up at Chiara.

"I can't quite make out what your mother's last name is. Is it Buono...."

Chiara can see there is something different in her way of questioning. "It's Buonoforte. Anna Buonoforte," Chiara quickly interjects.

"Was your father Enzo Buonoforte? Oh yes, I see that. And did they live on East Clifton Avenue?"

"Yes. How did you...." Chiara feels something is changing the tone of the conversation and she begins to feel hopeful.

"Oh my God, Mrs. Fonte. Your mother is Anna Buonoforte. My grandfather and grandmother lived on East Clifton Avenue and were very good friends with your parents who lived down the street." Mrs. Avero's attitude and voice change as she realizes the connection. "As unbelievable as this may seem, Mrs. Fonte...." Mrs. Avero can't make eye contact and keeps looking through the papers, because what she believes is too coincidental. She looks directly at Chiara. "Mrs. Fonte, your mother is my godmother. I can't believe this. I haven't really seen your parents in years because my family moved to Florida when I was young."

For a few moments, Chiara is taken aback. "I can't believe it! You're Anna. Mr. Fassino's granddaughter? Your father and mother...."

"Yes. Avero is my married name. My mother is Christina Caputo. My grandfather was Tommaso Fassino, and my grandmother was Bella; Isabella, that is. I am named after your mother, Anna. Unbelievable."

At this point, Mrs. Avero gets up from behind her desk and closes the door to her office. Instead of sitting back behind the desk, she sits on the chair next to Chiara. As they exchange family histories, the administrator reaches for her phone and dials her secretary.

"Mrs. Peterson, did Mrs. Deluca ever get back to you? Yes, I know.

She had until yesterday. You see her file...yeah, I'll hold on." The administrator puts her hand over the phone and whispers to Chiara as if they are old, school friends, "This woman has been driving me crazy. She wants to place her mother, but every time her mother comes, she cries and puts up a fuss and they leave. She can't make a commitment. I feel bad for her, but...."

Then she gets back on the phone. "OK, good. Call Mrs. Deluca. It's the second phone number with the first three numbers 791, the first number is her husband's work. If you can't get her, call her husband and tell her, or her husband, that the spot has been taken, yes, that's right. Tell her we couldn't wait any longer. If there are any problems, I will speak to her, but please try to handle it yourself. Thanks. Also, get the paperwork for Mrs. Buonoforte; the new resident application paperwork, and the cost sheets. OK. Thanks." Then she hangs up the phone.

"Mrs. Fonte, I will admit your mother. There is no way I could not."

Chiara starts to tear up, and Mrs. Avero moves her chair closer to try to comfort her, reaching for both her hands. Chiara is trying to make sense through her tears.

"I really appreciate it. It has been very difficult to even come to do this. I never thought it would come to this. Families are supposed to get closer as parents get older, but it seems to be the opposite."

"I know, Mrs. Fonte. You are not the first and won't be the last. For my part, this is a very difficult job, not only with having to disappoint people but also seeing the conditions of the people who are residents and their decline. And then there are the residents who no longer get visitors because families don't care, or the residents have just outlived their families and there is no one. We have a wonderful staff who are very sympathetic and do their best to make our residents comfortable."

Mrs. Avero gets up from her chair. "Mrs. Fonte, how about I give you a tour? It will be a week or so before your mother's room is ready because it is being refurbished."

Chiara gets up, fixes the position of the chair, and is led out of Mrs. Avero's office.

Mrs. Avero is more formal assuming her administrative role and gestures to the right.

"This is the administrative area. To the left is a small infirmary for visiting doctors and emergencies. There is a separate entrance for an ambulance if the need arises. There is the pharmacy. All medications are dispensed from there and then distributed to the residents."

Mrs. Avero leads Chiara to the right, toward the main area, where residents are sitting at tables playing games with staff members; other residents are reading, and some in wheelchairs are watching television.

"When did your parents move to—Florida, you said?"

As Mrs. Avero leads Chiara through the main area, she answers, "We moved there when I was very young. My father got a job—actually, my stepfather—in Fort Lauderdale with his brother building condos and homes. Unfortunately, he passed away a few years ago. I met someone from this area who was down there when I was in college, and we got married and moved back here where his family lives and where their family business is."

She leads Chiara into a large room. "Here we are. As you can see, this is the main common area. We try to get the residents to socialize as much as possible. We also have a daily schedule of events, like bingo and other group activities. We have people do what we call a "drop-in" and entertain, like local magicians, or singers—anything to keep the residents occupied. Through that area is the dining room."

As they walk through the area, Chiara becomes more comfortable, observing that her mother is not just going to be put in a room and forgotten. She wants to ask Mrs. Avero about her mother and grandparents but thinks it would be too personal at this point.

"As you can see, we have it set up like a nice country restaurant. Most residents eat here, but some have to eat in their rooms for various reasons. We have a nutritionist and we keep records of the dietary restrictions of each resident."

As she is explaining the operation there is an announcement on the loudspeaker: "We have a code 90, I repeat, we have a code 90."

"Mrs. Fonte, please sit here. I will be back as soon as I can."

Chiara reluctantly and slowly sits at the table. She doesn't know what code 90 means, but by the look on Mrs. Avero's face and the screaming and commotion she hears coming from the common area, she presumes it is very serious.

Mrs. Avero arrives in the common area to witness one of the younger residents going into another epileptic seizure. One of the male nurses calls out to him, "Come on Danny. Look at me, Danny. It's OK."

Mrs. Avero realizes the timing of the epileptic episodes is getting closer together, and his medication may have to be changed again. The facility is not equipped to handle this type of patient, but because there was a large gift left to the facility by Danny's parents after their death, the board decided that Danny would have to be taken care of for the rest of his life. It was not an altruistic decision. Other moneys were put into an annuity and are given out yearly as long as Danny is alive and living in the facility and is managed by the family's lawyer. Danny was in his thirties and it was thought because of his muscular dystrophy he wouldn't live that long anyway, especially since his seizures were happening more often. After all, as one of the board members put it, "business is business."

Chiara sees the commotion is under control, and as Mrs. Avero is walking over to her, Chiara stands up and walks to Mrs. Avero to meet her halfway. Mrs. Avero doesn't want to elaborate on the situation, which is fine with Chiara, who is already very uncomfortable.

"I am sorry. Everything is under control. I tell you what, Mrs. Fonte. You go home. I'll give you the paperwork to go over with your husband and then call me and make an appointment to finalize everything. If you agree to admit her, I would recommend you bring her with the intention of leaving her; it is easier that way."

Chiara nods.

Mrs. Avero guides Chiara to the front door. "Mrs. Avero..."

"Oh, call me Anna."

"Anna, I was so sorry to hear that your grandfather passed away. It was a real loss for my parents."

Mrs. Avero looks down for a moment. "Yes. I miss him every day. My grandmother is still alive and doing well and we go to see her every chance we get, and my mother, of course."

Chiara and Mrs. Avero walk toward the front door.

"Chiara, wait. Come back to my office. I have to give you the admittance papers and cost sheets."

They walk back to Mrs. Avero's office. Chiara stands in the doorway while Mrs. Avero grabs the papers that were left there by her assistant. She walks over and hands them to Chiara. Then she hugs Chiara, and they kiss each other on the cheek. Chiara has mixed feelings, now that the situation is a reality.

Mrs. Avero takes Chiara's arm. "I will walk you out. I need some fresh air." Mrs. Avero smiles and both women silently walk toward the entrance and onto the large front porch. After Mrs. Avero says goodbye, she stops Mrs. Fonte, "Mrs. Fonte, I have a question."

Chiara waits. Earlier, while she was sitting waiting for Mrs. Avero to return from the Code 90, she had begun to remember everything that her father told her about what happened years ago with the Fassinos and the scandal that almost was. *How could this be? How could we come together at this time for this?* She prayed Mrs. Avero would not bring anything up. There were so many rumors at the time. *What had she heard? What does she know? What will she ask me?* Chiara is afraid of any questions about Mrs. Avero's background.

Chiara turns toward Mrs. Avero, who is looking down, and asks Chiara in almost a whisper, "Well, maybe you don't even know the answer, but since you knew my parents and grandparents, I figured I would ask you." She hesitates and again avoids making eye contact. "I know this may seem strange, but ...." She hesitates again but looks directly at Chiara. "When I was born, there seemed to be some kind of mystery surrounding my birth. I know I was born in Florida and my father died in a car accident there right after I was born. There are really no pictures of him and me. When I brought it up to my mother, she seemed so uncomfortable. That and other things just kind of nagged at me over the years. Some people even acted strangely around me when I was young. Sometimes they would even whisper."

Chiara knows everything. *Could Mrs. Avero see it in her eyes?* She has to say something. "I really don't know if there is anything. I just remember my parents going to your Christening when you and your mother and grandparents came back from Florida. I was young at the time. It was sad because your father was killed, so things were quiet. No one talked about what happened. Then when you moved to Florida years later. I saw you a couple of times when you came to visit your grandparents, then they all moved to Florida.

Mrs. Avero seems to be convinced. *Would she bring it up again?* Chiara hopes she won't because Chiara *does* know the truth and it is so awkward. Chiara hates to lie. She hopes that Mrs. Avero will not ask her again. Regardless, it isn't her place to say anything, or is it? Even if Mrs. Avero asks her again, there would be no point in telling her the truth. She is doing her a favor, or that is what Chiara thinks at this time? But Chiara has the proof. The proof that old man Fassino gave Enzo and that Dean found.

Mrs. Avero realizes she may be embarrassing Chiara, so she decides to end the conversation.

"Never mind. I guess at this point it doesn't matter anymore. Anyway, wait till I call my mother tonight, I think she will be excited about this coincidence."

That sends a chill down Chiara's spine and she tries to hide her nervousness.

"Thank you so much for all your help, Anna. I will call you," Chiara says before she walks down the stairs of the nursing home toward her car.

She turns around, looks at the building, and tears up. *How can I do this to my mother?* She tries to fight off a feeling of resentment for her brothers and sisters allowing this to happen. But as much as she tries to reason with the situation in her mind, the resentment lingers. She tries to put the feelings out of her mind and just get home.

As she drives off, she remembers what Mrs. Avero asked her. Chiara hopes she will never ask her again. Then she thinks about what her father told her. *Maybe Mrs. Avero should know. What harm would it do? Didn't she owe it to her to let her know the truth?*

As Chiara drives home, for a while she forgets about her mother and the nursing home. She arrives home, pulls into her driveway, shuts the car off, and sits there thinking about what her father told her about the Fassinos. Now Chiara will have another struggle to deal with. She wishes she didn't know the Fassino family secret. *Damn. Why do I feel she doesn't believe me?* Chiara gets out of the car and goes into the house with a plan. She doesn't want to wait till tomorrow to call back Mrs. Avero in case something goes wrong. She goes into her bedroom and in the bottom drawer of her clothes bureau. She takes out the envelope marked Fassino and brings it into the kitchen. She calls the nursing home and makes an appointment with Mrs. Avero to make the final arrangements. There is no point in discussing anything with her husband, there is no other choice. She is going to call her sister Rita but then figures what is the point. If any of them wanted to know anything, except for her brother Donny, they could call her.

Chapter 21
Mrs. Avero takes the envelope that reads, Fassino family—Confidential

It is raining hard as Chiara parks the car, opens the door, and quickly walks to the entrance of the nursing home. She has the large brown envelope under her jacket so it won't get wet. A man coming out of the entrance sees Chiara running and holds the door open. As she climbs the stairs, she thanks the man. Once inside the lobby of the nursing home, she tries to fix her hair and shake the rain off her jacket. The nursing home is less intimidating and more familiar to her now. She walks up to the reception area and is surprised at Mrs. Petersen's greeting.

"Good morning, Mrs. Fonte! Mrs. Avero is meeting with one of the staff psychiatrists and she asked me to show you where your mother will be staying."

Mrs. Petersen leads Chiara to the north wing of the nursing home where the older rooms are refurbished.

"The room for your mother is private and it was just redecorated. You see, we have a board of trustees and some of them have the means to redecorate a room with new wallpaper, new curtains, whatever is needed to make it look 'more homey.' We do have fundraisers but sometimes those monies have to go to general maintenance."

They stopped outside Room 101.

"This room was recently redone by one of our trustee's families."

She points to a brass plaque next to the door: *This Room Redecorated by Emil and Leogadia Mully and Family*

Mrs. Petersen signals Chiara to step into the room.

"This is beautiful and you are right, very homey."

Chiara is even more nervous about the financing. With the news of her mother's acceptance into the nursing home she and her husband quickly reviewed the fees. *This room must be really expensive*, she thinks. *I hope this room is what we read about the boarding costs.*

"See, there is a large closet here and there is also a private bathroom with a large sit-in shower. All the curtains and bedding are new."

Chiara walks over to the large window where there is a small round table and two chairs. There is also a recliner that can spin around to face the window or the room. Chiara is pleasantly surprised at what she is seeing.

"What a wonderful view of the gardens. This is a beautiful room. What a wonderful donation they have made."

Mrs. Petersen sees Mrs. Fonte getting teary-eyed and takes Mrs. Fonte's arm for support and to lead her out of the room.

"Yes. The donors are wonderful people."

As they leave the room, she turns to Mrs. Petersen. "This is wonderful. I don't know if we can afford this."

Mrs. Petersen doesn't make any comment regarding the fees and leads Mrs. Fonte to Mrs. Avero's office, who has just walked into the room.

"Thank you, Mrs. Petersen. Please sit down, Chiara. I want to get the exact time and day your mother is going to move in. We always have something special planned to make the transition more fun and easier. Let me get my calendar and some papers I want you to take with you."

She goes to her desk, brings her calendar and they both sit down at the table. Chiara hands the admittance papers to Mrs. Avero and places the brown envelope face down on the table.

Mrs. Avero looks at the old brown envelope.

"Is this envelope for me? Some papers you want me to hold for your mother?"

Chiara touches the envelope for a second. "Well, not exactly."

There is silence for a few seconds, and Chiara sees the puzzled look on Mrs. Avero's face.

Chiara breaks the silence saying, "Do you remember yesterday when I was leaving, you asked me if I knew anything about your birth father and that situation?"

Mrs. Avero looks intently at Chiara and slowly nods.

"Well. I wasn't entirely truthful. Not because I didn't want to be. What is in that envelope was told to me in confidence. I didn't think it was my place to say anything. After my father died, there were a bunch of papers and this envelope with your grandfather's name on it was with his papers. I didn't open it because it was sealed heavily with tape and again, I didn't think it was my place. I don't even know why I didn't burn it or throw it away. I can kind of guess what is in it and now, well...I talked to my husband and my sister Rita and we all agree that we think you have the right to know about your life. So, we decided that you should make the decision to see what's in this envelope. If you don't want to know, I will take it home with me and burn it in the fireplace and it will never be spoken of again."

Mrs. Avero looks at Chiara and touches the envelope. Mrs. Avero tales the envelope that reads, *Fassino family—Confidential* and a chill runs down her spine. Mrs. Avero doesn't make eye contact.

"Thank you."

Chiara feels she did the right thing. Now it is for Mrs. Avero to decide to read what is in it or throw it away. Chiara remembered that a heavy sense of sadness came over Enzo after he heard that old man Fassino had died. Tommaso Fassino, his wife, and his children were friends from the first time they met at the Mussomeli Society.

Enzo told Chiara that he remembered clearly as if it was a few days ago, that on a cold winter Sunday in January, he was shoveling the snow from the sidewalk and he saw old man Fassino walking uncharacteristically fast toward him. His name was Tommaso but he was always called "old man" because even when he was young, he acted and moved like an old man, worrying, and complaining about everything, but with a heart of gold. Enzo and Tommaso were close and Enzo loved to tease Tommaso, who really loved it. Even so, he would curse, especially when he lost to Enzo at poker, even though it was just for pennies. It was a matter of Sicilian pride. But Tommaso and Enzo became even closer friends for another reason. There was a family secret that Enzo and Anna were part of, and this secret came to mind again after hearing of Tommaso's death.

As Tommaso was approaching, Enzo yelled to him, Be careful! Don't fall! "Che fai?" "What's wrong?"

Old man Fassino waved his hands and breathlessly shouted, "Malle, malle, molto malle; Bad, very bad!" They walked through the back of the house and into the dining room.

Enzo yelled to his wife. "Anna! Prende il café, bring the coffee, subito!" Then he looked at the exasperated Fassino, "No. Forget the coffee. You better bring the grappa."

Enzo helped the old man take off his coat and hat, brushed off the snow, and hung them in the closet. The old man was still breathing heavily as he sat at the dining table. He took a handkerchief from his back pocket and wiped his brow. As Anna put a cup of hot espresso and a bottle of grappa in front of the old man, she looked at her husband, shrugged her shoulders, and whispered, "Che?" Enzo shrugged and pulled over a chair closer to Tommaso.

"My friend, what is so bad that you are going to have a heart attack running to my house?"

The old man had tears in his eyes and slapped his two hands together as if to pray and just shook them up and down to God. "I should be so lucky to die, then I wouldn't have this shame!" He poured some grappa into his cup, stirred it, took a sip, and shook his head.

Anna was becoming impatient at this point. "Alright, Tommaso! Please, this isn't opera. What is wrong?"

Old man Fassino looked away, shaking his head. "When they are young children, they are such a joy and a comfort. It is when they are older, they can send you to your grave."

Anna took a chair and sat next to Enzo. "Per favore paisano. Please, tell us what happened."

He kept shaking his head and finally began to explain. "You know my granddaughter, Christina?" Again, he was hesitating.

"Yes, yes. Is she alright?"

He didn't answer the question. "She was seeing this boy from Englewood. What we thought was a nice Sicilian boy. They're so young!"

Anna spoke up. "Yes, we met him at our anniversary party. Very nice boy, very handsome."

Enzo yelled, "That's the problem? His age?" Then Enzo remembered. "Ohhhh. Someone said he's Jewish. Is that the problem?"

The old man waved his hands, yelling back, "Aspeta, aspeta, give me a chance to breathe! No. That isn't the problem. Well yes, that's part of it."

He tried to catch his breath. "They went out for a couple of months and…now he won't marry her!" he said, flinging his arms upward.

Again, Enzo yelled, "Is that the problem, he won't marry her?"

Anna hit Enzo in the back of the head. "Stupido!" She held old man Fassino's hand and softly asked, "Tommaso, is she pregnant?"

He looked at her with tears in his eyes and just looked down and shook his head.

Enzo was stunned. "Bastardo!"

This was something one only heard of. This didn't happen in their neighborhood. There was a long silence.

"What are your daughter and your son-in-law going to do?" Anna quietly asked. The old man sat up, now that the worst was said.

"I don't know. They went to visit his parents. They live up near Englewood Cliffs. The parents sent the boy to live with relatives in Florida. They are Jewish and we think they don't want him to marry her because my granddaughter isn't Jewish. Maybe because they are rich and we are not. The family says that he is too young and the baby is probably not even his. Christina is heartbroken. The boy is too scared or too stupid to speak up. The family thinks they are better than my daughter. All Christina does is cry all day. She cries day and night. He is the only boy she ever went out with. She cries that she loves him and she wants to die."

Both Enzo and Anna gasped simultaneously.

"Bastardo, Bastardo!" Enzo yelled.

Anna hit Enzo on the shoulder, "Basta, basta, don't make Tommaso more upset!"

Anna took Tommaso's cup to refill it, and Tommaso looked at her and said, "That isn't the worst." What could be worse, they both thought.

"If the boy doesn't marry her, my son-in-law is going to find a doctor in New York to...."

Once again, they both gasped. "Madonna Mia!" Anna said covering her mouth.

They all sat there for a few minutes in silence. Enzo stood up very erect, put the chair back in its place, and said, "I will talk to your daughter and son-in-law. There has to be a better solution. Does anyone else know of this?"

Tommaso shook his head. "They don't want anyone to know. They even forbid Christina from going to confession to tell Father Giorgio. I told my daughter and son-in-law that I was going to seek your advice, and they agreed. We know we can trust you."

Enzo put his hand on the old man's shoulder. He didn't say anything: The trust was well understood.

"Go home and try to calm down. We'll come to you tonight to talk about this."

That evening Enzo and Anna went to the old man's house, where he lived with his daughter, son-in-law, and granddaughter. This was not an unusual arrangement. It was mutually beneficial for all involved provided they could all get along. Anna brought biscotti and an almond cake, but no one wanted to eat.

They all sat for a short time and politely, and then Enzo sat up erect and spoke. He would not be interrupted.

"I know of your problem. The solution is simple, yet it will be difficult to maybe live through. Tommaso you have an older brother in Florida. You should call him and say that your granddaughter is pregnant and the boy won't marry her. She needs to get away to try to avoid a scandal. Tommaso, you said many times that your brother and his wife had a daughter who was around the age of Christina and died at the age of nine from influenza. There were many times that your brother wrote to you, and they always said that they would love to have Christina stay with them for a visit. Remember the summer Christina spent two months with them and it was hard for her to leave. They love her like a daughter. This now would be the perfect opportunity for everyone. You said your sister-in-law has very bad arthritis and didn't travel or get around that much, so she would love the company. She would welcome your daughter and your wife. Even you should go, Tommaso."

They all listened to Enzo's suggestion, and it seemed they were in agreement as Enzo continued.

"Christina will go and stay until the baby is born. You will tell every-one that your sister-in-law needs help because of her arthritis. You'll have to stay there for at least a couple of months after the baby is born. When you all return, you explain that Christina was married, she had a baby, and her husband was killed in a car crash or something."

It seemed like a far-fetched idea, but still a possible solution. Another option was to put the baby up for adoption, which they all agreed was out of the question. This seemed to be the only answer to a difficult problem.

"If anyone has any questions, just tell them it is too painful to talk about."

This was a very plausible plan because people never spoke of dead relatives. It is a taboo subject.

Enzo's suggestion seemed to be the only option.

Seven months later, a baby girl was born and baptized Anna, named after the baby's godmother-to-be, Anna Buonoforte. A year later, Tommaso, his wife and daughter, and their new granddaughter returned to Clifton and had another baptism so that Anna could be present. Friends and relatives had already heard the "fake story" of the death of Christina's make-believe husband with the last name, Caputo. At the Christening, no one asked any questions but just offered condolences and congratulations.

Christina was warned not to attempt to contact the baby's father. Lawyers had been involved to make sure that the baby's biological father had no rights to the baby, which was agreed to on both sides. The family also offered a check to help with the baby, which Tommaso refused to accept. There were also measures to make sure that when little Anna grew up, she would never be told the true story and she would not be able to find her biological father. All the legal papers except for the birth certificate, which listed the father as deceased, were hidden outside the Fassino home...with Enzo. The secret was kept as much as a secret of this type can be kept, but there were suspicions among the neighbors and relatives. Everyone knows old man Fassino has a terrible temper and no one dared to ask. After a few years the Fassinos, Christina, her parents, and baby Anna moved to Florida for good.

Years later when Enzo heard that old man Fassino died in Florida, he became melancholy about his friendship with the old man and his family. A few days after old man Fassino's death, Chiara was having tea with her father and she asked Enzo about the rumors. Chiara thought her father would get mad or would avoid the subject. But he didn't. He was feeling melancholy and needed to remember his old friend. He needed to tell someone the truth. Chiara was the right person at the right time. Enzo told the secret to Chiara, knowing that there would never be any point in revealing the secret. After all, who would even be interested? It had always been a heavy burden for both him and Anna that may be lighter if he could share it. He trusted Chiara. Anyway, who would Chiara tell? So, he told her the whole story, but not about the documents that were hidden all those years in the attic. He foolishly avoided letting anyone know.

After hearing the story, Chiara kissed her father on the cheek. Not only because of what Enzo had done for the Fassino family to help them years ago, but she suddenly realized that her father had gotten old. *When did this happen*, she thought? Now that old man Fassino had died, as well as some of Enzo and Anna's friends, Chiara came to the realization that her parents were going to die and it might soon. Most of the original founders of the Mussomeli Society had died, and even though some of the children kept it going, it wasn't the same. Their realized dreams of coming to America and making a life were forgotten. The stories of gratitude and appreciation of this country were long gone.

At that time, Chiara would put out of her head the inevitable. No. She would not let her parents die. She couldn't bear to think of it. After all, what would one do without the other? What would Chiara do without her parents? Her father? Unthinkable. She wouldn't let it happen. Dismissing the thought that one day her parents would die, comforted her.

Mrs. Avero, without a word, hugs Chiara and thanks her.

"Anna, do you want me to come on another day and schedule my mother?

Mrs. Avero, holding the envelope, shakes her head.

"That's not a problem."

"I really think I have to check with my husband and kids. The whole thing is going to be difficult."

Mrs. Avero places the envelope on the glass conference table.

"I understand. I will wait for your call"

Chiara leaves the office still wondering if she has done the right thing, but at this point, it doesn't matter. Mrs. Avero only waits a few seconds and looks down at the envelope trying to decide what to do. She gently brushes her fingers over the name: *Fassino family—Confidential.* With the distraction of the envelope, Mrs. Avero forgot to give Chiara more information before she brought her mother in. She quickly walks to the reception area.

"Mrs. Petersen, please call Mrs. Fonte now and apologize. I just remembered that she has to make an appointment to see Mrs. Rosenberg and fill out more paperwork and we need her mother's citizenship papers and medical records. Have her come in as soon as she can."

Mrs. Avero rushes back into her office, closes the office door, and grabs the letter opener on her desk. She sits down, takes the envelope on the table, and slowly opens it. She scans through the papers and begins to review them. She is astonished.

"Dear God. I knew it. I knew I was lied to all these years!" She feels she should be mad, but for some reason, she is just relieved she finally is getting at the truth.

She took out the Yellow Pages phone book from her desk and fingered through it until she came to the letter *S.*

"It's still the same damn address that's in these papers."

Then she picks up the phone and dials the number next to the address. Her heart is beating fast as if it is going to burst out of her chest. After what seems like an eternity, an older-sounding woman answers. Mrs. Avero tells the woman who she is and instead of the woman being annoyed or angry, she sounds relieved and happily surprised. They speak for a good while and the woman gives Mrs. Avero the information she needs. Mrs. Avero looks at the address the woman gave her and almost begins to cry.

"How will the rest of this family feel when they find out, I wonder."

Mrs. Petersen knocks on the door, comes into Mrs. Avero's office, and tells her that Mrs. Fonte will be in Friday with the information requested and to fill out the paperwork. Mrs. Avero quickly wipes her eyes and again asks about the day and time and writes it down. Mrs. Petersen sees the scattered papers on the table and she notices that Mrs. Avero is upset, so she leaves the room and closes the door. One of Mrs. Petersen's finest qualities is that she minds her own business and, unless necessary, asks few questions. More than any other time, Mrs. Avero appreciates that quality about her.

Chapter 22
"Pretty lady. What can we do for you?"

Mrs. Avero pulls her car into the crowded parking lot of the San Giorgio Supermarket and finally finds a parking spot. She looks at herself in the rearview mirror, wipes a small smudge of lipstick from the corner of her mouth, gets out of the car, and fixes her dress. *It is the perfect outfit for a business meeting,* she thinks, especially with her sleek black leather brief-case. She walks into the supermarket and is surprised at how big it is and the amount of people shopping. She makes her way around shopping carts bumping into each other, listening to people shouting, the smells of the different foods, and a loudspeaker with someone announcing sale items, which is almost indistinguishable from all the other noise. She walks past a long line of cash registers and people in line to check out. Some cashiers are screaming to get a price check. There is the smell of freshly baked bread as she moves closer to the bakery section of the store. Above the cashier are what look like offices with large windows offering a panoramic view of the whole store. As she walks into the produce area, she looks at some nice, large artichokes for a second that she thinks of buying, but then she remembers she isn't here for that. She thinks this would be a good place to ask for donations during the nursing home fundraiser, but that is not why she is here either.

She goes up to the service desk where a younger man is giving out information to the people complaining and returning items. As she waits in line for her turn, she notices the man has a great smile that he flashes at her. When he sees how she is dressed, he realizes she isn't a complaining customer. He asks if he can be of any help and continues flashing a flirting smile.

"Pretty lady. What can we do for you?"

Mrs. Avero is a little taken aback but smiles. "I am here to see Mr. San Giorgio."

The man nods.

"Oh yeah. You must be the lady from *The Shopper* for the ads in the paper. My father told me to watch out for you. I think he's in his office. Follow me."

Mrs. Avero doesn't correct him or say a word. She follows him, then stops, and thinks to herself, *Oh my God, it's his father. How many are there? I don't know if I can do this.* She follows him not knowing what else to do.

The man shouts to her above the noise. "Come on, it's this way."

They climb the stairs to the office. Once inside she is relieved to find no one is in the office. She is beginning to lose her confidence. She sees a whole wall of family pictures and walks over to them, happy to be distracted.

"All these pictures. Very nice. Are all these family pictures?"

The man comes over and stands next to her as he points out pictures from vacations, skiing, fishing, and older family portraits. Then she points to a group family picture.

"Is that you?"

He begins to laugh. "Yeah. Look how long my hair is. It's my Bar Mitzvah picture. You know what a Bar Mitzvah is?"

She nods, and then she is taken aback again. *Hmmm, Jewish. I'm in the right place and is he who I think he is . . . my brother?* she thinks.

He puts out his hand. "By the way, my name is Luca. What's yours?"

She shakes his hand. "Hi. My name is Anna. This is a beautiful family picture. That's your mother, I am guessing. Very pretty."

He gets a little serious. "Yes. She was. She died a few years ago."

Mrs. Avero quickly apologizes. "Oh. I am so sorry, Luca."

At this point, they hear two men talking as they come up the stairs.

"Oh. That must be my father and brother."

"How many of you are there?" she asks, laughing.

"Well, that's my brother Morris coming up the stairs and I have a sister, Loretta."

His father and brother enter the office and see Luca and Mrs. Avero.

"Hey, Pop. This is the woman from the paper, Anna."

His father looks at Anna as he sits behind his desk. "Oh, I met with someone different last week. What happened to her?"

Anna looks at Morris. He has her eyes; the shape and the color. She puts out her hand to him.

"Hello. You must be Morris. My name is Anna."

He shakes her hand and looks at his father. "Pop, what's going on?"

His father looks at Anna and doesn't know what to think. She looks familiar, but he knows he never met her. He tries to think how he would know her.

Anna walks over to the desk, opens her briefcase, takes out a large brown envelope, and places it on the desk in front of her.

"You *are* Mr. Stefano San Giorgio?"

She pushes the envelope toward Stefano and smiles as he nods. She is so nervous she is shaking but she is still smiling. He reaches for the envelope.

"Dad, are you being sued or something?" Morris asks.

His father ignores him or doesn't even hear the question.

"Do I know you? You look familiar. Have we met before?"

Mrs. Avero looks down for a second and then her eyes meet his.

"No. Not yet." She sits down.

Luca and Morris are staring at their father, who seems almost afraid of opening the envelope.

Mrs. Avero is anxious to get this over with.

"Avero is my married name, and my mother's maiden name is Fassino. Ring a bell?" She looks at Mr. San Giorgio, who freezes while holding the envelope.

Luca is getting impatient. "Pop, what is this all about? This doesn't sound good. Lady, who are you and what do you want?"

Mrs. Avero keeps her eyes on Mr. San Giorgio. "Should I tell him?" she asks, "or would you rather confirm it first after reading those papers."

Instead of opening the envelope or looking at Mrs. Avero, he puts his hands to his head. "I thought this was all behind me. But there were many times I thought about this."

Then he looks at his sons, who are waiting for an answer. "If what I think is in this envelope…it will confirm that this woman is your sister."

Luca screams. "WHAT! What are you talking about?"

Morris leans on his father's desk. "What did you do? Who is this woman's mother? Did you know her, or was this a one-night thing?"

Mrs. Avero bites her tongue. *How dare he?* she thinks.

Mr. San Giorgio shakes his head and leans over his desk.

"This was a long time ago before I even knew your mother. I met her mother at a dance and we started dating. One thing led to another, and…."

Luca looks at Mrs. Avero, who is staring at him as if looks could kill.

"How do you even know that you're her father?"

Mr. San Giorgio sighed. "Believe me, I know. She was a virgin. I was the only one. We were in love. When she told me she was pregnant, she thought I would be happy, but I was scared. I was too young to get married. I ran away. I went to stay with your Aunt Nora in Florida. Your grandparents were in a panic. They didn't know what to do. They covered for me. What else could they do? I know they were so ashamed. They wanted to help with money, but it was refused."

Mrs. Avero cuts him off. "Wait. You mean to tell me that *you* ran away? You mean it wasn't your parents who wouldn't allow you to get married?"

"I was young. I was scared. How could I take care of a wife? I was eighteen. I could barely take care of myself."

Mrs. Avero jumps from her chair and leans on the desk.

"Read what's in that envelope! I read it and cried for days. Do you know that I had to live a lie with my mother? I had to be born in Florida, probably only miles away from where you were, and my mother had to tell everyone that her 'fake husband' was killed in a car accident! My mother and my last name are fake; just made up. For all my life, all I had was a frame on a mantelpiece with a picture of a man who was not even my father! I used to make him Christmas cards and put them next to his photograph. I used to talk to the picture wishing he was with me."

She sits down and starts to cry. Luca goes over and tries to comfort her.

Then Morris speaks up. "Pop, how could you? What did you always teach us about taking responsibility? And we find this out? What have you done? What have you done to her and her family?"

There is a deadly silence for a few minutes. No one knows what to say. What can be said?

"Listen. I can't make up for the past. What can I do now? How can I make it up to you? What can I give you?" asks Mr. San Giorgio.

Mrs. Avero is calm at this point, but the anger she kept inside her all those years of growing up, starts to emerge.

"My mother cried, and not for my fake father. Now I know she cried for *you.* She should have known that it wasn't your parents. You turned out to be a real coward."

Mr. San Giorgio leaned back. "You're right. I really screwed up. What can I do? Where is your mother? Did she ever get married?"

"Yes, she married a real man, but he died a few years ago."

"Is your mother still in Florida?"

"Why do you want to know? What would you say to her? She would hate you if she found out the truth. She hated your parents. She lived an illusion. I lived an illusion and a lie all these years."

Luca has taken a chair, sitting next to Mrs. Avero. "I see the ring on your finger. You're married?"

Mrs. Avero wipes her eyes and nods her head.

"Do you have any children?"

She ignores the question, still staring at Mr. San Giorgio. There is silence again.

Mr. San Giorgio opens the envelope and reads over the papers.

"I have to make this right somehow."

"Don't you understand? I don't want anything. The only good thing to come out of this is now you're a real person who I can hate," says Mrs. Avero angrily.

Awkward silence again and then Mrs. Avero looks at her father. "I really don't mean that. At last, I have answers to questions that bothered me all my life. I have two brothers and a sister, growing up not knowing them. If I knew them, maybe I wouldn't have been so lonely."

Both Luca and Morris look at each other.

"We can always use another sister. And now that we see you, you look like us!"

Mrs. Avero smiles.

"Isn't there a third, a girl?"

Luca says, "OH MY GOD. Wait tell Loretta hears about this! She will flip. She has always said that she wished one of us was a girl because she always wanted a sister. She thinks we're real bores!"

"There is one thing I can do," Mr. San Giorgio says. "My father passed away a few years ago but my mother is still alive. She sometimes said to me she wondered what happened to you. If you were born, if you were happy. She only said something in the beginning, but I knew she was hurt. Both she and my father were ashamed that I ran away. So, I was punished in a way because I sensed they looked at me differently." He looks down for a few moments and wipes his eyes. "Would you like to meet her?"

"I already spoke to her this morning. That is how I got your address."

Luca looks at his father.

"Holy shit. Grandma must have almost had a heart attack and..."

Mrs. Avero cuts him off. "No. She was truly pleased to hear from me. We talked for an hour. We laughed and we cried...Believe me, she will talk to you tonight."

Mrs. Avero stands up from her chair and goes over to the wall with all the family pictures. Pictures proudly hung documenting years of family vacations, holidays, anniversaries, and anything that had to do with the San Giorgio family and business. As she carefully looks at each picture, she doesn't turn to make eye contact.

"These are all beautiful pictures that show a very close and happy family with a successful business. Let me tell you a little about my life now. I have been married for about three years. My husband is a very successful lawyer: A litigator." She turns to look at Morris and Luca. "That means he sues people."

Morris seems annoyed. "Yes, I know... we know what it means."

Mrs. Avero smiles. "Good." She turns back to the pictures and slowly moves down the line. "He works in the family business and comes from a family of lawyers. When I told him I was coming here, he asked me what your business is worth."

Luca gasped. "Wait a minute. You're gonna sue us or something? Pop...."

Mr. San Giorgio cuts him off. "Shut up, Luca. Is it money you want? Is that why you came here?"

Mrs. Avero takes the picture of the family Bar Mitzvah off the wall and goes over to Mr. San Giorgio's desk. "This is a beautiful family picture. These must be your parents and this is your late wife."

Mr. San Giorgio, Luca, and Morris all stand quietly trying to antici-pate what Mrs. Avero is going to say next. Why did she really come here and what does she really want?

"Money? You think I want money?" She takes the picture and slams it on the corner of the desk. Glass flies all over and Mr. San Giorgio and his sons back away.

"I don't need your money! I didn't come here for that. I wanted to see what I was missing as a child. I told you what picture I had!" She throws the picture frame on the floor and is pleased they are all startled.

"I told you. I have, had, a picture on a mantelpiece of a man who was supposed to be my father and died when I was a baby. That is what I was told, that he was killed in a car accident shortly after I was born. But after reading the papers in that envelope I gave you, there was no man. That man was *you*, and as I just found out you were hiding in Florida like a coward...I used to talk to that man in the frame. I wished him Merry Christmas, I made believe he wished me a Happy Birthday. I made cards and pictures that I would set up next to the frame. Sometimes my mother would see me and start crying. I thought it was because she missed him.

Now, I guess maybe she missed *you*. Maybe she felt sorry for me that I was being fooled."

She starts walking around toward Luca and Morris. They back up a little. She takes Morris's hand, leans up, and kisses him on the cheek. She does the same to Luca.

"I am happy to have met both of you."

Mr. San Giorgio starts to walk around his desk toward Mrs. Avero as she bends down to pick up her briefcase. She walks away from him. He gets the hint and stops in his tracks.

"What can I do? What can I say?"

She looks at him. "Do you have a time machine somewhere in a back room? Other than that, there is nothing you can say or do."

"What about your mother? Can I talk to her?"

She looks away. "I wish you could. She's dead."

They all gasp in their own way.

Mr. San Giorgio makes another step toward Mrs. Avero, but he senses she doesn't want him to touch her. "I am really sorry. Still, what can I do to try to make this right?"

She avoids looking at him and just smiles at Luca and Morris. "Well, gentlemen, give my best to your sister."

She walks around the boys and starts down the stairs. Luca looks at Morris and then his father. "Wait. When will we see you again?"

Mrs. Avero stops but doesn't look back. "I don't really know."

As she leaves the three of them go to the window to watch her. When she gets to where they can see her, she stops, turns around, and looks up to find them watching her. She stares for a moment and then walks out of the store.

Luca puts his hand on his father's shoulder. "Wow, Pop. She's something. What are you going to do?"

"You heard her. There is nothing we can do. Maybe just be here. The ball is in her court. You're right, Luca. She is some woman. She spoke to your grandmother and your grandmother is not going to let her go twice. I have hell to pay... again when I speak to your grandmother tonight."

Morris asks his father a question they all are probably thinking. "Pop. Do you wish now you would have stayed with her mother?"

Mr. San Giorgio turns and puts a hand on each of his son's shoulders. "If I had made a different decision, where would you two knuckleheads and Loretta be?" Then he kisses each of them on the cheek.

Chapter 23
"My mother will never live in a basement!"

As Mrs. Avero leaves the parking lot of the store and drives back to the nursing home, all she can think about is what to do next. She promised to meet the grandmother...her grandmother, in person, but how and when? And she lied about her own mother being dead but she doesn't care. Her father should suffer a little. She pulls into the parking lot of the nursing home, rushes through the front door toward her office, ignores her next appointment, and closes the door. Mrs. Fontanella, who was sitting outside her office, was early for her appointment. She throws down her briefcase on the glass table and grabs the phone. As she dials, she prays the call will be answered.

"Hi. It's me...No. Nothing's wrong. Listen, I am going to send you a plane ticket. I want you to stay for a while. Well, I was going to wait to see you, to tell you, but I am too excited...I'm pregnant...Mom! Please! Stop screaming! Yes, I feel fine...I will call you back with the plane reservation information. OK. I can't talk. I just got back to work. Bye, Mom. Love you. Start packing! I'll call you tonight."

As she hangs up the phone, there is a knock on the door.

"Come in."

Mrs. Petersen rolls her eyes, which is a sign that the next appointment is going to be a crazy one.

"Your next appointment is here, Mrs. Fontanella."

Mrs. Avero whispers,

"I know who she is after a dozen calls. Lord save me."

"Yeah. She's foaming at the mouth. She was here about 20 minutes early."

"OK. I am just in the mood to deal with someone like her. Bring her in."

Mrs. Fontanella is already letting herself in and moving past Mrs. Peterson, who leaves as quickly as she can. Mrs. Avero stands up behind her desk.

"Mrs. Petersen, please leave the door open and stay close in case I need a file or something." That meant she needed a witness to sit at the small desk outside her office, where Mrs. Petersen will make believe to do work.

Mrs. Avero motions to Mrs. Fontanella to sit down in front of her desk.

"Mrs. Fontanella. How nice it is to finally meet you. Please sit."

"I came early in hopes of seeing you sooner, but I guess that is not the case. I came to discuss my mother's evaluation and a date that she could take up residence."

As she is speaking, she takes off her mink stole, places it on the glass table, and puts her purse on top of the papers that are on Mrs. Avero's desk. She removes her white gloves and sets them next to her purse. Mrs. Avero smiles because Mrs. Fontanella placed her gloves and purse on top of Mrs. Fontanella's file.

"Mrs. Fontanella. Can you please remove your gloves and purse from my desk?"

She watches Mrs. Fontanella's expression of disbelief that someone would talk to her that way and before she can speak, Mrs. Avero cuts her off and smiles sarcastically.

"They are on your mother's file."

Mrs. Fontanella's expression changes. Acknowledging Mrs. Avero's silence, Mrs. Fontanella puts the purse and the gloves on her lap. Mrs. Avero takes the file, opens it, and leans back in her chair.

"Mrs. Avero, are you aware of my mother's situation?"

"I know Mrs. Fontanella. You must have called me a dozen times."

Before Mrs. Fontanella can object to the comment, Mrs. Avero continues, "Alright. I went over your mother's file and discussed the findings with the house physician and psychiatrist. I also had a long talk with your mother."

Mrs. Avero closes the file, places it on the desk, and slides it to Mrs. Fontanella, who picks it up and opens it. On the top is a rubber stamp stating, "Not Acceptable."

"Mrs. Fontanella, I will summarize the findings. There is nothing wrong with your mother that would warrant her becoming a resident in this or any other nursing home facility. Aside from her mild high blood pressure, which is under control with medication, she is of sound mind and body."

Mrs. Fontanella closes the file, puts it back on the desk, and shoves it hard toward Mrs. Avero, who catches it before it flies off the desk.

"I don't understand. My mother needs constant attention and care, which in good conscience I can no longer provide for her. It would be negligent not to see that she lived in an environment where she could get that kind of attention."

"Mrs. Fontanella, I have been in this business for five, going on six years. I have seen the different types of potential residents and the children of those potential residents. After careful study and observations, we have carefully developed a guideline for accepting patients, and your mother does not fit within that guideline."

Mrs. Avero senses Mrs. Fontanella is getting indignant, and she is just in the mood to confront her.

"I am sorry. I don't understand. My mother doesn't talk. She stares into space. She doesn't seem to have a good appetite. Something is obviously wrong."

"Yes. There is something wrong. Let me explain what I mean. There are several different reasons why a son or a daughter would want to place a parent in a nursing home. Of course, there is the obvious reason, that the parent needs constant care, because either their parent's physical or mental faculties are failing, and they need constant attention. There is also the case where a son or daughter has moved away and they just want to place their parent who is still healthy and functioning, and then put them in a nursing home instead of trying to relocate them with them or closer to them. We don't accept that type of patient. There is also the case when a family just doesn't seem to care and the parent is more of an inconvenience. We don't accept that patient either. It is unethical. You see, Mrs. Fontanella, that is your case."

Mrs. Avero knows Mrs. Fontanella is about to loudly protest.

"Mrs. Fontanella. Before you get angry, I am not saying you don't care. In your case, your mother is just an inconvenience. I had a wonderful discussion about food, cooking, and about her grandchildren, who are now all grown up. Of course, it was a little easier because I do speak Italian, however, when she was speaking to the doctors and the psychiatrist in English, she was perfectly understandable and lucid. Now you say she doesn't talk. It seems that when you have company, you don't like her to speak in a broken Italian accent around your so-called friends. I say "so-called" because if they were real friends they wouldn't care. You make her stay in her room. You say she doesn't eat. You no longer allow her to cook and she doesn't like the rich French food that *you* cook just because you went to French cooking classes. Do you ever..."

Mrs. Fontanella quickly interrupts her.

"This is nonsense. You have no right to judge what goes on in my home and determine what *my* mother's needs are."

"Like hell, I don't! I have a responsibility to our residents. Anyone who comes into this facility is a person who needs our help. Not someone who is going to be *dumped* here because they are an inconvenience. I am just *too* familiar with *that* scenario."

Mrs. Fontanella stands up.

"Sit down! I am not done yet!"

"How dare you! I want to talk to your supervisor or the owner."

Mrs. Avero opens her desk, takes out a business card, and hands it to Mrs. Fontanella, who grabs it and sits back down, not knowing what else to do.

"Here. Be my guest. Explain your situation to my *father-in-law*. I am sure he would love to hear from you."

Mrs. Fontanella reads the card. "Oh, I get it," she says.

"What do you get?"

"You can do anything you want and get away with it!"

"No, Mrs. Fontanella. I can say and do what is right for this facility and the care of its residents and make sure there is room for the people who really need us. I say and I do what I feel is right as *revenge* for all the sons and daughters who have no use for their parents and now they, or their spouses, want them "disposed of.""

Mrs. Avero leans forward over her desk toward Mrs. Fontanella, who backs away. She is still upset about the meeting with her father and whether fair or not, she is projecting her anger.

"Look at you. You come in with your "country club airs," wearing a mink stole on a hot day, dumping your fake alligator bag and cheap white gloves on my desk like you own the place."

Mrs. Fontanella stands up again. "I have never..."

"No, Mrs. Fontanella, I don't think anyone has ever told you what they really think of you, but I have no problem because someone has to make you realize that now that your children have gone and you don't need your mother's help anymore, she is now just an inconvenience. By thinking you can place her in a nursing home, you can make yourself look like the caring loving, daughter that you really...are *not!*"

"I am going to call the Better Business Bureau! I am going to call my lawyer!"

"No, you're not, Mrs. Fontanella. What are you going to say to them? That I won't place a healthy woman in a nursing home? Sure. Let's go to court. What you *are* going to do, if you have any heart at all, you will let your mother live at her cousin's, regardless if it's in a basement apartment like your mother explained to me. Maybe it's your mother who should get a lawyer!"

"My mother will *never* live in a basement!"

"No. But you would put her *here.* Do you know what some people call this place, Mrs. Fontanella? It's God's waiting room. The residents have no hope of ever leaving and their next destination is the graveyard. And you want to put your mother here rather than living with her cousin in a basement apartment? I understand from your mother they just refinished it and it is lovely and she would be with family. You would rather put your mother in a place that breaks hearts...it breaks the hearts of caring children who have no other recourse because their parents need this kind of care. This place breaks hearts when I have to inform a son or daughter that, although their mother or father needs this kind of care, there isn't any room for their parent...at least not until someone dies. This place breaks the hearts of the people who are living here and are abandoned by their families, have no visitors, and are alone. And except for the staff on Christmas and other holidays who voluntarily stay with them and let others who have family stay with their families, some residents would be alone with no family. Shame on you, Mrs. Fontanella. I would rather not have children than have a daughter like you."

Mrs. Avero gently brushes her hand over her stomach, remembering what she has just told her mother, and hopes she will never feel abandoned by her children. For a moment, Mrs. Avero thinks maybe she is getting through to Mrs. Fontanella, who is looking down fondling her white glove, but alas, no.

Mrs. Fontanella grabs her purse and her gloves and starts to leave. "There are plenty of other nursing homes. You're not the only one, you know!"

"Yes, Mrs. Fontanella. And I know them all. My father-in-law's family owns all of them, and I will be sure to give them a call when you leave."

Mrs. Fontanella goes to leave the office.

"Mrs. Fontanella. Don't forget your mink. It's *hot* out there, you know."

Mrs. Fontanella, embarrassed, grabs her mink stole and leaves without saying a word and without looking at Mrs. Avero, who stands up grinning.

The next moment, Mrs. Peterson runs into the office almost knocking over Mrs. Fontanella as she is leaving.

"Mrs. Avero! Come quickly...it's young Danny!"

Danny is having a seizure and by the time they get to the reception area the nurse is attending to him and everything is under control. As Mrs. Avero is getting closer to Danny, she sees Mrs. Fontanella standing there watching. Mrs. Avero asks Mrs. Petersen to escort Mrs. Fontanella politely out of the building. When Mrs. Petersen returns, she asks Mrs. Avero how things went with Mrs. Fontanella.

"I am afraid she is trouble."

"Yes, I could tell. I could hear most of it. You were pretty forceful."

"I could have put that woman through the wall. By the way, did you talk to Mrs. Fonte?"

"Oh, yes. She will be here Friday morning at 10:00. Mrs. Rosenberg will see her first and then bring her to your office"

"OK, great. Thanks. Now please try to get everyone back to their seats or where they belong."

Mrs. Petersen dutiful as ever, nods and does what Mrs. Avero asked her to do.

Chapter 24

"Time does not heal all wounds.
Time just goes by. The wounds stay."

"Good morning, Mrs. Fonte. We were expecting you. Mrs. Rosenburg, the head of our staff psychiatrist is waiting to meet you. Let me call her."

Before Mrs. Petersen can pick up the phone, Mrs. Rosenburg comes from around the corner. extends her hand, and introduces herself.

"Good morning, Mrs. Fonte. I am Mrs. Rosenberg. Mrs. Avero wanted me to go over some things first before you finalize arrangements with her. Please follow me to my office. Would you like some tea or coffee?"

Chiara, still somewhat surprised by the reception she is getting, says she doesn't want anything. Things are moving fast now; maybe too fast. As they walk into Mrs. Rosenberg's office, she sees framed diplomas hanging on the wall, as well as what look like awards from different organizations. Mrs. Rosenberg pulls a chair out from under a small round glass table next to a large window and asks Chiara to have a seat. Mrs. Rosenberg can tell Chiara is nervous and tries to put her at ease.

"This weather is terrible today, but it looks like it is starting to clear up."

Mrs. Rosenberg puts down the folder she is holding, opens it, and shuffles through the papers.

"Now, I understand your mother is moving in very soon, so we want you to know how things will progress. When we have a new resident, we just don't move them into a room. There are many things we do that help, not only to orient the new resident, but also help the family adjust to a new and emotional situation."

Mrs. Rosenburg looks down and reads some of her notes as Chiara sits silently.

"I see that your mother has been living with you for a little over three years."

"Yes. A few months after my father died. It was hard for her to live in her house alone, even though she insisted she didn't want to leave. She was alone and because of her age, she needed help due to her arthritis. Even though I tried to go as much as possible, I have three sons and a husband...."

Mrs. Rosenburg interrupts her, seeing how Chiara is becoming emotional.

"Yes. We understand. We have seen many similar situations, but there is one thing I want you to know. You are doing the right thing, and I think after I explain how we do things, you will feel much, much better."

Mrs. Rosenberg explains how Anna will be fully examined and monitored daily by a physician for the first few weeks she is here. She will also be talking to a psychiatrist who will help with the adjustments to living in the nursing home. If there is a language problem, she tells Chiara that Mrs. Avero speaks fluent Italian. Mrs. Rosenberg hands a pamphlet to Chiara outlining everything the nursing home will be doing on a daily and weekly basis.

"You see, Mrs. Fonte, we like to refer to our home here as a "residence" rather than a nursing home. What is wonderful is that your family is very supportive of your mother's well-being. That is a very important element in the adjustment to the new living environment. There are those residents who either don't have any family left or the family, for lack of a better word, "abandoned" them. Your mother is fortunate and you should feel very good about that. Here is my card, and if you have any questions before your mother becomes a resident, please call me."

Mrs. Rosenberg stands up, signaling that the meeting is over, and hands Chiara her card.

"I will be here when she arrives and we will make that day as special as possible."

Chiara stands, shakes hands with Mrs. Rosenberg, and thanks her. Mrs. Rosenburg looks at her watch.

"I do have a question," Chiara says. "What about the finances? Mrs. Petersen did give me some information but I want to get everything settled."

"Mrs. Avero will be taking care of that. I see you have an envelope. Is that the information Mrs. Avero requested you fill out?"

Chiara hands the envelope to Mrs. Rosenberg.

"Thank you. I will take care of that. While you're waiting to see Mrs. Avero, let me take you into the conservatory.

Mrs. Rosenberg leads Mrs. Fonte down the hall to a table near the window.

"Here you go. Would you like to have some coffee or tea?"

"Thank you, no. I'm fine."

Mrs. Rosenberg smiles and leaves.

Teary-eyed, Chiara gazes out the window at the clearing sky and the beautiful gardens and flowers. She instantly thinks of her father. Once again, she is haunted by his death and the wake that followed. *Would those memories that are still so clear on those fateful days in January ever fade?* Her mind wonders, as it has many times before about her father's death. She whispers to herself, "Time does not heal all wounds. Time just goes by. The wounds stay. The wounds from my brother are still there, now my father." She sits there and thinks about what brought her here and what happened three years ago. She tries to block the thoughts from her mind like she has so many times before, but for some odd reason, maybe sitting where she is, her mind keeps returning there. *Was it an eternity ago, or was it like yesterday?*

Chapter 25
Papa's Mass Cards

With Chiara's mother's situation finally settled with her living in the nursing home, Chiara and Joseph can turn their attention to the boxes they took out of the East Clifton Avenue house and stored in their basement. Since the basement in Chiara's and Joseph's home is now being finished, they need them out of the way and are forced to go through the boxes and either store or throw away whatever they can. When Joseph is at work, Chiara goes through a few boxes with her parents' old pictures and then comes to a box that is sealed and has written on the top, *Papa's Mass Cards 1963.* The family originally went through the sympathy, Mass cards, and sign-in book to send thank-you cards, then the box was packed, sealed, and labeled. Chiara decides to go through them again. She would ask her brothers and sisters if they wanted to go through them and then would decide what to do with them.

She unseals the box and takes the cards out, stacks them according to size, and then reads them. There are also the cards that were attached to the many flowers and plant arrangements that were sent to the funeral home, so she stacks them the same way. She can still smell the heavy scent of the flowers that after a while can become nauseating. She works through her anxiety and begins slowly reading the cards. After a few minutes, the memories start to flash through her mind. Now, instead of rejecting them, she sits back embracing the bits and pieces of thoughts and feelings that have haunted her since her father's death, letting them flow freely through her head. When she is done once and for all, she will shut them in the back of her mind for the rest of her life, hoping over the years they will eventually fade. She sits back in her chair, closes her eyes, and recalls the thoughts and events after her father died.

She thinks back to January of 1963. She tried to block it out of her head for so long. At last, she wants to remember and resolve her feelings. The first thoughts that come to her are when, on the day of the wake, Chiara and Joseph arrive at the East Clifton Avenue house. Anna was already dressed, sitting in Enzo's recliner wiping tears from her eyes. Rita brought out an expresso and gave it to Anna who took it without a word.

"Ma. Are you OK?" Chiara asked.

Anna just waved her hand. She didn't want to engage in any conversation. She wiped her eyes and placed her hankie in her sleeve.

"OK, Ma. Relax for a little while. Did you have lunch?"

"I'll eat later. Do you need the money for Johnny's?" Anna asked.

"No. We can pay him after the repass."

"Good. I have the money upstairs. I will give it to you later."

"Don't worry about it, Ma. Did you hear from Don Carlo's daughter if they are coming?"

"Your sister Rita got a call. I think she said maybe Thursday. He is still not feeling well. Rita said that his daughter sounded nervous." Anna shook her head. "Where have all the years gone? I never knew things would end up like this. I hope Don Carlo comes. I would like to talk to him about the old days. It seems the older I get the more I remember things from years ago. I want to talk about the old days and the happy times. How would I know then that they would be the happy times when your brother was alive and we were all together."

Chiara began to see that Anna may get some comfort from reminiscing, or would it be too painful?

"Ma, you could talk to Bruno Sessino. He remembers everything. Remember the time he was with Don Carlo when he brought his father to hide in our house? You remember us talking about that?"

Both Chiara and Rita nodded.

"Oh my God, was Papa mad about that. But you're right. We

laughed about it, years later. Even your father." Anna shook her head and laughed. "Oh my God. Did Papa swear up a storm. I remember when Bruno and your father would go to the opera together in New York. They would get in somehow and sneak in a bottle of wine and cheese."

Chiara was happy to see that these times were now fondly remembered, but her mother would have to tread carefully because some memories could trigger a depression.

Just then, Maria and Antonino walked in with some trays of food.

"Momma, some of the neighbors brought food over by us so I brought some here," Maria said, then looked at Chiara, "Did she eat lunch?"

Anna looked annoyed. "I'm not hungry. I said I will eat later with everybody."

Chiara took a comb and hairnet from the table and handed them to Maria.

"Here. Finish fixing Momma's hair. I have to go to the bathroom and get Momma's sweater and coat," Chiara said.

Rita said, "By the way, Bruno is up here from Florida. He is staying with his sister Theresa because she isn't well and he wants to take her back to Italy."

Chiara and Joseph got to the funeral home earlier than the two o'clock viewing in order to go over the funeral arrangements and car placement when they drive to the cemetery. When they pulled into the parking lot, except for the funeral director's car and the hearse, the parking lot was empty. Joseph helped Anna get out of the car, and when they got inside, the first thing they saw was the directory with Enzo's name directing people to the east viewing room. When Chiara and Anna saw his name, it was at that point that they knew his death was a reality. They knew that he was gone. Just the simple directory with Enzo's name made it real.

Joseph didn't let Anna or Chiara linger at the directory and walked them to the funeral director's office. Joseph ushered Anna to a chair inside the office. They talked with the funeral director and went over all the final arrangements. They also paid the balance for the wake and the funeral. It was just one more thing they wouldn't have to worry about and also not have to return to the funeral home. The funeral director shook both Chiara's and Joseph's hands, offered his condolences in Italian to Anna, and helped her out of her chair. As they left the office, he continued.

"We would again like to offer our condolences and both my son and I will be with you to take care of everything. Father Ludovico will be here in the evening to say prayers before the wake is over. Would you like to see your father at this time?"

Chiara thought it was such an odd question. It was as if he were a piece of art or a piece of furniture that was being unveiled.

"Thank you but I will wait for the rest of my family. And thank you again for everything you have done."

Then Joseph quietly whispered to Chiara, "Maybe you should go in and make sure that everything looks OK."

Chiara just shakes her head. "No, I want to wait."

Joseph can see her eyes are teary and wants to change the subject.

"By the way, who is Father Ludovico? I thought Father Brunelli was going to do the service."

Chiara wipes her eyes. "My parents have liked Father Ludovico ever since he did my brother's funeral. He's so handsome and charming, I think my mother has a crush on him. I even..." Chiara shrugs her shoulders teasing Joseph who ignores the gesture and teasing.

"Wow, this Father Ludo..."

Chiara cuts in. "Ludovico."

"Whomever. He must be really something for your mother to have a crush on him," Joseph says. They both smile thinking of Anna having a crush on anybody at her age.

Around twenty minutes later almost all of Anna's children arrived with their spouses and some with the older grandchildren. Some people went down to the restroom area where there was a place to smoke. It wasn't long before the smell of smoke began to waft upstairs as well as the talking that was getting louder. It was annoying Chiara, who asked Joseph to go downstairs and tell the family to keep the noise down. At the same time, they could hear Margo's loud voice as she was giving Jack instructions to help her get her coat off. They could hear the annoyance in her voice. The funeral director also looked toward where he heard someone "shushing" Margo.

Anna, Chiara, and Joseph were then escorted to the glass doors of the viewing room, where the family somberly greeted each other as they arrived, making sure they first greeted and kissed Anna. The newly arrived people began coming from downstairs and waited behind the Buonoforte family. The doors to the viewing room were covered with lace curtains, and through the blur of the curtains, you could see the flowers lining the walls on either side of the coffin. There were touché lamps on each side of the coffin that had pink light bulbs that gave off a soft glow on the coffin and Enzo's face. The coffin was closed halfway so you could only see Enzo's upper torso. Because he didn't suffer from an illness, he looked as if he was just sleeping, although he looked small in the coffin.

As Chiara was standing in front of the doors, she realized she couldn't remember if it was the same with her brother Pietro's wake. *Did I just block it out of my mind?* she thought to herself. Her thoughts were suddenly interrupted when she saw the funeral director coming from the doorway inside of the viewing room. He looked at the coffin for a second and then walked toward the glass doors to open them for the family. As he came closer there were a few moments of silence and nervous anticipation and then began the sound of crying. Turning around, Chiara saw it was her sisters, and Chiara tried not to get emotional. She gave them a look to stop, motioning to their mother. She was holding Anna's arm on one side, with Joseph on the other. Then suddenly Anna started to wobble as if she was going to fall.

"Momma!"

Joseph could help Anna on his side of her, but she was too heavy for Chiara. Maria and Rita screamed but they just stood where they were. Jack scrambled to help Chiara as Anna started to fall backward. Jack and Joseph caught her and helped her stand. Chiara could see the funeral director coming toward the door and waved to him not to open the doors.

He understands and instead of opening the glass doors, he runs to the side door of the viewing room and comes into the waiting area to help. Joseph and Jack helped Anna to a nearby couch and the funeral director came over with a paper cup of water. Anna took a few sips and then waved it away.

"Look at what your father is doing to me. Even when he's dead, he..." She then broke down and cried. Chiara sat next to her and held her hand.

"It's OK, Momma."

"No. It's not OK. I always thought we would die at the same time. I don't know why, but I just did. Who am I going to talk to? Who knows me? What am I going to do without him except maybe be a burden? I can't live by myself and I don't want to go to a home."

"Momma, don't worry. We'll take care of you. I promise you'll be fine. Don't worry. I promise."

Anna took Chiara's face in her two hands and kissed her.

"I know. Ti amo bella."

Rita walked over and motioned for Chiara to come over to the side with her. Chiara got up and Maria took her place next to Anna and held Anna's hands. Chiara was a little annoyed that Rita wanted to see her at this specific time. *What could be that important?* she thought. "What do you want?" she asked.

"I didn't want to tell you before in front of Momma, but I think I should tell you. I just talked to Don Carlo's daughter. She called the funeral home. I think he died last night."

"What do you mean you *think* he died?"

"A few minutes ago, his daughter called here and you were busy so I spoke to her. She said she went into the den carrying a tray with the expresso and a few cookies, it looked as if her father was sleeping. She said she called to her father. His head was to the side and his mouth was open. She went to place the tray down but when she saw his face, she realized he wasn't sleeping. The glasses that were dangling in his hand dropped to the ground. She missed the coffee table and everything crashed to the floor. There were a lot of people there when I was talking to her and there was a lot of noise and it sounded like she was crying and said something about the funeral home and the other line on the phone started to ring and I told her I would call her back and I hung up."

"I don't have time for this now. Jesus. Don't tell Momma anything."

Rita stood silent and then Joseph signaled for Chiara to come over to him because Anna wanted to get up and go to the viewing room.

"OK. Tell me later. It looks like Momma is getting up to go in."

Rita walked in front of Chiara and pointed toward the stairway entrance.

"Chiara. Look who just came in."

Chiara turned to look past the people walking up the stairs from the entrance. "Jesus Christ," Chiara said. "What the hell is he doing here? How did he get here?"

About the Author

Dr. Frank Plateroti earned his Doctorate Degree in Education Research and a Master's Degree in Communication, with a concentration in psychology. For the past twenty years, Dr. Plateroti has taught in the communication department at William Paterson University in New Jersey. Some of the courses he has taught are television production, media studies, and his specialty; intrapersonal and interpersonal communication.

Prior to his teaching, he worked in public relations and was a television producer, writer, and director working with network and cable news companies and formed his own international production company. Today, Dr. Plateroti has further established his writing career by republishing the 2024 updated and expanded first book of his trilogy, *East Clifton Avenue, Origins, Second Edition,* which he has self-published under Plateroti Communications. Book Two of the series, *The Next Generation*, will be released at the same time as Book One. *East Clifton Avenue*, Books One and Two, are available on Amazon and other online book websites.

He has also published *Speak No Evil, In Search of Our Self-Esteem, Self-Identity, and Self-worth,* and is currently writing a second edition which will also be available on Amazon and other online book websites. *Speak No Evil* is the culmination of twenty years of teaching the university communications course he developed. Dr. Plateroti describes his teaching experience as "the most rewarding period of my total adult career."

Dr. Plateroti is active in award-winning home renovations, maintaining his real estate and financial investments, and is also a recording vocalist.